Also by Linda Francis Lee
Published by Ivy Books:

DOVE'S WAY
SWAN'S GRACE
NIGHTINGALE'S GATE
THE WAYS OF GRACE

Looking for Lacey

Linda Francis Lee

IVY BOOKS • NEW YORK

Looking for Lacey is a work of fiction. Names, places, and incidents either are the product of the author's imagination or are used fictitiously.

An Ivy Book
Published by The Ballantine Publishing Group
Copyright © 2003 by Linda Francis Lee

Ivy Books and colophon are trademarks of Random House, Inc.

ISBN 0-7394-3317-2

Manufactured in the United States of America

For my hometown,
with love

CHAPTER ONE

BOBBY MCINTYRE wheeled up to Bobby's Place in a rugged, black four-by-four. A panther-tight coil curled inside him when he saw the reporters and fans standing by the door.

As the starting quarterback for the Texas Lone Stars, Bobby was legendary around the state, and practically a god in his hometown of El Paso. But two Sundays ago in the game against Cleveland, he had been taken down by all 350 pounds of the defensive tackle known as The Bathtub—famous for washing up careers. In a moment of mind-splitting pain, they had slammed together, helmet to helmet, crashing to the turf in a slow-motion ballet of inevitability.

Now hand-painted signs welcomed him home, and television crews tried to stay on their feet as the horde rushed to him.

"Bobby Mac, how's the knee?"

"When do you expect to be back in Dallas?"

"How many hearts have you broken this season?"

The questions came at him all at once as he pushed out of the vehicle. Barely using his crutches, he gave the women a devilish wink as if he didn't have a care in the world. With reporters everywhere, the last thing he needed was to appear vulnerable. Even hurt, Bobby Mac never showed weakness. It was one of the things that made him such a formidable player.

The corner of his mouth tilted in a crooked grin as he raked his dark hair back from his forehead. "I'll make this easy. The knee is healing fast, you can bet I'll be back in Dallas for the playoffs,"—his smile widened, flashing at the crowd—"and why aren't you asking me how many lovely ladies broke *my* heart?"

The reporters hooted, and the women melted. There wasn't a female in all of Texas who had been able to resist the combination of endearingly mischievous boy and sensually confident man that embodied Bobby McIntyre.

For the first time since the injury, Bobby felt the tight coil start to ease. El Paso did that to him. Maybe it was knowing his sister was here, or that Bobby's Place proved a safe haven. Or maybe it was the fact that El Pasoans adored him at the same time they gave him his space. That was just what he needed right then, peace and the ability to heal in private.

His surgery had been a success, and now he would put in his weeks of physical therapy. Then he would return to Dallas and get back on the field, taking the Lone Stars to yet another Super Bowl victory.

He didn't care what the doctors said; he knew he'd return in time for the play-offs. He had been hurt before, the injuries never causing more than a ripple of interruption to his season. This time would be no different, he had told himself and the coaching staff. And Bobby McIntyre always got what he wanted.

He worked the crowd and made his way into the sports bar he had opened three years ago. In the last twelve months, he had been in and out of El Paso, but never with the time to oversee the establishment as he should. At thirty-five, he had to spend more time training, and most mornings he was sorer than he liked to admit.

But walking up to the comforting flash of blue-and-red neon lights of Bobby's now, he smiled his famous Bobby

Mac smile. He had known that coming home was the answer instead of staying in Dallas while he went through physical therapy. He couldn't wait to see his cherished sister, Beth, and her family, suspected that she was probably inside the bar right now.

A young fan who looked like a high school fullback pulled open the door for him, and he shook his hand.

"You're the greatest, Bobby Mac!"

Bobby smiled genuinely. "Thanks, kid."

But just before he could cross the threshold into Bobby's Place, one last question was tossed out.

"Hey, Bobby?"

Just Bobby, not Bobby Mac. Always a sign that the question wasn't a good one.

"What do you think of Mark Sutter throwing that Hail Mary pass last Sunday?"

Bobby forced himself not to flinch as he thought of the rookie quarterback who was his backup. Twenty-three, star player out of Florida State, with a strong arm and even stronger ego. Sutter had been breathing down Bobby's neck all season, just waiting for his chance to get into the game. The fact that the kid had gotten his chance and had managed to step into the huddle and do well made Bobby's jaw clench in a way he didn't like.

He had every intention of calling Streamer, the Lone Stars' head coach, to find out what the hell was going on that they'd let a rookie throw such a crazy-ass pass. Sure it worked out, but had the other team intercepted the ball, the game would have been lost.

He refused to think about how that was the way great players were made. Taking chances. The daring. The guts. That was exactly how he had made his name. Doing what he wanted and succeeding. Because deep down he had known he had nothing to lose. If he failed, he had already been down, had spent a lifetime knowing he had nowhere to go but up. And if he won, if he connected in a moment of startling glory, he would be added to the ranks of great quarterbacks in history.

Bobby forced his smile to remain in place as he turned back and looked right into the camera. "That sure was one helluva pass. I'm damn proud of the boy."

Then he escaped, stepping inside, thankful when the door swung shut behind him.

"Bobby Mac!"

A welcoming chorus rose the minute he strode into the sunlit bar, his name echoing against walls lined with larger-than-life photographs of him. Trophies glittered, awards dangled inside glass cases, footballs were mounted like passes in midflight. Bobby's Place was a shrine to his success, created and decorated by Beth. Tall swivel stools pushed up against a four-sided bar of fine wood and brass railings that stood in the center of the room, a stained glass, over-sized Tiffany chandelier hanging overhead like a multi-colored crown.

All the regulars were there. Nick, a science teacher from one of the local high schools. Herb, the accountant who considered Bobby's Place his home away from home. Jazzy, the waitress who had been serving beer since the day the doors opened. And a whole host of others who came in early just to welcome him home.

He shook hands and laughed, kissed cheeks and slapped backs. But when he looked around, he didn't see his sister.

"Where's Beth?" he asked the bartender.

"She called thirty minutes ago to see if you were here yet," Peter said. "Sounded kind of frantic. I know she really wanted to be here when you arrived. Seemed really important, in fact."

Peter set a tall draft on the bar in front of him. Bobby didn't mention that he hadn't had a sip of anything but pro-tein shakes and alfalfa-sprout smoothies since that first day back to training camp when Sutter had run circles around him.

"Where's Gator?" Bobby asked.

Gene Hatley, otherwise known as Gator, was the manager of Bobby's Place.

Alarm flashed in Peter's expression. "Didn't Beth tell you?"

"Tell me what?"

Peter shifted his weight and grimaced against Bobby's sudden narrow-eyed intensity. "Why don't you wait till Beth gets here?"

"Let's not. What the hell is going on? Remember, Peter, you work for me, not my sister."

"Ah, man," the bartender lamented. "Technically I work for you, but we both know that I answer to Beth, and your sweet sister will tan my hide if I upset you."

"Peter," Bobby said, his tone warning.

The bartender hung his head. "She fired him."

"She what?"

But Peter didn't appear concerned about Bobby's outburst; he threw up his hands in dismay. "It's on your head, man, if she fires me, too."

"What the hell is going on around here?"

Bobby grabbed up his crutches and headed for the office. Suddenly his trip home wasn't going at all as he had planned. His knee hurt like hell, that damned reporter had to bring up that pussy-faced rookie, and now he learned that Beth had fired Gator. Gator, who had been with him since they were in high school. They would have gone on together long after that if Gator hadn't ruined his ankle their senior year when college scouts were out looking.

Gator had never gotten over it, falling into a life of drinking and gambling. He had been a mess until Bobby hired him. After an assortment of jobs, Gator had finally settled into running the bar a year ago.

Beth knew all that, but Bobby knew that his sister had always thought his best friend was no good. With his attention focused on getting ready for the season and drifting away from the bar, she had obviously taken the opportunity to fire the guy.

"Hell," he muttered, and then crutched his way toward the back hallway leading to his office.

He had just reached for the doorknob when he heard the front door fly open.

"Bobby!"

He couldn't see her, but he knew Beth's voice. By the time he leaned back on his crutches and turned around, his sister had raced through the bar and stood at the end of the hallway, her hair kind of wild, her expression even wilder.

Instantly he was on alert. "What's happened?" he demanded, an all-too-familiar fierceness rising up in him. "Are you all right?"

Beth was a beautiful woman, with dark hair, blue eyes, and a full, easy smile that was genuine where Bobby's was practiced. At thirty-six, she could pass for twenty-eight easily, not that she cared to try. She had a great life with a man who loved her and two kids that were her proudest accomplishment. She was the greatest mother Bobby could ever imagine. But even after creating such a perfect world for herself, she had always made sure that Bobby was as much a part of her life as he allowed himself to be.

"Am I all right?" she asked, one hand on her hip, trying to look calm as she caught her breath. "Of course I'm all right."

She smiled, but he knew it was fake. Something was wrong. Though maybe she was simply feeling guilty for firing Gator.

She shrugged. "I'm just disappointed that I wasn't here the second you walked through the door." Her smile went wide and innocent. Too innocent.

"Boo, tell me what's up."

He saw the minute she melted. It never took more than him using the nickname he had called her since they were little. Then she was in his arms, wrapping herself inside the crutches, holding on tight.

"God, I've missed you," she whispered. "I thought I'd go crazy when I saw you go down on the field. I love watching you play, but I hate that damned helpless feeling when you get hurt."

At first he tensed, but then he chuckled softly. "I'm too tough to hurt."

She sniffed. "Too ornery is more like it."

In the quiet hallway, shut off from the rest of the world, he let himself feel the warmth of family, at least for a second, and suddenly nothing seemed too daunting. It was always that way. He found an ease when he was with his sister that he didn't feel the rest of the time. Though even Beth didn't ease him entirely. There was a piece inside him that remained closed and locked, a place that neither his beloved sister nor his much-loved football had ever been able to fill.

"I've missed you, too." He kissed her forehead, then set her at arm's length. "Do you want to explain why you fired Gator?"

He felt the wariness return.

"Well . . . why don't we go for a drive or sit down so we can talk?"

"Spit it out, Beth."

"Oh, all right. Gene had to go. I've told you a thousand times that he wasn't doing you any favors."

"And I told you that it didn't matter to me."

Beth planted her hands on her hips and leaned forward. "It should matter to you. For the life of me, I don't understand how you can let a good-for-nothing louse like Gene Hatley take advantage of you. You don't let *anyone* take advantage of you. Anyone who has ever crossed the hard-as-nails Bobby Mac has learned the hard way not to do it twice. But with Gator . . ."

She sighed, dropping her hands to her sides. "I just don't get it. Why do you put up with so much from such a loser?"

"Because he's my friend." He stepped away.

"No, he's not, Bobby. He stole five thousand dollars out of the operating account and lost it gambling in Vegas."

Bobby went still.

"When I confronted him about it, he only laughed in my face and said, 'So what? Bobby's too busy fighting off women, smiling for photographers, and throwing money away on any little thing that catches his eye to notice. He won't care if I throw a little away, too.' "

Bobby felt the tight coil of anger resurface. Hating the impotent fear of being poor, he had fought and scraped and paid with blood to get every penny he had ever made. He didn't throw away a cent of it even now when he had more than he could spend in a lifetime. But then he forced himself to calm down. Gator was Gator. Gator was his friend. He'd talk to him about the money.

"He's had it rough, Beth."

"We all have! But you let him get away with this kind of stuff because you feel sorry for him. He said as much, and I knew if I left it up to you nothing would have been done about it. He'll only get worse. So, yes, I fired him. And he's lucky I didn't call the police. Though I should have."

His jaw cemented. "I will not report him, do you understand?"

"Yes, but understand this. I love you, Bobby—you know I do. But if I'm going to keep helping you with Bobby's Place when you're out of town, then I have to be able to make some decisions."

He looked at her hard. She had never stood up to him

like this before, had never made demands. She knew how he didn't put up with people when they ticked him off. But there she stood, pushing him, as if daring him to force her out of his life.

He hated how suddenly his world seemed to be spinning out of control. For decades he had worked to create a life that filled the cracks he knew ran deep inside him. He had found football when he was young, and he was good at it. When he had started throwing touchdown passes in front of crowds, the void had filled even more. The cheering fans and the coaches and the other players who he could always depend on were his life. What would he do if he no longer had football?

He thought of what the doctors had told him. The warning. The frank discussion about his age and the toll a sport like football took on the body. The accumulated injuries over a lifetime. The consequences.

The memory burst through him, and he felt a cold sweat break out on his forehead. He would be back for the playoffs, he told himself firmly, and he would win another Super Bowl ring. Then, maybe then, he'd start thinking about life after the game.

His thoughts settled, and he started to turn away, but Beth jumped between him and the office, plastering herself against the closed door, the gleaming brass plate just above her head glistening with his name. BOBBY MAC.

"What's it going to be, Bobby? Do I get to make decisions, or do I walk?"

His heart took a hard pounding jar, and his eyes bored into her. But she didn't shrink away. She stood up to him, and as always with Beth, he felt the anger tamed by his devotion to her—tamed because he knew that there was no one in the world who understood him like she did. No one knew what they had been through. No one.

Despite himself, he felt the smile curve on his lips. "Okay, Boo, you win."

He saw how relief filled her, though she'd never admit it. She was every bit as stubborn as he was. If he had said no, she would have walked, no matter how much it would have hurt her.

Her gaze softened, and he would have sworn her throat worked with unshed tears. He leaned down and locked his forefinger with hers. A child's game. Together forever, they had always said. "I couldn't do it without you," he said, "never could."

She closed her eyes. "I'm glad you're home."

"So am I. Now step aside, I've got things to do."

Her head jerked back, and her arms actually came out to block the way.

"Come on, Beth. You've won the battle; now let me get to work. I've got to call Streamer."

Levering himself on the crutches, he gently set her aside, smiled, then turned the knob.

"Wait!"

Bobby sighed. "Beth, what the hell is wrong with you today."

"I . . . I hired a new manager."

He cocked his head. "Without a word to me?"

"You just got through agreeing that you have to give me some power to make decisions. Well, I made a decision."

Just by looking at her, puffed up and defensive, Bobby knew he wasn't going to like her choice. Now he knew what she was all worked up about. And well she should be.

"If you've hired one of those girly restaurant guys who'll want to serve beer out of fancy glasses, I'm going to—"

"You're going to what? Fire me? Besides, I didn't hire some guy who likes fancy glasses."

He scowled, then headed inside.

"I hired a woman."

That stopped him. Slowly he turned back. "You what?"

Her chin rose. "I hired a woman with great credentials and a wonderful work history. She started last week. I gave her the apartment upstairs to stay in."

"You know I don't want some woman in here running my business."

"I'm a woman, and I've been involved in plenty of your business decisions."

"You're my sister. Big difference, and you know it."

"She's really good, and she's had great success. And the minute you want to take a look at the books, you're going to realize Bobby's Place needs someone really good to turn things around."

"I couldn't care less how good she is. Get rid of her."

"You haven't even met her."

"And I'm not going to."

"Yes, you are. I'm telling you, Bobby, if you mess this one up, you're going to regret it. I'm serious."

Bobby swore, and sure enough when he pushed through the door, he came face-to-face with a woman he had never seen before. She stood behind his desk, a discordant array of potted plants, macramé, and a china teacup replacing his trophies, game balls, and favorite SWEET THANG coffee mug.

He stopped dead in his tracks. She was small, at least compared to him, and delicate, with big brown eyes and the palest skin he'd ever seen, making her look like a deer caught in headlights. His first thought was that one harsh word from him and she'd melt right there on the office floor.

She wore a pale blue sweater with tiny pearl buttons, and had her hair pulled up in a loose bun, making her look prim and proper—nothing like any woman he had ever known, and certainly unlike any he'd ever dated. Though it was her mouth that was at odds with the picture she presented. Full and sensual. The kind of mouth that made a man get hard just looking at it.

He muttered an oath at the direction of his thoughts. Hell, the last thing he needed was some repressed little librarian with a mouth meant for sin complicating his life. He had enough problems as it was.

"Ah, um," she said uncomfortably, fiddling with a pencil that she stuck in her hair, "you must be Mr. McIntyre."

"Bobby," Beth said through clenched teeth, "this is Lacey Wright, the new manager of Bobby's Place."

Tension radiated from the tight brace of the woman's shoulders. But she made an effort to hide it when suddenly she raised her chin, her brown eyes taking on a determined glint. She extended her hand, small with short sensible nails, and he could only stare at it until Beth nudged him in the back.

Their palms slid together. Despite her resolute expression, he instantly felt the heat, like a jolt rushing through him, and his eyes narrowed. Then she gave him a hard, businesslike shake. He nearly smiled in relief. His center regained. Despite how delicate she looked, her grip was firm, and he thought about all those female corporate types he had met who bent over backwards to prove they had balls. He really hated it when a nice soft woman tried to act like a man.

He refused to think about how he berated her for being too soft, then berated her for being too hard all in the space of a half dozen seconds. This woman did something to him, made his blood heat low and deep in a way he didn't like.

It was on the tip of his tongue to tell little Miss Priss that she was wasting her time, to get the hell out of Dodge. Then he caught a glance of Beth's obstinate face, and he grumbled. There wasn't anyone Bobby was unwilling to go up against—anyone but Beth.

The fact didn't sit well until he realized that just because he couldn't fire the woman on the spot didn't mean this little mouse in front of him would want to hang around any longer than she had to once she started working for him.

Granted, he thought, his lips tilting arrogantly, it might be hard to get this prim little thing to hate him. Hell, he didn't know a single female who did. But he'd just have to run her ragged, wear off the rosy glow women looked at him with. Once she got over the infatuation that she no doubt felt, she would start seeing how this job wasn't so great and she'd quit. Then Boo would have to accept that she had been wrong about Miss Wright.

He nearly smiled at the thought.

CHAPTER TWO

LACEY WRIGHT stood on the opposite side of the massive desk and tried not to gawk at the equally massive man staring back at her. She felt hot beneath the primness of her clothes as she clasped her hands together in order to keep from wringing them. For one startling second she could only stare at him.

He was tall, much taller than she, with wide shoulders that tapered down into a slim waist. He had the brooding good looks of a movie star, and dark hair just long enough to sweep back from his forehead and brush against his collar. He wore a white button-down, long-sleeve Polo shirt tucked into hard-pressed Wrangler jeans and the round-toed roper boots she had noticed were popular with the strong Texas men. His eyes were blue, his lips full, and not a broken nose or playing field scar spoiled his strong, square jaw. Just the kind of man who could make the average woman go weak at the knees.

For half a second, she wished she were prettier, taller, thinner, not wrapped up in a sweater and high-collared blouse. He was beautiful in a ruggedly sensual way, making her feel hot and cold, her skin tingling at the thought of reaching out and touching him—just the sort of thought he must make most women have.

The realization brought her up short, and she bristled. She was not like most women. In recent years, she had worked hard to rise above foolish infatuations with the kind of man who turned sensual prowling into an art form. And this chiseled athlete wasn't going to undo all her efforts.

"Beth," Bobby said to his sister, with a sweetness that didn't meet his eyes, "I know you need to get back to the kids. Why don't you leave me and Miss—" He let the word hang, and he glanced at her bare ring finger.

Lacey gritted her teeth over a strained smile. "Yes, it is Miss. Though I prefer Ms."

"Of course, you would, *Ms.* Wright."

His slow, sweet Texas drawl wrapped around her as he caught both crutches in one hand and leaned his jeaned thigh against the edge of the desk. He stared at her with those sharp blue eyes, and she had the fleeting thought that this was not a man any sane person would cross.

Yesterday, Lacey had been sitting in the office when Beth came flying in with the news that Bobby was returning to town. Beth had paced and worried, then in the end had decided a surprise meeting between the two of them would be the best approach to a sticky situation. Lacey hadn't been so sure, and was even less sure now. Despite his honey-slow grin, Mr. Bobby McIntyre didn't look like he was enjoying the surprise.

Not for the first time Lacey wondered how she had gotten herself into this mess. She could hardly believe she was the manager of a sports bar—the epitome of male misogyny coming to light in the form of oversize photographs, prominently displayed trophies, and excessively large egos. In the short week she had been employed in this farthestmost reach of Texas, she had seen more barely clad females and puffed-up male egos than she had experienced in a lifetime—and that was before the main attraction had even arrived.

Now that crowd-pleaser stood before her, his bold gaze

taking her measure like he had stripped away her clothes. Heat rose through her, though it wasn't the same searing embarrassment she was used to. This heat was more like a sweet burn as his eyes ran the length of her, making her feel hot and unsettled.

Flustered, she pulled her shoulders back.

Bobby chuckled, then pushed away from the hardwood edge and came closer, his gait predatory despite crutches and a knee brace. "You don't mind if I set down here at my desk, now, do ya, sweet thing?"

"*Your* desk?"

"Yep, it's my desk. Didn't my sister tell you?"

Lacey glanced at Beth, who cringed.

Bobby shrugged. "When I'm in town, I work right here."

He glanced around with quick efficiency, and she could tell he was taking in the few additions she had made since her arrival. The African violet, the macramé plant holder, her favorite china cup. Then she winced at the sight of the New York Philharmonic poster she had tacked up over one of the many life-size photos of this man that lined the walls. Having his towering likeness looking over her shoulder every second had started to grate on her nerves.

But she never would have imagined how much more unnerving the real-life man could be. Thankfully she hadn't gotten around to having the bench press and stacks of weights removed from the corner. Though she had started hanging her jacket on the handles of the stair-stepping machine, and just then, her plastic-wrapped cleaning hung on the weights.

When Bobby saw this, his blue eyes flickered with a sharp flare of impatience. But he didn't say a word about it. He turned back with a tight smile and said, "My friend Gator preferred to work out at the bar."

"Drinking, no doubt, based on what he did to your ledgers."

That wiped the good ol' boy smirk right off his too-handsome face, and Lacey would have preened her triumph if she hadn't been too busy cursing her stupidity. Beth had told her there was only one thing she had to do when she met Bobby McIntyre. *"Do not, under any circumstance, antagonize him."*

At the time, Lacey had been instantly alarmed, and had asked what he would do if riled. Beth had patted her arm and offered a reassuring smile, saying he'd just get mad as Hades, probably curse—and in her case, maybe fire her. But if she'd just stay calm when faced with his bluster, everything would be fine. He was a pussycat beneath his hard exterior.

Standing there now, it was all Lacey could do not to snort in disbelief. This was no pussycat.

"Well, well, well, a mousy little woman with a razor-sharp tongue. What a surprise you are, Ms. Wright."

She wasn't crazy about being called mousy, not that "sweet thing" was any better, but she needed the job. She really, really had to make sure she didn't antagonize him again. "Please call me Lacey," she said, giving the edges of her sweater a crisp tug and raising her chin, determined to make the best of a bad situation.

When you're delivered a crate of lemons, make lemonade. When clouds muddy up the sky, look for the silver lining. When—

"Ms. Wright?" He waved his hand in front of her face. "Are you there?"

Lacey blinked, and nearly jumped out of her skin when she realized that the man stood barely a foot away from her, so close that she could smell the scent of him. Hot and rugged, not perfumed, but clean, like soap and sun-dried grasses, so blatantly sensual that she felt it like a brush against her skin.

"I said, let's get acquainted over lunch," he repeated, the low, deep rumble of his voice drifting down her spine like a caress. "I'm starved."

His searing gaze ran the length of her like he was starved for more than food. He also looked amused, like he enjoyed her discomfort. An all-too-familiar embarrassment surged at the realization that he was toying with her.

She didn't miss the warning glance Beth shot her brother. But Bobby ignored the look, only kissed his sister on the forehead and herded her out the door. As soon as he turned back, Lacey braced herself for the onslaught of harsh words and intimidation. But it didn't happen. He only shot her a smile that she had seen more than once in the newspaper articles she had scoured after she had accepted the job, then he held the door for her like a perfect gentleman and gestured for her to come along.

The welcome-home crowd had thinned, and even the regulars had gone back to wherever it was they went during those few hours they weren't at the bar. But she knew they'd return later. It was Saturday, and Bobby's Place enjoyed the committed patronage of a handful of men, with a whole slew of people who came regularly. Lacey had the fleeting thought that with Bobby back, the place would no doubt be jammed every night.

Mentally, she started tabulating the numbers. Bobby's Place hadn't made money since it opened its doors, which was absurd based on the number of people who frequented the establishment. The customers drank—though she had fast learned that for the most part, they drank for free. A fact Lacey had every intention of changing.

That is, if she could keep the job.

"Hold down the fort, Peter, while Ms. Wright and I get some lunch. I'll be at Casa Grande if anybody needs me."

"Sure thing, Bobby Mac."

They stepped out into the startling brightness of the sunny fall day. She had lived in northern climates her whole life, and was used to biting cold and cloudy skies. The beauty of this desert town had surprised her. The towering mountain peaks combined with the lush river valley made a spectacular contrast.

In what had quickly become a habit in the bright Texas sun, without thinking, Lacey put on the sunglasses she had bought since arriving. A hot pink pair of cat-eye frames with rhinestones. A splurge. The one foolish indulgence she had allowed herself that had nothing to do with sweater sets and pearls.

Bobby slanted her a look. "You in hot pink and rhinestones?"

Then he shrugged and continued on, not saying another word as he crutched across the parking lot to a Mexican food restaurant called Casa Grande.

Lacey had yet to adjust to the consistent diet of spicy food people ate in Texas. But she didn't think it would be such a great idea if she asked to go somewhere else. The Ice Cream Shoppe at the front corner of this rectangular square, with its tiny, too-cute curlicue chairs, probably wasn't high on Mr. Bobby McIntyre's list of places to go.

Once at the restaurant, yet again Bobby held the door for her as they entered into a terra-cotta-tiled foyer with a running fountain and paintings of gaily dressed Mexican men and women selling flowers and strumming guitars, the rich smell of chili surrounding them. An excited buzz started to build the second they stepped inside. Lacey had never seen anything like it, the sudden burst of attention, people clamoring to get close. And they noticed her, too, seeming to look at her differently by virtue of the fact that she was with this man.

No one ever noticed her when she walked into a room, at

least not in the years since she started wearing demure clothes. She had all but forgotten what it felt like to be noticed. She had to stop herself from smoothing her hair.

They were directed to a burnt-red Naugahyde booth along one wall, and once Bobby had greeted several people by name and signed a few autographs, he settled onto the bench seat across from her, his crutches laid out of the way, on the floor.

Lacey sat nervously, toying with the tiny top pearl button of her dainty sweater. When she realized what she was doing, she folded her hands in her lap. After one dire misstep sixteen years ago, she had worked hard to be the perfect lady. Good manners and a prim style had become as much a part of her as breathing.

"They like you," she said sincerely.

His crooked grin was infectious, and he clearly appreciated the attention. She'd give him points for that. But then a sultry, dark-eyed waitress with a peasant blouse uniform barely covering ample breasts sauntered up and all but groped him. Bobby chuckled and made suggestively appreciative comments about the woman's anatomy, and Lacey marked off every point he had garnered for being humble. He was an overgrown boy posing as an adult, just as she had known the minute she sat beneath his oversize smiling face on the poster.

"*Hola,* Bobby Mac," the woman purred. "Have you missed your little Yolanda?"

His little Yolanda?

Lacey must have made a face, because Bobby shot her a warning scowl.

With a raised brow and the promise to herself that she would not, under any circumstances, utter a single word— no matter how much this little display disgusted her—she turned her attention to the menu while he held the woman's hand. When finally the waitress strutted off, Lacey couldn't help but shake her head. Bobby, however, ignored her.

Thankfully, a different waitress arrived to take their order. This one looked like she had spent a fair amount of time eating the rich Mexican fare rather than serving it. She was plump, with a sweetly smiling face and plenty of gray hair, her glasses dangling on a long gold chain around her neck.

After only minimal fawning, the older woman asked, "The usual, Bobby?"

The corner of his mouth tilted seductively at the rotund grandmother. "That depends, María, which *usual* you're talking about?"

The woman batted him on the shoulder with her order pad and giggled like a schoolgirl. Then Bobby gestured to Lacey. "What would you like, Ms. Wright?"

Wondering if there were a woman in the whole state of Texas who didn't turn to jelly at the sight of Bobby McIntyre, Lacey turned her attention to the menu. She bit her lip and considered her choices for one last second, then plunged ahead. "I'd like a number three, with no sauce or beans, and coleslaw on a separate plate, unless your slaw is made with oil and vinegar instead of mayonnaise, in which case, I don't want any slaw at all." She flipped the menu closed and extended it.

The waitress stared at her, her pencil poised. Bobby looked at her with a furrowed brow.

"You want chicken enchiladas without any sauce?" the waitress asked.

"Exactly."

"And creamy slaw?"

"On a separate plate."

"Whatever you say." The waitress gave Bobby a look and raised a penciled-on brow as she retrieved the menus.

Bobby shook his head. "I'll have the usual," he said simply.

The waitress walked away, and Lacey sat back in her seat, smoothing her napkin in her lap. When she glanced up, Bobby still stared at her.

She went stiff. "What?" she demanded.

"Are you always this much trouble?"

"What did I do? I ordered. It's a waitress's job to make customers happy."

"It's customers like you who make a waitress's life a living nightmare."

"I'm not surprised you believe that. After only a week in your establishment, I can see how ordering more than a simple tap beer would cause your staff excessive aggravation."

He leaned back with a grim chuckle. "You're causing me excessive aggravation, lady."

She opened her mouth to defend herself, but closed it just as quickly. She would ignore his tone if it killed her, because, as she had to remind herself again, aggravating him was exactly what she *wasn't* supposed to be doing. She couldn't afford to lose this job. She had been looking for three months when she saw the advertisement for the position in West Texas. A chance to start over.

Truth was, over the last sixteen years she had started over more times than she cared to count. She was tired of starting over, tired of living without roots, tired of her stomach churning every time she arrived in a new town, whispering to herself that every place was a new adventure—even though she had stopped believing that many years ago.

"Mr. McIntyre—"

"No one calls me Mr. anything."

"Oh, that's right. What do they call you? Something Mac. Ah, I remember, Big Mac. Like the burger." She tilted her head. "How did you ever get a name like that?"

She decided Big Mac was wrong when that chiseled jaw

of his cemented. She nearly sighed at the thought that she wasn't doing a great job of getting him to like her.

"So," she began, racking her brain for some engaging form of conversation that might interest him. "You've hurt your knee?"

He eyed her suspiciously. "Yep."

Just that, and he didn't look like he was on the verge of expanding.

"I'm trying to remember," she added, determined to forge ahead with or without his help. "What position do you . . . do . . . have . . . ah, play?"

"Quarterback."

But suddenly, catching her off guard, he got chatty. "Enough about me, let's talk about you."

Or not.

"Where are you from?" he asked like a prosecutor, all traces of Texas twang gone as if it had never been there.

Out of habit, she considered her answer carefully. "Minnesota."

"Do you have family there?"

She debated. "Nope." She doubted her mother or father would mind that she didn't acknowledge them. They hadn't acknowledged her in years.

"Why'd you leave?"

Why couldn't he have stayed with the easy questions longer? When Beth had interviewed her, she never even got to the hard questions. In fact, there had been something fishy about the way Beth had hired her, but Lacey had been too grateful for the job to be concerned.

Bobby McIntyre obviously wasn't as easy as his sister.

"I got tired of the weather," she explained.

"But how, out of all the cities in the United States, did you end up in El Paso, Texas?"

She shrugged, then tilted her head, and hoped her smile

looked real. "If I hadn't come here, I never would have gotten this great job at the world-famous Bobby's Place."

One eyebrow lifted as he looked at her. "Funny. Now, tell me the real reason you're here."

She sat very still, her mind racing, hoping for nonchalance. "I saw the ad—"

"Beth put an ad in a Minnesota paper?" he demanded.

"Actually, I saw it on-line with a job-search firm. When Beth and I spoke on the phone, she said she didn't want anyone from Texas. Something about everyone here being too enamored of you to do a good job."

"And I suppose you're not."

"Going to do a good job?"

"No, be too enamored of me," he shot back.

Without warning, a wary anger flared, combining with a shuddering fatigue at the thought that this wasn't working out.

Lacey had connected with Bobby's sister from the second they started talking on the phone. When Beth flew to Minnesota to meet her, they had hit it off like sisters. Beth had loved her résumé, but she had also loved the fact that Lacey hadn't known a bit about football, didn't know a tailback from a taillight, and had been unaware of Bobby and his place until the day she saw the position listed. It was only after they talked, after Lacey had agreed to take the job, that she had gone to the library and looked up the sports archives on the woman's brother. Sports star extraordinaire. Ladies' man. Rich beyond belief. Treated like a god and thought he was one.

Lacey had also read that he spent over half the year in Dallas, another quarter in San Antonio during training camp, with little more than three measly months of the year in El Paso. And even then he was known to travel. How often would she have to see him, anyway? As a result, how could it possibly matter that she didn't want to work for an arrogant football player. She was perfectly happy to work for the sweet sister of that overconfident man.

But now with him glaring at her, all her hopes seemed like a dream gone awry. Frustration sliced through her as disappointment surged in—the feeling more familiar than the ones she had experienced during those fleeting days when she had thought that here, in this place, she could be happy.

"If you want me to be enamored," she said with a fake, strained cheerfulness, "I'll be enamored. If you want me to ask for your autograph every morning, no problem. I aim to please."

No sooner had the words passed by her lips than she gasped and slapped her hand over her mouth. Ack! What was happening to her? Her mouth was working independently of her brain. Worse than that, she realized she was being mean.

She had her faults, she knew that, but she'd never had a mean bone in her body. "I'm sorry," she said sincerely.

But it was too late. Whatever traces of good humor had lurked on his face turned dark and stormy, and she could tell that what little patience he had fought to maintain had evaporated.

"What will please me, *Ms.* Wright, is for you to pack your briefcase and your idiotic pencil in your bun—"

Her hand flew to her hair.

"—and get your prissy ass out of my life."

"What?" she gasped.

"I don't care what Beth said," he muttered more to himself than to her. "You're fired."

"You can't fire me!"

"Oh, yeah? Why not?"

"Because Beth promised."

Bobby laughed coldly. "She promised, did she? Well, did you get that in writing?"

Lacey blinked. "Well, yes. I did."

"You what?" he demanded.

Several heads turned their way, and just then the waitress came up to the table with their order. Bobby sat very still, and she knew he was reining in his temper with a sheer ironclad control as María set the plates down. Lacey's plate had both the sauceless enchilada and the slaw.

María started to turn away.

"Excuse me, miss. You didn't give me a separate plate for the—"

Bobby cut her off. "Forget the enchilada. Tell me what you signed when Beth hired you."

"An employment contract, guaranteeing me employment as long as I met or exceeded expectations."

"Bar managers don't get contracts."

"This one does. I made it part of the deal. No contract, and I wouldn't take the position." She still didn't know where she had gotten the nerve to make such a demand. "Clearly your sister believed I was the best qualified candidate."

He eyed her, his expression cold and grim. "Clearly my sister wanted you for the job. The question is why."

His gaze bored into her like he wanted to look deep enough to find the answer, and Lacey felt a piercing unease. The restaurant had filled up, and it was hard to continue the discussion with so many people looking and pointing. She could tell that he worked to find his smile. But whatever success he managed faltered the minute someone called out to her.

"Mom!"

Lacey's heart stilled in her chest. She turned slowly and saw her fifteen-year-old daughter coming toward them through the crowd of tables. Her sweet, caring daughter whom she loved with every ounce of her being. The one person that she would do anything for—even travel from city to city, job to job, until she found her child a better life.

And based on the happy glow on her face, the first in ages, Robin had finally found that place.

"Mom!" Robin raced up to the booth, but she hardly gave Lacey a glance. "Oh, wow! It's Bobby Mac!"

The girl squealed, and restaurant patrons smiled indulgently.

Bobby looked back and forth between Robin and Lacey, his brow creased. "Your daughter?"

"Yes, this is Robin."

Lacey was concerned that Bobby would take out his animosity for her on her daughter. But he surprised her when he smiled his famous smile and flirted innocently with her child.

"Peter said you were here," Robin explained.

"Is anything wrong, sweetie?"

"No, no." Robin giggled. "I just wanted to meet Bobby Mac."

"Your mom and I have some business to finish up," Bobby said with a kind smile. "It'll just take us a few minutes. Why don't you go on back to Bobby's and wait for her in the office. I'll come over in a minute or two and sign some posters for you."

She squealed again, then started out, but not before Robin leaned close and whispered, "This is so cool! Thank you, Mom."

Lacey watched her go, felt a love she could hardly fathom and a breathtaking joy at the genuine happiness she saw on her daughter's face.

"I thought you said you were a miss," Bobby said, his voice low and dangerous.

She drew a deep breath. "I am."

She knew what was coming, what always came even in this day and age of supposed enlightenment.

"Are you saying that you aren't married?"

"No, I'm not."

He hesitated, and he had to know he was treading on precarious ground. But even so, she knew what was next.

"Have you ever been married?" he asked quietly.

She pressed her spine into the booth, like somehow she could disappear. "No, Mr. McIntyre. And in answer to the question that is no doubt racing through your head, yes, I am an unwed mother, as I was called in high school." She felt the bile rise up in her throat, tasted the fury against the unfairness of having to fight the same battle over and over again since the day she got pregnant.

Why did people still care, she had wondered so often that the words must be imprinted on her brain.

But they did care, she had learned again and again. She had also learned that trying to cover up the truth only gave people one more thing to count against her when inevitably they found out who and what she really was. And they always did. Sooner or later there'd be some slipup. Robin would forget that she'd said her dad had blond hair, when the next time she said it was brown. Or the school principal would find some discrepancy and want Lacey to clear it up. As hard as the truth was to deal with, it was easier than trying to live a lie.

"So," she began, folding her napkin in perfect right angles. "I guess this means that contract or no, I'm fired."

He stared at her long and hard, his elbows on the table, his startling blue eyes boring into her. The sharply drawn planes of his face took on an unfathomable darkness, and mixed with what she would have sworn was an odd vulnerability. And when he leaned forward, she couldn't imagine what this man was feeling, much less what he was about to say.

CHAPTER THREE

"HELL, Beth really knows how to get her way."

Lacey's eyes widened as she tried to understand. Of all the things she had thought he might say, that wasn't one of them.

"What?" she managed.

He shrugged with a nonchalance that didn't seem to match the emotion she was sure she saw on his face.

"Nothing," he said, picking up his fork, tapping the end of it against the table like he had forgotten she was there.

"Mr. McIntyre?"

Focusing, he looked up at her. "Eat your lunch, Ms. Wright. Looks like we're stuck with each other. At least for now."

Lacey could only stare at him, trying to assimilate his words. "You're not firing me?"

"No." He didn't sound happy about it. "But stay out of my way. If you cross me, I'll fire you so fast that you won't know what hit you."

She was too relieved to care that he was back to being rude and boorish, that moment of stark vulnerability gone. She didn't care because she still had a job. Forget the fact that it was with an arrogant, way-too-cute brute of a football player. She had known that would be the case all along. No news flash there. She could deal with rude. She could handle boorish. She was a little iffier on the way-too-cute part. But the fact was she wasn't going to have to move on and start over yet again.

Her heart expanded as relief built and swelled. Impulsively, she reached across the table to grab his hand in thanks. The minute their fingers touched, she froze. His eyes narrowed in something close to confusion as he stared at their hands, hers on top of his, as if he didn't understand something.

She felt that same startling heat she had felt earlier, saw it flash in his eyes. Without warning, her lips parted and she inhaled sharply. Something darkened his face, something deeper than sensuality, and when he slowly met her eyes, her breath caught. She had the startling thought that the rudeness was a cover for something she couldn't define. It left her off balance, and with a start, she pulled away.

Laughing self-consciously, she fumbled around and grabbed hold of a water glass. "Ah, um, yes, I completely understand. One wrong move and my job is no longer secure."

She said the words while she struggled to regain her sudden loss of composure. Obviously she was rusty when it came to reacting to simple, unfettered moments of joy. "Thank you for not firing me."

He sat back, pulling his hand off the table. "Don't thank me yet, Ms. Wright. My guess is you'll soon regret the day you took a job at Bobby's Place."

She didn't like the sound of that, but before she could manage a response, he said, "I need to get back to the bar." He called out to their waitress. "Could you wrap our food to go, María?"

After waiting a few minutes, he tossed several bills on the table, then leaned over and grabbed his crutches, levering himself out of the booth. Fortunately, by the time he stood, the waitress had the meal packed. Since Bobby had his hands full with his crutches, Lacey gathered the chips, salsa, and the meals. Despite his injury, Lacey had to scramble to keep up as a new, unsettling thought began to take hold. "Mr. McIntyre, why didn't you fire me back there?"

Bobby grumbled, but kept going.

Finally, Lacey stopped and just stood there. He had gone several yards before he realized she wasn't beside him. With a lamenting sigh, he turned back.

"If the only reason you're keeping me on is *because* I'm an unwed mother, I don't want your pity," she stated proudly.

He eyed her, that unfathomable darkness flaring for one long second before it was gone.

"Good, because if anyone deserves pity, it's me. I'm the one who has to deal with a prissy-ass bar manager who probably doesn't know the first thing about pleasing a man."

She gasped.

"Like it or not, sweet cakes, Bobby's Place is a man's world."

Her mouth opened and closed as she tried to come up with a blistering response. "I'm—I'm—I'm not prissy." That was the best she could do?

"Oh, yes, you are. Prissy, uptight. It's written all over you."

He walked back to her, stopping mere inches away. She could feel the heat of him, hard driving like the blazing Texas sun that shone behind him. His gaze drifted to her lips, and for a second she thought he would reach out and trace her mouth. Breathing ceased to be an automatic function.

"But don't even think about changing anything around my bar," he said in a gruff whisper of sound.

Air surged back into her lungs and about knocked her over. "What?"

"Your job is to take care of the books, and to stay the hell out of my way."

Then he turned and crutched the rest of the distance to Bobby's, never looking back, even though she stood there, watching the rippling strength of him as he disappeared through the front door. A strange feeling rushed through her. Part nerves, part indignation . . . part heated awareness.

She told herself that she was getting the flu. But sick or not, she didn't have to be told that she was in over her head. Bobby McIntyre was everything she disliked in a man. He had an arrogant chiseled strength about him with a sleepy-eyed sensuality that should be a crime, coming together in a way that burned her up with frustration. Or at least that's how she explained away the heat that licked through her like fire.

Lacey entered the bar and immediately saw Robin holding out a photograph for Bobby to sign. The teenager wasn't allowed to spend time in Bobby's Place, but one quick autograph wouldn't hurt, she reasoned.

Bobby smiled and joked in a way that both charmed Robin and kept her at a polite distance at the same time. Lacey knew instantly that despite the worst she wanted to think of him, this was not a man who seduced young girls.

A slew of unkind thoughts about the sort of women he *did* chase after leaped into her head, though the images halted at the rapturous look on her daughter's face. Girlish joy crinkled her eyes, making her child look like the young girl that she was.

Lacey knew that Robin was doing well in school, enjoying her classes, meeting some girls. It was only a matter of time, she felt certain, before her daughter made friends.

A happy intensity tightened her chest at the thought that her daughter was happy, finally, after so many years of slowly spiraling downward. For that one smile, Lacey had to admit that every smart-aleck quip and arrogant swagger would be worth it if they could truly find a home here.

When Robin saw Lacey, her precious hazel eyes widened. "Look, Mom, Bobby Mac signed it to me!"

Lacey walked over, set the lunch tins down on a table, and wrapped her arm around her daughter's shoulders. "That's Mr. McIntyre, sweetheart."

Robin blushed, and Bobby started to say something, no doubt a protest. But Lacey cut him off. "You're an adult, and my daughter calls all adults Mr. or Mrs."

After a second, Bobby shrugged, and Lacey had the flicker of thought that he actually respected her dictate.

"Fine," Bobby said with one of his devilish grins.

But then Lacey noticed that he shifted his weight, and his smile dimmed. No one else would have noticed, but Lacey was watching. She realized his knee must be in pain, but he didn't want to be rude—at least he didn't want to be rude to anyone but her, she amended.

For half a second she thought she'd just let him suffer, but her conscience wouldn't let her. "Robin, don't you have some homework to do?" she asked.

"Mom, it's Saturday."

"Homework or not, you don't belong in a bar. Upstairs, young lady."

"I'm going, I'm going."

As soon as she was gone, Lacey saw a bone-deep weariness hit Bobby. For a second, it seemed every ounce of his weight was supported by his crutches, his massive body giving in on itself. But when he glanced over at her and saw that she was studying him, the fatigue vanished like a dove beneath a magician's cape.

Without a word to her, he tossed off some salty quip to Peter, then headed for the office, hardly using his crutches at all. Clearly she had been imagining things when she thought he had appeared spent. She must be looking for some weakness, she conceded, some vulnerability beneath the hard carved exterior. Anything to make him less intimidating, she reasoned.

Bobby leaned back in his office chair. He didn't want to think. He wanted to get Streamer on the phone and find out what the hell was going on in Dallas. But memories fought their way to the surface, memories that he had kept long buried until the minute Lacey and her daughter walked into his life—making his mind spin back to him and Beth. To their mother.

Bobby closed his eyes and suddenly he was there, years earlier, as if decades hadn't passed. Five years old and watching his mother as she stood on the curb, her beautiful long dark hair catching in the breeze.

"Mama?"

Little Bobby tugged at her skirt, and after a second Cheryl McIntyre looked down. She seemed surprised to find him there, Beth at his side.

"Mama, what's wrong?" he asked.

His mother blinked, then inhaled so hard that her chin tilted up and he could see the black spot she called her beauty mark. He started to point it out, tell her the favorite thing she liked to hear about how she was the most beautiful woman in the world. But she turned abruptly, cutting off anything he would have said, then walked with determination to a redbrick building a half block away.

Bobby grabbed his sister's hand. "Come on, Boo."

The children hurried to keep up, Beth silent, her rag doll in the crook of her arm, her dark curls framing her tiny face, Bobby growing tight-lipped and grim.

"Where are we going, Mama?" he demanded sullenly. "I wanna go home."

"I've told you. We're going to a nice place that has lots of kids your age."

"I don't wanna go."

Mama sighed, but kept going. "Don't make this any harder than it already is." Her voice caught in the hot West Texas air. "Please, Bobby, be a good boy."

She pulled open the heavy metal-and-glass door of the building, and herded them into a long, cavernous corridor, the distant sound of children playing echoing against the walls. After adjusting to the light, Bobby walked with his mother and sister into a small office that sat off to the right. A receptionist looked up from her typewriter.

"May I help you?"

"I'm Cheryl McIntyre," his mother said, smoothing back his hair with a dab of spit. "And these are my children, Beth and little Bobby."

"Of course, Miss McIntyre. We were expecting you."

The sound of a chair scraping against the floor somewhere down a hall caught Bobby's attention, and he looked up in time to see another woman walk out from an inner office. She was large with tightly curled gray hair and old-fashioned glasses hanging on a long gold chain. She smiled at the children, and Bobby pressed close to his mother's side.

"Miss McIntyre. I'm Nancy Reager, the director of The Sisters of Sacrament. We have some paperwork for you to fill out."

He saw his mother glance at the clock on the wall, and her worry lines got deeper on her brow.

"It will just take a second, and the state requires it. Then you can be on your way. Come into my office. Mrs. Harper will watch the children."

Beth and Bobby sat in two hardback chairs, their short legs dangling. They could see their mother through a glass partition, and they could see when she started to cry.

Reaching out, Beth locked her forefinger with Bobby's

as he watched through the window. He knew Beth was watching, too, and he could feel her finger hold tighter.

Suddenly it felt really hard to breathe. It wasn't their mother's tears that worried him, she had been crying a lot lately. It was when she nodded her head, took a deep breath, and stood that his heart started to pound.

"What's happening?" Bobby whispered to Beth.

"I don't know."

Something wasn't right, and he knew it, and he could tell Beth knew it, too. But they never could have imagined when their mother came out of the little room and kneeled before them, dabbing her eyes with a tissue, and said, "You are two of the greatest kids, really. Bobby, you're as cute as they come, and you're going to grow up to be big and strong one day. And Beth, you're just as sweet and smart as can be. There are lots of mamas out there who'd be tickled pink to have kids like you." She sighed, her pretty eyes darkening with worry. "But I can't do it anymore."

"Do what?" Bobby demanded. "Come on, let's go."

He started to push up, but his mother stopped him. "Bobby, love, your mama has to go away."

Beth started to hum.

"Go away?" His forehead furrowed and his eyes squinted as he tried to understand.

"Yeah." She touched his cheek. "I'm not any good at being a mama, I'm too young to be a mama. You're better off without me."

"You're not too young, you're old," Bobby declared, his voice rising.

Beth started to rock.

Their mother smiled, her eyes watery. "But I'm not old, not really. I just feel old right now. It's hard being a mama when there isn't a daddy to help. Can you understand that?" Then she shook herself, as if remembering her purpose. "You're both really great. And you deserve a mother and a father who can take care of you." She leaned over and hugged him fiercely, kissing his brow, then Beth, holding on for long seconds before pulling back abruptly, her face wet with tears. "Always remember that I love you."

Bobby could hardly register what was happening when his mother turned and headed out of the office without telling him to come along. Beth buried her face in her doll, still humming, still rocking.

Bobby leaped up. "Come on, Boo." Then he started to follow Mama. But the two women from The Sisters of Sacrament blocked the way.

"You're going to live here with us, now, Bobby," Mrs. Reager instructed.

Beth stopped rocking, ceased humming, as if shock froze her. Bobby jerked and broke free, refusing to understand. He ran after his mother, his worn canvas high tops squeaking on the linoleum floor, his shaggy mop of dark hair falling forward into his eyes.

"Mama!"

The single word echoed crazily through the long corridor. Adults and children leaned out of doorways to see what was happening. Three older boys walked along the hallway, and Bobby crashed into them.

"Mama, wait!" he shrieked.

The boys snickered, then pushed him to the ground. "Great, we got another baby," one sneered.

Bobby didn't even glance at them. He looked up from the floor tiles, tears streaking his cheeks. "Mama, don't leave me."

His aching sob careened through the building, and his mother's step faltered. With her spine rigid and her shoulders stiff, she stood frozen at the exit, her back to him.

Bobby gulped for breath, tears strangling him. "Mama, please," he whispered.

But after one long second, his mother bowed her head, then continued on, out of the building, out into the crisp Texas day.

Bobby scrambled up and raced after her, throwing himself against the door just as a security guard pulled it shut.

"Don't go, Mama!" Bobby sobbed, tears streaming as he slid down the painted metal to the ground. "Please don't go."

But his cries went unanswered. Helplessly, he watched his mother through the wire-meshed inset of glass as she continued down the walkway, her steps never faltering, until in the end, she started to run.

"Knock, knock."

Lacey stepped inside the office as she said the words, but stopped in her tracks when Bobby jerked upright in her desk chair. His face was dark and troubled, the television turned to ESPN, the volume muted, his shoulders a hard line of tautly kept control. He looked furious—or vulnerable. Which was impossible, she reasoned, given the man, and she pushed the thought even further from her mind when he said, "What the hell are you doing in here?"

"Last I heard, this was my office."

He looked at her, his gaze hard and cold as he sat in the large, leather swivel chair. After one long, unnerving moment, he stood, his height unfolding from the seat like a rugged snap of leather. "It's time we get a few things straight."

This didn't sound good.

"I might be stuck with you," he stated, "but this is *my* office. This is my desk." He rummaged around in the bottom drawer and found his SWEET THANG mug, clomped it down like a dog marking his territory. He smiled, then he pointed to the corner of the room. "You can use that."

The *that* he referred to consisted of a small wooden desk, just this side of the stash of weights and exercise machines, the top loaded with an assortment of Bobby Mac paraphernalia and a ladder-back chair made from hard wood that looked like it belonged to a schoolteacher in a 1950s schoolroom. Lacey was on the verge of telling him just what he could do with his desk and his grinning likeness, when the image of her daughter came to mind. Smiling, happy.

She nearly hung her head. No matter how far he pushed her, she would not let this man run her off.

The things a mother will do for her child.

So she smiled, or she hoped she smiled, and headed for her new desk. "Perfect," she replied with sunny brightness.

"Just stay on your side of the room," he said with a pained expression. "And at night, keep it down."

Then silence. "Excuse me?"

"Didn't Beth tell you?"

Lacey watched, amazed, at the shift that settled across his face. Every trace of darkness or emotion washed away, and she was almost certain this strong man looked relieved, as if he had regained his footing.

After one crystal-clear heartbeat, his famous smile returned. "You're not the only person who lives upstairs, darlin'."

"What? You mean— You live—"

"Yep, my apartment is right across from yours."

"But you have a house! Your very own house. I heard all about it. Some gigantic mansion you built on the cliff above Rim Road."

He dismissed it with a wave of his hand. "It's not that big."

"Big. Little. What does it matter?"

He scoffed and looked at her with a heated sensuality

that made her knees feel weak. "That depends on what you're talking about."

It took her a second to absorb his meaning. "Your house!" She felt the panic start to take over. It would be hard enough to deal with this man in the office, but across the hall, too? "Why would you live over a bar when you have a perfectly good home on a hill, no doubt replete with some gaudily shaped bed set high on a rotating pedestal and a life-size blow-up doll to keep you company?"

He crooked a brow. "You stay awake all night coming up with that one, sweet cakes?"

"I'm serious!"

"So was I—your little rotating pedestal speech was a good one."

She started to preen. "Thank you." Then she gasped. "Wait a minute! Stop trying to avoid the subject."

"There's nothing to avoid, Ms. Wright. When I'm in town, I stay here, so keep out of my way."

The telephone rang again, and Bobby snatched up the receiver. "McIntyre here," he barked.

Lacey turned toward the window, her mind doing double time to squash the very real desire to launch herself across his massive desk and strangle him. Her day had gone from bad to worse. Was there no justice in the world? she wondered miserably. She'd never have a moment of peace with him so close twenty-four hours a day. She could just imagine the sort of late-night parties he would give, with loud music blaring from a complicated stereo system.

She shot around to say exactly that, but he was still on the phone. She watched as a visible easing settled on his face. After a second of listening intently, a reluctant though genuine smile hinted at one corner of his mouth, and he sat back down in the desk chair. Just the sight of that smile did something strange to her insides, and she had the startling thought that this was the look that made women melt.

Instantly she cursed herself, and must have glared, because by then Bobby had shifted his gaze to her and raised a dark brow.

"Yeah, she's still here," he said into the phone, looking Lacey up and down, his blue eyes filling with a sensual burn. "No, I haven't killed her. Though just about now, I'd guess she'd like to kill me, probably in some way that involves extreme pain and mutilation. No one bothered to tell her about my apartment upstairs," he added, his mouth curving at one corner. "From the looks of her, I'd say she's afraid of things that go bump in the night. But I'll be there to protect her."

The image of Bobby coming across the hallway leaped into Lacey's mind. She saw him opening the door of her bedroom, those eyes locking with hers as he drew closer. Then leaning over her as she lay in a tumble of comforter and sheets. His mouth. His touch.

A rush of heat made her skin go damp at the thought, and she whirled away, embarrassed, mortified, and confused by her body's reaction.

"Fine, fine," he said into the phone before his voice lowered into a surprising softness. "Yeah—me too, Boo."

He hung up.

"Boo?" she asked, embarrassment and midnight forays across hallways forgotten as she turned back, unable to help herself when curiosity got the better of her. "Who's Boo?"

This time he looked uncomfortable. "My sister. It's a nickname. An old habit."

"You call your sister Boo?" She didn't think she had ever heard anything so sweet, but she also found it hard to believe this brute of a man had a sentimental bone in his body. "The two of you must be close. I think that's wonderful."

"Yeah." Just as his tone had softened, now his expression did, too. "She's great." Then he stiffened when he noticed her studying him. "But she's as big a pain in the ass as you are."

"I can't imagine Beth bothers anyone."

"Hell, she got me tangled up with you, didn't she?"

"Shows the mark of a sister's true love."

Bobby snorted. "She called to make sure I hadn't killed you and wasn't going to spend the rest of my days in the slammer."

"You, in jail? Pretty boy that you are, my guess is that you'd be popular."

This got another raised eyebrow.

Yet again she cringed. "I don't know why, but you bring out the worst in me."

His surprise was replaced by a slow teasing laugh. "You think I'm good-looking, do you, doll face?"

Lacey sought words, welcoming disdain. "Leave it to an excessively egotistical football player to latch on to anything that could be construed as a compliment."

Bobby only grinned. "Can I ask you something?" he said, studying her.

"Ask me what?"

He stood and came around the desk, leaning back against the edge. "How often do you have sex?"

"You can't ask me that!" she blurted out.

"Why not?"

She choked on indignation. "Do the words 'sexual harassment' mean anything to you?"

"Now, now, Ms. Wright, don't have a coronary. It would be harassment only if I were making a pass at you, and believe me, I'm not."

She looked at him like he had grown two heads. "And

you came across that definition where? From the triple-X porn postings of perverts on the Internet trying to justify everything from Peeping Toms to sexual peccadilloes?"

"Huh?"

"Don't play stupid with me, Mr. McIntyre. I've read all about you. After four years at Coronado High School, where you spent every semester on the honor roll, you went to University of Texas at Austin on a full football scholarship. Then you surprised the sports world, not to mention the academic staff, when you turned out to be as smart as you were athletic. You graduated in three years at the top of your class, went pro when you should have been a senior, stepped into the starting quarterback position for the Lone Stars a year after that, opened the bar, managed your own money, invested well, until *Texas Monthly* named you one of the state's Top Men of the Year. If I recall correctly, you have been on that list every year since."

"I'm impressed."

"With yourself?" she asked with an unladylike snort.

"With you. You have a remarkable ability to regurgitate exceedingly useless facts that have nothing to do with the issue at hand."

"Which is?"

"Since you asked . . ." His lips quirked at one corner, and he held up his palms with a look that said as clearly as words that he was only responding because *she* had requested the answer. "You're uptight and have that pinched, no-sex look about you that makes for an antagonistic bar manager who grates on everyone's nerves."

Her mouth fell open, though coherent thought, much less speech, seemed beyond her.

"As I see it," he continued as calmly as if they were talking about weekend sales figures, "we've got to work together. And the only way we are going to manage to do that and not kill each other is for you to ease up. I, being the caring, helpful man that I am—"

Surely he was toying with her.

"—would simply like to suggest sex as a means of accomplishing the task."

"And I suppose you are offering your services?"

The words were out of her mouth before her brain had a chance to catch up. Bobby crossed his arms on his chest, and his blue eyes sparked with humor. "Ms. Wright, I'm surprised at you," he responded, his grin widening. "I'd have to say you're the one veering into harassment territory now. Though if you insist, I might be persuaded to make a quick trip across the hall some night, and—"

The image of him doing just that tried to surface once again, his strong body slipping beneath her covers, the feel of his heated skin against hers.

"Stop!" She slapped her hands over her ears. "I am not having sex. Not with you, not with anyone. I don't need sex. I don't want sex. I have a daughter to raise, and it's my job to set a good example. As a single woman who has a teenager living at home, having sex does not set a good example."

The devilish planes of his face grew knowing. "Everyone needs sex. Single or married. Young or old. And there is such a thing as being discreet. In fact, honey, I'd let you slip across the hallway to my apartment, and not a soul would know, honey."

"My name is Lacey. I am not your sweet cakes, cupcake, doll face or honey, and I certainly will not be slipping off anywhere, most especially to your apartment. Furthermore, you and your overactive libido are certainly in no position to know what I do or don't need."

"Fair enough. But if sex doesn't do it for you"—he didn't look like he believed a word of it—"then what does, Ms. Wright?"

His question surprised her so thoroughly that she answered. "Chocolate."

"Ah, well, not a trade-off I'd make, but whatever it takes to get you through the night."

The phone rang again, this time the chirp of a cell phone. He opened the handset and glanced at the number, then grimaced. He seemed to weigh his options, then finally, reluctantly, answered.

"Hey, sweet thang." The accent was back, and he all but purred the words into the phone.

"Ah," Lacey muttered, her skin still tingling traitorously, "the coffee mug's namesake."

"I heard that." He returned his attention to the phone. "No one, Darla, no one you need bother yourself with."

While he cooed into the receiver, Lacey returned to her new desk and stared at the jumbled mess. Not knowing what else to do, she got to work. She found a cardboard box and filled it with stacks of photos, trophies, plaques, more profane coffee mugs, and footballs. As much as she tried to put the man out of her mind, it was hard to do given the deep rumble of his voice as he talked on the cell phone.

"I'd like nothing better, Darla," he cajoled. "And we're gonna do just that. But right now, I've got a ton of work to do here."

Lacey glanced over her shoulder and gave him a silent scoff. Bobby shot her a warning scowl, though his words were still honey sweet when he spoke into the phone.

Once she got the desk cleared, she started to pull it away from the wall. If she turned it just so, she'd have a nice view of the mountains out the window. Her first tug didn't so much as budge the piece of furniture.

Within seconds, he crutched and talked his way across the room, and waved her aside impatiently. Then he started to move the desk, the phone clutched between his ear and shoulder, his body balanced precariously on his crutches.

"Are you crazy?" she hissed. "You're hurt."

When she tried to push him away, he growled. But she didn't miss the grimace of pain either.

Not knowing what else to do, she flew out into the bar, retrieved Peter, who managed to get between Bobby and the desk. Bobby didn't look too happy about it.

With their boss looking on, still offering incoherent grunts to the woman on the phone, Lacey and Peter arranged the desk so that she had half the room, and Bobby had the other half. She felt smugly pleased with the arrangement.

But whatever smugness she felt fled the minute the door burst open.

"Bobby Mac!"

A woman stood in the doorway, a cell phone held in her hand. She wore a thick fur coat that came to the middle of her thighs, barely covering the short skirt that Lacey could tell fit her like a second skin. She had bleached blond hair, large eyes, and even larger breasts gaping through the low-cut blouse and open coat. The minute Bobby saw her, he clicked his phone shut, as did the woman.

She threw her arms up in the air in a Marilyn Monroe pose. "Surprise!"

Indeed, Bobby did look surprised, though not pleasantly so.

"Now, Darla, I told you I was busy."

"You're always busy." She pouted.

"But—"

"No buts." She sauntered across the room and draped herself over Bobby as if Lacey and Peter weren't standing there watching. "It's time to give you that welcome-home . . . party I promised over the phone, the party that starts with this."

Darla leaned forward on tiptoes, pulled him down to her, and then she bit his ear.

Lacey about choked, coughing in shocked surprise. Okay, she reasoned, the woman really only slid her tongue along his ear, but right there in plain sight without a shred of decency or embarrassment. Bobby glanced over at Lacey and winked.

"Now, Darla, let's not get carried away. We're not alone."

Darla stood back and for the first time she noticed her audience. "Peter," she cooed.

The bartender puffed up at the attention, though within seconds the woman turned away and looked Lacey up and down. An amused smile tilted her full lips, her green eyes flashing. "Who's the Girl Scout?"

Lacey's shoulders came back, and her chin came up. This got a smile from Bobby.

"I'm Lacey Wright," she said, using her most imperious voice and extending her hand.

The woman didn't even notice. She leaned up against Bobby, rubbing slowly against him. It wouldn't take much before they were sending Lacey's macramé plant holder crashing to the floor.

"For weeks I've been dreaming about the feel of your hot, slick body pressed up against mine," Darla murmured. "Don't tell me you're going to send me away now."

Lacey's mouth fell open, and if she hadn't known better, she would have sworn Bobby actually blushed. But this was Bobby Mac McIntyre, written up in newspapers across the land for his infamous scoring both on and off the field.

As if to prove her right, a licentious glint flickered in his blue eyes and he wrapped his Neanderthal arms around the appalling woman, all but lifting her off the ground. Then he kissed her like he was putting on a show. How could Lacey have imagined that he was capable of feeling any higher form of sentiment? He was an oversexed football jock without a moral bone in his body.

Lacey gave an unladylike snort. "I believe your theme-park bed might be a more appropriate setting for your little tête-à-tête."

Bobby set the woman down and chuckled. "Come on, Darla. I'll buy you a drink." Then he let the woman take his hand and tug him out of the office. Just before the door swung shut, he glanced back and said, "Peter, Ms. Wright here, is looking a little hot and bothered. Do us all a favor and run over to the ice cream shop and get her the biggest, creamiest chocolate sundae they make."

Lacey glowered. "Why, you, you—"

"Spit it out, sweetheart. But really, thanks aren't necessary."

Then he disappeared through the closing door just before Lacey could retrieve the macramé plant holder and throw it at his head.

CHAPTER FOUR

As a rule, fifteen-year-old Robin Wright was never late. Ever. Her mom had pounded into her head that late was rude, and Robin had always learned her lessons well. But as the tardy bell rang, echoing across the Coronado High School campus, announcing that classes had begun, she groaned.

Throwing open the door of the math building, much too late to consider dropping her books off at her locker, she raced toward Trigonometry—a class she hated more than any other of the upper-level courses her mother insisted she take. Not that she didn't love math. She did. But she hated being the youngest kid in the class. The fact that she was only a sophomore in a class filled with juniors and seniors meant nothing to her mother. Peer groups, social skills, and fitting in meant even less. Which was why Robin found herself enrolled in Trigonometry, Physics, Political Science, and—God forbid—Comparative Analysis of American Literature.

A shudder ran through her at the thought. During fifth period that afternoon, she had to stand up in front of her English class to read her midterm paper. Foolishly she had chosen to compare and contrast *The Awakening*, by Kate Chopin, with "The Love Song of J. Alfred Prufrock," by T. S. Eliot. When she had come up with the idea, it had seemed inspired—love thwarted, lives destroyed. Robin snorted in dismay. She knew the class would hate it.

Yesterday, Mary Louise Simmons, the most popular girl in the class, had given a paper comparing and contrasting *Pride and Prejudice* and *Emma*. Not that there was a lot to contrast. So Mary Louise had spent her time comparing hairstyles and contrasting gowns. Even Robin had laughed. Mary Louise might have gotten a scowl from the teacher and an F on her paper, but she had tons of friends.

Robin cringed at the thought of popularity. She had learned early on that making friends was hard. Sometimes people were really nice, sometimes not, though it was really difficult to tell the difference when you first met someone. Up until a few weeks ago, she had made the determination that having friends was overrated. Now, starting over in this new school, she kind of wondered if she should rethink her position.

Her mom was totally great, and had tried her best to fill the shoes left empty by Robin's lack of girls to hang out with. But a mom was a mom, and not great friend material. As to her father, well, it was hard to say. She'd never met him, and suspected that if her mother weren't so amazingly proper at all times, she'd probably use the man's photo for dart practice since he hadn't married her. As a result, Robin never brought up the fact that she would have liked to meet him.

Her stomach got a weird churny kind of feeling every time she thought about her father. Dad. Daddy. She didn't let her mother know how much she had yearned to have her father in her life. Someone to sling his strong arm around her shoulders and tell her she's a great daughter. But that wasn't going to happen, especially not after her mother let her know that her father had married some cheerleader type ages ago, and now had, like, ten kids. Okay, maybe it was only three, but he had enough kids apparently. Clearly he didn't want to remember that he had another from a high school mistake.

But things were starting to change since she and her mom had moved to Texas. Her head of unruly brown curls didn't seem to faze anyone here; in fact, more than one girl had stopped her in the hallway and said they were totally jealous of her long mane of wild hair. She even seemed to be growing into her eyes and mouth. Certainly no one was going to accuse her of being pretty, but she was almost certain she didn't stand out anymore as some kind of awkward geek.

As to her lack of dad, she wasn't sure if the girls she was meeting would care or not. So far, no one had asked. It was like totally starting over, and this time, maybe, just maybe, their new life would turn out better than Robin could have hoped.

Of course, that was before the tardy bell rang for Mr. Martin's math class.

Robin gritted her teeth as she dashed down the hall, then skidded to a halt in front of room 103, her stack of books banging against the doorjamb as she tried unsuccessfully to make an unobtrusive entrance.

"Well, well, well. Miss Wright. How nice of you to join us." Mr. Martin's words sliced through the room as Robin grimaced and searched for an apologetic smile.

Mr. Martin was an unpleasant little man who Robin would have sworn didn't like teenagers. He was short and thin, with thick dark hair done up in some sort of elaborate Elvis pompadour. He harangued his students, making sarcastic remarks whenever anyone gave a wrong answer. Why he was a teacher, Robin would never understand.

Teeth set and head down, Robin started toward her seat. Her taken seat.

She froze at the front of the class, her mind unable to assimilate this latest dismal turn in a long line of dismal turns for the day. Even though Mr. Martin didn't believe in assigned seating, Robin had sat in the same place every day she had been there. But today Jo Beth Randall sat there, probably trying to get on Mr. Martin's good side after failing last week's pop quiz.

"We are waiting, Miss Wright," Mr. Martin said from his place in front of the chalkboard, where he stood poised and ready to launch into the day's lesson.

Furtively Robin scanned the room until she found a vacant seat—the only vacant seat, in the back row, in the back corner of the room. Right next to Kyle Walker. Bad boy extraordinaire. Robin felt weak in the knees.

Kyle Walker was a junior, and by far the most handsome boy on campus. He had dark hair and darker eyes, but he was also someone any sane girl should steer clear of. Not that any did. In the short time she had been there, she had learned that there was not a female at Coronado High who was immune to his dark good looks—and not a male who wasn't at least a little afraid of him.

He ran with a fast crowd, smoked in the parking lot, and always had a girl hanging on his arm. Rumor had it that he had seen the inside of the city jail more than once.

Kyle Walker was trouble. And everyone knew it.

Everyone also knew that Mr. Martin hated him.

Even though Kyle had never said so much as a single word to her, and despite the fact that it was none of her business, Robin hated the way Mr. Martin attacked him at every turn. She also hated the way Kyle sat there, his face an implacable mask, staring at Mr. Martin as the teacher got angrier and angrier, his voice rising, his words growing harsher with each silent minute that ticked by.

Mr. Martin wanted Kyle to react, and he was infuriated each time the boy didn't. Only when Mr. Martin finally stopped, his nostrils flaring, his face red, would Kyle speak, his voice cool, his tone a low taunt like he was daring him to come unglued. "If you're finished, Martin, why don't you get on with the lesson."

Mr. Martin's face would turn even redder, a telltale vein ready to burst on his forehead while the class waited in dread, each time wondering, Would this be the day? Would Mr. Martin finally lose control and lunge at Kyle?

Thankfully that day had yet to arrive. And for reasons Robin didn't understand, she hoped it never would.

Kyle's wild reputation was no doubt well founded, but Robin felt certain there was more to him than that. The fact that he was taking Trigonometry when, as a junior, he could have been done with math credits said as much.

She also felt that Kyle wasn't as calm about Mr. Martin's contempt as he appeared. Kyle Walker cared, Robin was certain, though he would allow himself to get kicked out of school before he admitted it. She had seen the stubborn pride in his dark eyes.

With her heart slamming against her chest, Robin slid into the desk next to Kyle. That morning she had hurriedly pulled on a white cotton shirt with a Peter Pan collar, a pale yellow cardigan, a forest-green-and-yellow tartan skirt, yellow socks, and clogs. It was one of her favorite outfits because she really, really loved her clogs. Though she could have been bald and lime green for all Kyle Walker noticed.

He sat low in his desk, his black-booted feet crossed, extended into the aisle, as unaware of her today as he was every other day.

"Now, then," Mr. Martin said with a dramatic sigh, "let us begin." He picked up his book with a flourish. "Please turn to page two-oh-four."

The class did as asked, at least everyone did but Kyle, and Mr. Martin was watching.

The teacher smiled, slowly, deliciously, as if the cat had finally gotten the mouse. "Mr. Walker," he said, his voice coy, "I see we have yet to find our math book."

Kyle glanced at Mr. Martin but didn't respond.

"As I recall," the teacher continued, closing his manual against his chest, "you were to have found your book or supply the money to pay for it by the twenty-third." He looked at the calendar on his desk. "Ah, look at that." He feigned surprise. "Today's the twenty-third. I take it since you don't have the book, you brought the money."

The air in the classroom grew charged. Mr. Martin stared at Kyle, and Kyle stared back. Mr. Martin's opportunity had arrived. Robin was sure of it. She was also sure, based on the way Kyle dressed, and his bad-boy demeanor, that her classmate must not have the money to pay for the book. She recognized the pride that covered embarrassment over the inability to pay for something. Robin knew all too well what it was like to be poor.

An impotent anger built up in her.

"Well, Mr. Walker? Do you have it?"

Slowly Kyle pulled his long legs in, then leaned forward and very coolly patted his jeans pockets. After one long tense moment he shrugged, his broad shoulders rising beneath his black T-shirt. "Sorry," he drawled, "I must've dropped it somewhere."

Mr. Martin's smile widened. "Well, then," he began.

In that second Robin acted. She didn't think about what she was doing. She took the twenty-dollar bill her mother had given her for two weeks' worth of lunch money, and she surreptitiously tossed it on the floor. With her breath stilled inside her, she pressed back against the wooden slats of her desk chair and prayed.

"It would seem, Mr. Walker, that you are in a spot of trouble."

"Excuse me, Mr. Martin," Robin ventured, her voice unnaturally high, "but maybe that's Kyle's book money there on the floor."

The smile on Mr. Martin's face froze, and he turned slowly to look at her. The entire class turned around to look at her, as well. Including Kyle Walker.

Her heart surged so hard in her throat that it felt like the Peter Pan collar was choking her. What had she done? What had she been thinking? She *hadn't* been thinking.

She met Kyle's gaze, a hint of surprise barely discernible in the normally obscure depths. Self-consciously she gave a tiny, defiant shrug of shoulders, before she jerked back to face Mr. Martin.

Still no one spoke. Mr. Martin stared at her as if she had suddenly grown three heads.

He stood there for what seemed like an eternity before he very slowly walked down the aisle, staring at Robin as he went. He stopped at the neatly folded twenty-dollar bill that lay on the floor at Kyle's boots.

After one long charged moment, he snapped his gaze over to Kyle and started to bend down. In a voice meant only for the junior, but that Robin overheard, the teacher said, "This isn't over, Walker." Then he snatched up the money, turned on his heel, and marched back to the front of the class.

The next fifty minutes were the longest Robin had ever experienced. The second hand on the clock ticked by with aggravating slowness. No longer were wrong answers the only answers that made Mr. Martin mad. He snapped at right answers just as fast.

When the bell finally rang, Robin had her belongings stacked and ready to go. She had no interest in confronting Mr. Martin—or Kyle Walker. Not that Kyle would say anything to her. But she was sure he had noticed what she did. The look in his eyes, that aching sadness she was sure she had seen, only confirmed that he cared about his life much more than he let on.

After that, the day didn't get any better, especially given the fact that without the twenty dollars she didn't have money for lunch. She was starved. Beyond which, she had been so nervous giving her comparative English paper that she had lost her place over and over again, making the upperclassmen laugh.

Physics class was a disaster—though even she'd had to smile at how her day could easily have been used as an example of Newton's First Law of Motion. Once matter got going in a certain direction—namely, in a bad direction—it was near impossible to get it stopped.

At three-thirty, Robin was finally free to go home. Just one more stop at her locker and she would've managed to avoid Kyle Walker for the rest of day. Tomorrow she would change her math class and avoid him for the rest of the year.

But her luck ran dry the second she rounded the corner to her locker. Kyle Walker stood directly in front of the blue metal door. Ever the optimist, Robin told herself that he was waiting for Webster Balestock, whose locker was just below hers. What Kyle Walker could possibly want with the president of the chess club, she couldn't imagine. But she *could* imagine what he would want with her.

On the outside chance that Kyle hadn't seen her, Robin pivoted on her heel and headed in the opposite direction. But Kyle's eyesight was better than she had hoped, and he was beside her in a few long strides.

He grabbed her arm firmly but with a gentleness that surprised her, and turned her around to face him. His dark hair had fallen forward, and with his free hand he raked it back.

He was beautiful. The words shifted through her mind before she could stop them. Up close, he was the most beautiful boy she had ever seen.

"Why did you do it?" he demanded.

Robin worried her lip. "What?"

"Damn it, why'd you do it?"

What could she say? That she was obviously as bad as all the rest of the girls, cooing after him like a lovesick puppy? Or truer yet, that she had seen a look deep in his eyes that seemed more like churning vulnerability than cool disinterest?

"Because I hated to see you get kicked out just because Mr. Martin has it in for you."

She saw the flicker of surprise in his gaze. But the surprise gave way, and the dark depths returned. "I can take care of myself. And I certainly don't need some little girl defending me."

He could have said many things that would have made her melt or cringe with embarrassment. But calling her a little girl only made her mad.

"I'll have you know that I am not a little girl," she shot back. "I am old enough and smart enough to get your sorry . . . behind out of trouble."

An amused grin quirked on his lips. "My sorry *behind*?" Kyle braced his hand against a locker, leaning so close that her collar started feeling tight again. "Don't tell me you're really such an innocent. It's a *butt*," he said, his voice a rugged growl. "Have you ever said *butt* before, little girl?"

She should have known. She obviously was dreaming if she thought she had seen a vulnerable look in his eyes.

Robin forced a smile. "Of course I have. And I can say worse. *Ass.* How about that? In fact, *you* are an ass."

With that Robin elbowed him out of the way, headed for the door with her chin held high, ignoring the boom of laughter that echoed against the cavern of metal lockers.

First thing Monday morning, she would change her math class, no matter what.

CHAPTER FIVE

ONCE BOBBY MAC determined he couldn't fire Lacey, at least not in good conscience, he assumed it would be easy enough to ignore her. But after being there little more than a week, he had already learned that there was nothing easy about Lacey Wright.

She drove him crazy.

She also made his abdomen grow tight with awareness every time she walked into the room.

He couldn't imagine why. She wasn't anything like the women he usually dated—soft and easy to get along with, their voices deep and sultry and making him think of hot, smoky sex. Over the years, reporters had called his women everything from angels to airheads. He preferred to think of them as uncomplicated and undemanding.

Lacey, on the other hand, was neither, which was made clear whenever she walked into the bar and the regulars at Bobby's Place sat up straighter and talked more quietly. One glimpse of her, and every one of them was on his or her best behavior—a best behavior that quickly turned to annoyance. No one went to a bar to shape up.

Today was no different when she strode out of the back office just as the regulars were starting to arrive, one of those damned ledgers in her hands.

"Bonjour," she called out, chipper as you please, oblivious of the low grouses that rumbled across the bar.

She wore a sweater set, with little white buttons and a pair of wool trousers cuffed at the bottom. Cream-colored sweaters, cream-colored pants, flat shoes, and a string of pearls around her neck. Her hair was pulled up in a twist of sorts at the back of her head, tendrils curling about her face, then more pearls, this time at her ears. She looked like she belonged in her backyard snipping roses for her dining room table, not working on accounting ledgers in a bar.

She looked prim, proper, and as much as Bobby hated to admit it, sexy as hell. Who would have guessed that the librarian type would turn him on. Clearly his injury had rattled his brain.

Bobby sat toward the back so he could survey the room. She didn't so much as glance his way as he took another sip of the whey shake that he had poured into a darkened beer stein.

Lacey walked behind the bar like she owned the place, crouching down to count the bottles. "Did you know," she called up to them, her voice muffled as she began one of what had become an endless supply of inane topics, "that the crawfish has no discernible brain?"

The group groaned, and Jazzy mouthed at Bobby to fire Lacey. Bobby scowled.

"Then shoot me and put me out of my misery," Jazzy hissed just as Lacey popped up from below.

"Yes, I thought a life with no brain would be a misery, too," she continued, jotting some numbers down in columns on her paper. "And did I mention the whole issue of English as a second language?"

"Yes!" the room called out in unison.

Lacey shrugged her shoulders and laughed daintily, stepping toward the storeroom. "Silly me, going on about such things. I'll just count the bottles in here; then I'll be out of your hair."

"Good," someone grumbled when she disappeared from view.

"Don't hurry back," another muttered.

"Maybe we could lock her in," Peter added.

"Come on, you guys," Bobby said, though he couldn't believe it. "She's not that bad."

Actually she was. His head throbbed just thinking about her stories. But the fact was, he felt a grudging respect for her. Despite having a child when she was only a teenager, she hadn't avoided the responsibility. She hadn't disappeared on her daughter. She had sacrificed to provide a home.

On top of that, despite the way she turned his thoughts upside down, she really was straightening out the books. At night after the bar had closed, he had been poring over them, and, sure enough, the more he delved into the matter, the more he found that Gator had done him wrong. At first he had been furious. But when he learned that his boyhood friend had pulled up stakes and left town, Bobby figured it was for the best. There was nothing left for them to say.

"Lacey Wright could bore a doorstop," Jazzy stated. "And she's cramping my style."

Bobby shook his head. "She's not cramping anyone's style."

Lacey reappeared. "Done!"

"She *is* cramping my style," Jazzy accused. "And yours, too, Bobby Mac. Since you returned, you've hardly had a single woman in here falling all over you. You have a reputation to uphold. Instead, you're sitting around this bar, drinking—" She swept up his mug and sniffed, grimaced, then slammed it down. "—smelly shakes."

Leave it to Jazzy to go straight for the jugular.

"Darla's been here," he stated, and even he could hear the defensiveness in his tone.

"Darla? You think Darla's a conquest?" She scoffed. "Peter could get Darla in bed."

Lacey held her hand cupped to her ear, her pen woven between her fingers. "Did I hear mention of our fearless leader's nubile inamorata?"

Jazzy snorted for good measure. "Great. Here she goes again."

Sure enough, Lacey began a thorough analysis of Bobby and his love life. Though he could hardly believe when she compared his dating skills to the mating habits of a prehistoric primate. Something about grabbing a woman by the hair and dragging her into his cave.

Bobby muttered when the regulars suddenly found their sense of humor and hooted their glee. Though they quickly covered their laughter with coughs when he shot each of them a blistering glare. Only Jazzy had the good grace to look incensed by Lacey's comparison, then disgusted as she turned away with a bemoaning shake of her head.

"But clearly there are women out there who thrive on the sort of brutish manhandling provided by our man Bobby." Lacey seemed pleased as she headed back to the office. "All bottles counted. Now to reconcile the statements." She looked pointedly at her employer. "That should prove interesting."

Lacey's low, sensible heels and damn cute butt disappeared down the hall, and Bobby muttered about women. Beth, Lacey—hell, even Jazzy was giving him grief today.

It didn't help Bobby's mood that his knee wasn't healing as fast as he had hoped. The days were ticking by, and he had to be back in shape before the play-offs started. But the knee's movement was still slim at best, the tendons strung as taut as piano wire, the swelling still not completely down.

Bobby refused to think about the pain. He concentrated on returning to the field. He reassured himself that his knee would loosen up. As soon as he met with the doctor, he had every intention of getting the brace off and losing the crutches. For tonight, he had a long, easy evening planned with Darla. She knew how to make a man forget his troubles.

Tired of the ribbing he was taking, Bobby pushed up from the bar stool and crutched down the hall to the office. As soon as he walked through the door he saw Lacey. She sat at her desk working on the books, and all thoughts of a nice, easy evening with Darla fled.

Lacey did that to him, tying him up in knots—making it impossible to look away. Her head was tilted in concentration, her hair pulled up in a damn frumpy bun, standing in contrast to the long column of her neck, creamy and white. Delicate. He felt a sizzle of heat race through him.

He shut the door harder than he intended. She glanced up and smiled in a way that made her eyes light. He had liked it better the day he told her to use the little side desk and she gathered her belongings like a political prisoner being sent to jail for her deeply held beliefs, then carted that damned macramé plant holder and china cup across the room. He could deal with tilting chins and biting scowls, but her sudden, unexpected smiles made his head spin and heat burn through him.

Bobby made his way over to his own side of the office, and she returned her attention to the ledgers. With each step he took, she started making noises. Indignant sniffs, outraged *hmmms*. *Thank God,* he almost muttered.

But he had the presence of mind to swallow back the words, and managed to get to his desk without even asking what was wrong. No telling what she had found, and right then he was in no mood to find out any more about what Gator had done. So he ignored her.

He fell back in his chair and tried to look busy. It didn't help that in the short time she had been there, she had taken over everything so completely and thoroughly that there wasn't a damned thing for him to do. But she didn't need to know that.

"Oh, my stars," she said to no one in particular, then flipped the page in the ledger.

Finally giving in, he hung his head. "What now?"

Lacey stood up from her chair, her outer sweater hanging on her shoulders, the ledger held opened, close to her chest.

"Do you know how many rum drinks this bar supposedly sold in September?" she asked, her tone stern.

He did, but he wasn't going to let her know that.

She peered down at the page. "The tallies show that one hundred fifty-seven rum drinks were paid for, which means that two hundred thirty-five ounces of rum should have been used, equating to less than seven liter-sized bottles of alcohol—six dot six eight bottles, to be exact."

"What's your point," he muttered, having a good idea where this was headed.

"It means that over five bottles of rum have been stolen, misplaced—" She hesitated and raised an accusatory eyebrow. "—or doled out for free. Based on the cavalier attitudes toward the dispensing of alcohol that I have witnessed since my arrival, my guess is that it's the latter."

The actual number of bottles missing surprised him. Even though he had gone over the books, he hadn't had time to reconcile the number of drinks sold to the amount of liquor used. He knew that they gave away a lot of free drinks. That's how you kept customers coming back. He had put it in the category of promotion. Goodwill. But hearing the exact amount of "goodwill" for a single liquor during one measly month jarred him to attention. But he didn't want her to know that.

"You're probably right," he said.

He turned away. She gasped indignantly, but he didn't

care. He'd had enough—of Gator, of the books. Of Lacey and her melting brown eyes and too-round mouth that made him hard.

He pushed out of the chair, grabbed up his crutches, and headed for the door. Even physical therapy was sounding better than hanging around here. But before he could make it safely out of the office, she stopped him cold.

"Don't you care?"

He whirled back around and stared at her, a fire he refused to name burning inside him. "No, I don't," he lied.

Her head came back, her eyes going wide—not because he had intimidated her, but because he had disgusted her. What kind of a man was he if he didn't care about wasting money? He saw it in her eyes, and he couldn't blame her.

He did care. Too much sometimes. The truth was, Bobby's Place wasn't about money, never had been. But if it wasn't about profit, then what was it about?

He stared at her, questions swirling in his mind—questions he didn't like. Until then, his life had been just fine as it was, and he didn't need this woman stirring things up.

"Leave it alone, Ms. Wright. I'm in no mood to talk to you about what I want or don't want. Go have your love affair with numbers and ledgers, and do what you've got to do. But leave me out of it. I have a knee to concentrate on."

He banged out the door, then made it through the bar with little more than a smile and a wave before he slammed into the Lexus and wheeled out of the parking lot. His blood pounded through his veins like a time bomb. He drove up Mesa Street toward the medical building, but not even the mountains that rose up on his left, then gave away through an apron of undulating hills to the river valley on his right, eased him.

He thought about calling Beth, but what could he tell her? That his knee hurt like Hades and he was ticked off about a woman who stirred up things better left alone? Besides, Beth had joined the enemy. Just yesterday he had come into the office to find his sister and Lacey leaning over a whole slew of clothes catalogs, laughing like best friends. The day before that, they had gone to lunch at the mall. His sister had lost all impartiality when it came to the new bar manager.

By the time he arrived at The Hip Joint, Physical Therapist, Inc., for his afternoon session, his mood wasn't any better. He levered himself onto the table, wound up so tight that when the therapist touched him he flinched. The young woman was a cute little number who had made it clear she'd be available for some evening therapy sessions. She spent the first part of the appointment doing little more than loosening him up.

Once she had stretched and prodded her fill, and the hour was nearly over, she leaned close enough so that he could feel her peppermint breath against his cheek. "Why are you so crotchety, Bobby Mac?" the woman asked as she eased her palm down his back. Her professional expression turned sultry. "I know just how to make you feel a whole lot better."

Bobby didn't think anything she could do would make him feel better, short of giving him a new knee, whacking off a couple years from his age, and planting him back in Dallas, taking the snap from his massive center, Donald Rommel.

"Thanks, sweetheart." He flashed her the famous Bobby Mac smile, slid off the table, then pulled on his shirt. "Maybe later, but I got business to attend to."

Hot-footing it out of there before he could get a full glimpse of her lushly lipped pout, he returned to the SUV and headed back to the west side of town. He nearly stopped at the Charcoaler for a burger and fries, figuring he deserved the treat for good behavior. But a burger and fries weren't going to help get him out onto the field any sooner. Irritable, he headed for the bar, where he'd have to make do with a whey shake, tuna fish sandwich without mayonnaise, lettuce without dressing, and a potato without butter. He grimaced at the thought.

It was early afternoon when the crowd started pouring in. A storm threatened, and what better place to be than inside with friends and liquid cheer on a cloudy day.

Lacey stood at the bar with an apron tied around her waist and a tray in her hands. She hadn't hired on to be a waitress, but Rose, who worked the Monday shift, had called in sick. During the time it took Lacey to figure out what she could say to the woman—namely that she didn't believe for a second that Rose was indeed ill—the woman had hung up.

Then had come the threat of bad weather, which brought a swarm of business crowding in. Peter made drinks as fast as he could, and Jazzy, a full-time veteran of the trade, had been run ragged with patrons calling out, wondering where their drinks were. One couple had already left after they had waited fifteen minutes, then ended up with the wrong order.

Lacey couldn't have that, and she determined that the only thing to do was pitch in and help. For half a second, she thought better of it. She was good in the back office; she had proved that. But actually serving drinks? She shook the concern away. How hard could it be?

Nearly every table was taken, and the crush of voices and laughter competed with the music blaring from the jukebox. Glancing at the clock, she had the fleeting thought that Robin was going over to a new friend's house after school, with the promise that the mother would bring her back by five. A frisson of concern raced through her.

When it came to her daughter, Lacey didn't know how

to stop the worry. Some days it consumed her. But she was given little chance to think about it when another customer called out for a drink.

That was an hour ago, and now she had more beer splashed on her favorite cash*near* sweater than in mugs. She had found the sweater at the mall when she and Beth had gone to lunch. It had been like two best friends having fun when Lacey had a few hours free and Beth's twins were in preschool.

But now the cashnear appeared *near* to ruined, and Lacey was faced with the very real certainty that working in the bar and working in the office were two very different kettles of fish. Drink trays loaded with hefty steins of beer, not to mention unwieldy margarita glasses, were heavy. Jazzy had looked at her oddly when she had picked up the first order of drinks and nearly pitched it to the floor for the surprise of the weight. Lacey had laughed. "Guess I'm a little rusty." If only the woman knew how rusty.

Fortunately, Lacey had managed to deliver drinks without incident, learning to balance the tray on the palm of one hand, then hold the rim with her free hand to keep everything steady. But three hours into the shift, she picked up a tray lined with three margaritas on the rocks and three tall, pale ales, and her arms began to shake. Taking a deep breath, her top sweater long forgotten in some dark corner, she picked up the order. Balancing carefully, she turned. Too fast.

"Watch out!" Peter bellowed, just before the top-heavy drinks wobbled.

Lacey yelped as the margarita mix and ice sloshed back and forth, spilling over the sides like a gale swirling the seas. Instinctively, she let go of the rim to reach out and steady the glasses, but that only made things worse since the tray was too heavy for her to hold on her palm. The world seemed to shift into slow motion, sound rushing with exaggerated slowness through her ears. She watched, helplessly, as one margarita after another tipped over and crashed into the beers, liquid leaping out like a wave rising in a foamy curl, before the whole jumble plunged to the floor.

Sound exploded in startling clarity the minute glass shattered. The bar went silent, the only noise coming from the scrape of chairs as people turned to get a better look.

"Way to go," Jazzy jeered.

"You been doing this long, Lacey?" Happy Horowitz chimed in with a hearty belly laugh.

Peter just shook his head.

Panic raced through her, but before she could do a thing, the door pushed open and a gust of chilly damp wind raced across the bar.

"Bobby Mac!" the crowd cheered.

Lacey gasped, twirled around in hopes that he hadn't seen her, then sank down to the floor so fast that her blouse fluttered against her skin. As quickly as she could, she started piling broken glass and lime wheels onto the tray, using small napkin squares to mop up the mess.

"Please, please, please, don't let him see me," she whispered to herself. She couldn't afford to let him see her when she was doing a terrible job.

But her prayers went unanswered when she reached out and the next thing she grabbed was not an errant ice cube, but the toe of a roper boot. She jerked her hand back as if burned, leaving the distinct mark of three wet fingerprints on the pristinely smooth leather toe.

"Lacey?"

There was no mistaking the smooth, deep tones—or the way her heart slammed against her chest at the sound. A sliver of heat rushed through her, making her light-headed.

Gathering a calm professionalism around her like a heavy metal shield, she stood, and found Bobby.

"Hello," she said brightly, holding back a grimace when she smoothed her hair with margarita-sticky fingers.

As always, he stood tall and handsome, making her heart beat faster.

"What are you doing?" Bobby asked, studying her in confusion.

Embarrassed, wishing she was any place but standing there in front of him, she forced a calm bravado into her voice. "I'm serving drinks."

"Looks to me like you're wearing more than you've served." His lips tilted mischievously. "My guess is that when you do your little numbers routine for the day, you'll find that the quantity of drinks sold compared to the amount of liquor gone isn't getting any better with you behind the tray. Have you gotten a single drink to a customer?"

"Ha, ha. Very funny. The fact is, I was doing great until I had a little problem with this last order. Who thought to serve alcohol in such top-heavy glasses, anyway?"

"Next you'll be saying we need to serve drinks in those plastic cups with straws and kid-proof tops."

"Not a bad idea," she sniffed.

Bobby grinned, then started to turn away, but suddenly his head came back and his hand circled her wrist with a firm gentleness that caught her off guard.

"You're bleeding."

Startled, Lacey looked down and couldn't have been more surprised when she saw the blood that dripped onto the floor from the distinct slice that gaped open between her thumb and forefinger.

"Oh," she said faintly.

She had never been all that great with blood, not with her daughter as a child, not this time as a hot flash streaked along her skin, making her break out in a cold sweat. Telling herself that this was absolutely not the time to show an ounce of weakness in front of her employer, she steadied herself, told him she'd be just fine, stepped over the ice cubes, margarita mix, and lime wheels with her heart pounding in her ears, and then headed for the office. But just before she got through the door, she made the mistake of glancing at her hand. At the sight of all that blood, her stomach pitched and her head roiled, and she had the distinct thought that if beer hadn't already ruined her favorite cashnear sweater, plummeting to the floor would.

CHAPTER SIX

BOBBY CAUGHT HER before she hit the ground, his strong arms circling her waist. In some recess of her mind, she could tell he was going to pick her up. For half a second her head cleared enough to worry about her weight. Not that she was fat, but no one had ever picked her up before, and there was a moment of sheer terror that he'd stagger, grunt, groan, then drop her.

"Peter, get a clean towel and the first-aid kit."

Bobby lifted her with ease, and she could feel the incredible ripple of muscle as he cradled her body against his broad chest, his crutches tossed aside with a clatter.

The noise brought her senses back. Crutches, surgery, bad knee. "You can't pick me up! You're injured."

His body flinched as if she had hit him, and she could tell her words didn't sit well. His jaw tightened, the muscles leaping beneath the taut skin, and she nearly said something about men and their unreasonable need to be strong at all times. But for the first time since meeting Bobby McIntyre she managed to rein in her tongue as he set her down on the office sofa.

Peter raced in with a red metal box and a clean white towel, then all but tossed the supplies next to them. "If you can handle this, I've got to get back to the bar."

"I can do it," Lacey stated, feeling awkward, grabbing for the box.

But the sudden movement brought a fresh surge of blood, making her head swim. Bobby took control, pressing her back against the cushions, then pouring a generous portion of rubbing alcohol on the towel to clean the wound.

"Ow!"

"It doesn't hurt that bad."

"Easy for you to say. You're not the one with a gaping slash filled with alcohol. I think you're doing this just to get back at me."

"Don't be such a girl."

"I am a girl!"

"You're supposed to be a woman."

She would have rolled her eyes, but just then he sat down next to her, making it hard for her to breathe, much less think, when he held her rag-wrapped fingers up against his chest.

"You've got to keep your hand up to stop the bleeding," he said.

His explanation was lost, however, in the tangle of sensation that raced through her at the thought of how wonderful he smelled—warm and very male, like long hours of heat on hot smooth stones. Then there was the feel of him underneath the back of her forearm as it crossed down over his ribs and abdomen, his muscles hard and solid. Their hips pressed together, the startling intimacy making her breath catch painfully in her chest. Cuts, blood, and crutches were forgotten, and whatever light-headedness remained had little to do with her injury.

"See," he said, as if reading her thoughts. "I took your mind off the pain."

"Yep," she said guiltily, "you being the bigger pain has distracted me."

Watching his startled surprise turn to a grudging respect, he threw back his head and laughed, a deep rumbling sound that washed over her. If she hadn't already disliked him so much, she might have felt a tiny stirring in her heart.

In a matter of minutes, he cleaned the wound and held her hand up to look at it.

"It's a superficial cut, but that part of your hand bleeds a lot. Fortunately you don't need stitches."

So calm, so professional, so different from the ultraconfident jock.

"Why were you waiting tables?" he asked unexpectedly.

"Rose called in sick."

"So you stepped in."

"I didn't see that I had a choice."

"Rose is taking advantage of you."

She sighed. "I was afraid of that."

"For all your ability with numbers, you're not so great with people—employees or customers." Bobby looked at her closely. "Are you sure you've managed a bar before?"

The question made her nearly as light-headed as the sight of all that blood had. "What are you talking about?" she scoffed, forcing her voice to be calm. "You've seen my résumé."

"Yes, I have. It's as impressive as Beth said it was." He considered a second. "It just seems like you should be better with a tray of drinks—and better with people who frequent a bar."

Thankfully, blood started to seep again, and Bobby instantly took her arm back and held it up in the air.

"You know, if you'd stop trying so hard to keep everyone at arm's length," he added, "they'd treat you better."

"My job is to make sure people do theirs—not to be their friend."

"But if they liked you, and felt that you liked them, they wouldn't call in sick."

"Don't be naïve."

Bobby chuckled grimly. "I am many things, but I can't say naïve is one of them."

"Then you're fooling yourself. If you think being nice to people is what makes them nice to you in return, then you're wrong. At least that's not how it works for the rest of the population. You're a star. You could be mean and they'd still want to hang around you as long as you're the world-famous quarterback, Bobby Mac."

His face clouded up with a glower. "We aren't talking about me, we're talking about you. Loosen up, then Jazzy'll be more help, Rose won't call in sick, and the regulars won't try to ignore you every time you walk into the room. Hell, it's as if you don't want people to like you, as if you intentionally try to keep people at a distance."

The words hurt more than they should have, not because they weren't true, but because it had been a long time since she had let anyone get close enough to say anything that could hurt her. Not that this man was close to her in any sense other than physical proximity, but for reasons she didn't want to examine, she cared that he could peg her so easily.

The wind had picked up outside. A bolt of lightning sliced through the sky, thunder rumbling close behind. The very air in the room seemed to change around them, like a slow electrically charged dance of emotion.

He turned a bit to face her. "Just try being friendlier for a change, and see what happens."

But she hardly heard. She had never been so close to him, had never noticed how his blue eyes were shot with shards of deeper color, brightening, growing intense as his gaze drifted to her lips.

"I am friendly," she managed. "In fact"—she looked at him through lowered lashes—"yesterday I made a point of talking to the regulars and the staff."

His gaze went lower to the line of her neck. "I'm not

talking about being friendly as in polite," he said, his voice a rasp of sound. "I'm talking about being friendly as in having fun."

Slowly, like a long ray of sun stretching out over the sea, he reached up and brushed a strand of hair from her face. Instantly the heat of his finger seared against her cheek, the intensity surprising them both. Their eyes met, and she could feel her breath expel. His brow knotted, a battle ravaging his features as something shifted inside him. She could feel it, feel a tautness rising through his body.

"What is that supposed to mean?" she asked, her voice shaky and barely heard. "I'm fun."

His hand slid lower. "Like a stick in the eye."

She choked, though it was lost when his fingers trailed along the line of her jaw. Alarm bells went off in her head, and she knew she should leave the office, escape to the safe environs of the bar with its crush of patrons. But her heart was beating so hard, it was difficult for her to move.

"You don't know the first thing about fun," he said, his gaze drifting back up to her lips.

"And I suppose you're going to show me?"

His eyes met hers for half a second; then he leaned down and captured her mouth with his.

Her breath caught and her mind reeled. The feel of his lips on hers was exquisite, warm and heated, gentle but demanding. Her eyes closed, and she exhaled, like she had been waiting—waiting to breathe, waiting for this—this deep heavenly touch that made her body come alive in a way that she hardly understood. But when his tongue grazed her lips, coaxing them to part, she stopped thinking.

She refused to concede that the soft mewling sound had come from her. Though that became difficult to do when the next sound she heard was his deep, rumbling chuckle of satisfaction.

Insulted, embarrassed, and stunned by her behavior, she

pushed at the broad expanse of his chest, determined to put an end to such exceedingly inappropriate behavior. But when he started to move away, her fingers curled into the starched cotton of his shirt. And passion exploded.

He pulled her into his lap, her bottom cradled between his thighs as his mouth claimed her once again. The sensation was hot and enveloping, mind-spinning and exhilarating. She felt herself melt into him, his strong arms capturing her against his massive chest. This, she understood in an instant, was what women across the country sought. This was why women lined up for his attention.

When their tongues touched, fire burned through her, his lips brushing gently at first, then with demand, his strong thighs spreading just enough so that she was cradled against the unmistakable hardening of his body. Desire reached low between her legs, throbbing with heat. Wrapping her close, he consumed her. He tasted dark and dangerous, like a slippery slope between sanity and decadence, making her want more. Making her want to give in, forget right from wrong, lose herself in the intensity of emotion.

"This is crazy," she managed.

"You're right." But he didn't let her go. He brushed his lips along hers.

"We have no business kissing."

She told herself to leap up and run as far away as fast as she could. But sensation locked out coherent thought.

"You're probably right about that, too."

"Of course I'm right, and you know it," she replied, reveling in the heat of him as his strong hands trailed down her spine. "I don't even like you."

At that, he chuckled, then ran his hands up her arms and over her shoulders until he touched her lips with the pads of his thumbs. "That's okay, I don't like you either."

Instantly her mind froze, before she started pushing at his chest. "You can't not like me! Everyone likes me."

He glanced meaningfully toward the door that led to the bar.

Lacey sniffed. "Okay, so not *everyone* likes me. But that's only because they don't really know me."

"I think they do."

She sliced him a narrow-eyed scowl. "You're insufferable."

"You're a snob."

"Well, you're . . . you're . . . a sex-crazed jock who thinks that a kiss solves everything!"

As soon as the words were out, her heart stopped. She couldn't believe what she had said, but more than that she couldn't believe the clouds that formed on his features.

"We're both being childish," she whispered. "But you really do bring out the worst in me."

With one easy movement, he set her aside and pushed up from the sofa. He walked to the door, his brace stiff and awkward, and Lacey felt a tremendous regret. After years of hurtful stereotyped words about an unwed mother and her out-of-wedlock child, she couldn't believe she had done exactly the same thing to someone else. "Bobby?"

Stopping at the entrance, he didn't look back.

"My last comment was completely uncalled for."

Slowly, he turned and looked at her. Long seconds ticked by as he stared at her; then a smile started to tug at his lips. "Just the last comment? You mean you don't take back calling me insufferable?"

"Only if you take back calling me a snob," she responded in a strained whisper.

His eyes sparkled with reluctant humor. "I'll think about it."

Then he disappeared out the door, leaving her with a strange tingling that she tried to tell herself had everything to do with loss of blood, and nothing to do with that horribly endearing Bobby Mac smile.

She refused to think about how her hand had curled into

his shirtfront. About how forward she had been. How even after telling him they had no business kissing her mouth had run amok. No telling what they would be doing right that second if she hadn't said such hurtful things. She didn't need a man, didn't want a man, especially one like Bobby Mac McIntyre who was known for his conquests.

Disgruntled, good waitress or not, she decided she had to return to the bar and see what needed to be done. The crowd seemed surprised when she reappeared. She thought about Bobby's words that she was too standoffish with the crowd, making it hard for them to warm up to her. But how to loosen up?

Like an athlete getting ready to compete, she rolled her head, shook out her arms, then did a double-fisted power salute in the air like she was Rocky, grimacing over the sting of pain that leaped underneath the wad of gauze she had wrapped around her hand.

She came up to the bar. "Hey," she said, her voice like a rusty squeak. But at least it was better than her traditional "Hail, hearty fellows" or "Bonjour."

Brows furrowed suspiciously, and the regulars curled their drinks closer like she was about to take them away. "Hey," came the ambivalent response.

Only then did she see Bobby—his famous smile pulled on his lips, his blue eyes glittering as that awful woman named Darla clung to his arm.

A sharp stabbing sensation shot through her, centering in that sensitive place between her eyes. But she wasn't jealous. She wasn't.

"He sure is seeing a lot of Darla," Herb the accountant commented.

"Yeah," Ned the telephone repairman replied, "I've never seen him so interested in one woman for so long. It's been a week."

Lacey looked back and studied Bobby and his date. *This*

was more interested? She'd hate to see the opposite. Then she groaned. She had seen less interested. In the back room, minutes ago. A kiss that clearly meant nothing to the man since now he was out here with that woman.

She felt a low growling sound bubble up from her chest, loud enough that the others heard.

"What was that?" Herb asked.

Embarrassment flashed through her cheeks. "Indigestion," she offered.

"Been eating too many of those buffalo wings," Ned said with a knock to his chest with his fist. "I know the feeling."

The long line of regulars got a kick out of that, the sound interrupted by the distinct peal of a woman's sensual laughter.

The men swiveled on their stools to eye Bobby and Darla. Lacey looked, as well.

"I say this one's serious," Rupert chimed in as he brought his mug to his lips.

Lacey glanced between the men and the couple. "You mean to tell me that a week is a long time for him?"

"Ages."

"He's not known for lasting relationships."

"Though this one's different," Herb reiterated as the men swiveled back to the bar. "I say this one's gonna last a month."

"I give it two months," Ned offered. "Look at those—"

The men glanced sharply over at Lacey.

"Those big green eyes," Rupert finished for him.

The men cleared their throats.

"So what do we have?" Ned asked, pulling out a blunt-nosed pencil and scratching out some numbers on a paper napkin. "I've got a buck on two months. Herb?"

"I'll go with one month."

"Nick?"

The man named Nick didn't hear. He was staring at Lacey, and when she finally noticed, she jumped with a start. Nick smiled.

"Nick," Ned demanded.

"Ah, I'll go with a month," he answered hurriedly, then turned back to Lacey with hopeful eyes.

But Lacey ignored him. "What are you doing?" she asked.

The regulars perked up and turned to face her. "We run a pool on the women Bobby dates. How long he'll stay with them, how he'll break up. Those sorts of things. It's the best entertainment in town."

"That's ridiculous," she stated before she could stop herself.

The men turned away from her, and she groaned silently.

"I'll put a fiver on this one getting a ring," another man from the very end of the bar called out.

"No way."

"Look how she's rubbing up against him."

Sure enough, Darla was pressing up against Bobby like a cat in heat, the promise of more to come made clear by her provocative body language.

"Tonight I have a surprise for you at my apartment," they heard her say, her voice a full purr of promise. "It involves lots of whipped cream and cherries. But first I told my parents we'd stop by. Just for a few minutes. Then it'll be just you and me, and a long night of—"

Rupert whistled over whatever else she said. "Yep, this one's gonna last for a while."

Ned shrugged. "Maybe I should go with two months."

The men mumbled among themselves, until Lacey surprised herself and the regulars when she picked up her tray, refused to grimace at the sting of pain in her hand, and said, "I give the relationship—" She glanced at her watch.

"—until sometime this afternoon. And you can count me in for a dollar on that."

"What?" they demanded.

She wasn't sure if they were more surprised that she had placed a bet or that she had given the relationship only a matter of hours.

Herb's lips quirked. "Till this afternoon, huh?" he mused, eyeing her like she wasn't so bad after all.

A silly thrill raced through her at being part of the crowd. The feeling was foolishly gratifying.

"Are you insane?" Ned asked.

Lacey just smiled and turned away, concentrating on three draft beers that she refused to let fall.

The shift ended, giving Lacey a few hours before the evening business started to file in. The weather had only gotten worse, and where better to warm the body than at Bobby's Place.

The thought of Robin loomed in her mind, that all-too-familiar prick of fear and concern swelling. She worried about her daughter, always did, couldn't help it. Since coming to El Paso, it seemed her worry had changed. It was different, more intense, if that was possible, at a time when everything was getting better for her child. It hardly made sense.

Lacey had the unexpected thought that there was more to her anxiety than simple concern for her daughter's whereabouts. She had hoped they would spend some time together, just mother and daughter. But since arriving in El Paso, Robin always seemed to have something to do. Homework, Spirit Club, and now this friend who had invited her over.

Suddenly they had very little time to spend together. Lacey knew that she should be thrilled, and she was. But that didn't completely take the sting away from the fact that her daughter no longer thought she was the most important person in the world.

Robin was growing up. Lacey was proud and saddened all in one big tangle of confusing emotions.

Shaking the thoughts away, she started to head back to the office, and the front door pushed open, a gust of wind rushing in with it. Instantly she turned back in hopes that it was Robin.

"Bobby Mac," came the normal echoed greeting.

Lacey felt that same leap of awareness at the sight of him, the same flash of heat she had felt when his fingers ran along the fullness of her lower lip. And she certainly didn't need to be having, thinking about, or tasting such behavior. It was her job to set an example for her daughter.

Robin was at an impressionable age, subject to teenage hormonal pressures. Lacey knew. Lacey had been there and had fallen prey to the worst kind of good-looking senior who had wooed her with sweet words of love everlasting.

And look where that got her. Running, fighting, trying to build a life that never seemed to work out. Anyone who said that times had changed, and unwed mothers were no longer thought poorly of, had never been an unwed mother. Rich and famous people in New York and California might have children without the benefit of a father, but the whole country in between wanted mothers to be married, and children to have at least the father's last name—even if he wasn't around any longer.

If Lacey hadn't seen for herself the prejudice against unwed mothers, she might not believe that kids and even parents still thought of any child born out of wedlock as a bastard. But she had seen the judgment in neighbors' eyes. She had moved her child to new town after new town to start over too many times not to understand that truth all too well.

"Hey, Bobby, come join us," someone called out.

"I have some work to do, but how about later we shoot some pool?" he suggested.

"What about Darla?" Ned asked, his tone a lament. "I thought you were going out with her tonight."

"Yeah, well, plans changed."

Lacey stopped in her tracks, then turned back with a raised brow.

The regulars shifted on their bar stools.

"Plans changed?" Rupert inquired.

Bobby never missed a beat as he crutched down the steps. "Yeah," he said with casual uninterest. "We're not seeing each other anymore."

"What?" came the echoing chorus from the long line of regulars who had swiveled around on their stools to face Bobby. "Not more than a few hours ago she was all over you."

"Why do you care?" Bobby asked, looking suspicious for the first time since walking through the door.

Lacey returned to the bar and couldn't help the knowing smile that slid across her face.

Bobby's jaw ticked. "What's going on?"

Her grin quirked mischievously. "You told me to be more a part of the crowd. I'm nothing if not a quick learner. So when they started laying wagers, I joined in."

Bobby's eyes went wide. "You've been betting with the guys?"

"Are you proud?" she asked, her voice silky. "Do I get a gold star for doing as the teacher said?"

"Funny. What the hell were you betting on?" He glanced from man to man, and each in turn looked sheepish.

"Now, Bobby, what does it matter?"

"Herb?" he said, his tone warning.

"We were betting on you," Lacey chimed in proudly.

Bobby's face took on an apoplectic hue. "You what?"

"We bet on how long you and Darla would last," she explained, enjoying herself immensely. She refused to acknowledge the thought that she might actually be pleased because he was no longer seeing the woman.

Bobby gaped at the crowd of regulars like he had been betrayed.

"Now, don't get hot, Bobby Mac," Herb cajoled. "We were just having some fun. You know how it is. You've bet with us plenty of times."

Lacey extended her hand. "Pay up, gentlemen."

Grumbling, they started pulling bills out of their pockets. Bobby looked as if he had swallowed a chicken wing whole as each man paid up.

"How'd you know?" Rupert asked, forgetting Bobby for a second as he handed over his ante.

Lacey made a great production of counting the stack of bills. "It was the mention of parents that did it. Specifically *visiting* with parents. I knew our Mr. McIntyre wouldn't last long with that kind of pressure."

Then she shoved the bills in her prim little pocket, turned on her sensible heel feeling devilishly pleased, and headed for the office. But whatever satisfaction she felt evaporated when she caught a glimpse of the time. Nearly five o'clock without a word from Robin, and she felt a surge of worry leap up and overwhelm her.

CHAPTER SEVEN

KYLE WALKER sped up Thunderbird Drive in his old Chevy truck after the manager of Garvey's Service Station told him to head home. Dark clouds had threatened all afternoon, until finally the swollen skies let go of a bitterly cold fall rain, and no one was stopping for gas.

His stepfather hated that he pumped gas with a bunch of guys he called low-class grease monkeys. But then again, his stepfather didn't like much about what Kyle did since he and his mom had moved into the gigantic house in the Coronado Country Club two years ago.

Fortunately, Harold traveled constantly, which meant Kyle hardly ever saw him—or his mom, for that matter. She was always going somewhere, either with Harold on a trip or to some women's meeting. When he did see her, he always felt her sudden, unexpected surprise, as if just then she remembered she had a son. Not that she remembered often. Last December his stepdad and mom had gone to some fancy place in France for a "quick getaway." But one week turned into two, and then two turned to three. When they had returned the day after Christmas, Kyle's mom had breezed into the room and hugged him, her brown eyes filled with tears as she asked for his forgiveness. "I'm just sick you were left alone for the holiday, but we met up with this fabulous European couple who had access to all the best places, and they invited us to come along. How often does that sort of opportunity come my way?"

Not that he cared, he told himself firmly. He didn't. He was happy that his mother left him alone, and she did as long as he wasn't doing something that would give Harold an aneurysm.

Staying out of the way was made even easier since he worked every day after school at Garvey's for gas money. Regardless of his mom's newfound monetary status, Harold didn't believe in the trickle-down effect. The man provided a roof, three squares a day, and a meager allowance that wouldn't keep a grade schooler supplied with bubble gum. And now Kyle owed a certain little girl twenty bucks.

Kyle downshifted the three-on-the-column with smooth efficiency through the driving rain, turned left onto Cherry Hill, then accelerated past the country club golf course and sprawling mansions. He shook his head, his low chuckle grim as he thought of Robin Wright. He had noticed her the first day she showed up at Coronado High. Smart, funny, and cute. Real cute, with strange golden brown eyes, lots of wild brown hair, and a body that her odd clothes couldn't hide. But she was a sophomore. Too young as far as he was concerned.

He had meant to give her the money after school on Friday, but her smart mouth had made him forget. He couldn't remember the last time a female of any age hadn't sighed and smiled at him. But Robin hadn't done either.

The wipers slid along the glass, the world going clear for half-second intervals time and time again as he pulled up to his home. The house was as large as the others on the street, as stately, with its slate-gray roof absorbing the dark sky, the manicured gardens and lawns reflecting a gardener's attention to detail. Brick walkways lined with fall flowers led to a massive front door inset with etched glass. So different from the boxy apartment he and his mom had lived in on the northeast side of town before she met and married Harold.

Downshifting again, Kyle started to turn left into the granite brick circular drive when he saw someone walking in the rain, huddled against the wind.

Kyle wondered who would be fool enough to be out in this kind of weather. The person was going slowly, soaking wet, and was no doubt freezing cold. A second later, Kyle couldn't have been more surprised when he realized it was Robin.

Just as the thought registered, she tripped. It happened fast, real fast. Her eyes went wide as she started to fall. She put her hands out. But there was nothing to grab hold of, and she went down.

Braking sharply, he threw the truck into park and leaped out into the street. "Are you okay?" he demanded, picking her up.

Her eyes focused, raindrops clinging to her long dark eyelashes. "Kyle?" she asked, her breath coming out in a puff of white, her voice barely heard over the chatter of her teeth.

"Come on, get in the truck."

It was as if her brain were sluggish with cold, and it took a second for his offer to register. "Oh, thanks."

He helped her climb in, not without effort. As soon as he slammed into the driver's side, he saw that her lips were kind of blue, and her knees and one of her palms were pretty banged up from her fall.

Kyle didn't think about what he was doing. He bypassed the circular drive and accelerated down the side of the house to the garage. In seconds, he helped her from the truck, took her hand, and headed for the kitchen and the back set of stairs that led to his bedroom. No one would be home, Harold still at work, his mother at a society meeting. On the second floor, he pulled her down a wide, carpeted hall, ornately framed paintings lining the way.

Inside his bedroom, he took her straight into the adjoining bathroom and put her bad hand underneath warm water. Instantly she flinched.

"Sorry, but you've got to get the grit out."

She only grimaced and groaned, dropping her head like she was miserable, her teeth still chattering, her clothes starting to form a puddle of water on the tile floor.

Once her hand was clean, without a thought for modesty, he tugged off her soaking sweater and wool skirt. Undressing girls was nothing new to him, but this was different. This wasn't about sex.

"My clothes," she squeaked. "What are you doing?"

"Getting you warm and dry," he grumbled. "But that's not going to happen as long as you're wearing wet clothes."

He hoped like hell his stepfather or mother didn't show up. They still hadn't gotten over the condom they found in his bedroom two months ago—or at least his mother hadn't gotten over it. Kyle suspected Harold had actually been amused.

Kyle grimaced at the thought, then felt a slice of anger over the fact that Harold and his mom hadn't believed it wasn't his. He wasn't stupid enough to leave a condom lying around in his room. Hell, he kept a box under the seat in his truck.

The one in question had been his cousin's, though Kyle doubted Mert even knew what to do with the damned thing. The kid was a sophomore at Irvin High, back in the old neighborhood. Mert was from his mother's side of the family. There was a whole slew of aunts and uncles his mother didn't like to admit she had. Every once in a while, though, she'd feel guilty and invite them all over. Something always went wrong. That time it had been Mert bragging about all the girls he'd been banging, then pulling out the condom like that was proof. Both their mothers had walked in right then. Kyle's mother had stood stock-still, her face set. Her sister had gone into meltdown, shrieking like a maniac. Mert had tossed the rubber at him. "It's his, Mom, I swear."

That had been that. The party broke up, and Kyle had one more mark against him. He wasn't sure which was worse to his mom, that he might have had a rubber, or that he ruined her party. Either way, the last thing he needed right now was more trouble.

He should have known the second Robin sat down next to him in class that she was trouble. Regardless, Kyle could hardly believe that she had come to his defense in class. No one ever defended him—not his mom, and certainly not his stepfather. Not that he needed it, he told himself sharply. And he certainly didn't need some little girl defending him.

Kyle grabbed a towel out of the linen closet in his bathroom. He wrapped Robin in the length then started to rub.

"Ouch!" she mumbled, trying to pull away, though with little strength.

Between the heat in the house and rubbing her dry, before long Kyle saw color start returning to her lips. He sat her on the toilet lid, then used a washcloth to wipe away the rest of the grit from her knees.

"That hurts," she squeaked.

"You should have thought of that before you went out in the cold rain. What were you doing out there, anyway?"

Her perfect skin creased with concern, Robin looked at him—just looked as if considering how much she could tell him. "I was walking home."

"I didn't know you live around here."

"I don't." She looked at her hands like she was embarrassed. "I live on Mesa."

Kyle couldn't imagine that anyone lived on the main

drag that was lined with businesses, shops, and gas stations. "And you thought you'd walk all that way?"

Her pert little nose wrinkled, and she pulled a deep breath. She didn't seem to remember that she was sitting there in little more than her underclothes. But he didn't forget—couldn't forget the slim waist and just-right-sized breasts pushing against her cheap wet bra. He took a second towel and wrapped it around her, the first towel secured around her hair.

"I met this really nice girl, Amber, in my English class, and she invited me over to her house this afternoon. Her mom was supposed to take me home, but Amber and her mom got in this really big fight."

Amber Rueben lived farther up the mountain in the Casitas. Kyle knew her, but she seemed spoiled and selfish to him. So they never talked.

Robin grimaced. "They were yelling, and I didn't know what to do. I didn't see how I could stay there with them going crazy and all."

"Why didn't you call someone to pick you up?"

"My mom works. And when I asked if I could go over to Amber's, she said no until I promised she wouldn't have to come get me."

"Then you should have called your dad."

Her teeth sank into her full lower lip. White teeth, straight, though he'd bet she had never worn braces. When he glanced up, he saw that the gold in her eyes had darkened.

"I don't have a dad," she said, her chin rising.

"Your parents are divorced, too? No big deal, mine have been for years."

She looked at him forever, and he would have sworn her pupils dilated. "No, I don't have one at all, at least I don't have one that I've ever met."

She said the words half-defiant, half waiting for the other shoe to drop. He'd bet money that she'd been given a ton of grief for not having a dad. He wondered if Amber knew. She could be the biggest snob he had ever met—worse than his mother, and that was pretty bad.

But that certainly wasn't any of his business. His only concern was getting Robin warm and dry, then taking her the hell home. He glanced at the digital clock on his desk and realized his mother would be home any minute.

"Sorry about the dad thing," he said. "It's probably been hard."

She shrugged, but didn't comment.

"Come on, let's get you into some dry clothes."

He found an old pair of jeans and a heavy pullover sweater from a million years ago. That would have to do. But when he started to pull away the towel he had wrapped around her, she came to life, her eyes widening, and she gasped. "I'll do it."

She did, though slowly like she was coming down with the flu. She made Kyle turn away.

"Don't you dare look, Kyle Walker."

Kyle smiled. He didn't need to look. He had already seen. He didn't mention that. But when he could tell she was pulling the jeans over the remaining wet stuff, he stopped her.

"Take off everything, or you'll still be wet," he instructed.

"You're looking!"

"I am not. Just hurry up. And keep that towel wrapped around your head."

"You sure are bossy."

"You sure are taking forever. Are you ready yet?"

She didn't answer. When Kyle turned around, she was sitting on the bed, her elbows planted on her thighs, her head in her hands. "I feel awful."

"That's what you get for walking in the freezing rain."

"Are we back to that again?"

"Yep, now come on, I'll take you home." He made sure

he still had his keys. "My mom will be here any time now, and you don't want to witness her finding a girl in my room."

"Does this happen a lot?"

When he glanced back at her, he saw the faint glimmer of a smile. "No, it doesn't happen a lot."

"Then how do you know how she'll act?"

"It happened once. I think I traumatized her for life."

He looked at the scrape on her hand one last time, saw that it wasn't so bad, then pulled her up. For a second they stood facing each other, so close that he could have kissed her. The thought surprised him, especially since she wasn't his type.

He had dated a lot of girls. Most let him know they were his for the taking. And he did take them.

He had been thirteen when the woman next door had asked if he could come over to help her with a few chores. Her husband worked long hours, and there were just some things a woman couldn't do alone, she had said. Those *chores* had changed Kyle's life forever, introducing his body to things most boys didn't learn until adulthood—if ever. He visited her every day after school, losing his heart with each stroke and caress of her fingers.

A month into the affair, Kyle had sworn his love to Mrs. Sandefer, promising at age thirteen to quit school, get a job, and marry her. Mrs. Sandefer had smiled softly, then pulled his mouth to her full breast, holding him tightly and making him forget anything but a consuming need.

Kyle had left later, anxious to find a job so he could spend his nights with her as well as his afternoons. But the following day when he returned after school, a man introducing himself as Mr. Sandefer answered the door. Mrs. Sandefer had come up behind her husband, to peer over his shoulder. "Oh, hi, Kyle," she had said simply, giggling when her husband pulled her close. "I don't have anything for you to do today."

Kyle had stood perfectly still, too stunned to move, wounded to the core. Foolishly.

In hindsight, he realized he had learned a valuable lesson. About love. About women. His mother was no better, leading his stepdad around by the nose, fighting like cats and dogs, then going off to their bedroom to screw. Like he didn't know what they were doing.

And they wondered why he spent so much time away from the house. No kid should have to listen to his mother crying out for more.

He guided Robin out of the bathroom and into his room. But they didn't get farther than the end of his bed when he heard his name.

"Kyle!"

Robin gasped.

"Kyle, where are you?"

"Fuck."

"Who's that?"

"My mom."

"Oh, no! I've got to get out of here," Robin said, panicked. "Or maybe I should hide."

Kyle swore, his mind racing. "You aren't going to hide. I'll explain."

"What do you mean, you'll explain. You just got through telling me your mom wouldn't understand. She'll take one look at me wearing your clothes, and she won't believe for a second that nothing went on. Then what if she calls my mom? Oh, God! You think your mother won't understand. My mom will freak. I've got to hide."

She swiveled around, like she was going to find a place to do just that. But it was too late.

Merriam Simmons opened the door without knocking,

a smile on her face. "How many times do I have to tell you to clean up this—"

Merriam froze at the sight of Robin. Robin froze as well, her big eyes huge, her full lips rounded in a silent gasp.

"Mom," Kyle said, "let me explain."

"Explain?" she said, one perfect brow arching in a way that meant trouble.

Kyle looked at the woman who stood in the doorway, and he saw her as a stranger would. Her hair was swept up in a fancy bun, and pearls wrapped around her neck. It was moments like these when he was struck by how much she had changed since her marriage to Harold Simmons, moments when his mother suddenly appeared, giving Kyle no time to prepare. Someone seeing Merriam now would assume she had been born to money, no doubt a member of the Junior League, perhaps even the president. But Kyle knew differently. Kyle knew his mother had been born in Las Vegas, grew up in Albuquerque, had never graduated high school, much less college, and the only club she had ever been a member of was the *700 Club*, which she had joined looking for a miracle. That miracle had come in the form of Harold Simmons.

With Harold's money and her willingness to spend long hours doing every sort of charity work in town, she had managed to make inroads into El Paso's better society, making it possible to put her past firmly behind her at all times except when guilt surged up and she had her family over for dinner. It was like his mom had reinvented herself, wanting to erase the woman she used to be. There were times when he wondered if she wanted to erase him, too.

"Well," Merriam said, her smiled strained as she stared at Robin. "I don't know what to say, Kyle. You know how your father feels about you having girls in your room."

His jaw cemented. "Harold is not my father, Mom. And this isn't what you think."

Merriam sighed. "I don't see how it would hurt you to call Harold father. It's not like your real father has ever given you a house like this."

Like that was what made a father.

She must have noticed the mutinous set of his shoulders, because she said, "Fine, but don't take me for a fool with this girl. The last time it happened, you said it wasn't what I thought, and as I recall, that young woman has gone to live with her grandmother in Southern California for the remainder of the year. With *Harold* footing the bill."

For half a second, Robin seemed to forget that she had been caught in his bedroom, and she studied him. He could feel her intense scrutiny as she looked at him much as she had looked at him the day she tossed down the twenty bucks.

"Mom," he said, his own voice deep in warning.

"Don't get that tone with me, young man."

"Robin's just a friend from school. She got caught in the rain. She needed to dry off and change into some dry clothes. It's nothing more than that."

Merriam glanced between her son and Robin, looking Robin up and down. Kyle could tell that his mother didn't entirely believe him, but she didn't entirely disbelieve him either.

"She's new in town," he explained, "and she was walking home from Amber Rueben's when it started to rain. She tripped and fell, I helped her out. That's all."

Instantly, Robin held out her hand in proof.

Merriam's lips tightened as she studied the girl.

"I better get her home, or her mom is going to be worried. See you later."

He herded Robin toward the door, his mother still standing in the way. It was like a battle of wills, but at the very last second, Merriam stepped aside.

"It's nice to meet you, ma'am," Robin said softly.

Kyle could feel his mother watching them as they hurried down the hall.

They were down the stairs and outside before his mother could rethink her position and do anything else. Kyle helped Robin into the truck, then raced around, before reversing down the drive as he had done a thousand times before.

Robin groaned.

"Are you okay?" he asked, glancing at her as he shifted into first and headed down Cherry Hill.

"No, I am not okay. Your mother hates me."

"No, she doesn't."

They rode in silence for a while before he remembered the money. He fished around in his pocket and pulled out a ten and two fives. "Here's your twenty," he said.

She took the bills, wadding it in her hand as she hugged herself to keep warm. "Thanks." She hesitated. "Will your mom tell your stepdad that she found me in your room?"

"Hard to say."

"Will you get in trouble if she does?"

"Probably."

"Sorry."

"Don't be. I'm used to it."

She gave him directions, and he swallowed back surprise when they pulled up to the sports bar, Bobby's Place.

"What are we doing here?" he asked.

"This is where my mom works. She's the manager, and we live upstairs." She peered up through the windshield. "See that window?"

Kyle leaned forward.

"The one with the white lace curtains. That's my room." She pressed back into the seat. "At night I look out and can see the mountains and the moon and the stars. Bobby Mac's sister gave my mom the curtains to put up."

"Have you met Bobby Mac?" he couldn't help from asking.

"Yeah, he's totally great. You'd like him. Everyone likes him, at least everyone except my mom. She thinks he's an oversized kid."

Robin smiled, and her face lit up in a way that made Kyle feel young. But he wasn't young. He hadn't been young in ages. And he didn't need to get tangled up with a little girl like this.

"Do you want to come in?" she asked. "Bobby might be there. I could introduce you."

"Nah, I've got to get home."

"Okay, thanks." She pushed open the door, then hesitated. "Kyle," she said quietly. "Does this mean we're friends?"

Kyle felt his chest tighten. He stared at her for a long time, filled with emotion—emotion he didn't begin to understand. What was it about this girl that made him feel so hot and cold all at once? Like he wanted to hug her tight and push her away at the same time.

"Sure, kid," he said gruffly. "We're friends."

Robin smiled and climbed out of his truck. She stood in the parking lot, looking up at the sky. "Look, Kyle. A rainbow."

He smiled and shook his head, then pulled away after she had shut the door. At the end of the parking lot he looked in the rearview mirror. She stood there, her hand raised in farewell.

Despite himself, he smiled, then accelerated, shifting gears in a way that eased his mind as he raced up the street toward the rainbow.

CHAPTER EIGHT

BOBBY ENTERED the office and found Lacey pacing. As always, just the sight of her made his skin go hot. Over and over again he found himself thinking of her—her hair, her smile, those lips that were so at odds with the rest of her.

The scent of her filled him—nothing cloying or perfumed, more like spring water and roses. Innocent and pure. It made him want to pull her close and sink deep inside her until he was lost.

He told himself to stay the hell away, told himself that he should take his papers and phone calls to his apartment upstairs and not see her. But that didn't happen.

He was obsessed, he lamented. Obsessed with a woman who turned his thoughts upside down.

"Where could she be?" Lacey whispered to herself.

"Where could who be?"

She whirled around at the sound of his voice, her eyes wide with hope until she saw that it was him. Her shoulders slumped. "My daughter. She went to a friend's house and was supposed to be back thirty minutes ago."

His knee was sore, and as nonchalantly as he could, he made his way over to his desk and sat down. "She's a kid," he said. "And kids aren't always on time. Besides, I hardly call thirty minutes late. Relax. She'll show up."

"But what if she doesn't?" Her voice spiked with worry.

He studied her, and she grew uncomfortable. Abruptly

she turned away and looked out the window into the rain-soaked parking lot, the overhead lights just starting to flicker on. "Robin isn't just any kid."

"How so?"

"She's mine."

The words whispered through the room like a half-spoken thought, barely heard, partly imagined.

"Ah, so that makes her what? Better? Special?"

"It makes her *not* late." She turned around, her chin thrust out. "I raised her right. Robin would never be late unless she had a good reason."

"I take it having fun and losing track of time isn't a good reason."

"Absolutely not."

He shrugged, trying again for nonchalance, though in truth he felt none. He didn't understand what this concern of hers made him feel. Alone? Jealous?

That last word came out of nowhere, and he felt his nostrils flare. He wasn't jealous; he didn't want this woman's attention. And even if he did, he certainly wasn't someone to begrudge a daughter the affection of her mother. But still, he couldn't deny that seeing Lacey like this, so concerned for her daughter, tightened something in his chest.

The thought of his own mother surged in his mind. Beautiful, full of life. Gone.

His jaw clenched. "If you're so worried, call her friend's house."

"I did! And she's not there. Amber said Robin left over an hour ago."

"How did she leave?"

"She didn't know."

"What?"

"I know, I know! It makes no sense."

She resumed her march back and forth across the floor.

"Pacing isn't going to help," he said. "Go out and look for her."

Lacey drew a deep breath. "I can't."

"Sure you can. I'll hold down the fort here."

"My car's at the service station."

"Again?"

"Yes, again. They're returning it in the morning."

Bobby cursed, pushed up from his chair, and snatched up his crutches. "Then I'll go. Where should I look? Where does she like to hang out after school?"

"Robin doesn't *hang out*."

He looked back at her with his leather jacket pulled halfway on. "She should. Hell, Lacey, it doesn't take a genius to see that Robin is an uptight kid."

From the look on her face, he doubted he would have insulted her more if he'd called her baby ugly.

"Hey, look," he added. "All I'm saying is that Robin's a teenager, but the two of you act like she's forty with responsibilities of her own. She should laugh more, and not have to be so obsessive about time and rules and a zillion other things you two worry about."

Her expression went from bad to worse. "How dare you tell me how to raise my child?"

"Sometimes it takes remembering what it was like to be a kid to figure out how best to deal with one. Turning her into an adult this soon doesn't do anyone a favor except for you."

"What is that supposed to mean?" she asked coldly.

"It means that having a little adult who doesn't hang out or doesn't do anything wrong makes your job easier. But being a parent isn't supposed to be easy. It's about turning kids into responsible adults *when* it's time for them to be, though not a second sooner."

"Ah, and I suppose that your parents have decided you aren't old enough to be an adult yet."

They stared at each other, and the room around them grew charged with emotion. The skin of her pale cheeks burned, her brown eyes suddenly shot through with green and gold fire. He had always thought her nice-looking in a simple sort of way. But emotion made her intense and beautiful. It was the responsibility and worry that dragged at her, making her weary, he realized.

Without warning, his body began a fiery tingle as it hadn't since he'd been hurt—at least not this kind of heat, making him want to spread her legs and taste her. He felt a need to be closer, deeper than a simple joining.

It had been the same earlier when he found her in his lap, their faces so close. He couldn't remember the last time he'd had such a hard-on for a woman. When he had kissed her, she had been a dizzying mix of innocent and temptress, hot and cold. The way she had pushed him away, only to have her fingers curl into his shirt and not let him go, had lit a fire in him that would have ended with them on the floor making love, had she not doused it. Just thinking about it now made him want to lay her out on the sofa, peel off her clothes, and bury himself inside her until he'd made them both come.

If he'd had a beer handy, he would have ditched the health kick and downed it in one rapid gulp. As it was, he needed a cold shower.

Unaware of the direction of his thoughts, she cleared her throat. "Bobby?"

Reality surged back, and his body fought the need to pull her into his arms. But then in the next second, she caught him off guard.

"I'm sorry," she said softly. "I'm upset, and I keep taking it out on you. That is unforgivable."

He didn't respond, couldn't think of what to say. He wasn't used to apologies, given or received.

He shifted his weight uncomfortably. "Where does the friend live? I'll drive up that way and see if she's walking."

"In this weather?"

"Hard to say."

"She lives in a place called the Casitas. It's—"

"I know where it is."

Thankful for any means to escape both his desire and the confusion her simple apology made him feel, he grabbed up his keys and headed out the office door.

After a frozen moment, Lacey followed. "I should go with you to help look."

"No."

The single syllable echoed against the wall, harshly, unfairly. He bowed his head, his hand on the brass handle as he used the ironclad willpower he had mastered years ago to still his raging thoughts and body.

"No," he repeated, this time quietly. "You stay here in case she calls." He wrote something down. "Here's my cell number. Let me know if you hear anything."

But whatever Lacey felt about his outburst, whatever she would have said was lost when he opened the door and they saw Robin tiptoeing down the hall, as if she could make it to the back stairs that led to the apartments above without anyone noticing.

At the sight, all three of them froze.

Lacey stared at her daughter, who stood with her hair damp and wearing someone else's sweater and jeans.

"Hey, Mom," Robin said, her smile forced and guilty.

The first thing Lacey felt was relief, the kind of knee-weakening joy that sent her flying forward and pulling her child into her arms. "I've been worried sick."

"Sorry," Robin mumbled into her mother's shoulder.

Then Lacey jerked back, holding her daughter at arm's length. "I've been worried sick," she repeated, this time relief giving way to something else. "Where have you been?"

Lacey didn't think about Bobby standing there; she was pushed on by the competing emotions of panic, relief, and now a bubbling anger and accusation. Someplace deep inside her, she had the glimmer of thought that she was over-reacting. But too many years of running and moving and caring, and ultimately, being taken advantage of herself kept the thought at bay. "Whose clothes are these? And why weren't you at Amber's house, like you said?"

Robin raked her hair back from her forehead, her eyes suddenly sparking to life in a way that Lacey had never seen before.

"Look what time it is," the fifteen-year-old demanded. "I'm barely thirty minutes late."

Lacey felt her lips compress into a hard line, and her spine stiffened.

"Mom," Robin lamented, her face riddled with frustration and love and the need to be understood. "Don't get like that. I'm just pointing out that I'm hardly late at all, and you worry too much."

"Too much? Then tell me why I shouldn't be worried when you weren't where you said you would be, and when you do finally show up you're in someone else's clothes."

"I *was* at Amber's. But she and her mom got in this huge fight and it was really weird and I didn't know what to do except leave, and I couldn't call you because I knew you had to work, so I started walking. Then the next thing I know it's raining like crazy and I trip like a stupid klutz and I'm soaked and probably going to die of pneumonia, but then Kyle Walker comes along and takes me to his house and . . . and—"

"And?" Lacey asked, her breath catching in a hard knot in her chest.

Robin threw her hands up. "And he let me clean up and

dry off and he gave me some old clothes to put on. That's all!"

"Who is this Kyle Walker?" Lacey heard the chill in her voice, felt it deep down into her bones.

"Mom, he's nobody. He doesn't matter. But he helped me out, then as soon as I was dried off, he drove me here. Would you rather have had me walk the rest of the way in the rain?"

"Don't get that tone with me, young lady. You should have called me from Amber's house."

"You were working!"

"I would have made other arrangements, then I would have come to get you."

"Your car's in the shop!" Robin shot back in a way that she had never done before.

Lacey felt her head spin from fear and a certain strangeness that she didn't understand. This couldn't be her daughter. She had raised Robin to be sweet and kind.

Suddenly she remembered that Bobby was standing there witnessing this, and Lacey felt a glimmer of embarrassment. "Robin, we will finish this discussion upstairs."

"No! I want to finish it now." Without warning, Robin started to cry, and with each word that she spoke, her voice rose an octave.

"I'll just head out," Bobby said.

"Why?" Robin suddenly demanded. "Because you think I'm bad, too. Well, I'm not." She turned to Lacey. "You have to give me some room. I'm a good kid. I make good grades. But you're smothering me. If you have your way, I'll never date or drive."

"Robin, I've told you that I will consider teaching you to drive once my car is in better repair. It would be irresponsible of me to allow you behind the wheel of a vehicle that is undependable at best."

"That's just an excuse, and you know it. You don't want me to grow up and have a life of my own."

Lacey's head came back like she had been slapped, and the fear reared up, full and raging. Her chest felt like it would explode, but she didn't know what to say. She faced the sudden and very real thought that she might lose her daughter. And if that happened, what did she have?

"If this is what friends and El Paso have done to you, then I see no reason for us to stay here." Lacey started through the doorway, intent on the back stairs—intent on escaping this horrible scene.

"Stop running, Mom!"

At the sound of raised voices, several regulars got off their bar stools and drifted their way, until they gathered in a clump at the end of the hallway.

Bobby shifted his weight. "Back to the bar," he commanded, and instantly every one of them turned and fled. "Why don't both of you take this upstairs."

"There is nothing to take anywhere," Robin cried dramatically. "I'm going to be sixteen years old next month, but Mom won't teach me how to drive, won't even let me take driver's ed. You live in Texas, so you know that everyone learns to drive at fifteen and gets their licenses at sixteen. I'll be the only sixteen-year-old left who's still getting dropped off by her mother! And forget doing anything else besides going to school. I had to beg to go to Amber's house, and even then I'm timed and worried about."

"Yes, and look what happened?" Lacey stated. "You had to leave without a ride and walk home in the rain."

"But it all worked out." She extended her arms. "See, I'm here, safe and sound. You've got to stop worrying so much, Mom!"

Robin's face was mottled as Lacey looked on, and she could hardly recognize her own child. It was as if her daughter were changing before her very eyes. *Blossoming* was too clichéd a word, too ordinary. With Robin, it was like the Texas sun had burned away an outer shell, the years of ice melting and cracking away until she leaped full-blown into a young woman. The child was gone. When it first started, Lacey had felt excited and thrilled. Now she felt devastated.

Lacey tried to tell herself that she was upset because Robin was growing up too fast, but even Bobby had pointed out that she had wanted her daughter to act like an adult. Lacey wanted it all: a responsible child who loved and needed her.

Deep down she had a flicker of understanding—she was unable to let her child go. For every one of Robin's nearly sixteen years, it had just been the two of them. Mother and daughter against the world. Now it was as if Robin had thrown her arms wide, finding a whole new life—reaching out and grabbing it. And Lacey understood in that moment that she was afraid that she would be left behind.

This new daughter, one she couldn't control as easily, would leave, breaking their bond. For half a traitorous second, Lacey wished they had never moved to this place that had transformed her daughter.

Then she felt sick with guilt. How could she think such a thing? This was her daughter, and she wanted nothing more than for her child to be happy.

"Mom," Robin said, her voice lowering, though sounding terribly old. "I'm sorry I yelled. I just want you to stop worrying about me every second of the day."

"That's my job. I'm your mom." She tried to sound light and funny, but a choke of tears got in the way.

Robin sighed and came up to her, close but not touching, like she was too old to hug her mother. "You've done a great job raising me. I'm a good kid. Really. And I wish you'd start worrying a little more about yourself and a little less about me. I'm happy, Mom. But it's hard to be really happy when you're so miserable."

Lacey's breath caught.

Robin lowered her head, suddenly interested in her hands. "I feel responsible."

Lacey couldn't believe what she was hearing; she also felt heartsick. "But I am happy, Robin."

"No, you're not. Though maybe you don't even realize it."

How had her daughter gotten so old and enlightened? How had they come to this place that unraveled what little control she had tried to gain—first with the burning need that flared when Bobby kissed her, and now with her daughter.

"Come on, Mom," Robin said, a tiny bit of a little-girl whine returning to her voice, "I hate it when you get that look. I think what you need is some time when all you have to do is have fun. You need to go out on a date."

Lacey felt like she swallowed a horse. "A date?"

She would have sworn that Bobby made a strange strangling noise, as well.

"Bobby, tell her," Robin implored. "She's young, she's beautiful"—she smiled shyly—"and Mr. Palmero is totally hot for you."

"What?" Bobby and Lacey said in unison.

Robin chuckled. "You know Mr. Palmero, the science teacher who's always here."

"Nick?" Lacey asked.

"He totally has a thing for you. He asked about you yesterday in Biology."

"About me?"

Lacey felt hot all over. And her state wasn't helped when she noticed Bobby's raised brow.

"I can't imagine what a little wimp like Nick Palmero

would be doing talking about you at school. Seems unprofessional to me," he ground out.

"I hardly think you're in a position to talk about unprofessional behavior," she offered.

Robin glanced between the adults, then took her chance. "I'm going upstairs to change."

The teen was halfway up the steps before Lacey reassembled her wits. "We'll finish talking about this later, young lady."

"About Mr. Palmero?" she inquired hopefully.

"No, about you being late . . . and this boy you mentioned, Kyle Walker."

Robin groaned. "Mom, he's no one."

But the glitter in her daughter's eyes told a different story before she bounded up the rest of the stairs in the stranger's outfit, her own still-wet clothes bundled underneath her arm as she disappeared behind their apartment door.

Lacey didn't turn around. She stood staring at the steps, at first too distressed to move, then all too aware of the man who stood behind her.

"She's right, you know," Bobby said, his voice deep and rumbling, running down her spine with an electrical charge.

"About what? About going out with Nick Palmero?"

She turned slowly and caught a glimpse of tension in him. Then he laughed. "No, that's not what I was talking about. You need to get a life."

Her face burned. She was so pathetic that her teenage daughter and irresponsible employer were giving her advice on how to live.

"I hardly know you," he continued kindly, his tone making her throat tighten with something she refused to believe was unshed tears, "but I've seen enough to figure out that your whole world revolves around your daughter and this job."

"I'm a mother and a good employee."

"Do you really think that's enough?"

"Of course it is. My job is to raise my child, mold her into a responsible adult."

"So you keep saying. But why does that have to exclude you having some time for yourself? Go out, have some fun. Join a club, go to the movies, learn to play tennis. Loosen up."

"I believe we've had this discussion before."

His smile broadened. "True. Though last time I think I was telling you to have more sex."

Her chest puffed up, and he held his hands out to ward off a barrage of words. "I won't mention it again. You do what you want."

"For someone who espouses the virtues of loosening up and having fun, I don't see you doing a whole lot of either yourself," she remarked.

"What are you talking about? I have more fun in an hour than you've probably had in a lifetime."

"I beg to differ. You just tell people that you're having lots of fun. You toy with women, you backslap and pretend with men—when really all you care about is your sister and football. I've never seen anyone more dedicated to a purpose. Don't think I don't hear you through the walls at night, exercising, the blender going at all hours. And given the smell of those awful shakes, I can tell you aren't in there making piña coladas or daiquiris."

He stared at her hard.

"I've been around you long enough, Mr. McIntyre, to have seen that you care about little else in your life."

His jaw ticked.

"It's easy to guess why *I'm* the way I am," she mused, tapping her finger to her cheek. "I'm an unwed mother with a daughter to raise in a world that is even more sexually promiscuous than it was when I was her age. A more difficult question is what has made you this way." She stared at him, trying to understand. "Who would have guessed that you and I would have so much in common?"

Then she headed for the office, but just before the door swung shut, he called out to her. "You don't know what you're talking about. I'm nothing like you."

CHAPTER NINE

"YOU SHOULD give some serious consideration to retiring, Mr. McIntyre."

It was Tuesday morning, and Bobby sat stone-faced across from one of the top physicians in the country. Dr. Andrew Blitzer was known for cutting-edge technologies and a magician's understanding of the human body. He was the best of the best, and since Bobby's return to El Paso, the doctor had been telling him he should retire.

"I am not giving up," Bobby said, his teeth clenched, his voice low in an attempt to fight off the panic he felt rising up inside him. "You said yourself you've never seen a turnaround like this in such a short period of time. I've worked hard. I've taken care of the knee. And I'm young, damn it."

"Not in football years."

The doctor was good at what he did; he also never pulled any punches.

"They say," the man continued, "that Wall Street is a young man's business. Football, then, is a really young man's business. It's kids, Bobby, who are playing, kids who don't think about what the future holds. They hit and tackle like there's no tomorrow, and no human body can sustain that kind of punishment for long." He looked him directly in the eye. "Not even you."

Pushing up from the chair, Bobby felt both weighted

down and free. Not more than fifteen minutes ago Dr. Blitzer had removed the brace, divested him of his crutches, and pronounced him ready to resume normal activities with his knee. Bobby had nearly done a victory dance until Blitzer asked him to have a seat in his office.

"I'll give it some thought, Doc," he said.

"Bobby, my prognosis is no different from the one you received in Dallas. Your knee injury is one thing. But the concussion you sustained is a very different matter."

"I completely recovered from the concussion before I ever left Dallas, without a word about it leaking to the press. And I want it to stay that way."

"This isn't a matter of public debate. This a medical matter. If you'd like a third opinion, I can give you the names of some fine doctors."

"Hell, I trust you, Andy, I just don't like what you have to say."

Bobby smiled as he said the words, but unlike reporters and pretty women, the doctor wasn't won over.

"I truly hope you do as I say," the man said.

Out in the hallway, Bobby ran into Dr. Blitzer's nurse, Natalia, a beautiful woman who treated him like a bad boy who needed a good reprimand, though she always did it with a smile.

"Be careful with that knee," she instructed. "Think regular activities of a normal guy."

"Normal's no fun, Natalia," he quipped, winking. "In fact, dance with me, right here. That big brawny husband of yours won't mind," he teased.

She laughed easily. "You are a bad, bad boy, Bobby Mac."

"I try."

After a quick good-bye to the doctor's secretary, Debbie, he left the office, his black leather jacket open to the breeze. He had to adjust to a freedom of movement he had nearly forgotten. No more crutching around, no more careful steps. Though he had to admit his first inclination was to be wary of the knee. He didn't trust it yet, which the doctor had told him was normal.

The day was clear and cold, brisk, and instead of heading to the bar, he drove to the Upper Valley, where Beth lived. Within minutes of leaving the doctor's office, he pulled up to a sprawling ranch-style house made from adobe with a terra-cotta-tile roof situated in a copse of trees across the street from the El Paso Country Club golf course. He had to brake nearly as soon as he turned in to avoid running over the clutter of tricycles and toys.

He threw the SUV into park, then ambled up the drive. He had always loved the valley, with its giant cottonwood trees and sprawling lawns. Such a contrast to the rugged desert mountains only a couple of miles away.

Instead of going to the front, he took the flagstone breezeway that connected the garage to the house. He entered through the back door without knocking, as he always did, and stepped over another slew of toys, this time Barbie dolls and G.I. Joes. Beth had twins, a girl and a boy, and he knew his sister didn't want her kids to discriminate between boys' and girls' toys. But no matter how hard she tried, it never ceased to amaze him that little Jason always went for the G.I. Joes, and little Jackie always went for the Barbies—unless she needed a dad for her make-believe adventures.

Kids.

The thought sizzled through his mind, filling him with a bittersweet and unexpected ache followed closely by the doctor's warning. But he didn't want kids, at least not yet; he wanted the football field.

"Hey, stranger."

When he focused, he found Beth sitting at her kitchen table, oblivious of the mess around her. A mug sat in front of her, and her smile was soft, her dark hair pulled up in a loose ponytail that made her look like a teenager. She wore not a speck of makeup, and one of her husband's oversize crewneck cable-knit sweaters with jeans washed so many times they were nearly white. The late-morning sun hit her, drifting in through the multipaned bay window that overlooked the flowing, picture-perfect backyard. In the summer, when the grass was green and the willow trees were in bloom, Beth's house looked like a watercolor painting.

"Hey, yourself," he replied, walking over, kissing her forehead, then sitting down across from her. "Where are the kids?"

She smiled. "At that glorious place called preschool. I adore my children, I do. But I can't tell you what heaven it is to have a few hours each day to do as I please."

"And not have to deal with the bar anymore."

Her smile crooked at the corner. "That, too."

She tilted over to get a better look at his leg, which he had stretched out under the table. "I see the doctor's appointment went well."

Not really. But he didn't tell her that. "Yep, good as new," he announced.

"How soon before you head back to Dallas?"

"Probably a month. I'll start seriously training now to make sure I'm a hundred percent. I need to up my weight and take my workout to the gym, do some running. Typical stuff."

"I hear swimming is good for rehabilitation."

He felt a flare of long-forgotten yearning at the thought of a pool. One of the things that he had missed growing up. Something that other kids took for granted.

Silently he cursed. This whole issue of his knee was throwing him for a loop, not to mention bringing up a past he'd rather forget. He didn't wallow in history. He had moved on and made a great life for himself. "No thanks. Swimming's for lightweights."

She looked at him oddly. But he headed her off. "I should be back in Dallas in plenty of time for the play-offs."

"I'm happy for you," she said, though she didn't look happy, at least not until she curled her hands around her tea.

Bobby could see the ease seep back inside her as they sat together in an always-comfortable silence.

"Penny for your thoughts," he said after a while.

"It'll take more than a penny, buster."

They laughed, but then she pulled a deep breath.

"I was just thinking how happy I am," she offered.

"You say that like it's a bad thing."

"No, of course not. It's just—"

"Just what?"

"It's scary to be too happy . . . for fear that it'll be taken away. Like holding on too tight, afraid to do anything wrong for fear that this wonderful place will disappear like a perfect dream evaporating in the morning."

"You deserve happiness, and I can't imagine yours going away." His face darkened. "Nothing's wrong with Ray, is there?"

"No, no." Her expression turned dreamy, and she held her cup close in both hands. "Ray's great."

She had met Raymond Hargreave in high school, and she had never been with any other man, as far as Bobby knew. A love match like they write about in novels—true and meant to be. If she weren't his sister—and he could truly see how happy they were—he wouldn't have believed it possible.

"And the twins are doing really well in school." She sighed then. "I can't believe that next year they'll be in kindergarten."

"Beth, it's barely November now. You make it sound like they're going next month. It's almost a year away."

"Yeah, but mark my words, the years zip by and before you know it they'll be old and married, and I'll be left to my own devices because little Jason's wife will hate me and refuse to let me visit my grandchildren."

Bobby blinked.

"Thank God, Jackie's a girl," she continued. "Daughters stay true to their mothers."

"So that's why you're upset?" he ventured.

"Upset!" Her chin came forward. "I'm not upset. I'm just thinking." Then she giggled like she just became aware of all that she had said. "I was sitting here thinking about how I'd like to freeze this moment in time. The holidays are just around the corner. My family is healthy. You're home." She hesitated and reached across and laid her hand on top of his. "I wish you'd stay this time. Forget football, find a wife, have kids of your own."

"Beth," he said, his tone warning.

Automatically, she held her hands up in surrender. "Fine. Far be it from me to meddle." She took a sip of her tea. "I just want you to be happy . . . to find what I have with Ray, to find someone to love."

"You and Ray are an exception."

"That is not true. One of these days you're going to realize that not everyone will hurt you."

Bobby pushed up and walked over to the refrigerator. "You've been watching too many soap operas. I'm not worried about getting hurt."

He found a container of plain vanilla yogurt, pulled it out before rummaging around in the drawer for a spoon.

"Then why don't you let anyone get close to you?" she asked. "Especially women."

Taking a bite, he shook his head, his famous Bobby Mac smile tilting his lips. "Don't worry about me with women."

"I'm not talking about mindless sex." She eyed him as if considering how much she should say. "I have no doubt you are good at that. It's true intimacy I'm talking about. Truly touching. Truly letting someone touch you."

He looked at her like she had lost her mind. "This is not a subject I have any interest in discussing. Especially with my sister."

"Fine, far be it from me to lecture. But face it, Bobby, you go from woman to woman, dropping every one of them the minute they get serious. You're happy to make them feel, perfectly content to pleasure them—"

"Cut it out, Boo."

"But God forbid if any woman tried to break through that hard heart of yours and make *you* feel. Have you ever felt any emotion other than sexual satisfaction when you have an orgasm? The fact is, there *is* no other emotion to feel unless you have truly connected with a person. And you won't allow that to happen."

His jaw ticked. "I'm warning you, Beth. You're skating on thin ice."

She studied him, and he hated how she had the ability to make him uncomfortable. Little Jason had been born two minutes after Jackie, and for years Bobby had been telling his nephew not to let Jackie get the upper hand. "If you do," he had warned, "you'll regret it for the rest of your days. Women love bossing us guys around, so we need every advantage we can get."

Jason always giggled hysterically, then attempted to boss little Jackie around, who gave him a look like who in the world did he think he was, then pronounce that Unca Dobby was silly. "You tell him," Beth loved to say.

"I'm sorry, Bobby. Really I am. I just felt I had to say it. I love you, and I hate to see you lock your heart away." She looked at him with poignancy spilling over. "Get yourself back in shape, and get back to the field, if that's what you have to do. But then, soon, think about coming home to family. That's all I ask. Okay?"

Their eyes met.

He took a deep breath as he calmed his thoughts and fought to find a smile. "Okay." He put his spoon in the dishwasher and threw away the empty yogurt container. "I've gotta go."

"Sure. But remember, I'm having Thanksgiving here," she said before he got more than a few steps away.

"Count me out."

"Bobby!"

"Hey, if it hadn't been for this knee, I wouldn't be here anyway."

"But you are here. You have to come."

Hanging his head, he asked, "Who's going to be there?"

"Us, of course. And Mr. Olson from across the street. He lost his wife last summer, and at eighty it's hard for him to travel to California to be with his daughter, and she isn't coming here. So I invited him."

"Still taking care of everyone, I see."

"Don't criticize."

"I'm not. I think it's great. Who else will be there?"

"Nigel and Hannah." She said the words with a guilty cringe. They both knew that there was no love lost between the older couple and Bobby.

"No thanks. You might want Nigel and Hannah to be a part of your life. But they aren't a part of mine."

"Come on, Bobby, you know you love Thanksgiving dinner. Besides, they're not that bad, and whether you believe it or not, they care about you."

"Oh, yeah, right. Nigel and Hannah Hartley care about me."

"Please, Bobby." She walked up to him and hooked her forefinger with his.

"Ah, man. That isn't fair, Boo."

"Do it for me. The kids miss seeing their Uncle Bobby.

And you know how much Ray loves it when you come around."

"Yeah, at least one person in this house understands me. Your husband doesn't like Nigel and Hannah any better than I do," he groused, though as with so many things between them, they both understood he was just being ornery. With Beth he could do that. With Beth he could be himself and not have to worry that people were disappointed in him when the Bobby Mac face slipped—the Bobby Mac that the world loved and expected. The Bobby Mac he was afraid he was losing the ability to be.

Unexpectedly, the thought of Lacey came to mind, and he nearly smiled. Lacey didn't like him in any incarnation. Not when he was ornery, not when he pushed her, not when he was being Bobby Mac. *Especially* not when he was being Bobby Mac.

He thought about her comment that all he cared about was his sister and football. He didn't like that she had said it any more than he liked that she had figured out it was true. No one but Beth had ever understood that—not the press, not the women he dated. And that's how he wanted it. Bobby Mac McIntyre was about an easygoing fun. No worries. Nothing to make anyone remember that he was the kid without parents who'd had to fight and scrape and claw for everything he got until he found football.

Just one more thing that ticked him off about Lacey Wright.

"All right, I'll come. But if I end up drop-kicking and punting Nigel, it'll be on your head."

"I'll take the chance."

He headed for the door.

"One more thing," she added.

Stopping, he sighed. "What now?"

"Lacey and Robin."

"What about them?"

"I thought it might be nice if they joined us, as well. I can't imagine they have anywhere to go, and trying to cook a big meal in that tiny apartment can't be easy."

He thought of Lacey in the office, in the bar. In the apartment across the hall. He had seen the way she had turned the tiny space into a home. She might be overprotective, but no one could accuse her of not loving her child.

The gauzy, dreamlike image of toys lying about leaped into his mind, tricycles in driveways, and dolls sitting at imaginary tea parties, tiny arms circling his neck, catching him unaware. Followed by another image, not foreign, not welcome, of wire mesh in glass, linoleum floors, and tears.

"Mama!"

The memory hit him out of nowhere, and for half a second it was hard to breathe, as if he had taken a blow to the midsection, sacked by a past that haunted him.

"Bobby?"

Off balance and angry, he forced the thoughts away and looked at Beth. "You really like to push me to the limit, don't you?"

Reaching out, she touched his arm. "Is Lacey really that bad?"

Lacey. So different from his own mother.

Beth bit her lip. "I like her so much. But did I make a mistake when I hired her?"

"Lacey Wright is a pain in the butt." His smile returned and curved at the corner of his mouth, bringing with it a tremendous sense of relief, the past once again gone. "She's nearly as bad as you."

She choked on a relieved burst of laughter. "Then she must be pretty good after all. Just as talented as her résumé stated."

"Hmmm," he said, distracted as he remembered Lacey crouched on the floor scrambling to clean up the tray of drinks she had dropped. Then another memory, of those hot pink sunglasses pulled on over eyes snapping with fire, and the realization that there was more to her beneath those prudish clothes than met the eye. "Truth is, I haven't figured out Lacey Wright just yet."

He shrugged his shoulders. "But I will."

CHAPTER TEN

ROBIN YANKED OPEN the door to the library building at school. If there was one thing she was going to do that day, it was get out of her math class—to put some distance between herself and Kyle Walker. And if it meant switching around her entire schedule, so be it.

She had been embarrassed last week after dropping money on the floor like a country mouse who had just fallen off the turnip truck. But she was mortified this morning at the memory of being practically naked in his bedroom.

"Please," she muttered, "let it all be a bad dream."

But try as she might, she couldn't deny the fact that he had found her soaking wet, sprawled out on his street like a clumsy dork, had taken her into his house, then stripped off her clothes. And she had let him.

To make matters worse, his mother had walked in on them. But what really made her want to cringe was her dopey question. *"Does this mean we're friends?"*

Robin squeezed her eyes closed and shook her head. *Hello!* What had she been thinking? She hadn't been thinking. She had been so caught up in his dark-eyed gaze and half-smile that she had acted like the kind of besotted idiot he probably dealt with all the time.

She had spent the rest of Monday trying to forget the unfortunate incident. Finding her still damp clothes strewn across her floor could have been explained away, but waking up in the middle of the night to the remembered feel of his fingers tugging off her sweater was a little more than even her really great imagination could rewrite.

Heat stung her cheeks. He had seen her without her clothes on—or at least without most of her clothes on. Robin groaned, and as she hurried toward the Admissions building, she decided then and there that changing math classes wasn't enough. She would have to change schools. El Paso High School wasn't too far away, she reasoned, her head down, her books clasped to her chest. But then Robin snorted in dismay. She would be lucky to get her math class switched around. The chance of actually changing schools was slim to none, and slim was out of town.

"Robin?"

Robin's head shot up, and she nearly dropped her books when she found Kyle standing against a pillar in the A-building courtyard with Mary Lou Rivers practically plastered against his side. This time when Robin blushed, she blushed for a great many reasons. Embarrassment, no doubt—but there was a strange coiling discomfort, as well. The word *jealousy* snaked through her mind, but she immediately discounted it.

But still . . .

"Wait up," Kyle called out.

Mary Lou looked both curious and disgruntled. *Great.* Robin stifled a groan. Just what she needed.

Kyle stopped in front of Robin, close, too close, and thoughts of Mary Lou fled. He tilted his head to the side and took her in. She felt hot and cold, and her stomach did cartwheels.

"How are those scrapes?" he asked.

He said the words with a possessiveness that made her breath catch. Sobering quickly, Robin shrugged her shoulders. "They're fine, really fine, never been better."

Kyle took hold of her arm, turned her around, and steered her away from Mary Lou's curious eyes.

"I'm serious," he stated. "You had me worried yesterday." He shrugged. "I just wanted to make sure you were okay."

"I don't see how that's any of your business," she said, embarrassment making her words overly sharp.

"You made it my business when you pitched facedown into the street right in front of me."

Robin groaned. She guessed it was too much to ask that he would have completely wiped the incident from his mind.

"But," she began, "look at me now."

He glanced over at her, his grip never lessening. "I am. You look awful."

Robin's cheeks burned. "Gee, you really know how to make a girl feel great."

"Damn it, Robin." Kyle wheeled to a stop, turning her to face him. His eyes were intense, like a deep brown velvet licked with fire. "You could have gotten run over, broken something, froze your ass off."

Robin shifted her weight uncomfortably. "Well, I didn't."

"Only because I showed up."

"You know," she said wryly, "it seems to me that you are making more of this little incident than need be."

"Where the hell did you learn to talk?"

"Obviously not where you did in Curses and Slang 101."

Kyle groaned, shoving his fingers through his hair, then he reached down and grabbed Robin's hand. "Come on, we're going to be late for class."

Robin would never be quite sure how she ended up in the very math class she was determined to steer clear of, sitting next to the very guy she had sworn to avoid. But she did. After that, he waited for her at her locker after school, then again the next morning.

It was amazing to walk through the school with Kyle, as she told him jokes that he never laughed at, only smiled with a disbelieving shake of his head, then sitting together in class. She wasn't interested in examining the really tur- moilish expression she saw in his eyes when she caught him looking at her. It reminded her of that first day when she had thrown down the money, and she had seen a loneli- ness that most people wouldn't have believed about a guy who was considered cooler than cool. For the first time that she could remember, she was wildly happy.

At the end of Wednesday, Kyle showed up at her locker. She had only ten minutes to get to the bus before it left, but she couldn't seem to make herself move.

His crooked half-smile dazzled her. When his large hand curled around hers and he said he'd give her a ride, at first she hesitated. The last thing she could afford was to get home late again. But the bus took tons longer than a truck, which gave her a few extra minutes.

With her heart beating hard, she let him lead her to the parking lot. And when he opened the driver's side door for her to get in next to him, she did, sitting in the center of the bench seat, their bodies so close she could feel the strength of his arm when he shifted the gears.

Kyle needed to stop by his house before he took Robin home, then had to head for work. After he pulled the truck down the narrow drive to the back of the house, he turned to face her. Her heart raced and her palms grew sweaty. This was the moment. He was going to kiss her. She had wondered about and wished for this moment every second since he started walking her to class. But he had always been the perfect gentleman, in an older, mature sort of way. Touching her hand, her shoulders, just barely—just enough to make her want more.

But instead of kissing her, he tilted her chin with the crook of his finger. "I'd invite you in, but I'll only take a second. It's hard to say when my stepdad or mom are going to be home, and I don't want you to have another run-in with either one of them."

Robin had to force her mind away from the sheer disappointment she felt about not getting the kiss. "No problem," she said with a sigh. "I'll wait here. I've already been through the 'no one's home' scenario with you."

Kyle grinned. But just when he leaped down from the truck, the vehicle's door gaping open, a man stepped out the back door of the house. He wore a navy blue pinstriped suit like ones Robin had seen in movies. She could tell he was shorter than Kyle, with wiry gray hair, and an angry red face.

"I told you to meet me at the bank," the man bellowed.

"And I told you I couldn't make it."

At this, the man turned a baleful eye on Robin. Robin pulled her lips back in what she hoped resembled a smile and gave a quick wave. She had never seen, much less met, such an angry-looking man.

"Who are you?" he demanded.

"Robin Wright, sir."

"Ah, yes. The girl my wife found in Kyle's bedroom. So that's why you couldn't make it."

Robin was mortified.

"Cut it out," Kyle said, his voice low.

Kyle and his stepfather stood facing each other, heat and anger and fury shimmering across the fine brick drive.

"I'm your parent," he said with cold fury.

"*Step*parent."

The muscles in the man's jaw leaped around, and for half a second Robin thought he would race forward and punch Kyle. But he held himself together, which was a darn good thing, she thought, since Kyle could probably make mincemeat of the little guy.

"As long as you live under my roof, you do as I say."

"Believe me, as soon as I graduate, I'm out of here."

The man visibly restrained himself before a smile parted his thin lips. "I'm counting the days, let me tell you. Just imagine the life your mother and I will have once you're out of our hair."

Something twisted in Kyle's chest, and his throat felt tight. He hated the feeling, had it all too often since they had come to live in this rich man's neighborhood. "You're full of shit," he muttered under his breath, turning away.

Robin cringed.

"What did you say?" the man asked ominously.

Kyle wheeled back. "I said you're full of shit."

"Don't you dare talk to me like that."

"How do you want me to talk to you? Do you want me to roll over like everyone else or kiss your ass? Don't hold your breath, because it will never happen."

The man looked on the verge of bursting, his face red, veins bulging in his neck. But Kyle didn't care. He vaulted back into the truck, banged the door shut, then didn't say a word as he started the engine.

"Kyle," Robin ventured when he threw the shift into reverse and raced down the driveway. "What was that about?"

No answer. He jammed the gear into first, accelerated, and let out the clutch. He drove with cool certainty and a great deal faster than Robin was comfortable with. He shot down Thunderbird Drive going well beyond the speed limit and gave no indication that he was going to slow down as they approached the left-hand turn on to Shadow Mountain.

Robin braced herself, but Kyle downshifted like a professional, took the corner smoothly. In seconds he careened to a halt in the parking lot of Bobby's Place.

"Kyle, tell me what's wrong," she insisted, her brow knitted with concern.

"Nothing's wrong," he ground out.

He was around the car and opening her door before she could say another word. Her heart began to sink. No sooner had he come into her life than she was losing him. She could feel his growing distance.

Very carefully, she slid down off the high seat of the Chevy. "Don't bother yourself to walk me to the door," she said, her tone cold and tight.

With that Kyle grabbed her and turned her around to face him. And there was the look. Dark. Devastated. Vulnerable. If Kyle hadn't had such a grip on her arms, she would have reached up and touched his cheek.

"I'm sorry," he said, his voice hoarse. "It's just that—"

"Robin!" a voice called out.

Robin's mind shifted, trying to understand.

"Hey, there, Robin!"

Kyle's grip tightened on her arms before he turned around to see Bert Burroughs loping across the asphalt in his Coronado High letter jacket.

Robin groaned. Bert Burroughs had been asking to come over since she met him. From the look on Kyle's face as he glared at Bert, Robin knew the opportunity to talk about what had gone on between Kyle and his stepfather had passed.

Kyle slowly released his grip on Robin's arms. Bert came to an abrupt halt when he finally got close enough to realize who was standing next to Robin. The tall sophomore began to stammer, but Kyle paid him no mind, only transferred his intimidating glare back to Robin.

"I said I'd introduce him to Bobby," Robin offered lamely. "Do you want to go with us?"

"Hell," was all he said before he turned on his booted heel, and slammed back into his truck.

Robin watched as Kyle's car disappeared, a sinking feeling in her heart.

"What was Kyle Walker doing here, Robin?" Bert asked, his voice a cross between outrage and concern.

"Nothing. He was just giving me a ride home."

True to her word, Robin introduced Bert to Bobby. Her mother stood in the doorway eyeing Bert as if he were a leper. If she didn't like Bert, the all-American, straight-A athlete, Robin knew that she'd hate Kyle.

But whether Lacey hated him or not, Robin promised herself that tomorrow she would *make* Kyle talk to her. Because despite her mom, she didn't want to lose him.

CHAPTER ELEVEN

LACEY HAD A DATE.

She stared at her reflection in the mirror, her nerves as jittery as butterflies under glass. Turning from side to side, she examined herself with a critical eye. She knew she had a nice figure. For years, men noticed her body, praised her shape, but they never said anything about her face. What she would give for less figure and a bit of confidence about her looks.

But the confidence had never come, though right after she had Robin, before her sweater sets and sensible shoes, Lacey had foolishly tried to find it through sex with men who claimed they loved her.

It had never been passion that had gotten her into bed, rather hope—hope for a future, hope for that promise of love. But hope diminished when the phone never rang a second time.

Years had passed since then, and she had worked hard to cover the mistakes with the shield of propriety. No one even guessed that she had ever looked for love in the furtive encounters in motel bedrooms or backseats of old cars while Robin was staying with a neighbor or kindly older woman. Lacey tried not to remember, tried to blank it out until there were days when she thought of herself as virginal and pure.

The clothes helped. Who could possibly be promiscuous in soft wool and pearls? It had been years since she had heard the kind of suggestive compliments that offered nothing more than a one-night stand. Since then, not until Bobby McIntyre walked into his office, she hadn't given any man a second glance. But for reasons she didn't entirely understand, she *saw* Bobby, just as he saw her.

Did he see through her façade? Did he see through her desperate wish that she had never made mistakes? And why hadn't he fired her?

Because Beth had boxed him into a corner, she told herself firmly. It was as simple as that. He couldn't see who she once was. He didn't want anything from her.

Then how to explain the kiss?

She shook the memory away. It had happened in a moment of weakness, for both of them. The proximity, her sitting on his lap. A recipe for disaster.

Which reminded her of her date.

What had she been thinking when she had agreed? she wondered dismally. But the truth was that when Nick Palmero had asked her out to dinner with all the stuttering awkwardness of a teenager, Lacey had been too flattered and surprised to think straight.

It hadn't helped that the regulars had overheard, and had proceeded to hoot and holler lewd encouragements, flustering Lacey, making it virtually impossible to come up with any response other than an awkward yes. The crowd had cheered, though when she had glanced over and saw Bobby standing at the bar, he had only lifted a whey shake to her in salute, then turned away and returned to the office.

Later, Lacey had racked her brain to come up with a means to extricate herself from the prickly situation. She barely knew Nick, and wanted to go out with him even less. Besides, it was a school night. But when she made the mistake of mentioning the ill-advised date to Robin, her daughter had danced around her tiny bedroom, adding that she had Spirit Club that night and wouldn't be home until nine. The gaiety had made it difficult for Lacey to say that she was going to cancel, and even more difficult to bring up the awkward subject of her being late. In hindsight perhaps she had overreacted.

In the end, she hadn't said a word, simply reveled in her daughter's glowing happiness. Besides, an early dinner on a weeknight hardly seemed like a date at all.

Now, with only a few hours remaining before Nick picked her up, and with Robin already having dashed out the door to decorate the bleachers with posterboard signs, Lacey paced nervously. She hadn't dated in years. She felt out of sorts and had no idea what to wear.

Frantically, she went through her closet, flinging things out one after another, but nothing seemed right. Grabbing up the phone, she called Beth's house to ask what sort of outfit would be appropriate for a local sporting event, but she got the answering machine.

To calm her fluttering stomach, Lacey walked through the cozy, L-shaped apartment, intent on brewing some tea. Despite the small size, she loved this new home. It had Beth's joyful touch everywhere. The comfortable sofa with a scatter of fluffy pillows, the cheerful curtains with bow-tied swags. Two bedrooms and one pale blue-and-white-tiled bath. But it was the kitchen that Lacey loved best.

White painted cabinets, which matched a country table that stood just to the side of the room, opened up the space. The kitchen would have seemed cramped had the wood been left dark. The stove was small but adequate, the refrigerator old-fashioned but cute. Perfect for two females who'd never had a place of their own to call home.

She pulled out the teakettle in hopes that the familiar ritual would help her nerves. When she turned off the water, she heard a television set come on in the distance, the volume loud enough to wake the dead. Wrinkling her nose in thought, she listened. Since the day Bobby arrived, she had learned that certain noises meant certain things. The brooding low sound of the stereo inevitably indicated female companionship. Grunts and banging warned of weight-lifting or any number of exercises to rehabilitate his knee. The sound of the television, tuned to his perennial favorite, ESPN, was a certain sign that he was alone.

Desperate and without thinking, she set the kettle aside, dashed to her room, gathered up three possible outfits, banged out her door, and then knocked on his.

"What the hell is all that?" Bobby asked, glowering at the pile of clothes she held when she entered.

He sat in a reclining lounge chair with a newspaper, his feet up on the attached footstool. He started setting things aside so he could get up.

"No, stay there. I'll just be a minute."

He wore a royal blue sweatshirt with TEXAS LONE STARS emblazoned across the front in a yellow gold, and cotton shorts that showed off well-defined thighs and calves, with just enough hair to make him look manly rather than barbaric.

"What do you think?" Bobby asked, showing off his leg, making it clear he noticed that she was gawking.

Lacey's mind jarred, and her eyes shot up to his face. "What do I think?"

"About the knee."

"It's beautiful." She blinked, then gasped. "I mean, your crutches and the brace! They're gone."

"Yep, the wonders of arthroscopic surgery."

"That is wonderful news."

"Yeah."

"Which means you'll be returning to Dallas."

"Don't look so excited."

She had the good grace to look abashed. "I'm simply thrilled for you that you are healing so well."

"Sure you are."

Deciding that she'd do well to let the subject drop, she said, "I need help."

He eyed her armload of clothes. "Why am I not surprised?"

"Amusing. But really, I can't figure out what to wear." She set everything on the sofa, then hurried over and turned down the TV.

"Make yourself at home," he said dryly.

She disregarded his tone and studied his apartment. It was the first time she had actually been inside, gaining a better perspective than she had when peering in from the hallway. It was identical in shape to hers, only everything was in reverse, and it lacked Beth's feminine touches. But it didn't have all the posters and trophies that he insisted on downstairs, either. This space was simple, utilitarian, clean and comfortable, with every electronic device known to man. One whole wall was covered with stereos, speakers, the largest television she had ever seen, and a number of other devices she had no clue about. Of course, he also had the extensive weight set and exercise machines. All said, she couldn't imagine where he kept his bed.

She glanced toward the back.

"Looking for something?" he inquired with a teasing tilt of lips. "Want to see for yourself about the shape of my bed?"

She choked and coughed, then looked back. "Nope, no, no thank you. My imagination works well enough—though it doesn't seem to be translating into what I should wear to dinner. Robin has already left, your sister isn't home, and I'm stumped."

"And you think I can help?"

"It seems to me that you've visited plenty of restaurants around town."

"Sure, but I spend my time eating, not taking notes on women's apparel."

All of the sudden, she couldn't imagine why she was there. The whole idea seemed stupid, idiotic. Why in the world had she thought he would help? "I'm sorry. I wasn't thinking." She started to gather the clothes.

Bobby groaned and gave a long-suffering sigh. "Let me see what you have."

That perked her up.

Hurriedly, she took one outfit at a time and held it up to herself. "The camel slacks and cream sweater?" Two abrupt side views, then a quick change. "The gray slacks with the gray sweater?" Side to side, then another change. "Or the blue slacks with the red sweater?"

She set each outfit along the expanse of his sofa, even taking one wool arm and folding it with a bent-arm pizazz, then lined up three sets of shoes. Each were low-heeled pumps, only in different colors. Standing back, she did the Vanna White thing. "Ta da."

Bobby looked at her with bemused chagrin. "They all look pretty much the same to me."

She huffed. "What do you mean?"

"Pants and a sweater. The only difference is in the color. Brown, gray, or blue. One is boring, two is better suited for a funeral, and three will make you look like a flag."

"Your sarcasm isn't appreciated."

"Hey, you asked."

"True. Okay." She held up her palms like dual stop signs, her head slightly bowed. "Let's start over." She drew a deep strengthening breath. "Since I am not inclined to wear necklines down to my waist or skirts short enough to bare my backside à la the infamous Darla, which of these outfits do you hate the least?"

Bobby growled, then moved the lever to lower the foot-stool portion of his lounger. The movement made him grimace.

"That depends on who you're going with," he said.

"Nick Palmero."

Bobby glanced up at her as he maneuvered himself out of the chair. "I can't believe you said yes to that guy. You complain about the women I see. He puts me to shame. Plus, he's as cheap as they come."

"I find that hard to believe. Sweet, shy little Nick? He's harmless. And no matter where he takes me, it will be far more enjoyable than throwing something together for myself."

Bobby scoffed. "I don't want to be the one to say I told you so."

"You won't be. Now, tell me. Which one of these should I wear?"

"What do I look like?" he asked, pushing up from the chair. "Your girlfriend?"

"Actually, no, but you're all that's available, short of going downstairs to the bar and asking Jazzy." Lacey snorted. "I can just imagine what she'd have to say if I asked for her opinion."

"And you think I can do better?" he asked dryly.

"Not really. But I'm desperate."

He headed for the kitchen. "The gray."

"You said it looked like I was going to a funereal."

The sound of opening and closing cabinets rankled. "Then wear the blue."

"You want me to look like a flag?"

"Hey, I don't care what you look like."

"Why are you so ornery?"

"I was born ornery," he replied, returning empty-handed.

"That doesn't surprise me. But tonight you're more ornery than usual."

Just as she said the words, he took an awkward step, and she saw him grimace.

At the sight, she made a frustrated noise deep in her throat. "Why didn't you tell me your knee ached. No wonder you're in such a bad mood."

Instantly she started bustling around. "Get back in that chair, and I'll get whatever you need. Have you eaten?"

His glower provided the answer.

"You must be starved."

Within a few minutes, despite Bobby's annoyance, Lacey had him back in his chair, and she was banging around in his cabinets.

Returning, she said, "You don't have anything in there but ice cubes and some awful-looking sprouts."

"I'll have cereal later," he said.

"You don't have any milk."

His stomach chose that moment to grumble.

Lacey shook her head. "I'll be right back."

Bobby watched her go. He heard her light footsteps as she crossed the hall, opening but not closing the doors behind her. Then quiet, no sounds coming up from the bar downstairs, despite the fact that he knew the early crowd would be showing up by now.

Sitting there, waiting for Lacey to return, he wasn't certain why he felt so edgy. He didn't like the idea of her going out with Nick. She might work in a bar, but she was innocent in a way that Nick wasn't. For all the science teacher's dopey, schoolboy looks and stammering ways, he was a known rake. Bobby was half-convinced that it was the way he acted that reeled women in.

Bobby felt a foolish need to protect Lacey, had since the day her daughter walked into Casa Grande restaurant. And that really set him on edge.

For as long as he remembered, he had felt wild and brash, standing on a cliff, screaming into a stormy sky, rubbing raw against the conflicting need to feel safe and loved. But safety and love didn't exist, not really, not in any way that did anything other than bind and hurt. He knew that, but he had never found the means to keep that knowledge from aching like a dull throb behind his eyes.

If he'd had anything in the apartment to drink, he would have damned his health regime and thrown back a tall one. Hell, he might even consider Lacey's Rx of chocolate. But somehow the sound of Lacey across the hall, soft footsteps on the hardwood floor, the barely heard click of cabinets, drawers gliding open and shut, all lulled him until his head relaxed against the plush cushions of the chair and the dull ache seemed to lessen. When she returned, he started, realizing he had nearly fallen asleep.

"I have tuna or turkey, and soup. I didn't have any mustard or mayonnaise, but I saw you have both. Which would you prefer?" she asked, her arms filled with an assortment of lunchmeats and potato chips and Fritos.

"Turkey sounds all right. And the Fritos. But I can do it."

"Absolutely not. You look beat. You had therapy today, I take it."

He grimaced.

"How is the knee progressing?"

"Great."

She studied him. "I'll just get the mayonnaise."

"You could make the sandwich here," he suggested before he could think straight.

They looked at each other for a second, and Bobby tried to find his ready anger to wrap around him. But she didn't give him a chance when she nodded her head, dashed back to her apartment, returned with her arms filled with the rest of what she needed, and then disappeared into his kitchen.

Once again sounds soothed him. The whirl of the electric can opener. The clink of a spoon in the mayonnaise jar.

And ice. Lots of ice, though he couldn't imagine what she would do with that.

Soon she returned with a tray he had forgotten he had, and set it down in his lap. At the center was a steaming bowl of creamy tomato soup sprinkled with some kind of green on top. A spoon and a cloth napkin, folded perfectly. Next to that he found a tiny dish of cranberry sauce and a sandwich piled high with turkey and a melting slice of Swiss cheese, lettuce, and tomato, cut diagonally in half, so neat, so homey that the pressure behind his eyes returned. But if Lacey noticed his discomfort, she didn't let on.

She placed the TV remote at his side along with the cordless telephone and a tall glass of iced tea with a sprig of mint floating on top. Then she surprised him even more when she secured an unwieldy bag of ice on his knee.

"There," she said, standing back, pleased. "That should tide you over for a while. Let the ice do its work." She gathered her assorted outfits, then started out of the apartment.

"What did you decide to wear?" he asked at the last minute, not understanding the sudden need to have her stay.

"I don't know yet. But I have an hour before I have to get dressed. Use the phone to call me if you need anything."

Bobby watched her go, appreciating the demure swing of her slender hips—and the unaccustomed feeling of being cared for.

Over the next hour, Lacey buffed, waxed, soaked, and powdered within an inch of her life. When she was done, her skin felt raw and oversensitive. But by the time she had decided on a pair of rather fitted black pants instead of any of the more conservative woolen trousers that Bobby had derided, then added a beautiful blue and black floral sweater set, she felt amazingly good. Pretty in a sensible sort of way. Not too wild, not too dowdy. A fine balance.

Her eyes narrowed as she stared at her reflection. A balance. Was that what she was achieving here in this desert town with its mix of jagged mountains and lush river valley?

The thought startled her. Could she find a balance here, the kind that had nothing to do with dependence on another person? And when she looked in the mirror, for the first time she saw more than a girl who had made too many mistakes. Before her stood a woman who didn't look half bad for someone with a teenage daughter.

With a lightness to her step, she came out of her bedroom, only to squeak in fright when she found the backside of an overlarge male sticking out of her refrigerator. It didn't take long to realize it was Bobby leaning over, perusing the contents, his arm lining the top of the appliance.

"How did you get in here?" she demanded.

Bobby straightened, holding a quart of chocolate milk in his hand. Just when he would have opened it up and started drinking, she gasped. "Get a glass!"

He actually looked chagrined at that, his lips tilting, his blue eyes glowing. "Sorry, forgot where I was."

She bustled over, retrieved a glass, poured the milk, then extended her hand. But Bobby didn't take it. He stared at her, those eyes taking her in. Earlier, in his apartment when she had returned with the food, for half a second she had seen a wild loneliness in his expression. It had been that reason more than any other that she had stayed and made the sandwich there. She couldn't explain the need to make that darkness go away. When she had returned to the living room, the look had been gone. But now his eyes glittered with something else, something she had never seen before.

He stood so close that she could smell his rugged scent, like soap and leather. The intense heat of him startled her, like a fire burning just below the surface. She felt an urge to reach out, run her fingers along his skin. Melt into the core of him.

How was it that the shapeless clothes she wore like armor didn't stop this man from seeing her? She wanted to touch him, feel the hard sinewy muscle, drag her fingers through his overlong hair.

His gaze traveled down her body, like he was stripping her naked, and she felt seared. "That's what you decided to wear?" he said, his voice rumbling along her senses.

Lacey's breath went shallow in her chest.

"What happened to the gray, blue, or brown?" he wanted to know.

After a moment, she looked at her outfit. "You made them all sound terrible. What's wrong with this?"

"Hmmm," he mused, taking the glass from her hand, their fingers brushing.

"Hmmm?" She had to clear her throat. "Is that a good *hmmm*, or a bad *hmmm*?"

"I didn't know there were different kinds of *hmmm*s."

"Of course there are. And yours sounded like a bad *hmmm*."

He only shrugged, making her crazy.

With a huff, she pulled back her shoulders. "How can you not think I look great?" she demanded. "I look great!"

"If you say so."

"I do!" But of course her confidence started to waver. "You really are a horrible man. What is wrong with how I look?"

He leaned back against the worn but sparkling clean linoleum counter, a barely audible sigh slipping out from his throat. "You look fine."

She could tell he wasn't sincere.

"You're just being mean because I have something to do and you're staying home alone."

"That isn't true. In fact, I'm glad you're going out. And

believe me, if I wanted something to do, I could find plenty."

He gave her a horribly sly look, then pushed away from the sink and started going through her kitchen. He went from cabinet to pantry before he found a box of Oreo cookies. Just when he reached for them, she flattened her palm against the door and banged it shut.

"Why in the world don't you have food in your own apartment? In fact, I really don't get why you don't stay in that mansion of yours I keep hearing about." Curiosity got the better of her. "Does it really have an indoor pool sur- rounded by glass walls and a glass ceiling?"

Bobby scowled. "There are just a lot of windows that make it look like it's surrounded by glass."

"But it's true!" She shook her head. "You amaze me. Why in the world wouldn't you be there now?" Her thoughts took on a hazy softness. "For years after I had Robin, I used to dream of the perfect existence, go there in my head every night as I was falling asleep. I wanted a house. A kitchen with windows looking out over a yard. And a swimming pool. Somehow the idea of a pool made it seem like life was in order." She blinked and looked at him. "Silly, I know. But I can't imagine why you don't stay there."

He shifted his weight. "It's too far."

"A house overlooking Rim Road can't be more than ten minutes away."

"Yeah, well," he said, his tone belligerent. "It's easier to stay here."

She studied him. "I find that hard to believe, but what- ever. Just tell me what's wrong with what I have on?"

He shrugged, a barely perceptible relief passing over his features when she moved on to another topic. "The pants are tight."

"They are not!"

"They are, and it accentuates your hips."

She looked at him hard. "Accentuates in a good way or bad way?"

"Do you define everything in terms of good and bad?"

"Don't go all irritatingly philosophical on me. Just answer the question."

"Depends if you like your hips big or not."

"Eek!"

"They also make you look loose."

"They do not!"

"I know how Nick is." He tilted his head and appeared to give the situation some serious consideration. "For all his womanizing, Nick Palmero likes his women really demure. Saintly." He gave her a knowing look. "The Catholic thing, you know. If you want to make a good impression, I'd say you should wear one of those outfits you showed me earlier. The brown, I think."

"You said it was boring!"

"Then the dark gray. Maybe with a little white collar."

"I'm not interested in reminding him of church."

Bobby shrugged. "They say dark clothes make you look slimmer. If you wear the brown, maybe he won't notice the size of your butt."

"You're horrible."

"I prefer to think I'm honest."

He shrugged like he was apologetic, holding back a smile as she muttered a few words that he would have sworn didn't belong in any church he knew. Then he chuckled when she stormed out of the kitchen, figuring she'd return in one of the outfits she had shown him earlier.

But he wasn't laughing for long when she reappeared seconds later in the same black pants that gave him a hard-on just looking at her, and had added a silky, nearly sheer white blouse with big flowing ruffles at the tapering neckline and cuffs. She looked both sexy as hell and angelically innocent.

That was his undoing. When she walked past him with a look that he could only term sassy, he caught her hand. Instantly, her smile vanished, her breath catching as her lips parted. Slowly he pulled her to him, her eyes going wide, before focusing on his mouth. They stood facing each other, and he reached out and ran the backs of his fingers along her jaw.

"You know when I said that your hips looked big?"

"Yes," she answered, the word a puff of breath.

"I lied."

Her head came back as she inhaled deeply.

"What I should have said," he added, "is that you look better than fine. Your hips are perfect, your hair is great, the outfit . . ." His voice was low, gruff with the heat she made him feel. "Too damn fine for Nick Palmero. Too damn classy."

He could see the wild flutter of her pulse in her neck, could feel the beat where his hand circled her delicate wrist.

"I'm thinking perhaps there's a compliment wrapped up in all those *damn*s," she managed.

Bobby grinned, his hand running up her arm, the shimmering material so thin he could feel her softness. "Nothing like a good *damn* to add emphasis."

Her body melted against him as one hand slid around her back and the other cupped her face to tilt her to him. He touched her with his lips then, barely, softly, his teeth nipping at her mouth. The feel of her instantly made him hard as a rock, the fullness of her breasts that up until that night had been so completely covered, the slimness of her waist giving way to the perfect round hips. He hadn't been able to get her out of his head before, something about her making it impossible to look away. And that was before he had a taste of the sweetness of her body beneath all the clothes.

He groaned into her mouth, tasting her, the hint of peppermint mixed with the dusky scent of a simple bath powder. No perfume, nothing overpowering, just Lacey. He could hardly believe the intensity of the desire for her that burned through him, felt weighted down by the sheer hunger that drove through his body.

"You do something to me," he said, the words a gruff accusation as he trailed his lips back to her ear.

Her head fell back, exposing the long column of her neck, and he sucked gently, relishing the feel of her fingernails curling into his shirt. He stroked her skin with the backs of his hands, lower and lower until he came to the V of her blouse. Holding her securely, he traced her lips with his tongue and undid one button after the next. When his hand slid inside and he cupped her breast, she gasped. For one long second she tensed, but when he ran his thumb over the thin lace of her bra, her mouth opened in a silent gasp.

Her resistance faded away, and when he slipped his palm into the cup, she only ran her hands up underneath his sweatshirt. In an explosion of passion, they couldn't seem to get close enough. Their mouths slanted together; their hands explored. Never letting her go, he leaned back against the edge of the kitchen table, pulling her between the hard brace of his thighs. The gentle curve of her abdomen cradled his hardness, and when she moved just so, sensation shot through him. He wanted her. There, now. And he could tell she wanted him, too.

But just when he would have crashed napkins and place mats to the floor and laid her on the kitchen table, the phone rang. At the sound, Lacey jerked back, and he saw the minute she remembered just how much they didn't get along. Her fingers came to her love-swollen lips, and red seared her cheeks.

But he was given no chance to comment when she grabbed up the receiver, spoke briefly, then hung up.

"That was Peter," she said with a gulp, fumbling with the buttons on her blouse.

Bobby gently but firmly moved her hands aside and did the fastenings with quick efficiency. "What did Peter want?"

His fingers stilled, and she practically leaped away from him.

"My date is here," she said, her voice still glossed by passion. "I've got to go. Lock up when you're done raiding my kitchen."

CHAPTER TWELVE

"FIND OUT everything there is to know about Lacey Wright."

Bobby's lawyer scribbled a few notes on his yellow legal pad. It was the following morning, and the two men sat alone in the Bobby's Place office, Lacey having run downtown to Albert's House of Liquor to discuss a questionable bill face-to-face with Albert himself.

The lawyer studied his longtime friend and client. "This sounds serious. Are you thinking about marrying her?"

Bobby couldn't have been more surprised. "Marry? Hell no. She's an employee, nothing more."

Clint didn't look like he believed him.

"I'm serious. She's running Bobby's now. Beth hired her to replace Gator."

"Is she doing a good job?"

"For the most part," Bobby admitted grudgingly, "though something doesn't add up."

"How so?"

"She's supposed to have been this great bar manager for a whole slew of places, but it's taken her weeks to learn the most elementary things about serving drinks."

"Serving and managing are two different things."

"True. But I've never met anyone managing a bar who hadn't first worked their way up through the ranks. I'd swear she had never seen the inside of a bar before she set foot in here."

Clint made a few more notes. "How deeply do you want me to look?"

Bobby glanced over at Lacey's perfectly kept desk, the tiny vase with purple violets, the china cup. Then he thought of those sunglasses she had put on that first day. Wild and pink, as if there was something very different hiding beneath the perfect surface. "If there's something to find, I want you to find it. And find it fast."

"Done." The lawyer stood, his cashmere sport coat and flannel trousers settling without a wrinkle. "I'll call with an initial report in a couple of days."

Once Clint departed, Bobby considered the woman in question. He told himself that once he found out all there was to know about her, she'd lose the hold she seemed to have on his imagination. As much as he hated to admit it, he thought about her all the time, whether he was working his knee or making phone calls. She fluttered through his thoughts.

What would he do if he found out she had lied?

He'd be relieved, he told himself. She was a complication he didn't need, and if she had fabricated a story about her past, it would give him a reason to fire her without guilt. He wanted it done before Thanksgiving. Beth had called last night after Lacey had left him in her apartment. His sister said she was going to ask Lacey to the family dinner, though she added it might be nice if the invitation came from him. But as far as he was concerned, the new bar manager was becoming too much a part of his life.

He'd probably do well just to sleep with her and be done with it. That certainly would be the less expensive route— his lawyer's time didn't come cheap. Sleeping with her would no doubt prove to be the quickest way to get her out of his head. End the speculation, be done with the intrigue of an elusive woman. He couldn't remember the last female who had proved a challenge. That's what Lacey was, he reassured himself. A challenge, nothing more. And once he got her in bed, he knew women well enough to spot an ice queen a mile away.

Or was she?

Just the memory of her walking out of her bedroom in those black pants and silky top made him wonder who really was beneath the prim layers of her work clothes.

He had nearly dropped the carton of chocolate milk on the floor when he saw her. Gone was the uptight pain in the ass, and in her place had been a woman with a body that would stop men in their tracks. Including him, a connoisseur of every sort of female.

But that wasn't what he couldn't forget. It was those few moments when her guard was down, when she had raced into his apartment wanting him to help her with her clothes, that haunted him. The fun, the smile. A happiness that he wanted to see on her face every single day.

Hell.

He needed to focus on getting back on the field, and he wasn't doing that. He needed to put Lacey, and all women, out of his head so he could get on with the business of recovery. The brace was gone, and now the really hard work was just beginning. Weights and workouts. Running. Flexibility. A laundry list of issues that he'd hired a team to help him work on in order to get back to Dallas as soon as possible.

When he came out of the office, Peter was setting up the bar for the day.

"Hey, Bobby. How's it going?"

"Good."

"Good."

Man talk. Plain, simple, no emotion. Just how he liked it.

Peter snatched up a set of keys.

"Are you leaving?" Bobby asked.

"Nah, just moving Lacey's car. After her date last night, she ran over to the store because I forgot to tell her I was nearly out of olives." He grimaced. "Who knew so many people were drinking martinis these days? Anyway, when she returned, her spot in the back was taken." He laughed. "She doesn't think it's a good idea for her heap to be sitting out front. Says it will give the place a bad reputation."

"Her car's here? I thought she went downtown."

"She did, but after she bailed me out last night, I told her to take my Acura. That piece of crap of hers is on its last leg." He headed for the door.

"I'll move it," Bobby offered. "You've got plenty to do before we open."

"Great, thanks."

Peter tossed him a set of keys attached to a fuzzy rabbit's foot. Bobby grinned in spite of himself; then he stepped out into the crisp fall air and saw Lacey's lone Ford. It had to be ten years old if it was a day, and he wondered how the car had made it cross-country.

With a shake of his head, he levered himself into the front seat and nearly jumped out of his skin when he turned the ignition and the Fairlane roared to life without the benefit of a muffler. Once he got over the shock, he pulled the column gearshift into reverse and chugged and jerked backwards. When finally he had the car facing forward, he manhandled the shift into drive and accelerated. But when he came to the turn that would take him around the back of the building, he muttered a curse and kept going out of the parking lot, like a sluggish ship sailing off into the sea.

"I'm telling you, Robin. It's not that I don't think you're mature enough to drive," Lacey said as calmly as she could. "It's just that as you well know, our car has been acting up since we crossed the Texas border. Maybe you can sign up for Driver's Education this summer. By then I'll have it thoroughly repaired."

"Mom!" Robin had a way of dragging the word out into a multisyllabic lament. "That isn't fair!"

Lacey knew it wasn't fair, but still, the car not working properly had provided her with a reasonable excuse for keeping her daughter out from behind the wheel of an automobile.

"Robin, I'm doing the best I can."

Lacey hated using those words, but as usual, they were just the thing to make her daughter back down.

Bobby chose that moment to walk into the office. She hadn't seen him since she left for her disastrous date last night. She still could hardly absorb the heat she had felt in his arms, the tingling desire that felt like it would burn her up.

The minute he saw her, she saw the same heat ignited in his eyes. She could tell he was remembering their kiss, remembering how she had run her hands over his body, unable to get close enough. She cringed just remembering.

It was easier to think about the horrid Nick. Granted, she hated that Bobby had been right about the man. But the science teacher had been a wolf in sheep's clothing, his paws groping around like an inexperienced schoolboy when he had taken her not to a nice or even decent restaurant for dinner, but rather to the drive-through at the Charcoaler for a hamburger and a Coke. Parked underneath the awning at the very back of the drive, she had leaned closer and closer to the door as he leaned closer and closer to her, until she all but fell out of the car when he made his passionate plea to kiss her.

An *accidental* elbow to the jaw had cured his desire. Lacey could only hope that Nick wasn't the sort of man who told tales around the bar. Bobby's "I told you so" look if he heard would be mortifying.

"What's going on in here?" Bobby asked, a smile replacing the heat. "I could hear you two clear out in the bar."

Robin crossed her arms on her chest with a *hmmph.* "Mom is making up excuses why she won't let me learn to drive."

"I am not making up excuses, Robin."

"Hey, hey." Bobby walked over to his desk. "That Ford of yours is a disaster waiting to happen."

Both Lacey's and Robin's eyes slanted suspiciously, each wondering where this was headed.

"So you're agreeing with Mom that I shouldn't learn how to drive?" Robin asked cautiously.

Bobby looked at Lacey. "I don't think your mother cares whether I agree or not."

Lacey started to nod in agreement, but Bobby's private phone line rang, cutting her off.

Just before he picked up the receiver, he tossed her a set of keys. "I took care of your car."

Lacey caught them automatically, and could only stare at the ring she didn't recognize. "These aren't mine."

"They are now." He turned away. "McIntyre, here," he barked into the phone.

Lacey stared at his back. "What is this?" she asked very slowly. When he kept talking, she only raised her voice. "Bobby, who do these belong to?"

Robin glanced over, then clasped her hands to her chest as if silently hoping.

"Bobby!" Lacey bit out.

He stopped and looked at her. "They're the keys to your new car." Then he scoffed. "No, Vernon, not your new car." He continued on with his conversation as if he hadn't just unloaded a bombshell the size of Texas.

Robin started leaping around in the room. "Oh, my gosh! Oh, my gosh! Are you kidding me? A new car."

Bobby waved them away. "Go have a look."

Robin didn't need any other encouragement. She snatched the ring away and raced out the door.

"Just look," he yelled after her. "No driving for you, young lady."

"No problem!" Then the teenager disappeared.

"How dare—?"

"Not now, sweet cakes. I'm in the middle of an important discussion. Go have a look, then you can come back and yell at me later."

"I was not going to yell."

"It doesn't look like you're on the verge of thanking me either, which, by the way, is what you're supposed to do after you receive a gift."

Lacey's chest expanded with . . . what? Fury? Anger? Dismay? She tried to find words.

"Yeah, Vernon, I'm here." He turned away and sank down into the chair.

With her mind paralyzed, Lacey left the office and walked in a daze out to the parking lot. Robin was already sitting in a brand-new, cute as a button, silver automobile.

"This is so awesome! A Jeep four-wheel drive, no less!" Robin enthused. "Get in!"

Lacey couldn't breathe. She recognized what was clearly anger burning through her, yes. But something else was there as well that made her nerves tingle with emotion. Bobby's sudden and unexpected generosity left her off balance. She felt invisible and on display, angry and thankful, all mingling together in a volatile mix.

"Can you believe it?" Robin practically sang, her brown eyes glowing with life. "He bought us a car! Bobby Mac bought us a car! This is so cool!"

Like it was that easy.

"Let's go for a ride!" Robin shot her a crooked smile. "Can I drive now?"

"You don't know how to drive," she answered automatically.

Robin rubbed her hands together. "That won't be the case for long."

"What?"

"You said the problem was the car. Now there's no problem, so I get to learn how to drive!"

Lacey took a step back and had to steady herself on a low wall. Her baby. Her excuses gone. Her ability to keep her child a child bit by bit chipping away. But she was saved from having to do or say anything when a maroon Cadillac pulled up. Robin's friend Amber popped her head out the window.

"Hey, Robin. Hey, Mrs. Wright."

Lacey's mind snagged on the word *Mrs.*, and on the spark of guilt that flashed across Robin's face.

"Oh, wow, I forgot. Gotta go, Mom. Amber's mother is giving me a ride to the library. Amber and I are doing an extra-credit project together for English. I'll be home by seven. I promise." She gave her a quick kiss, handed her the keys, then was gone.

Lacey stood there, her heart pounding, her mind racing with too many conflicting thoughts. Did Robin have friends because they didn't know that her mother was an unwed mother? Had Robin decided that the best course of action in this new town was to make up an alternate history— with her being widowed or divorced?

But she had no answers, didn't want to face the possibility that Robin was embarrassed of her.

Numb, she turned back to the bar. She didn't stop in the main room, barely heard Peter's comment that they were running low on rum and tequila. She continued on, slamming into the office with such intensity that Bobby swiveled around in his chair, one dark brow raised in surprise.

"We need to talk," she stated.

He gestured to the phone that he still held to his ear, his smile self-satisfied, his slouch ruggedly sexy, and she wanted to slap the smile right off his face. Short of that, she marched forward, leaned across the desk, and pressed the hang-up switch.

"Hey," he bellowed, glancing with disbelief between Lacey and the now dead receiver. With a curse, he stood. "What are you doing?"

"What the hell are *you* doing?" she fired back, relishing the distraction of Bobby's latest misdeed. "How dare you buy me a car?"

Bobby only smiled that four-color smile. "Now, Lacey, don't get your panties in a twist."

Her eyes went wide with fury. "You low-life, gutter mouth, domineering . . . boar!"

"Boar?" He had the nerve to chuckle, his sunny good nature returning full force. "Surely you can come up with something better than that."

"Aggghhh!"

"Or maybe not."

He replaced the receiver with a cool nonchalance that made Lacey want to kill him.

"Now, tell me," he said, coming around the desk. "Why are you so ticked off? You said yourself that your car was trouble. I solved your problem. It's as simple as that."

Of course, Bobby knew that it wasn't as simple as that. He hardly could believe he had bought the damned thing. But as always with Lacey, she twisted him up like a pretzel. One minute he was driving that heap to the service station at the corner, and the next he kept going and headed to the Jeep dealership. The owner was an old friend, and within the hour Bobby was headed back to the bar driving the brand-new car.

"You've been concerned about Robin behind the wheel, and what safer vehicle is there than a four-by-four with dual airbags and antilock brakes?" he added.

"You can't just get rid of Betsy!"

"Betsy?"

"I love that car! And you have no right to go off and buy me something else."

"Why not?"

"Because!"

"That's it, just because? Listen, it's not that big a deal. I got it for cost. The dealer's a friend. And believe me, I've spent a hell of a lot more on cars in my day than I laid out for yours."

Lacey screeched, grabbed her pocketbook, then marched out the door.

"Hey!" he called after her.

But she was gone. For long seconds he stood there. He knew he had stepped over some boundary, but to his way of thinking, better she stay mad. When she was angry, she tore into him in a way that made him remember what he didn't like about her. Everything. Everything except the way her eyes lit up when her daughter walked into the room. Everything except the way she sometimes forgot he was a football player and saw the real him.

As much as he hated it, he understood that she saw him, saw to his core. He had come to realize that it was more than her simply having figured out how important football really was to him. She saw below the surface to the deepest part where he kept his hopes and fears. She understood how he tried to hammer and mold his world into the shape he wanted, and how he couldn't bear the way it suddenly was spinning out of control. And the only times he saw a flicker of respect in her eyes was when she did see those things, however fleeting. It was the surface that others wanted, needed, the same surface that Lacey had no need or liking of.

That was why he had bought her the damned car.

Which was ridiculous. Because when he really thought about it, he probably imagined the whole thing and she really hated him all the time, which she had aptly demonstrated seconds ago.

But still, with a lamenting shake of his head about how he was going soft, he couldn't help but follow her. He went upstairs, but she didn't answer her apartment door. When he returned to the bar, Peter guessed what he wanted and nodded toward the parking lot. "Lacey dashed out of here a few minutes ago." The bartender smiled. "She had that look about her that said she was heading for The Ice Cream Shoppe. That look and the fact that she didn't take a coat. She couldn't have gone too far."

"Hell."

Bobby crossed the tarmac to the ice-cream parlor at the opposite end, muttering as he went. The quaint little store, with tiny round-topped, red and white tables, was crowded. The minute he entered, fans started clamoring around, wanting autographs and to say hello, ask about his knee. He caused such a ruckus that Lacey looked up, and he saw the moment she realized he was there. With a gasp, then a curse, she sank down in her chair and grabbed up a menu, pretended to study the offerings.

Bobby smiled and made small talk with customers as he headed across the room, intent on Lacey. She didn't so much as glance up when he stopped at her table.

"You forgot your coat."

With an irritated groan, she straightened and made a great show of looking at his empty arms. "So you brought it to me?" she asked with a lilting sarcasm. "No? You just thought you'd let me know, in case I hadn't realized."

He shrugged, then sat down in the too cute and too small wrought-iron chair across from her.

"Go away," she said.

"I want to talk about the car."

"Too bad, there is nothing to discuss," she stated crisply. "I want mine back."

"That is yours."

She counted to ten. "I want my Ford."

He sighed. "The Ford is gone."

"Gone! It can't be gone. That's, that's theft!"

"Then call the police." He pulled out his cell phone. "You want me to dial?"

She slapped his hands until he put the phone away. "Just stop." She drew a deep breath. "Return to wherever you got that car and get mine back."

"I don't see why you won't accept a small token of my appreciation for your work at Bobby's Place."

"Please. What do you take me for? You don't appreciate anything I do at Bobby's Place." She looked around, then leaned forward. "Besides, a car is . . . an inappropriate gift. I can't accept it. And I sure can't afford to pay for it."

"Panties are an inappropriate gift."

The waiter chose that second to come up to the table. He was a pimple-faced teenager, and he blushed red at the words.

"What are you ordering?" Bobby asked Lacey.

Lacey's face burned with mortification. "Nothing."

The waiter's face lined with concern. "But you already said—"

"Yes, fine, all right, I've already ordered. But the gentleman," she grimaced at the word, "won't be staying."

"I'll have whatever she's having. Write that down, then leave. I want to get back to the subject of panties."

The boy blanched, looked confused, and then hurried off with a stunned helpless look.

Her eyes lit with fire once again. "You . . . you . . ."

"Boar, I believe you said earlier. I think the word is growing on me."

With that she lunged across the table. Hands out, fingers splayed, and this time his eyes went wide. For half a second she caught him off guard, and she actually got her finger curled into his thick sweater at his neck. People turned to stare.

"Whoa, there, doll face. If you want a hug, all you have to do is ask."

Her long thin fingers curled and he felt the bite of nails in his throat. Squeezing was one thing; scratches were another. His hands flew up and grabbed her by the wrists. "Tsk, tsk, Ms. Wright. I never would have thought you were the violent type."

Her face was red and her eyes were wild. She was beautiful. No buts about it, not just sexy or sultry like she had been last night. This was a soul-deep beauty, and Bobby felt his body grow hard with desire right there in the damned little ice-cream parlor with elementary school kids all around.

Exerting control, he willed his body into check; then he took her hands and forced her back in her chair. They stared at each other. He saw the instant she realized what she had done, must have seen the red marks on his neck where he felt the burn. He watched as the wildness turned to panic, followed quickly by remorse.

"Oh, my God, I'm sorry," she breathed.

She touched him before he could stop her, her hand pressing on top of his. The touch was not the kind he was used to, the kind meant to entice. This was different, making his heart jar in his chest.

"Don't worry about it," he managed, pulling away, sitting back until he felt the swirling wrought iron bite into his spine. "It's nothing."

"It's not nothing. Let me ask for some ice."

"No need."

Her brown eyes were deep pools of despair, and when the waiter returned, looking like he wanted to be anywhere but there, he carried two of the largest ice-cream extravaganzas Bobby had ever seen. Hot fudge, whipped cream, chopped pecans, all piled high on three scoops of chocolate ice cream.

"Chocolate," Bobby said, remembering her honesty the day she told him about her favorite food. "The cure for what ails you."

He had hoped to bring a smile to her face, but if possible, her expression only got worse.

"Ah, come on, Lacey."

But she wasn't listening. Suddenly she fumbled in her purse, rising out of her chair at the same time she pulled out a handful of dollar bills.

"Hey, don't worry about it," he said gruffly, waving the money away. "I'll get it."

Her fist of money came down on the table, her eyes flaring, a tendril of hair falling loose from her perfect bun at the back of her head. "Stop paying for things! I don't need your money, or your cars, or your smart-aleck remarks." Her chest rose and fell with her breath, agitated just like her expression. "You might be able to buy other people, but you can't buy me."

Then she pushed through the crowd, leaving the ice cream untouched.

A harsh fury shot through him at her words, and he didn't stop to think. He added to the pile of bills and dashed after her. When he got out the door, she was only a few yards away.

"Lacey!"

She didn't stop.

"Damn it, Lacey, you're crazy if you think I'm trying to buy you!"

She never missed a step.

Swearing, he caught up to her. "I don't buy people," he stated vehemently.

"Don't you? Isn't that why you give away more beer than you sell? Isn't that why you let the old manager waste your money like there was no tomorrow? Despite all your nonchalance, you want people to like you."

"I don't give a damn about what people think of me."

"Oh, really?"

She shot him a narrow-eyed glance, but he hardly noticed for the sudden bite of pain that shot through his knee as he kept up with her. The ache made him alternately angry and scared, and he hated both emotions.

"Then why do you smile and act nice when reporters ask questions that upset you?" she demanded, not easing up. "Why don't you tell them it's none of their business when they ask personal questions?" She drew a deep breath. "Why are you so afraid that people *won't* like you if you're honest?"

He didn't answer, couldn't, as he fought to regain his hard-won control. He forced the muscles in his body to relax, then said, "Don't confuse me with yourself. Unlike you, I don't try to make people like me, they just do."

"Bastard," she hissed, her hand whipping out, and she would have slapped him had he not caught her wrist.

But her words were lost when the sudden contact nearly sent them both to the ground. For a heart-stopping second, Bobby realized his still-weak knee was giving in, and he was losing his balance.

Despite her upset, Lacey didn't hesitate. She grabbed him, trying to steady his weight, but he was too big, and together they faltered. They landed with a thud against the hard adobe that coated the pet store's wall.

They stared at each other, surprise riddling through them.

"Are you okay?" she asked, anger slipping into concern.

His lips tilted at one corner, and he shrugged. "Never been better." He grimaced at the feel of adobe biting into his back.

He held her, and didn't let go. He knew he should; he knew that giving in to his wild desire for this woman wasn't smart. Beth had said that he never allowed himself to feel anything for a woman. Deep down he knew she was right. He gave pleasure, but he took nothing other than satisfaction when he was with a woman—no true feeling.

But with Lacey, again and again, she made him want to give in to more. No matter how many times he told himself to steer clear of her, he wanted Lacey Wright, wanted to feel her body curled into his embrace.

Slowly, as if he had no will of his own, he pulled her close with a guttural groan that echoed against the cool adobe walls.

"What are you doing?" she asked, concern replaced by a palpable wariness.

Her voice grew breathless, and he could see the pulse of her heart in her neck. Wild, just as her eyes had been. He told himself to leave. To fire her. Something, anything to stop this mad careening of his emotions.

With considerable effort that he made look easy, he tugged them into the narrow alleyway that stood between the ice-cream parlor and the pet store. He caught her against the wall, his palms flattening on either side of her head, capturing her. His breathing was ragged, and he was so close that he could smell her fragrance, sweet and innocent and hot. Hot from anger and wariness, hot from fire that he saw start a low burn in her eyes.

"I'm touching you," he said, stating the obvious, brushing his hips against the gentle curve of her abdomen.

He trailed his fingers down her neck to the edge of her sweater, downy soft. Her lips parted.

"I want to kiss you."

Lacey heard the raw sensuality in his voice. She understood that he wanted her, and she knew as well that his desire was barely controlled. She saw it in his eyes, could hear it in his voice. His meaning was clear. He was warning her, not inviting her.

Lacey understood that he hated the wanting—at least he hated wanting her. She was everything he felt he didn't need in his life, because she didn't make him feel like the man he pretended to be. Only the young, sexy ones did that. She doubted he knew anything about a long-term, committed relationship. And why should he if he had women like Darla throwing themselves at his feet all the time?

He wanted her despite himself. Even knowing that, she couldn't deny that she wanted to lean into him, felt a blind, irrational desire to lose herself in this moment of heady sensation. Forget the car, forget the past, forget for a moment that the world was more complicated than a single kiss.

A flicker of shame raced through her, but only a flicker until his forefinger drifted lower, along the curve of her breast. If she didn't stop him, as his gaze was both daring and demanding she do, his touch would graze the nipple beneath her bra.

He hesitated, giving her one last chance to pull away, before his finger dipped, circling. She couldn't help it. She closed her eyes, exhaling as if she had been waiting for this, just this, his touch, the gentle circling.

"You like it, don't you?"

His voice was gruff, dragging along her nerve endings like a caress. Her eyelids fluttered open, and she saw the demand in his expression. In answer, she leaned into him. But that wasn't enough. He wanted more.

"Say it, Lacey." He leaned just close enough so that his lips were close to hers, a brush of his warm breath. "Say the words," he demanded.

The words were hoarse, and she knew, at least, that he wasn't immune.

"Yes, damn you. Yes, I like it."

With that his mouth came down on hers possessively. He kissed her hungrily. He devoured her, his mouth slanting over hers. His strong hands pulled her closer, the heat of him searing through her clothes. His arms were like bands of iron, holding her securely as his hands caressed her back, then settled lower, and he cupped her hips.

She gasped at the undeniable feel of his erection pressing insistently against her abdomen. Shock swept through her, yes, but mostly there was desire and a rush of titillating power that she could have this kind of effect on this intensely sensual and beautifully virile man.

The world was forgotten completely, the shops and people just a few yards away in the sunlight beyond the dim cocoon of this alleyway erased, as if nothing else were real.

"Don't be scared, Lacey."

She almost laughed. She was many things, but not scared. She felt like she was diving into life.

"I won't hurt you," he added.

The sensation of his breath against her ear made her tremble. Her head fell back when his mouth seared a path to her neck. Then he bent lower. Lower until he kissed her breast beneath the wool.

Wrapping her arms around his broad shoulders, Lacey melted close, letting her fingers feel, roam. Take him in. But her breath caught when she felt his hand slip beneath her sweater. Skin to skin. So real. Then he unsnapped her bra with an ease that snagged in her mind.

Her thoughts jolted, then reeled when his large palm closed around her breast. Cupping, lifting. His erection matched his desperate groan into her neck as he pressed against her.

"God, you are so beautiful," he murmured, his hand

pressing her breast high. "Why you hide yourself beneath layers of clothes, I'll never know."

It hit her from every direction. Her wantonness, the answer to his question. She knew the answer. All of which reminded her of Robin. Her responsibility. Reminded her she was a mother and not this . . . person she couldn't afford to be.

With force, she tore herself away. "This can't happen."

They stared at each other, each breathing hard.

"I work for you," she managed. "And even if I didn't, we have nothing in common. Neither of us can offer what the other one wants."

"And what is that?" he asked dangerously.

"You want a woman who is young and beautiful, who in turn makes you feel young and virile."

His features hardened. "And what do you want?"

She stared at him for an eternity. "I'm not sure anymore, but I do know it can't be you," she answered earnestly.

CHAPTER THIRTEEN

SOMETHING WOKE HER.

Robin lay in bed, the cotton sheet and downy covers pulled up to her chin as she stared at the ceiling, her vision murky from the scrim of a deep sleep. It took a second for her to remember where she was, and only when the electric blaze of blue and red neon seeped through the cotton curtains did Texas come to mind. El Paso. Bobby's Place.

She closed her eyes and sighed with a deep contentment she had never known before. Texas also meant Coronado High School and Kyle Walker.

Rolling over, Robin pulled her pillow into her arms. Kyle. So incredibly cute. So full of life as if he had leaped off the pages of a book. Standing in front of her at her locker with one hand braced beside her head as he leaned close to talk to her. He was also a puzzle. It was as if there was a really caring guy beneath his hard, tough-as-nails surface.

Suddenly she heard something again, a light knock on her window. She didn't have a chance to get really scared because she heard her name.

"Damn it, Robin, wake up!"

"Kyle?" she gasped.

Robin nearly tumbled to the floor when her legs tangled in the sheets, blankets, and the soft flannel of her long nightgown. She raced across the room, whipped back the curtains, and stared out through the glass. Kyle was perched on the tiny overhang of the roof in front of her window.

"Oh, my gosh, how did you get up there?"

"Not as easy as I'll get down if you don't open the window and let me in before I fall," he replied, his voice muffled.

Robin squeaked, then shoved open the glass pane.

Kyle climbed through, long silver rays of moonlight spilling in with him as he jumped down into her bedroom. "Damn, it's cold out there," he said, rubbing his hands together to get warm, cupping his palms against his breath.

Robin stared at him. Shock that he was standing in her bedroom raced down her spine like a warning. She glanced at the clock, saw that it was eleven-thirty, and remembered that her mom had said she had to work late tonight.

"You can't be in here," she whispered incredulously, glancing frantically at her door.

Kyle turned and closed the window. "I didn't think you'd ever wake up. You sleep like the dead," he lamented. "I've been knocking for ages."

Hackles rising, Robin forgot about her mother. "If you came over to be mean like you were yesterday, you can just leave and take your chances getting back out of here."

His eyes glittered with humor in the silver-lit room. "I didn't come to be mean."

He took a step toward her, moving slowly, determinedly, his eyes never leaving hers, and Robin felt the sudden need to run. "What are you doing, Kyle?" she asked carefully, taking a step back.

With her eyes wide, she stood in the middle of the room, her brown hair tumbling around her shoulders, her favorite white flannel nightgown—a holdover from junior high— dotted with sprigs of purple flowers. Her feet were bare, peeking out from beneath the folds of her gown.

Robin watched as his gaze took her in. She couldn't tell if he was noticing her little girl's nightgown or the fact that she had developed curves underneath, and she blushed. At that moment, he stopped and sighed. "Jesus, you make me crazy."

"*Now* what did I do?"

Kyle looked at her long and hard before he shook his head, then he started moving around her room.

She had an unobserved moment where she could just look at him. He was tall, but not too tall, and more handsome even than Josh Hartnett or Freddie Prinze Jr. Her mom would have said he was more handsome even than John Travolta a hundred years ago when he was in *Grease*. Robin loved that movie even if it was old. The bad boy trying to make good.

She felt a strange tightening in her chest. The world seemed to close in around her, her thoughts echoing in her head. Kyle was beautiful. So beautiful, and he was there with her, in her room.

His strides were smooth and unhurried. His hair was kind of long. The jeans he wore were clean and soft from wear. His T-shirt was white beneath his black leather jacket that molded against broad shoulders.

In short, he looked like trouble. But excitement raced through her at the sight of him. He was totally dark and sexy and dangerous—everything she shouldn't want, but did.

He picked up her old, stuffed bear, a hint of a smile pulling at his mouth before he set it down. He flipped through her meager CD collection. "The Carpenters?" He grimaced.

"Bobby Mac's sister gave it to me. I don't think she's really up on what's cool these days."

"The Carpenters were never cool."

Then he found The Rolling Stones' *Sticky Fingers*. He

looked impressed, so she didn't clarify that it was Beth's, too. Major old music that Beth had bought on CD, then decided she didn't want. She had brought over the stack, along with the CD player and told Robin to enjoy.

Moving on, Kyle studied a photograph of Robin and her mother, though he didn't say a word, and he didn't stop again until he came to her latest project.

"What's this?" he asked.

"My butterfly jar."

He held it up to the moonlight streaming into the room.

"It's a cocoon," she clarified.

"I can see that. I take it you're going to watch it turn into a butterfly."

He said the words with an amused smile, like she was an eight-year-old with a third-grade science project. Robin took offense.

"It is a photographic depiction of the fundamentals of life beginning. A transformation. For art class."

"Do you ever talk like regular kids?"

She shot him a very regular dirty look. "How do regular kids talk?"

He laughed. "Like me, I suppose."

"Ah," she began, her tone wry, "I'll see what I can do. Perhaps tomorrow I'll buy a leather jacket. And how about a pack of cigarettes? Would you like me to drop my art class? Though wouldn't that be considered a *regular* class?"

"Hey, I like that you take art. Shows you're smart *and* creative."

"I'm glad you approve," she responded with a scowl.

After he had roared off yesterday afternoon without so much as a word of good-bye, she had gone from concerned to mad. If he had been upset, he should have talked about it.

"I'm also smart enough to know you shouldn't be in my

bedroom," she added. "Though my guess is you don't care about shoulds and shouldn'ts."

His grin widened and he raised a brow as he set down the jar. But he didn't respond, simply continued on, unhurried, his hands shoved in his back pockets. In spite of herself, Robin really wanted to cross the room to him. Of course that would be insane, especially with her wearing only a nightgown. But still, she wanted him to hold her hand, smile at her. Kiss her.

Appalled at her own thoughts, she leaped back to her bed and pulled the covers high.

He stopped at the window, and for a second she thought he was going to leave. Just like that. Here one second, gone in the next, no reason given as to why he came in the first place. But then he walked over and dropped down on the bed.

"I'm exhausted."

Her breath caught in her throat at the sight of him next to her on the twin-size bed, his eyes closed, his leather jacket so black against her white eyelet comforter. His legs hung over the side, one foot planted firmly on the floor.

"Tough day at the office, dear?" she asked.

Kyle opened one eye and shot her a brief dry glance. "As a matter of fact, June, it was."

He rolled over on to his side to face her, propping his head on his palm. A devilish smile pulled across his lips. "And if Wally and the Beaver are asleep, I see no reason not to give me a better welcome home, *dear*." He reached across and took hold of her covers, and very gently started pulling them away.

Oh, dear.

Her thoughts spun, and it was really difficult to breathe because her heart pounded so hard. But her thoughts were cut short when he started to talk.

"I'm sorry you ran into Harold yesterday."

"Harold?"

"My stepdad."

"Do you really call him Harold?"

"Just when I'm ticked at him." He snorted. "Which is most of the time. Anyway, I shouldn't have acted like an ass to you."

Robin smiled softly. "Thank you for the apology."

Kyle groaned. "I hate him," he suddenly spat out.

And she realized that he truly did. Deeply, completely.

"Don't do this to yourself, Kyle," she whispered.

"Do what? Don't hate him?" He turned and looked into her eyes, his own dark and troubled. "Why not? He hates my guts, too."

She tilted her head. "Why would an adult hate you?"

"Because I get in his way. It's my mom he wants, and unfortunately for him, I come as part of the package. He tried to send me to military school in Louisiana. It was the one time my mom got mad at him since they met. And I'm talking really mad, not the kind of weird fight-and-make-up stuff they do all the time. The next day, I got the truck."

"He bought you that truck?"

"Yeah," he groused.

"If you don't like that he bought it for you, then why did you accept it?"

"I didn't, at first. But my mom went crazy, got all weepy saying that I was ruining everything for her. Shit. I want her to be happy. I really do. But I hate how she's changed. It's like she's someone I don't know anymore."

He cut himself off, like he was surprised by how much he had said.

"Maybe she feels the same about you. I know my mom has started looking at me real weird—like a stranger's moved in with her. Maybe it's a teenage thing. As to your stepfather, maybe the only way he knows how to show his feelings is by buying things for people."

"Yeah," he stated harshly. "And I'm just an ungrateful prick who doesn't appreciate what I have handed to me. I know the story, have heard it a thousand times before. From Harold himself. Like yesterday when he shoved me against the wall and told me I was a pissant and it wouldn't be long before he convinced my mom of that."

"You're kidding! That's horrible."

He jerked up from the bed and headed for the window. "I've got to go."

She raced forward and grabbed his arms, forcing him to look at her. "You can't just leave like this. Not again. I'm sorry, I shouldn't have defended your stepfather. I just didn't realize. What can I do to help?"

The hard lines of his face eased, and for half a second his eyes closed. When he looked at her again, he pressed his forehead to hers. "You're too young to be trying to save the world."

She could hardly think much less respond from the way it felt when he touched her, the cold night air seeping in through the thin glass—cold brushing against the unexpected heat that she felt emanating from Kyle.

"I'm not trying to save anything," she whispered.

"Aren't you? First you tossed down the twenty bucks to save my butt from Martin. Now you're standing here trying to figure out how to get me not to hate Harold, like somehow that's going to make everything better."

She started to protest, but he stopped her. "I can see it in your eyes. You think that with a little help and talk everything will be fine."

She thought of how she and her mother had moved and moved, ending up here, and how what had for so many years seemed hopeless, now seemed so exciting. "Sometimes out of nowhere, things do change, Kyle. Sort of like you take an unexpected turn and a light springs up at the end of a tunnel."

Kyle groaned and wrapped his arms around her, fiercely pulling her close. Robin loved the feel of him, loved the beat of his heart against her ear. And the smell of him. The leather of his jacket, the faint smell of motor oil and the soap he had used to wash it off his hands.

"You're a crazy kid, Robin Wright. Crazy and innocent and too damned much trouble. You should have stayed in the front of the class where you belong."

"Why?" she murmured against his chest, her knees feeling like jelly in a totally great way.

He put her at arm's length. "Because I'm not into innocent little girls, and you're too innocent to hang out with me."

Her mind finally cleared and her chin rose, a flicker of obstinate anger surging. "You don't know the first thing about me, Kyle Walker."

"Don't I?"

She sliced him an aggravated look.

"Okay, let me tell you about you," he said. "You're fifteen, think you're treated like a child, have an over-protective mother, are way too smart for your own good, have never been kissed in your life. And you like me." At this last statement, he smiled with devilish pride.

Her mouth fell open as amazement, indignation, self-righteous anger, and the need to kick him in the shin all raced through her mind.

Kyle only chuckled, then lined her face with his hands. "Shut your mouth, Robin, so I can kiss you."

Anger, indignation and every other emotion besides shock drained out of her. He was going to kiss her. Finally!

Her heart lurched, scared and intrigued at the same time. But coherent thought cut off when he leaned forward and pressed his lips to hers.

The touch startled her with its intimacy, and she sucked in her breath. He pulled back and looked at her with a faint smile.

"Close your eyes," he instructed.

"Oh!" She squeezed them tight, only to hear him groan.

"Jeez, Rob, relax."

Her eyes shot open as embarrassment washed through her. "I didn't know there were so many instructions involved. Had I known, I would have bought a book and read up."

Kyle hung his head and muttered a curse. "I knew this was a mistake. I'm out of here."

He stepped away.

"Don't go!" The words blurted out of her.

He stopped and looked back.

"I'm sorry," she said, too desperate for him to stay for better sense to make a dent in her brain. "When I get nervous or embarrassed, my mouth runs a mile a minute and I don't say anything right. Stay and I promise I won't utter a single other word." She pretended to zip up her lip and throw away the key.

All cool fled when he looked at her like she had lost it.

"Oh, great! That was the wrong thing to do," she lamented. "See, I don't do anything right. I'm just trying to get you to stay. You can't leave, at least not before you've really kissed me."

Robin gasped, then slapped her hand over her mouth. "I mean, I mean—," she began, the words muffled.

"Hell," Kyle muttered, then he took her hand and pulled her close so quickly she didn't have a chance to think.

His mouth came down over hers, and her mind reeled. He kissed her hard, determined, before she felt his body ease. Then he truly kissed her, gently, patiently, and she felt her body melt. This was a kiss. This was heaven, and without thinking, her fingers curled into his coat.

"Robin," he groaned against her skin.

His hands trailed up her arms, then around to her back,

pressing her closer. He kissed her again. Her fear and uncertainty were overcome by his gentle touch. Without warning, he opened his shearling-lined jacket and pulled her
inside. At the startling intimacy of little between them but
his thin shirt and her softly worn nightgown, she melted
against him. He cupped her jaw and brought her mouth up
to meet his, and he coaxed her into knowing—teaching her
how. And she understood that he was showing her what he
wanted in a kiss.

Her body began to tingle, to yearn for Kyle in some in-
tangible way that she couldn't name. She held on tighter,
lost herself to the feel of his lips brushing over hers. She
gave a start when she felt his tongue glide across her lips.

"Open for me, Robin," he murmured.

She could no more imagine opening her mouth than she
could imagine screaming, but something deeper than in-
tellect overrode her mind, and she parted her lips.

The instant she felt his tongue on hers she jolted with
shock. And when he gently circled and sucked, shock fled
completely.

"Oh, my gosh!" she breathed.

"You like that, don't you?" he whispered.

"Oh, my gosh!"

Kyle chuckled, then leaned back against the windowsill.
He pulled her with him, pulling her between his thighs,
nestling her against him in a way that made her feel loved
and cherished at the same time she felt hot and cold, and
like she was going to get in really bad trouble. But even
knowing that, she could have stayed that way forever.

But then his hand lowered to press against the curve of
her hips and her mind shuddered with belated understanding. She felt the hardness, the desire. And reality hit her
square in the chest. Everything her mother had ever told
her about what boys were after. About how they wanted to

use girls for one thing, and one thing only. That very hardness was proof that he wanted more than gentle kisses and to cherish her in his embrace.

"Kyle!"

"It's all right," he groaned against her hair, pulling her back to him.

"No, it's not all right! Let go of me, Kyle."

With another groan and a curse, he did as he was asked. He didn't move, remained silent, his head down, and for a second Robin thought he was praying. Then he took a deep breath, his head falling back.

"You really are innocent, aren't you?"

First, he called her little girl, now innocent. And again it made her mad. "I am not innocent," she shot back at him. "I know enough to understand what . . . what you . . . what you wanted."

Kyle looked at her with one dark brow cocked. Then he chuckled. "Yeah, understanding that you've gotten out of a book somewhere, or from some sex discussion with your mom doesn't make you any less innocent." He reached out and curled his arm around her shoulders and pulled her back to him. "But I'm glad." His smile disappeared, and he looked at her intently. "I'm glad as hell that you don't know the first thing about sex. And you better tell Bert Burroughs to stay away from you, or I will." His voice lowered. "And I'm not sure you'd approve of my choice of words."

"What in the world is wrong with Bert Burroughs?" she asked, half in outrage, half-confused. "He just wanted Bobby's autograph."

"That's what he said. But if he doesn't stay away from my girl, he's going to have something very wrong with him."

Robin's eyes widened. "Your girl?" she asked on a burst of breath.

"That's right. You're mine, Robin Wright. And I don't share."

With that, he kissed her again, pulling her to him, his strong arm holding her secure. "Either you tell him, or I will," he breathed against her lips.

Then he kissed her on the forehead before he disappeared out the window, his footsteps sounding against the roof until he lowered himself to the ground.

Robin stood very still, staring through the empty glass, infuriated, incensed. Stunned.

And strangely breathless.

Kyle shoved his hands deep in his pockets and headed for his truck. He had parked toward the back to keep out of sight of the entrance to Bobby's Place.

He was hard as hell, and even the cold wasn't settling him down. God, he had wanted to sink into Robin, still did. She was different from other girls, so different that he had almost told her about his stepdad.

At the thought, he suddenly felt the bite of cold. Harold was a dick, but his mom really seemed to like the guy.

Kyle hated himself for taking the truck, but what else was he going to do. Tell his mother that Harold was only giving him things to make her think that he cared? What would that solve? Nothing, because he had learned that his mom wanted to believe Harold. She didn't want anything to disrupt her country club world.

Instead he stewed, simmered in anger that he didn't know how to relieve. Until he met Robin. Somehow she made him feel okay, like a regular kid.

He scoffed. Maybe she made him feel regular since she didn't have a father and she lived above a bar. Whatever the reason, he knew he didn't want to lose her.

Kyle smiled into the night at the thought of seeing Robin

at school in the morning, completely unaware of the woman who sat in the car next to his, studying him with her brow furrowed in confusion.

CHAPTER FOURTEEN

LACEY SAT in the brand-new Jeep, staring into the rearview mirror, watching the truck disappear into the night. Despite the young man's confident gait and dark good looks, he didn't look old enough to belong in a place like Bobby's.

She'd have to make sure Peter was carding anyone whose age appeared questionable. She was not about to allow serving beer to underage kids. But this one must have just come out of the bar, since nothing else in the square was open at that time of night.

It was late, and Bobby had gone out for the night, so it had been safe to sneak out and slip into the car and have her first real good look. She shook away the oddly concerned feeling that the sight of the boy had caused, and curled her fingers around the thick steering wheel, inhaling deeply. The smell of leather and new car filled her. She hated that she loved sinking down into the plush upholstery, hated that she loved the feel of the cool enameled knob on the gearshift between the bucket seats.

For years she had relied on the bus, buying the Ford only three years ago from an old man who rarely drove. Betsy, they had named the Fairlane. But three years and a trip from north to south had taken their toll on little Betsy. This new vehicle was an answer to her prayers.

Reverently, she turned the key just far enough so she could listen to the stereo. Heaven, as a Stevie Nicks song swelled, the deep bass drumming deeply.

If only she didn't feel compelled to give the car back.

Bobby McIntyre really knew how to get under her skin; he seemed to have a sixth sense about how to bring out her weaknesses—touching her in a way that made her want more. Giving her the kind of gift that would be the hardest to refuse.

Turning off the ignition, she locked up, huddled close against the winter night, then dashed through the parking lot, and returned inside.

"Lacey," several patrons called out in chorus.

She couldn't deny the silly pleasure she felt at being recognized by people she was coming to care for. And maybe, just maybe, they were coming to care about her, too.

There was Frank, who just yesterday had asked how Robin was liking school. Over the weeks she had been there, Lacey had learned how much the man loved his wife and kids.

And Melvin, forty-five and a single dad who rarely got to see his son. He had a whole wallet full of photos that regularly came out after beer number three.

She couldn't forget Herb. Sweet, kind, bookish Herb.

Then there was Nick, who thankfully ignored her whenever she came into the bar. Not a single word had been uttered about their disastrous date.

Now, standing in the midst of Bobby's Place, she felt a sense of peace that was as foreign as it was reassuring.

"Peter," she said, leaning up against the bar. "Who drives an old blue pickup truck around here?"

The bartender cocked his head in consideration. "Can't say that I know. Why?"

She pushed away. "I think we better start doing a better

job of carding people before we serve them drinks. I saw a young man leave here who I feel certain was underage."

"Tonight?" His tone was incredulous.

"Yes, Peter. I saw him no more than a few minutes ago. I'm not blaming you. We've been busy. But in the future, I am simply suggesting that we ask for identification on a more discerning basis."

"Lacey, I didn't serve anyone tonight that was even questionable. Whoever you saw, either you mistook his age, or he wasn't leaving Bobby's Place."

"Hmmm. That's odd." She tried to recall the boy, but suddenly she wondered why she had been so concerned. "You're probably right. But be on the lookout, just in case. Everything under control here?"

"Yep, I'll lock up."

"Thank you. I am rather tired."

She said her good nights and walked up the stairs. A foolish fissure of disappointment raced along her senses when she saw that no light shone from underneath Bobby's door. But neither was the stereo crooning melodies, which would have indicated he had made up with Darla and brought her home. She hated that she was pleased.

Quietly, she clicked into her own darkened apartment. Leaning back, she closed the door, taking in the dim surroundings. The quaint living room was filled with the moon streaming in from the dark crystal sky that was rapidly filling with clouds and the promise of snow. Her sense of joy and contentment grew.

Pushing away, she set her purse and keys aside, then headed back toward the bedrooms. She almost stopped at Robin's door to talk, catch up on their days, but it was late. Though when she continued on, Robin called out.

"Mom?"

"Yes, sweetie?"

Robin pushed up against the mound of pillows on the

bed as Lacey came into the room. Moonlight fell across her daughter, making her look so young, so vulnerable. Lacey felt her heart expand with love.

"Can we keep the car?"

Lacey sighed. "It's not the kind of gift we can accept. At least I don't think we can. But let me sleep on it. How was school?"

"Fine."

"How did the government paper go?"

Robin smiled proudly. "I got an A."

"You deserved an A. It was a good paper."

"Thanks."

Lacey sat down on the side of the bed and smoothed back Robin's hair. For a few wonderful moments, it felt like old times, just the two of them, like it always had been. Lacey hated to think that this closeness had become fleeting.

"How are your other classes going?" Lacey asked.

"Great. Really great." Robin's eyes lit in the darkness. "I got invited to Janie Phillips's birthday party. It's a sleepover, and she's one of the most popular girls in my class."

Lacey smiled, happy for her daughter.

"I can go, can't I?"

Lacey hesitated, though only for a second. "Will an adult be there?"

"Yes." Robin dragged the word out.

"Then fine."

"Great! As long as we have the car, can you take me, and we can pick Amber up for a change?"

A belated sense of embarrassment shot through Lacey at the thought that this had been a problem. But then Robin launched into a series of tales that held huge importance for the teenager, like the change from hamburgers to pizza on Fridays in the cafeteria, some popular girl's new hairstyle, and a freshman who put up campaign posters touting

Louis the Lizard for sophomore class president. The lizard, apparently, had won.

Lacey listened to every word, loving the sound of her daughter's happiness. She was so wrapped up in the calm tranquillity of the day that she almost didn't hear Robin's last comment.

"What?" Lacey asked, sitting up straight.

Robin shifted around, folding her arms over the top of the covers. "When do you know if you're really in love?"

Lacey inhaled sharply as if she had been physically hit. "Why are you asking?"

Robin shrugged. "Just wondering."

Lacey forced a laugh and stood. "You are much too young to be thinking about love."

"Mom, I am not a baby anymore."

"Of course you aren't." Lacey tried to smile over the lump in her throat. "But you're only fifteen. And fifteen-year-olds don't fall in love."

"Mom! I'm almost sixteen, and you know it. You can't keep me from learning how to drive a car any more than you can keep me from noticing boys. I am going to get a license. And I am going to date. Those are things teenagers do."

"Robin, please, let's talk about this in the morning." She headed for the door.

"But we won't! That's your answer for everything. One of these days you're going to realize that you can't keep me a baby forever."

Lacey whirled back. "This isn't about you growing up. This is about keeping you safe! Boys will hurt you."

The words echoed in the tiny moonlit room, the feeling of happiness dissipating much as the light faded when the clouds shifted in front of the moon.

"Oh, Robin. I don't want you to get hurt, and when you're

young, it's hard to understand that one mistake, one deceptively simple moment in time has the power to change your life forever."

They stared at each other, and Robin's face flared with red. "I'm sorry that you got hurt, Mom. But I am not you," she said with a painful certainty. "I'm me, and I'm different, and you can't constantly judge me by your mistakes."

Lacey's heart felt like it stopped.

"I'm sorry that you got pregnant and I ruined your life—"

Lacey fell down onto her knees before her child with a determined vehemence. "Never, never say that. You are my greatest joy. You ruined nothing."

"Isn't that what you're talking about when you say one moment in time can change your life forever? If you hadn't had me, you would have had a very different life. You would've had girlfriends and gone to your prom. You would have graduated from high school. Gone to college—"

"But I did have you, and I wouldn't trade that for all the high-school girlfriends and proms in the world." Lacey took her daughter's hands. "You believe that, don't you, Robin?"

Robin shifted uncomfortably.

"Robin, tell me that you believe me."

"Sure." She rolled away. "Good night, Mom. I'm really tired and school's tomorrow."

Frozen, Lacey didn't know if she could move, but when Robin didn't relent, she pushed up from the floor. She went to her own bedroom, stripped off her clothes, trying her best not to think, then went to the bathroom. She turned the water on as hot as she could stand it, then stepped into the shower.

Her daughter thought she was a mistake, and Lacey realized in hindsight that she probably had made Robin feel that way. In her attempt to keep her child safe, she had made Robin feel like a burden. On top of that, Robin had asked about falling in love.

How was it that every time she felt like things were starting to go right, out of nowhere she got blindsided?

But no amount of questions or answers were going to help. The reality was, her daughter was growing up. Her daughter would fall in love. But not yet, she pleaded silently. Not yet.

Instead, as if bargaining with God, she promised herself she would find a way to keep Bobby's car, and start teaching Robin how to drive. A concession. And when she finally slipped into bed and a deep troubled sleep overcame her, she dreamed of love and cars. And Bobby Mac McIntyre's stereo playing softly, surrounding her, as he pressed her against the wall, his desire hard and persistent against her.

Lacey knocked on Bobby's door.

The building was quiet; Robin was sound asleep in her room. Lacey had tried to fall back to sleep, but after that fleeting dream, she had woken with a panting start. Lying there, she realized she could hear Bobby next door through the paper-thin walls. Despite the late hour, she could hear his voice, though she couldn't make out what he was saying. At the thought of him with a woman, she had slammed the pillow over her head to drown him out.

Unfortunately, after a handful of seconds, she felt like she was suffocating. So she had gotten up and gone into the living room, only then realizing it was the television she heard droning through the walls. The television Bobby played when he was home alone.

A sizzle of awareness raced through her at the thought of him across the hall. She wanted to see him . . . and she did owe him an apology, after all, regarding her outburst about the car.

She half believed herself, and half, for now, was enough. She couldn't remember the last time someone had been kind to her for no other reason than because they wanted to help.

Months ago, she had read about his notorious generosity to charities, sick children, the Big Brother foundation that provided fatherless boys guidance from men, but she had conveniently ignored those articles that had sung his praises. It was easier that way. But now with the evidence of his kindness sitting out in the parking lot, she couldn't ignore it any longer. And the only way to rectify the situation was to tender an apology.

At three in the morning?

Sanity tried to intervene, but something stronger than wisdom pushed her on. Besides, clearly he was up, as was she. And then a really good excuse hit her. Not only did she need to offer an apology, she needed to discuss what to do about the car. It couldn't wait a second longer.

With a decisive nod of her head, she pulled back her shoulders and knocked again, this time louder.

It took a second, but eventually she heard the television die down, and then the door swung open. Bobby stood in the entrance, the remnants of sleep softening his features, and she realized he must have drifted off watching some late-night show. He wore a deep blue flannel shirt that matched his eyes, unbuttoned down the center to show a broad chest covered by a dusting of dark hair that trailed low, disappearing underneath the barely buttoned jeans. She tried not to look, but when he yawned, his palm running down the strip of hair, her knees seemed to fuse, and her breath caught.

She told herself that her reaction was normal. What red-blooded woman wouldn't find this man attractive? But finding someone physically attractive was a very different proposition from a true and honest respect.

Herb, the accountant, was just the sort of man who was true and honest—and wouldn't make anything fuse, even if he wielded a blowtorch.

She cursed her errant mind and focused on her apology, doing her best to ignore this ruggedly sensual man's bare chest and trailing swath of hair. She told herself that she had no interest in him other than as her employer, her neighbor, and as a man who had given her an incredibly kind gift. Of course, there was the issue of his kiss, or kisses, but she refused to think about those or his chiseled good looks—that is, until he braced his forearm against the door, his head leaning against the edge, his famous crooked smile lighting his eyes.

"What's wrong now?" he asked.

"Nothing, not a thing." She shrugged, fighting for nonchalance, then glanced inside to make sure he was alone. But it was dark.

"No one's here."

"Not that I care. I'm only here to apologize."

One dark brow raised, and he glanced at the clock behind him. "At three in the morning?"

"Seemed as good a time as any."

Bobby smiled grimly, then stepped aside. "Come in."

She hesitated on the threshold.

"What? You'd rather say your piece in the hall?" he asked, then grinned wickedly. "Or are you trying to decide which apology to offer first?"

"Which apology?" she demanded, marching inside and closing the door with a bang.

Bobby chuckled and turned on one light that softened the darkness with a dim haze of gold. "Do you want some coffee?"

"No, thank you. I won't be staying," she said primly, even though she stood in his apartment in the wee hours of the morning, dressed in little more than a nightgown, robe, and slippers.

"Fine, have it your way, cupcake. What did you want to say?"

Her fingers curled at her side, and she felt the set of her jaw. "Must you call me cupcake?"

"Sorry, I forgot. You like sweet cakes better."

Why did she bother? How was it possible that her mind had turned him into some kind of knight in shining armor? "Just that I was horribly rude about the car."

"True, you were," he said, raking his hair back in a way that made his shirt part to show the muscles in his chest and the ripple of his abdomen. "But you've been rude most of the time since I met you."

Lacey had to force herself to look away from his body. She noticed the teasing twinkle in his eye, which only served to make her angrier. "You are the most aggravating man I have ever met. It's no wonder that you were run down by some barbaric brute since you probably weren't paying attention to the game, flirting with some woman in the stands, and never saw him coming."

Instantly, whatever easy cheer he'd had disappeared. But before he could get out a sharp rejoinder, she groaned.

"I'm sorry, I'm sorry! It's just that again and again you make me say things that I would never say to anyone else."

Their gazes locked, and Lacey took a deep breath. "I am sorry, and I truly appreciate all you have done for my daughter and me."

"It's nothing," he stated gruffly. "Besides, it's all Beth's doing."

"She didn't buy the car."

"Yeah, well . . ."

"And that day at Casa Grande, it wasn't Beth who didn't fire me. You let me stay on when we both know you didn't have to—regardless of my contract. You could have fired me."

"I should have."

"But you didn't. And that's the point. As much as you try to be ornery to me, deep down you are really very kind. Despite that, I can't accept your gift."

"Not this again. I'm telling you, your car is gone."

"I realize that, so I've come up with a plan."

"I have a feeling I'm not going to like this."

"There's no reason that you shouldn't. I'm going to make payments."

He groaned. "I don't want your money."

"All right, I'll make payments to Beth."

"Leave my sister out of this."

"Then I can't accept the car."

He sighed, a long-suffered exhale. "I take it there's no other way to handle this."

"Not one."

"Fine," he stated, disgruntled. "Make payments."

She scrunched her shoulders. "They might start out small, though. But if it takes the rest of my life, I promise you'll get every penny back."

He grumbled. "Save your impassioned Scarlett O'Hara vows for someone who'll appreciate them."

"You're impossible."

"I try." He glanced away. "Hey, it's snowing."

Lacey turned to the window. They stood side by side, each looking out as giant white flakes drifted down, the parking lot light illuminating the crystalline dance.

"It's beautiful," she said, "and so amazing to see it in the desert like this."

"I remember as a kid that I used to pray for snow. I loved the way it turned the world white and perfect, like a storybook."

She glanced up at him, taking in his strong profile, then

turned back to the window. "Robin says the very same thing about snow."

"She's a great kid."

"Yeah, she is." A soft sigh winged out of her. "She's doing so well here, that's really why I feel so thankful. She told me tonight she was invited to her first sleepover birthday party. I can hardly imagine spending the night with a bunch of girls. But she wants to go, so that's all that matters."

"Friends are important."

"I bet you had tons of them. Boys *and* girls. I can see you having huge birthdays overflowing with friends."

He stared out into the night, his body growing hot and tense despite the cold outside. Just when she thought he wouldn't respond, he said, "I only had one birthday party."

Her brow furrowed, and she could tell that there was more to this story than the simple words implied.

"I was seven, and I put it on for myself." His strong chin came up with a certain pride. "I saved every nickel and penny I could earn for a year, then I wrote up invitations, cut out party hats from colored construction paper, bought the best cake I could afford, then waited for everyone to arrive."

A chill raced down her spine at the sudden understanding of what would come next.

"No one came," he said so softly she almost didn't hear.

"Why?" she asked. "I can't imagine that you didn't have lots of friends."

"Yeah, the kids liked me. But none of them wanted to come to the orphanage for my party. I think most kids are afraid of places like The Sisters of Sacrament Home for Children, afraid that if they walk into one, they'll never come out."

"You were an orphan?" She could hardly believe it.

"Yep."

"But I don't understand. I've read so much about you, and no one mentioned anything about you being orphaned."

"Not many people know, and while that's just the sort of private tripe reporters like to showcase in pregame shows in this day and age, back when I started out in the league, personal was personal. People minded their own business."

Her mind staggered, and she turned completely to face him. "I just didn't realize," she repeated stupidly.

He shoved his hands into his pockets, his shoulders rippling beneath his soft shirt, his jeans pulling slightly lower. The power of his body always amazed her, drawing her in for reasons she didn't completely understand.

"No big deal," he said with a shrug.

"What happened to your parents?"

"I never knew my father. And I guess motherhood was too much for Cheryl," he answered.

Cheryl, not *mother*. She heard a calm numbness in his voice, as if he didn't allow himself to feel anything about the woman who had given birth to him.

"She left Beth and me with the sisters when I was five and Beth was six. I never saw her again."

Lacey could hardly breathe for the emptiness of his words. She also understood that there but for the grace of God, Robin, too, could have gone.

In the early years, it had been so overwhelming to care for a child and grow up herself, that there were times when she didn't think she could do it. But something always made her hold on—a deep abiding love, an untenable commitment that always kept her going.

"Sometimes," she said, "giving a child up is the only thing a mother can do."

He shot her a hard, cold look. "Yep, sometimes that's the case."

"How long before you were adopted?"

"I wasn't." Just that. No emotion.

"But you were only five!"

"Yeah, someone tried to adopt me once. But I was five and a handful. Five and wild. Five and furious at the world." He drew a face in the condensation left by his breath. "Five and certain that my mother would come back."

Her heart broke for the little boy, and she understood something about the man that she hadn't understood before. The loneliness. The fear of trusting.

"I used to dream that she returned," he said, his voice quiet, the hour and cocoon of darkness creating an intimacy they never had in the crisp light of day. "I used to dream of her arms holding me tight. I had broken her favorite cup the day before she took us to the sisters. She got so angry. I realize now that it wasn't just the cup that got her so upset. It was everything. But for years I was sure she gave us away to punish me."

Lacey didn't know what to say, how to reach out, how to make the hurt in his eyes disappear. "What happened to her?"

"About six years ago, just before Beth had the twins, she tracked her down. Some kind of maternal thing. Needing to see her own mother before she became one herself, she said. It was no easy feat to find the woman since she had changed her name. Turned out she married some rich guy in Albuquerque who didn't know she'd had two kids without the benefit of marriage. Not a pretty sight when Beth showed up at her door and said, 'Hi, Mom.' Apparently the woman turned white and denied knowing who Beth was. Later, Beth got a panicked phone call from Cheryl trying to explain. Her husband wouldn't understand."

Lacey wanted to reach out, but she didn't. "Bobby, I'm sorry."

"It is what it is. The past. I don't think about it much."

She wasn't so sure. "I'm surprised then," she said, "that when you found out about Robin you didn't fire me on the spot. I can't imagine you feel all that kindly toward unwed mothers."

He looked her in the eye. "I *didn't* fire you because of Robin. You can be a pain in the ass, a prim do-gooder who nearly ran off every customer before you started to ease up." His expression grew fierce. "But you didn't take the easy way out when it came to your daughter. You did what my mother wouldn't do."

The truth of his words hit her all at once. It wasn't about her. Not when she got the job in the first place, not when she kept the job once Bobby returned. Both brother and sister had seen something in her that spoke to their hearts.

And the car. It all made sense now. When he touched her, it wasn't because he couldn't resist her. He saw something in her that was different from what he found in the women he knew. Different from his mother. Different from the likes of Darla and her skimpy clothes.

She wanted out of there, because in that second she realized she had come to hope that he actually cared about her for who she was, not what she had done.

"I'd best get back before Robin notices I'm gone."

She turned to go, but he reached out, his fingers curling around the soft flesh of her arm. "Don't go."

She couldn't read his expression, but there was a hint of a smile lurking at the corner of his mouth. They faced each other, the snow outside brightening the world.

He glanced over at the clock. "Three-thirty. It's well into Friday morning, which just happens to be my birthday. I wouldn't mind some company."

Her heart raced, adrenaline pumping through her. She felt so much for this man in that moment, but she knew in the morning she would be filled with regret if she did anything other than leave.

"I really can't."

"Please," he whispered, all traces of humor gone, only the stark desolation of a little boy lost.

"Oh, Bobby . . ."

"Just for a little while." He scoffed, trying for lightness, but she knew better. "I don't want to be alone."

She closed her eyes and inhaled slowly. "A few minutes."

A deep groan rumbled in his chest, and he started to pull her to him. But she squeaked and slipped away. "Want to play a game? Cards?" She grimaced at the thought that she really didn't know any adult card games. "Go Fish or Concentration," she offered.

His chuckle was grim, and his eyes burned like blue ice.

"Those don't do anything for you?" she managed, twirling farther away. "Then charades. Charades is fun. Or we could sing. Singing's always good."

She launched into the birthday song every child sings at parties. Bobby hung his head.

"That doesn't put a pop in your tart?"

He looked at her as if she had lost her mind.

"Then how about this?" she asked.

She started croaking out "Raindrops Keep Falling on My Head," but she didn't get any further than the first few bars when he winced, then caught her hand and drew her close, pressing one finger to her lips.

"No sense in attracting every stray dog in the neighborhood." He stepped closer.

She took a step back. "Robin always wanted a pet."

"I'm not interested in playing games or singing songs," he said, his fingers curling around her upper arms.

Instinctively, her hands came up, her palms flattening on the hard planes of his chest between the edges of his shirt. His skin was hot and cold, like electrically charged marble, and alarm mixed inside her with a slow burning desire. "Then what do you want?" she couldn't help but ask.

"To hold you. To feel you in my arms, to feel that tonight, at least tonight, I'm not sitting here alone thinking about my knee and football and . . ."

His words trailed off, but she understood what he meant. "And birthday parties from the past with construction paper hats."

"Maybe so," he conceded, his voice a gruff whisper of sound.

When he leaned forward and she knew he was going to kiss her, she wondered for one fleeting moment if this was what she had come here for all along. Not to apologize, as she had told herself. Not to do the right thing. But to feel his hands on hers. To taste the pleasure of his lips against her mouth.

Shame scorched her cheeks, but that didn't help as her hands circled around his chest, her palms relishing the feel of him. He was virile, and she felt alive, no longer watching life pass by while she sat on the sidelines.

Awareness shimmered through her veins with an intensity and boldness that made her heart trip. Despite everything, she wanted him to touch her again. Perhaps it was the snow, or perhaps it was the hour, or maybe the story of the little boy he had been, but Lacey stepped out of herself, as if she could make the past slip away for both of them.

Their gazes never broke, and when he drew her near, her heart pounded wildly. She felt consumed by him. Hot and unmistakably sensual.

Then he kissed her, hungrily, desperately, his hands sweeping down her spine to her hips, until he pressed her against the hard ridge of his erection.

"I want you," he whispered against her ear. "I want you in a way that I have never wanted a woman before."

CHAPTER FIFTEEN

LACEY CLUNG to Bobby, and he kissed her again, his lips brushing back and forth, his deep groan like a gust of swirling wind against her senses. She felt his tongue slide along her lips, his teeth nipping as his head went lower. Gently he pressed her back against the wall, and she circled his shoulders with her arms as he pulled her up against him. She might not have weighed anything at all. She felt insulated from the world, as if its rotation had ceased.

He swept her up and carried her through the apartment to his bedroom. But he didn't take her to his bed. He set her down, his mouth covering hers as his hands framed her face.

He kissed her with a slow, heated passion, his palms just barely grazing over her, trailing down, his lips skimming to the pulse that throbbed in her neck. She gasped when he parted the opening of her robe, his hands cupping her breasts, and nothing separated them except the thin flannel of her nightgown.

Desire hit her like lightning, electric in a black sky, not civilized, not cautious. Her head fell back as his thumb swept over her nipple, bringing it to a taut peak, then circling before his hand moved to the long line of buttons that ran down her gown. One by one they gave way, though he

went only far enough to reveal her breasts, his fingers working the tiny fastenings with an expertise that gave her
pause.

For one long second he stood back and looked at her,
taking her in. "I knew you'd be beautiful."

An empowering boldness rose through her, and when he
caught her hands, pulling them away until her arms were
stretched out like wings, then bent his head to taste, she
forgot. Propriety. Decency. She only wanted to be held by
this man, give in to a hunger and longing, desperation and
a careening flight into ecstasy.

He captured one nipple, then pulled the other deep in
his mouth. Framing the fullness of her breasts, his expression clearly admiring, she felt an amazing power simmer
through her. She could tell that indeed he thought she was
beautiful.

The knowledge was exhilarating. And when he kissed
her again, his mouth coming down on hers, his tongue
seeking entrance, she opened to him, then shuddered with
intensity.

Sensation she had never experienced before filled her,
seemed to crack her open until she wanted to cry out for
the touch, to weep at the pleasure that she had sought but
never found. And it had been that quest that betrayed her.

Guilt and the past tried to rear up. But right or wrong,
she pushed it away.

With his arm holding her securely, he palmed first one
breast, pushing it high, then the other. He groaned into her
neck, his mouth tantalizing her throat, then sliding low
once again to close over first one nipple, sucking, teasing,
then the other, again pulling it deep into his mouth, making her body tingle and yearn.

She sighed, then gasped as his hand drifted low, over
her ribs, then still lower, her breath held. He worked the

remainder of the buttons; then the tips of his fingers grazed a path down the center of her torso.

Only to stop at her waist.

He froze. Suddenly, her mind clearing long enough to remember, she pressed her eyes closed and cringed.

"Mmmm," he murmured against her skin. "Can't remember the last time I encountered high-waist cotton panties. Do they even sell these anymore?"

Thinking of all the scantily clad Victoria's Secret types he was no doubt used to, she blushed crimson and tried to push away. But Bobby only chuckled, ran his finger underneath the heavy elastic, tugged, then let it snap.

"Ouch!"

"Oooo, I like the sound of that."

"You are so bad," she said without much conviction.

"I want to see. Are they the kind that have pink-and-blue flowers? Or plain white?" He tried to peek down her gaping nightgown.

Lacey gasped, and she slapped at his broad chest, humoring Bobby to no end. "Stop," she pleaded.

"Come on," he cajoled, his blue eyes wicked. "Who knew that kissing you could remind me of hiding in the broom closet at Sisters of Sacrament with Jenny Perkins and Racine Mendelson, and getting the show of my young life when they whipped up their skirts." He started to gather the nightgown, reaching down to find the hem, the material sliding up and up. "Just a peek," he stated, running his finger under the waistband once again.

But when she prepared herself for the next snap, it never came. Instead, she inhaled sharply when he wrapped both arms around her, his hands sliding low beneath the cotton to cup her bottom, and he pulled her to him.

They stood face-to-face, neither moving—not that she could have moved for the thundering sensation that seared through her paralyzed limbs. Then without a word, he lifted her, like slow molasses, their bodies coming together, hers higher and higher, until her face was level with his. They stayed that way for an eternity, only a hairsbreadth between their lips. But he didn't kiss her. He lowered her, slowly, maddeningly, the most intimate parts of her body gliding down over his erection.

Had it not been for the thin cotton and thick denim of his jeans separating them, the motion would have caused him to slide deep inside her. And just when her feet nearly hit the ground, he pulled her back up again, gliding, making her want to tear away the material that stood between them so she could feel the silken hardness of him slip inside her yearning body.

She felt primal and ravenous. He did this to her. Part of her understood that he was an expert at making women want him, and another part didn't care. It had been too long. She wanted sex. She wanted the physical act, consequences be damned.

A rumble of exhilarating laughter tried to bubble up through her.

"What's so funny?" he demanded.

She looked into his eyes, feeling bold and free. "I'd have to say that this is a tad better than chocolate."

His eyes shone with a predator's glint; then he lowered her to the floor and stepped away. "Just a tad?"

"Maybe more than a tad."

"Damn right, more than a tad," he preened, then slowly backed her up until her knees hit the mattress of his bed.

She sat back with a start, but he kept advancing, forcing her to lie back. He loomed over her, her hair spilled out on the deep green comforter and crisp white sheets. The bedding was rumpled, as if earlier he had tried to sleep, only giving up to sit in front of the television, and falling asleep there.

For half a murky second, she wondered what had kept

him up. She wondered what kept him from his bed. But then he lowered himself, covering her with his body and kissing her hungrily.

Her hands came up, searching, but he pulled back, as always, elusive. Once her hands were at her sides, he kissed her again. First on her brow, then on her nose. Chin, collarbone. Lower and lower, her nightgown parting. His lips followed his hands, until his fingers slipped beneath her cotton panties, and he expertly found the curls between her legs.

Despite her longing, she jerked, her hands flying to stop him.

"Shhh," he gentled her. "I'm just going to touch you."

But she couldn't relax.

"It's all right. Surely you've been touched before."

Silence. Embarrassment.

"Lacey?" He pulled back slightly and considered her. "You've had a child."

She exhaled sharply, twice, trying to find words. "I've had sex. Yes. More than once, I admit it. But it's never been anything like . . . this." She gestured to his head so low, his fingers parting her in such a way that it was hard to think. "I've . . . never been touched like that before."

"There's nothing wrong in this, Lacey. I want you to find pleasure in my touch."

"I want you to touch me," she admitted with not just a little embarrassment. "But just not like that. I want you to . . ." The words trailed off.

She pursed her lips. "I want to have sex. There, I confess."

His features hardened. "Sex is about more than body parts coming together in the dark." He studied her for a moment. "Have you ever had an orgasm, Lacey?"

Lacey groaned. "Where are all the self-centered, in-a-hurry sort of men when you need them? I've got to go," she said, scrambling to sit up, grabbing at her nightgown and robe.

His handsome face clouded with emotion. "No," he said gently, coaxing her back, touching her intimately. "Let me do this, Lacey. Let me show you what you deserve to feel. Don't be shy."

"I am not shy, Bobby McIntyre. I am sensible. And I really have to go. It's late, or rather early."

"Stop being so sensible," he whispered. "Let your hair down for a change. Let me show you what you've been missing."

Then he dipped his head, his lips grazing her mouth, before he once again parted her robe. The nightgown fell away, and he brought the surprisingly graceful power of his thigh over her, pulling her close to the heat of him. He found her breast, one finger circling in that way that made her forget thought, reason, and her long-held need to be sensible.

Within seconds, he returned her to that fevered pitch, his mouth capturing hers, distracting her as his hand trailed low. She felt on fire from the lean, sculpted heat of him, and she hardly noticed when he tugged off her panties.

Her arms were tangled above her head in thick folds of flannel and terry cloth, but he didn't free her. He touched her intimately then.

"You're wet," he murmured, his voice filled with awe and appreciation.

"You didn't have to point that out," she managed, though only barely, and when he slid one lean, slightly callused finger inside her she gasped, her body shimmering with sensation.

Her body rocked.

"Shhh," he whispered, boldly stroking, pulling out until the tip of his finger touched her most sensitive spot, then sliding deeper, making her body begin to move of its own volition.

"Lift your knees," he instructed, his voice low and passionate.

Her eyes fluttered open. He looked at her with a wealth of emotion in the deep blue depths of his eyes. "Yes, Lacey, open to me."

Slowly, dragging in her breath, she did as he said, lifting her knees until her feet were planted on the mattress. He studied her for one last, long second; then he nudged her knees farther apart. "Yes, sweetheart, just like that."

Then a shiver of heat ran through her as his hand slid down the inside of her thigh to the core of her, his palm cupping, before he parted her and slipped his finger deep once again.

Composure and common sense were lost, and all she wanted was more of what he was giving. When she thought she couldn't feel anything better, he kissed her. The thrust of his tongue was carnal, propelling her higher as he slipped a second finger inside her. She squirmed and wanted, seeking something that she knew of but had never experienced.

Their kiss turned hard and rough, hot and wet. She couldn't get close enough to his heat. She wanted all of him, his hardness inside her, his strength surrounding her. She wanted to feel his solid strength on top of her, her arms free to explore his body.

He broke the kiss, and she cried out.

"You liked that, didn't you?" he asked.

"Yes," she breathed, almost frantic.

"You want more of this?" He lowered his head to her naked breasts and his maddening tongue laved her nipples, attending to each lovingly. He whispered words of awe before he levered back.

"Yes!" And she did. She wanted to reach and fly.

"I want you to feel ecstasy."

"I do."

"Then trust me."

Suddenly the warmth of him was gone, leaving her bereft. Then he came down to kneel on the floor between her up-raised knees, his warm palms skimming along the inside of her thighs. The touch was electric, and her hands grasped the comforter.

His lips scorched a path along the tender skin, closer and closer, until his thumbs gently parted her.

"Bobby?"

"I want to make you come."

Shock riddled through her, though there wasn't much she could do about it with his head between her thighs. Then seconds later, she felt a whisper of cool breath against her moist center, then fire at the first touch of his tongue gliding along her.

"Bobby!" Her hands fought against the tangle of flannel and terry cloth until they came free. She clutched his head, her fingers raking through his dark hair.

"Shhh," he hushed her again, his broad hand splayed on her abdomen. "Don't think, just feel."

And when his lips closed over the tender nub, sucking gently, she could do little more than that. Feel. Fly. Cry out for the intensity that built and grew, threatening to consume her like a white-hot fire. Sensation coiled through her, and when he lifted her hips to take her more fully, her body exploded.

Crying out, she tensed as her world rocked, convulsing like wave after wave in a pounding sea. When finally the world righted itself, she felt suspended in those same consuming waters, floating, until she lay there, drained and empty.

When the sensation settled, her limbs felt luxuriously weak, and she stretched like a cat, sexy and fulfilled. She smiled, feeling altered, and she wanted Bobby to understand—she wanted Bobby to have the same experience.

But when she rolled over to touch him, feeling that he was hard against her hip, he only wrapped his arm around her and held her close.

"But . . . but what about you?" she asked hesitantly.

"This wasn't about me," he answered, kissing her forehead. "This was about you."

"I don't understand." Instantly she felt embarrassed that he didn't want her.

He must have read her thoughts, because he looked at her fiercely. "I want nothing more right now than to sink deep inside you until I'm lost. But I won't do that, not to you, because true intercourse is different for you than it is for me. You needed pleasure tonight. You deserved pleasure, Lacey. But having sex is different from simple pleasure." His face creased with a nearly palpable despair. "For you sex is a total giving—and I can't take that from you."

"Bobby—"

He cut her off by kissing her, one last lingering contact, before he pulled away. "It's almost five in the morning. Go home before Robin wakes."

Instantly, her mind jarred. "Oh, my gosh! Robin!"

She scrambled around, adjusting her clothes, and before he could say another word, she dashed across the room, sanity returning like an icy cold splash of water.

Dear God, what had she done?

CHAPTER SIXTEEN

ROBIN WOKE UP early and went into the kitchen for a glass of orange juice. It was five, still dark, and she about jumped out of her skin when her mom came flying in the front door wearing her robe and pajamas, her hair stirred up.

At the sight of Robin, her mom stopped dead in her tracks, her mouth frozen in a silent gasp, then burst out, "There you are, Robin!"

"Where did you think I was? In the hallway?"

Her mother laughed kind of loud. "No, silly me. I was looking for the *El Paso Times*."

"I didn't know we got the newspaper."

"We don't. But for half a second I forgot and went out there to look just the same." Then more weird laughter.

Robin told herself not to worry. Sometimes her mom got sort of frantic about work, and Robin couldn't blame her. Growing up and getting old seemed to be a total drag. Paying bills and dealing with things like insurance claims. Her mom always told her about stuff like that, though Robin had never met anyone else her age who knew the first thing about that stuff. So she had learned to keep it to herself. Other moms and dads clearly didn't talk about that with their kids.

Though most parents didn't seem to talk about the good things either. She guessed that somehow that made it kind of even.

By the time her mom dropped her off for school, even though it was really early, Robin forgot about her mom's weird behavior. In truth, it was actually fine with her since she wanted to get there early enough to go to her locker and get to class before Kyle ever pulled into the crowded parking lot.

After grabbing her books from her locker, Robin raced to first period. Her heart did a strange, staccato dance when she thought about Kyle sneaking into her room. She had been seconds away from forgetting every dire warning her mother had ever beat into her brain, and let Kyle do whatever he wanted. She had wanted him to. She had wanted to feel his arms wrapped around her, and if it meant his hands too, so be it. Something about the way he was when he was with her eased this, like, totally empty place that she'd had since forever.

But letting him touch her was impossible. Nice girls didn't do those kinds of things. If they did, kids like her were the result. Yep. No thanks. Fortunately her brain had finally kicked in and put the brakes on her raging hormones.

Heck, she swore, plunking herself down firmly in the first row of Mr. Martin's math class even before the teacher had arrived, she didn't need to repeat her mother's mistake.

As a result, Robin understood that Kyle was dangerous and she had to stop doing things like practically passing out in his arms and letting him into her room when he crawled up onto the roof.

When she had realized what she had to do, her heart had started a real awful dull ache. She didn't want to give him up, her first boyfriend. But she knew as she knew her own name that Kyle Walker wasn't interested in simply holding her hand, sweet kisses, and walking her to class.

Lost in thought, she was startled by the first bell. She sat up straight and focused on her opened math book while other students started filtering into class. But there was no sign of Kyle.

Jo Beth Randall, who had commandeered the seat that day the whole Kyle thing started, came in two minutes before the tardy bell and made a big sighing scene. "You're in my seat," she announced.

"There are no assigned seats, and you—"

Robin's words trailed off, because just then Kyle arrived. He stood in the doorway, filling most of it so that no one else could get past, his dark eyes taking her in. Her mouth went dry as he approached, then stopped directly in front of her.

"I waited for you at your locker." He spoke with cool, deliberate tones that sent shivers of a lot of things coursing through her hormone-ravaged body.

"Oops, I must have forgot." She hoped her smile looked genuine.

Jo Beth looked back and forth between them, her head swiveling from side to side like she was front and center at the Friday afternoon high school tennis match. Had it been under any other circumstances, Robin would have been amused.

Kyle ignored Jo Beth, just looked at Robin with that really closed-off expression on his face. "Come on," he said, gesturing toward the back where he always sat, where she had started sitting.

"That's all right." She turned the page to the day's lesson, her homework folded neatly in the crease. "I'm fine here."

Kyle sighed, then shrugged his shoulders. Just when Robin thought he was going to move away, he flipped her book shut, stacked it on his, then took her hand in that oddly commanding though gentle way of his, and *assisted* her out of her seat. "Let me help you," he said as polite as could be.

Robin was incensed, outraged, and damn near ready to give him a piece of her mind. And she would have. But just then the bell rang and Mr. Martin entered the classroom.

"Is there a problem here?" Mr. Martin asked in his way-too-feminine voice that didn't match his slitty, mean eyes as he glanced from Robin to Kyle.

Kyle looked at Robin. "Is there?"

Robin glanced between Mr. Martin and Kyle. She knew that while she might have saved Kyle with her twenty-dollar-bill episode, she could just as easily and more thoroughly do him in with a simple, *Yes, there's a problem.*

"No, no. No problem," she said with a huff. "Kyle was just helping me to my desk."

"Then get on with it," Mr. Martin snapped.

Robin scrambled to her desk in the back, slicing Kyle a murderous scowl.

"We'll talk about this later," Kyle said, his voice gravelly as he opened his book.

Mr. Martin gave them a list of trig problems to solve during class instead of boring them with a long lecture. Robin wrote out the equations with angry strokes, and ignored Kyle when he tried to talk to her. She was halfway through the third problem when Kyle leaned over and pointed out a mistake. Robin slapped at his hands. "Mind your own business."

Kyle tsked and had the audacity to smile. That heart-melting grin that Robin loved—though hated today.

"I was just trying to help," he said, returning to his own paper with a shrug.

Sure enough when she looked, her problem was incorrect. Damn him anyway for being so smart.

When the bell rang, Robin had already packed up and leaped out of her desk to race out the door. But Kyle had anticipated her intent. She hadn't gotten much farther than the stairwell when he caught her arm and pulled her around to face him.

"I'm sorry about last night."

So simple, so sincere, as if he was hurting worse than she was.

"I'm sorry I scared you when I showed up at your window," he added quietly, his voice gruff. "I don't know how the hell it happened, but I think about you all the time, Rob. I love your wild hair and great brown eyes. I love your laugh, I love your sincerity."

Then he leaned down to her and pressed his lips to hers, gently, coaxing her to respond.

Her head spun. He'd all but said he loved her. And she realized in that second that she loved him. Helplessly. Completely.

"Oh, Kyle," she murmured, excited but concerned, as well.

"Trust me, Robin," he whispered against her lips, his hands pulling her close. "Can you do that?"

"Yes," she whispered, looking into his eyes.

"Then don't be afraid of me."

She wasn't. Despite all the horrible warnings her mother had dispensed about boys, Robin wanted to be near him, wanted the feeling that she had when he held her close.

His sudden smile held relief, as did his dark eyes. Then he kissed her deeply, thoroughly, just as the tardy bell for second period rang. He kissed her one last time. "Go to class. I'll come over later."

"You can't! It's too soon. My mom will go crazy."

He gave her that smile again. "I don't plan to come to the front door, Robin. But this time leave the window unlocked."

Her breath caught, but she didn't say a word. Not yes, not no. Though her heart raced in her chest until her knees felt weak.

"I'll see you tonight," he said.

Then he was gone, leaving her to wonder what would happen if she didn't unlock that window. But more than that, what if she did?

CHAPTER SEVENTEEN

THE RINGING PHONE woke Bobby from a deep, dream-filled sleep. Dreaming of Lacey. The unexpected passion of her. In his arms. Bringing her to orgasm.

The phone rang again, jarring him awake to realize that he hadn't been dreaming. Lacey had been here, in his bed. He also realized he was sore as hell.

He had been working out every day since the brace was removed, pushing himself to get back in shape. Every inch of him ached, and there were moments when he wondered if he'd be ready to return to the Lone Stars this season. But he set uncertainty aside. He would be ready, and in time for the play-offs.

The ringing persisted, and rolling over, he saw that the clock read 12:15. The sunlight outside told him it wasn't the middle of the night. He had slept past noon.

Grumbling, he picked up the receiver on the fifth ring.

"McIntyre," he barked gruffly.

"Did I wake you, Bobby? It's Clint."

His lawyer greeted him with his typical good cheer, always managing to sound as if he had just stepped out of a nineteenth-century British novel.

"I'm not in the mood, Clint. What's up?"

"Well, it's about your bar manager."

For reasons Bobby couldn't explain, dread filled him, and he wished he had never asked the lawyer to look into anything. He didn't respond, but Clint didn't need any prompting.

"As usual, you were correct. From what I've been able to dig up so far, your Miss Wright has something of a past. You have a way of reading people, Bobby, that never ceases to amaze me."

"Meaning?"

"Meaning that you sensed something was wrong, and when I compared the résumé she submitted to what I've been able to find out about her, the two don't match up."

Bobby switched the phone to his other ear, nearly hanging up in the process. "Tell me what you found."

"Lacey Wright grew up in a middle-class family in Minnesota—her father is a professor at the local university. One of those religious colleges. When she was young, she was smart, if unexceptional. She definitely wasn't popular. That is until high school, when her popularity grew in direct proportion to, let's say, the dimensions of her figure. Suddenly, Miss Wright was the center of attention, at least with the boys. Classic case, from what I can tell, of a mousy young girl with a cold father who suddenly finds herself with curves and lots of attention. Not all girls handle that well, including your bar manager, it would seem."

Thoughts of his own mother came to mind. He remembered Beth telling him that during the furtive call Cheryl had made to his sister, she had said her high school boyfriend had gotten her pregnant, then broken up with her. After that, she had dropped out, and gone through a string of mindless affairs trying to find love. Only she'd gotten pregnant with Bobby instead.

Angrily, he pushed the thought away. "What does Lacey's sudden popularity have to do with anything, Clint?"

"Her newfound status left her pregnant, kicked out of school and her home, while the young boy, a star football player, went to college on a football scholarship."

"Shit. No wonder she hates football players," he muttered more to himself than to the lawyer.

"Miss Wright has a daughter out of wedlock."

"I already knew that. I can't believe I pay you for something that's as plain as the nose on your face." He was lashing out, he knew it, but couldn't seem to keep emotion in check.

"What isn't so plain, my good friend, is that I can find no trace that Miss Wright has ever seen the inside of a bar, much less run one. She lists jobs she doesn't appear to have had, and there's even one job she did have, that she didn't list. Her résumé appears to be a work of fiction."

A month ago, Bobby would have been glad for the news, at the confirmation that he was right. But now he felt a twist inside him that he hardly understood. He hated to learn that she had lied. To Beth. To him. He could deal with many things, but not lies.

The image of her in his bed, the sheets and blankets tangled, her long hair loose and wild, her inhibitions melting away, reared in his mind. The memory of her passion made him hard. He had burned to take her, but hadn't because he wanted her to feel something. He wanted to make her come. It had been an incredible gift to have shared in that moment.

Though now two images tangled together in a snare. Lacey, the innocent in all ways that mattered. And Lacey, the woman who had lied to him.

He had been so certain she was different from his mother, who had said she loved him, but left him and proved that her love was a lie. Different from the other women who inevitably wanted something from him. Gifts. To be associated with his name. To gain attention from the press when he dated them. Lacey wanted nothing to do with his fame, wouldn't even accept the car she needed badly without paying for it herself. But on the other side of that coin, Lacey had lied.

He hung up, then brooded as he shaved, showered, and made a dry tuna fish sandwich and a soy shake. Afterwards, he hardly realized he had eaten, until the plate and cup stood empty in front of him. Then he paced. Trying to clear his head. For half a second, he almost called Beth to tell her what he had learned. But somehow he couldn't. At least not yet.

After brushing his teeth, he finished dressing. When the phone started ringing again, he welcomed the relief of football business that consumed him the rest of the afternoon. But no sooner did he hang up from the last caller than Lacey returned to mind. And he knew what he had to do.

By the time he was ready to leave the apartment, it was nearly five. The bar would be filling up, but Lacey would still be in the office. He wasn't going to wait until tomorrow to confront her.

Grabbing up his keys and shoving them in his pocket, he opened the door. He stopped at the sight of Robin in the hallway. At the sound of his door, she whirled around.

"Bobby Mac!" she squeaked, her schoolbooks nearly dropping to the floor. "Hi!"

Bobby looked up and down the hall in confusion. "What are you doing out here?"

"Nothing, not a thing," she shrugged kind of goofy. "Just hanging out, doing homework. Trig equations."

"In the hall?"

"Ah, yeah!" Her nose wrinkled. "It's a great place to do homework."

He scowled in disbelief.

"The lighting," she explained, gesturing to the overhead fixture. "It's really, ah, well . . . light."

Had she lost her mind? That, or was she trying to

sneak out of the apartment? He remembered all too well the crazy things teenagers did to sneak around and avoid adults. Hell.

"Where's your mother?" he asked, though he didn't wait for an answer before he headed for the stairs.

"Wait!"

Stopping, he peered at her.

Robin laughed self-consciously. "I need to talk."

She glanced down the hall as if checking for someone, but Bobby didn't have a chance to question her before she grabbed his arm.

"Or better yet, rather than talk," she said, "let's go find my mom. I bet she's in the parking lot."

He looked at her suspiciously. "I'm sure she's out there looking at the car." She dragged him along to the set of stairs that led out to the back of the building. "Speaking of the car, did I tell you how ultracool it was of you to get it? Mom told me about making payments and all, and that's the right thing to do. But even so, I'm totally glad you got it because there is no way she would have ever gotten one herself. Especially not a Jeep. Not your regular carpool car for my mom."

Furtively, she glanced back down the hall, like at any minute someone might appear.

"Robin, what is this about?" he asked ominously. "Are you hiding someone in your apartment?"

"Me?"

Her voice squeaked again, and he had to steady her when she tripped.

"No way. You said you wanted to talk to my mom, and I'm almost sure she's back here." She tugged him outside, then slammed the door shut.

They took the back, outside stairway, Bobby holding on to Robin's arm like a father steadying a child. He had the fleeting thought that she was just like her mother, in no way intimidated by his stature—either physical, or in society. For reasons he didn't understand, both mother and daughter trusted him.

He didn't like that thought any more than he liked any other thought he'd had about Lacey since the day he walked into the office and saw her.

They came around to the side of the building, and the second he saw a woman half in, half out of the car, he knew that the backside could only belong to Lacey. God, she had a great ass.

"Mom!"

Lacey straightened out of the car. "Bobby," she said, her eyes lighting at the sight of him.

Robin was still acting strangely, glancing back and forth between them and the building. But for that second, he could only stare at Lacey. Something in his chest kicked, and everything around them seemed to fade away as their gazes met and locked. He knew she was remembering last night, the blush of red across her cheeks was a telltale sign.

For once at seeing him, she didn't look put out. Her expression softened, and for a moment he would have sworn she almost reached out to take his hand.

"I was just telling Bobby how cool the car is," Robin interjected. "And I was talking so much that I shut the door and forgot my keys. We'll totally have to go in through the front door."

Instantly, Lacey snapped to attention, her hand falling awkwardly to her side.

Bobby looked at the teenager long and hard. "Fine, but why don't you go in first, Robin. I need to talk to your mom."

"Great! Good idea!" Robin chirped. "I'll leave you two to talk." Then she whipped around, her long hair swinging out, before she dashed across the parking lot toward the front door.

They both watched her go.

"She's acting strange," he said.

Lacey's eyes went wide. "Robin? I don't think so."

Then before Bobby could say another word, Lacey stuck her head back into the car, pulled out a bag that she snatched away when he tried to help her, then locked up.

"Come on, let's get inside," she said.

She practically ran to the front door, stopping only to wait for him.

"Lacey," he said, his tone warning as he followed her. "I'm serious."

"I'm sure you are, but we can talk inside."

Muttering a curse, he grabbed the door handle. "If you want to talk inside, fine. But wherever we go, you better have a damn good reason for lying on your résumé, or I'm going to fire your ass like I should have that first day."

Lacey went still, and her face blanched. For half a second Bobby wished he hadn't been so blunt. But he was given no chance to say another word when he pulled the door open.

"Surprise!"

The loud chorus echoed through the bar, out the door, enveloping him in a cocoon of sound. Understanding came slowly.

"What the hell?" he whispered.

Lacey couldn't answer, couldn't find enough oxygen to breathe.

The place was packed with regulars, Robin standing at the front, proud of the part she had played in keeping him distracted. Beth was there, and her husband, Raymond, and Bobby's old high school coach. Nearly a hundred people who had been a part of his life over the years packed the bar. With Beth's help, Lacey had spent hours that morning gathering these people together. It was a testament to their love for Bobby that they would drop everything on such short notice and come to this impromptu party.

They laughed and cheered, then launched into a rowdy rendition of "Happy Birthday to You."

Bobby stood stock-still on the small landing, like an actor on stage, his face a careful blank. Slowly, he turned to look at Lacey. She felt his questioning gaze as a palpable dread rushed in. Her life flashed before her eyes. It was over, her new life crashing down around her.

How was it possible for life to turn upside down once again? But deep down she had always known the lies on her résumé would catch up with her eventually.

Shame reared up, and for a second she thought she would be sick. At the time when she had done it, she had been desperate. Her work history was anything but impressive, and the only jobs she had been able to obtain over the years were long hours at a paper plant in Minnesota. When she had been laid off, and she and Robin had inched toward welfare, suddenly she found herself *embellishing* her list of accomplishments.

But the truth was, embellish had turned to spin, and spin had turned to out-and-out lies. She had taken baby steps away from the truth, one bit at a time, so that it had never felt like lying. By the time sense returned, Beth had already made her fateful call with the offer of a job that seemed the answer to her prayers.

Now Lacey had to pay the consequences. Looking at the burning wrath on Bobby's face, she knew it would be severe.

The crowd launched into "For He's a Jolly Good Fellow" next, and Beth walked up the three steps to the landing and took Bobby's arm. He all but tore his gaze away from Lacey, and she saw the effort it took to muster a smile. In that moment, it was like a façade had come up, and he was once again Bobby Mac McIntyre, the legend this crowd of people adored. He didn't look at her again. He allowed himself to be pulled into the festivities.

It was then that Lacey noticed the surroundings. In her hasty planning, she had gotten Beth to call his friends, Robin to guard his door and bring him out to the parking lot, while she had been in charge of the food. Sitting at the bar early that morning, after she had written up a list of the games she wanted to play, Peter had coughed into his fist and said he'd be happy to take charge of getting what she needed for the games. He also said he'd get the cake.

But Peter's vision did not match her own.

"Hey, Lacey!" Ned called out. "Who would ever have thought you'd know how to throw such a great party?"

The regulars cheered, Bobby turned to look at her with a darkly raised brow, and her daughter stood in the middle of the room, her tiny rosebud mouth gaping.

When Lacey had requested a set of Hot Wheels, she had meant the tiny metal cars and orange track that little boys of Bobby's generation had loved. Instead she cringed at the sight of a tall, well-endowed, scantily clad woman with legs up to her armpits and a sparkly sign that read, I'VE GOT HOT WHEELS.

Pin the Tail on the Donkey had morphed into Pin the Tail on the Bunny—a Playboy Bunny. And just then the bunny was bending over with her hands on her knees, swishing her tail, the rowdy crowd of men hollering out, "Pin her, Bobby Mac, pin her!"

Lacey closed her eyes and groaned.

But even without looking, she couldn't forget the cake she had caught sight of on the bar. She had asked Peter to pick up one from Big Bert's Birthday Bakery. Instead it had arrived as *Big Boobs for Bobby Mac*, a cake in the shape of two large women's breasts, iced in flesh tones with bright red frosting swirls for nipples. Yes, she really was going to be sick.

She hadn't moved from the entrance landing, and she jerked to attention when Beth came up beside her and hooked their arms together. They stood side by side, looking out over the crowd.

"This was incredibly sweet of you," Beth said.

"After surveying the results, I'm not sure *sweet* is the right word. Racy. Crude. Obscene. Any of those might work."

Beth laughed. "Let's leave it at incredibly thoughtful."

Lacey's heart clinched hard in her chest. She loved Beth like a sister, and with that thought the shock of the party wore off and all that remained was shame at what she had done.

"I lied on my résumé."

Beth sighed, though she didn't speak or turn to face her. Neither did she unhook her arm from Lacey's.

"I know," she said finally.

Lacey whirled around. "Bobby told you?"

Beth seemed to debate her answer. "No, I knew from the very beginning. You don't think I would hire someone to work for my brother without checking them out first, do you?"

"Well, I guess not. Then how could you have hired me?"

Tilting her head to the side, Beth shrugged. "I met you. And I met you first, while I was having the check run— before I knew the truth. Perhaps if the timing had been different, I never would have gone to meet you. God works in strange ways sometimes, and the minute I arrived I liked you."

"So you hired me to manage the bar because of that? What if I had run the place into the ground?"

Lacey knew she sounded incredulous.

"The way I saw it, you couldn't have been worse than Gator. Besides . . ." Beth hesitated. "You needed us." This woman, who looked so much like Bobby, turned to Lacey and took her hands. "And I had this feeling that Bobby needed you. My brother needs a special kind of woman, one who doesn't care that he's a football player. One that can understand the kind of background he comes from. One who can make the little boy whose mother left him at an orphanage feel safe."

Beth looked out into the crowd and found her husband. He was a tall man, though not so tall as Bobby. Lacey had met him once before, and she had liked him immensely. Though at first he had surprised her because Beth was such a beautiful woman, and on first inspection, her husband might not have been called good-looking at all. But he had a joy about him, a strength and confidence that made him seem far more handsome than he was.

As if sensing his wife's gaze, he glanced over and smiled, and Lacey could almost feel the love that charged the air between the couple.

"That's what Ray makes me feel," Beth said softly, a wealth of emotion in her tone. "He makes me feel safe and loved and cherished. I want that same gift for Bobby."

"But your brother hates me! You should have seen his face a few minutes ago when he said he knew I had lied on my résumé. I doubt he's going to think anything about me is a gift."

"Perhaps not now, but only because he's too afraid to let down the walls he keeps around himself. Women with skimpy clothes and no brains don't threaten him. You do."

"That might have been the case before. But after all Bobby has been through, even I know he's not the type to forgive lies."

Beth hesitated as if she debated her next words. "Don't give up, Lacey. The truth is, my brother lives a lie."

Lacey couldn't have been more surprised.

"Not intentionally," Beth added hurriedly. "But he has created a life filled with characters who act out their parts, and he has made himself into a character that the world loves. The legendary quarterback. The man who every woman wants, but no woman can have. But that Bobby Mac isn't little Bobby McIntyre who I love with all my heart."

As soon as the words were out of Beth's mouth, Lacey saw tears burn in the woman's eyes.

"I brought you to Texas on a hunch," Beth added, "on the hope that Bobby might find a true happiness that I don't believe he has ever known. I found happiness when I met my husband and we created a family of our own. But as much as I want Bobby to be a part of my world, he keeps himself on the fringes—as if he feels like this is my family, not his. Lacey, he deserves more than that. Just as you deserve more. And when I met you, I had this inexplicable feeling that you were the one." Unexpectedly, Beth smiled the same devilish smile Bobby loved. "Nothing ventured, nothing gained, I've always believed."

Lacey didn't know what to say. An incredible hope expanded in her chest.

"Now go out there and ignore that damned Bunny and the crude cake, and don't let Bobby push you away—or fire you."

The words sent a shiver down Lacey's spine. "I'm surprised you didn't want to fire me when you took one look at this party. I never meant for it to be this way."

Beth laughed in a deep contagious way, a large laugh that was a contrast to her petite form. "Peter called and told me what you sent him out to do." She wrapped her arm around Lacey's shoulder. "As sweet an idea as pin the tail on the donkey was, it probably wasn't the best way to go with this crowd."

"But . . . but an indecent cake?"

"This is a bar, Lacey, not a bar mitzvah." Beth giggled, pleased when her husband raised a brow as if he had overheard; then she added, "I figured you wouldn't want Robin around this, so I gave her a stack of magazines I had in the car and told her she'd best go upstairs before her mother had a heart attack."

Had anyone other than Beth done such a thing, Lacey probably would have thought it presumptuous. But with Beth, she was only thankful.

"Now, go find Bobby. Talk to him. Explain why you felt you had to *fudge* a bit on your résumé. Don't let him push you away."

Beth nudged her forward, and suddenly she was enveloped by the crush of Bobby's friends. Compliments flew the minute she stepped into the crowd. Amazingly, the party was a hit. She got so caught up in the gaiety and game playing, that she nearly forgot the panic she had felt earlier. But fear and remorse hit her square in the chest when she broke through a knot of revelers and came face-to-face with the guest of honor.

Standing so close, as always, the height and sheer strength of him surprised her. If she didn't look up, she stared straight into his broad chest, so wide and all-enveloping that she could wrap herself close and always be safe.

The thought startled her. He had done nothing to make her feel safe, she told herself. But she knew that wasn't true. He hadn't fired her. He cared for everyone who stepped into his bar. He cared about Robin. But what she truly couldn't deny was his generosity and his kindness—a kindness that she hadn't expected from a man whom she had always thought of as selfish.

A rush of heat swept through her when she remembered those early morning hours when he had given her pleasure, refusing to take his own. Unselfishly. Giving to her. Not taking.

Could it have been simple kindness? Or had it been because he knew that if he had taken, eventually she would have wondered if he had given her the car as some form of down payment on what he wanted from her.

She looked up at him, wanting to know, wanting to understand. Could it be that simple? Or was there more to the way he held himself separate?

But his face was filled with such anger that questions dried up in her mouth. Then he turned on his booted heel and slipped away into the crowd.

Her mind spun, raced with what she should do. She caught sight of Beth, whose eyes implored her to go after him. Lacey pulled a deep breath. She really did want to talk to him, explain, tell him all the things she had never told anyone before. But to let down her guard, tell him her deepest secrets, was difficult to do. What if he still turned her away? What if he told her to pack up her daughter and her belongings and get the hell out of Dodge?

Those few words did it. Texan and daring. Centuries of larger-than-life people who were not afraid of anything. That's what she came here to be. That's why she had come to this far-off place. To be strong. And whether anything ever happened between her and Bobby again, all that mattered was that she explained. Truthfully, completely. Not holding anything back.

Lacey parted the crowd like she was parting the Red Sea. At first, she didn't see Bobby anywhere. But at the very last second, she saw the back of him disappear down the hall.

"Lacey, great party!"

"Let's put the tail on Lacey!" Ned cried out, his margarita sloshing over the side.

She gave him a look she had mastered since arriving at Bobby's Place.

"Or maybe not," he added, then the group hooted their laughter.

"Hey, Lacey," someone else called, though this time she wasn't distracted from her purpose.

She headed for the office, offering up a silent prayer before pushing through the door. But Bobby wasn't there.

Knowing that the only other place he could be was in his apartment, she went up the stairs and knocked on his door.

No answer.

She knocked again, harder.

"Bobby?"

His muffled voice came through the door. "Go away, Miss Wright."

"We need to talk."

He whipped open the door, and she automatically took a step back. His shirt was gone, as if he had ripped it off the second he got inside. He looked feral, caged as he stared down at her, much as he had in the bar. With a curse, he raked his hair back with both hands, the long line of muscles on his chest and stomach rippling, a flash of dark hair under his arms, before he dropped them to his side. Heat rushed through her, and her knees felt weak at the memory of his body cradling hers, his mouth closing over her most intimate center, making her cry out.

"No," he said coldly. "Not now. I want to be calm and sane when I fire you."

Then he slammed the door. But Lacey didn't care.

"No," she said, barging in. "We talk now."

CHAPTER EIGHTEEN

ROBIN HEARD the knock at her window, and her heart slammed against her ribs.

Surrounded by glossy magazines and piles of pillows, the sound of laughter and music from Bobby's birthday party drifting through the floor, she sat paralyzed with anxiety, outrage, and the tingling thrill of joy.

Another tap sounded, this time impatient, and she leaped out of bed. Nervously shaking, she dashed to her bedroom door, peered into the apartment, and confirmed that her mother wasn't home yet. Sending up a silent prayer—or perhaps a silent plea for forgiveness—she secured the lock, then dashed to the window, and whipped aside the sash.

Kyle crouched on the overhang, beautiful and rugged and smiling at her in the dark.

"You can't keep coming here like this," she whispered frantically when she pushed open the glass.

Kyle flashed his crooked grin and crawled in without being asked, then jumped down to the floor. The thud resounded through the room, and Robin caught her breath, then waited.

"No one heard," Kyle assured her. "With the music and partying going on downstairs, they won't hear anything we do."

Between his words and the look he gave, her knees went weak and her heart beat even harder.

"I'm serious, Kyle. You really can't keep doing this. If my mom found out, she'd freak. No, she'd do worse than freak. She'd pack me off to a convent, and I'd never see the light of day again."

"You've been reading too many books. Besides, I told you I wanted to see you."

"Whoever said I wanted to see *you*?"

Kyle laughed and leaned back against the windowsill. "That's what I like about you, Rob. You give as good as you get. But I didn't crawl up here to argue with you."

Robin couldn't help herself as she looked at his lips, slightly parting her own. "Then why are you here?"

"Like I said, to see you. And," he drew the word out, "to tell you about our date."

She met his gaze in a flash. "Our date? We haven't been out on a date."

"Yet."

"Yet. Yet?" she said in escalating tones. "You really are too much. You can't just come over here like I've already said yes."

"Why not?"

"You have to ask first," she said sternly. "Preferably over the phone. I might say no. Haven't you heard that rejection is harder to take in person?"

Kyle pushed away from the sill and stepped closer. "You're not going to say no." His smile was as boyish as it was assured.

Robin scoffed in disbelief. "You don't know that. I might already have plans." She crossed her arms and looked at him askance. "I might already have a date."

His smile flattened to a hard line, but his eyes glittered with challenge. "We've been over the other guy thing, Robin. You're my girl."

Okay, so he was archaic and a little over the top. But the thrill of belonging raced down her spine, even as it battled with the need for the kind of independence her mother had taught her was essential in this day and age. She shouldn't want this guy to be possessive of her, but she couldn't deny that his words and attention made her feel important and cherished.

He started to reach for her hand, but Robin jumped away.

"Playing hard to get, are we?"

"*We* aren't doing anything," she responded, moving back with every step he took forward. "I am trying to act like the level-headed girl that I am."

This time Kyle snorted. "You? Level-headed?" he demanded, taking a step closer, backing her up against the bed. "You who gets caught out in the rain, nearly killing herself? That you?"

Kyle lifted his hand toward her cheek. But Robin was too quick as she leaped up onto the bed, jumping across, landing on the opposite side.

"You're fast," he responded, impressed.

"I thought so—"

But her words were cut off when Kyle leaped around the end of the bed, scooping her up. Ignoring her laughing squeal of protest, he tossed her onto the mattress, then pinned her down in the scatter of glossy magazines. "But I'm faster."

She laughed in spite of herself, feeling free and alive, worries set aside, until she met his gaze and her laughter trailed off. Releasing her wrists, he supported his weight on his elbows. Gently he leaned down and kissed her. Like the first time, it was wonderful and exhilarating, and she never wanted it to end.

He brushed his lips against hers and she sighed, her body trembling with excitement and trepidation.

"You taste like peppermint," she whispered.

He smiled. "You taste like butterscotch."

Startling her, he rolled away, making himself comfortable against her pillows, and took a butterscotch candy out of the bag. Grabbing hold of both ends, he pulled, the candy spinning out to where he caught it. After he popped one in his mouth, he tugged off his leather jacket, kicked off his boots, then crossed his feet and picked up the first magazine at hand.

What about the kiss? she almost demanded.

But she held the words back, chastising herself for not being relieved he had stopped. She tried to focus, but it was hard given that this amazing guy was lying on her bed in his stocking feet. Somehow the socks made everything seem so real—made *him* seem so real. That is, until she got a really good look at the socks he had on.

"Did you know you have on *Power Rangers* socks?" she asked hesitantly, hating to embarrass him.

Kyle glanced over the glossy pages at his feet, then waggled his eyebrows. "My cousin left them at the house a hundred years ago, and somehow they ended up in my drawer." He shrugged. "I thought they were pretty cool." He went back to the pages, then grimaced. "Though this magazine is anything but. *Redbook*?" he asked. "I thought all you girls read *Teen People* or *Seventeen*."

"We probably do, but these are Bobby Mac's sister's magazines, and while Beth is really neat, I wouldn't call her cool. Though Bobby is totally awesome."

Kyle flipped through the *Redbook*, then started on an issue of *Good Housekeeping* without a word.

Robin curled her legs beneath her. "I think he likes my mom," she said pensively.

Kyle glanced at her over the top of the magazine. "Bobby Mac likes anything in a skirt."

Coming up on her knees in front of him, Robin furrowed her brow. "That isn't true," she said defensively.

He shrugged his shoulders and went back to reading.

"It isn't," she insisted.

"All I know is what the newspapers say, and they say he is known for loving 'em and leaving 'em, babe."

"Don't call me babe," she groused.

Robin got quiet, wondering if it were true. Would Bobby Mac make her mom fall in love with him, then leave her—or even fire her once he got tired of her? But surely with her mom and Bobby it was different. He bought her the car after all, and while her mom had made this whole big production about making payments, Bobby had wanted it to be a gift. She couldn't imagine he would have done that if he didn't love her mom.

"Hey," Kyle said softly, tossing the magazine aside. "What do I know? If your mom is anything like you, then she's different, and I'm sure Bobby Mac knows it."

He reached out and took her hand, tugging her toward him. He curled her close in his arms, holding her against his chest, then he kissed her on the forehead. Only when she sighed, leaning into him, did his lips trail lower and meet hers.

She felt the beat of his heart. Then there was the smell of him. Leather and soap. And now butterscotch. Tentatively Robin brought her hand up and touched his shoulders, her palms barely pressed against him.

He made a noise deep in his chest. "God, Rob, you do something to me," he murmured against her, his thumbs caressing her cheeks.

Boldly she ran the palms of her hands along the ridge of his shoulders until they met at his neck, her fingers tangling in his hair. She had never touched a guy. Ever. She had read about how hard and different they felt in books, the "rigid planes" and "musky scent." But words on a page had not prepared her for the intimacy she would feel when touching Kyle.

With a groan, he circled his hands around her, pulling her body to curve into his. He kissed her again, his lips brushing hers in a way that proved she wasn't his first girlfriend. But she already knew that, and when his hand slowly rubbed her back, her panic and concern slipped away with his surprisingly gentle touch, and she melted against him. When her tension eased, his mouth slanted over hers. Her body began to tingle in a way that was as unfamiliar as it was intriguing, and Robin felt herself starting to kiss him back.

The sensation was heady and forbidden. She felt older and desirable. Worries and concerns vanished. In that second, she wasn't the odd, smart kid with wild hair and way too many books.

"Yes," he murmured, his lips trailing to her ear.

Tentatively, she wrapped her arms around him, his long-sleeve T-shirt and her sweatshirt the only thing between them. He kissed her neck, his tongue sliding against her pulse.

But then his hand slid down to press against the curve of her hips, the touch intimate. Suddenly the pillows and magazines were in a heap on the floor, and Kyle rolled on top of her. One solid thigh came between her own.

"Kyle," she whispered, uncertain but somehow wanting more of this.

"Shhh," he murmured.

He kissed her neck, his touch teasing at her ear as his hand came up to cup one full breast. Robin gasped, but Kyle whispered sweet words, gentling her again.

Her head spun with so many new sensations. The feel of him, the tantalizing smell, the sound of his rugged voice making it clear that he was as affected as she.

He returned his lips to hers, his hand slipping beneath her sweatshirt, his palm gliding up over her ribs.

"Kyle!"

"Shhh, Rob. It's all right. Let me touch you."

"Kyle," she repeated, this time her tone uncertain.

He pulled back and looked into her eyes. "I'd never hurt you."

Their gazes locked and held.

"Do you trust me, Robin?"

She bit her lip. "Yes," she whispered.

Kyle pulled back until he kneeled on her bed above her. In one swift motion, he pulled his shirt over his head, leaving his hard-muscled torso bare.

Robin stared, her full mouth opening in a silent *o*. Instinctively, she reached out and ran her fingers along the rippled plane of sinew and hard muscle. She felt him tense, felt him draw a deep shuddering breath.

Strangely empowered, not thinking about what she was doing, her fingers traced the path of dark hair down his abdomen, only stopping at the waistband of his jeans. Kyle sucked in his breath, capturing her hand.

Robin realized suddenly just where that strip of hair led, and she blushed.

"Don't be embarrassed around me," he stated gruffly, lowering himself until he was over her, his weight supported on his elbows and forearms.

He kissed her again, drowning her uncertainty with the touch of his lips to hers. Slowly he deepened the kiss, coaxing her lips apart. This time when his thigh came over her, she lifted her knees so that the two of them slipped closer together. The palm of his hand slid up the bare skin of her midriff; then he pressed one full breast high.

Robin sucked in her breath at the contact, and Kyle groaned into her neck.

"Robin, Robin," he whispered as his thumb brushed against her rosebud nipple, bringing it to a hard peak.

"Robin," he groaned against her.

She lost herself to the feeling, refusing to think. But then the sound of pounding footsteps on the stairs filtered into her mind. A door banged shut. Bobby's door. Then more footsteps, lighter, and Robin was sure they belonged to her mother.

"My mom!" Robin gasped.

"Shit," Kyle hissed.

He leaped up from the bed as Robin scrambled to fix her clothes.

"Quick," she whispered, "out the window!"

Kyle grabbed his coat and leaped over the sill onto the roof, but before she could get the glass pane shut, he stopped her.

"Our date."

"Date? My mom will never let me go out on one."

"Tell her you're going to stay at Amber's."

Robin went stiff. "I can't do that." But then a thought occurred to her. "But she might let me go to the Winter Dance."

The Winter Dance was the single most important event of the fall semester. Every girl wanted to go, including Robin, though she couldn't believe she had been bold enough to ask.

She was so caught up in the thought that she didn't notice that Kyle tensed.

"You'd have to meet my mom first," she added, "but I think if you came over, talked to her for a while so she could see how really great you are, and because mothers love that kind of prom stuff, I bet she'd let me go." She grabbed his hands. "It would be so great!"

That's when she finally noticed how he stared at her.

"I'm not a Winter Dance kind of guy, Rob, and you know it."

Heat seared through her. "Oh. Oh, my gosh, I am so embarrassed. What was I thinking? I can't believe I asked you to take me to something that is totally the kind of thing a guy should ask a girl to. Forget that I said anything."

But her mortification was interrupted by the sound of muffled voices in the hall.

"Oh, man, it's my mom. You've got to go."

She wanted him gone so her mother wouldn't find him, but also because she didn't think she could stand that penetrating look he was giving her for one more second.

Thankfully, he didn't resist, he just looked at her then slipped away in the early evening darkness.

Quickly, she glanced at herself in the mirror, smoothed her hair, then drew a deep breath. Opening the door, she glanced out into the apartment, but she didn't find a trace of her mom.

Chapter Nineteen

Lacey faced Bobby in the doorway, her fingers clutching the doorknob.

"I'm sorry I lied," she stated. "It was idiotic and wrong, and I regret it terribly. But I'm doing a good job, Bobby."

"Ah," he breathed, the simple word a scoff. "And that makes it okay?"

"Why doesn't it?"

"Because you lied!"

His voice reverberated in the carpeted hall, against the ceiling and wood paneling. Lacey cringed and looked around, then tried to come into his apartment. But Bobby stood coldly in the way.

After a moment, she closed her eyes, panic making her bold. "I needed the job, and I stretched the truth. I was desperate." She met his hard gaze, her chin rising. "I wanted to find a home for Robin. I realize now that I wanted to find a place where I could stop running."

He looked at her with his steady, unreadable gaze. "Running from what? The law? Do you have a criminal record on top of everything else?"

"No!"

"Then what were you running from?"

"From me, from my past. Running from city to city, job to job. I didn't even realize it until my daughter pointed it out. I always thought of it as moving on, finding something

better. Now I understand that I've been running for years."
She let go of the door. "But sometimes it's easier to run
than face the hard stuff."

"That's what life is, Lacey, hard stuff."

She smiled feebly, hoping he'd soften just a bit. "Don't
you think I know that?"

But he stood like stone, his expression ruthless and un-
forgiving, and she sighed.

"I needed a job, Bobby. A good job in a city far away
from the whole list of cities and towns I had made my way
through in Minnesota."

"And you expect me to believe you thought working in a
bar was a good job?"

"Yes! I never graduated from high school, and my parents wouldn't have anything to do with me once I got pregnant. Suddenly I was on my own with a baby and no way to
support myself. No sooner would I get a new job than
Robin would get sick and I'd have to miss work, or small-
town gossip started heating up about the unwed mother. I
can't tell you how many jobs I lost because people assumed I was loose. If I told people I was divorced, they
eventually found out the truth, which only made it worse. I
went from factory assembly lines to cleaning motel rooms,
shampooing hair, sweeping floors, anything to keep food
on the table and clothes on Robin's back." She closed her
eyes remembering. "I could never get ahead."

"As long as you were lying your way into a job," he
asked bluntly, "why not get work as a secretary?"

"Because I can't type. But I've always been good with
numbers . . . and getting people to toe the line. A year ago,
I got this really great job as the assistant to a restaurant
manager. No typing involved. Just placing orders, keeping
track of time sheets, and the like." She looked him in the
eye. "I was good at it. And it was a good job. Once my boss
saw how well I handled the position, he gave me more and

more responsibility. Sure, he was getting me to do his work for no more pay, but I didn't care. To me it was on-the-job training. I was finally getting ahead, finally finding something to do that would make it possible for Robin and me to stop living hand-to-mouth."

"Then why didn't you stay there?"

She shrugged with an indifference she didn't feel. "When I wouldn't sleep with him, he decided I wasn't so well qualified after all."

Just that, as if it had been that simple. Her stomach churned with the same anxiety she had felt when the man's hand had slipped between her legs when she had bent over to pick up a pencil. As if she had asked for it.

Though regret was forgotten when she felt a sizzle of anger rush through Bobby, an amazing surge of protectiveness in him that made her certain that he blamed the boss, and not her. But whatever protectiveness he felt, his anger with her was still there, as well.

Determination to make him understand built inside her. "He fired me, and he certainly wasn't going to recommend me for any other job, but I had learned that I could manage a business. I knew I could be in charge of people who needed to keep on task in order to make something run smoothly." She refused to look away. "But it had to be big enough so I could make some money, far enough away from Minnesota so I could truly start over without anyone knowing me, and small enough that I wouldn't be dealing with a long chain of command."

He didn't look any happier about her confession, but he hadn't slammed the door in her face either. Encouraged, she plunged ahead. "I sent out hundreds of applications, through the mail and through e-mail at the local library. Only three businesses got back to me. Bobby's Place was one."

"Who were the other two?"

"A Red Lobster restaurant in Pasadena—"

"Too big," he surmised coldly.

"And a boutique in Oklahoma City."

"Too small?" he ventured with a sneer.

Lacey wrinkled her nose. "Owned by a lawyer," she conceded.

His face darkened even more. "I see. Too suspicious. He might have poked around and learned about your past . . . unlike a football player who wouldn't be smart enough to check your references."

She nearly cringed. "I didn't think a football player who owned a bar would care about my past."

"I do care," he said with low intensity.

Without thinking, she touched his arm. "I realize that now. You care a great deal. You cared enough to keep me on when you would have rather fired me on the spot, all because you wanted to help me."

He stared at her fingers against his skin. "I didn't want to help. I just couldn't turn you away."

"The end result is the same. You helped me. Then you helped me again by defending me to the regulars when they wanted me gone. Don't you think I know how much they disliked me in the beginning? After that, you bought me the car. Even now, you haven't slammed the door in my face. Beneath all that gruff bravado is a very caring man. I should have seen it sooner. Should have told you myself about the past so you didn't have to learn about it from someone else."

She bowed her head. "I'm sorry I lied. I'm sorry that it feels like I kicked you in the teeth just as so many others have done before me."

He held himself on a tightrope, emotion working in the tautness of his massive frame. "You want forgiveness, is that it? Why? Because you like the sex?"

Lacey flinched, dropping her hand away. But how could she blame him for saying the words?

With a shake of her head, it hit her that Beth was wrong. There wasn't anything here to fight for. There was nothing between them other than angry words, lies . . . and sex.

Stunned at the realization, she drew a breath. "I'm sorry, Bobby. Really I am. I was wrong to have lied on my résumé, and there is no reason for you to keep me on." She turned away and headed for her own door.

Bobby muttered an oath, then followed. "Damn it, I shouldn't have said that about the sex," he growled. "No matter how much you tick me off, it was uncalled for."

"No, you have every right to question my motives and character after what you have learned. I consider myself fired."

"Ah, hell."

When he tried to take her arm, she slapped him away, tears streaming down her cheeks. But before she could slam into her own apartment, he whirled her around, holding her by the shoulders, his eyes boring into hers.

"I'm sorry," he said, his own eyes burning, his rugged whisper echoing. "Every time I see you, you knock me over."

This time when he pulled her close, she went to him. Suddenly she was in his arms, holding on, their mouths coming together in a frantic search. They fell back against the wall, the overhead light flickering in the narrow hallway. They tangled together in desire, anger, and need.

Their hands sought each other, his palms cradling her face, tilting her to him. When their tongues met, she groaned into him, his arms coming around her, wrapping her so close that she could feel the beat of his heart.

It always seemed to be this way with Bobby. He knew how to touch her, pulling her in with the lost vulnerability in his eyes. She recognized it now, understood the call, couldn't resist even though she knew she should.

The feel of his hands on her body brought her to life,

blocking out all else. The slick wetness of his tongue, his hands pushing her breasts high beneath her blouse. The slow shimmer as his palms brushed back and forth across her nipples, teasing them erect.

She wanted to feel his skin, feel the intense heat of him, and she nearly cried out when one strong hand trailed down her back to her hips, then pressed her close. There was no mistaking how much he wanted her, the hard ridge sending a thrill rushing through her. She felt hot and wet, and when he picked her up, then slid her down over his desire, she only relished the sensation.

Everything was forgotten, as least for now. Her only thought was to get closer. But then something inside her jarred. In some recess of her mind she registered the sound of the dead-bolt lock on her apartment door sliding back.

Perhaps it was long years of being tuned to any sound that her daughter made, but in a matter of seconds, Lacey ripped herself away from Bobby just as the handle turned and Robin appeared in the hallway.

They stood in the small space. Her daughter looked radiant, flushed, and confused.

"Mom?" Robin asked. "Is everything okay?"

Bobby leaned back against the wall, pulling a casual smile into place, and Lacey would never have suspected what had just gone on if his eyes didn't still burn with the glint of fire. Lacey's hand flew guiltily to her hair. "Everything is fine, sweetie."

But of course it wasn't. Lacey felt devastated at what she had done, ending up in Bobby's arms yet again, sanity so lost that she was nearly caught by her daughter.

Robin started to back into their apartment, her hands up. "Okay, if you're sure."

But she was stopped when they heard footsteps on the stairs. "Hey, Robin."

All of them froze, and turned. This time, confusion cut

through Lacey at the sight of a young man who stood at the end of the hallway.

"Kyle!" Robin gasped.

Lacey turned to her daughter, whose eyes were wide with something that made Lacey's heart start to pound.

A boy stood at the top of the stairs that led up from the bar, his dark hair long enough to brush the collar of his black leather jacket. His dark eyes assessed the situation and seemed amused at what he had found. He looked ruggedly handsome and much too mature for Robin to know him. But when he walked closer, Lacey's heart went still. She realized immediately that he was the young man she had seen driving away from behind Bobby's Place—the young man in the truck who Peter swore couldn't have been in the bar.

"Kyle, what are you doing here?" Robin asked, her cheeks filled with a blush of color.

He strode closer with a predatory gait and looked at Robin with a knowing possessiveness. "I've come to meet your mom."

He said the words with a pointedness directed at Robin, but Lacey heard it. This was rehearsed. She knew it. Her stomach clenched.

Kyle stepped forward with the polish of a much older boy. Holding out his hand, he said, "Ms. Wright, I'm Kyle Walker."

Lacey stared at his hand, paralyzed.

Bobby looked back and forth between them, then extended his hand. "I'm Bobby McIntyre."

They shook hands. "Hey. Robin says how great you are."

Kyle turned back to Lacey, but still she couldn't speak. Robin hurried forward.

"Kyle and I are in math class together. He's really smart."

From the looks of him, Lacey thought, he appeared to be anything but. He looked like James Dean and a young Marlon Brando rolled up into one. A mother's worst nightmare.

"Not as smart as Robin," he responded, looking at her daughter with a mixture of pride and heat that took her breath.

This boy and her daughter were involved.

Kyle turned back to her and grew serious. "I wanted to meet you because I would like to take Robin to the Winter Dance."

Robin gasped, her eyes sparkling with joy.

"That is very nice of you, Kyle," Lacey managed. "But Robin is not allowed to date."

"Mom! That is not fair! The dance is almost a month way, and I'll be sixteen then."

Lacey ignored her daughter. "Thank you for coming by," she said to Kyle, and even she could hear the coldness in her voice. But she couldn't help it. She ushered him back toward the stairs.

"Mom!"

But Lacey didn't relent, and as soon as Kyle disappeared, Robin flung herself back into the apartment, slamming the door with enough force that the whole building seemed to shake.

Lacey stood there, suddenly aware that Bobby was studying her.

"Do you want to tell me what that was about?" he asked.

"I don't see how any of this is your business."

"Some kid comes by and asks Robin to the prom and you dismiss him without even getting to know him?"

"He is not the kind of boy Robin should go out with!" she spat.

"You just met him. How can you tell?"

"I recognize his type."

"Ah, so this is about *your* past, not about Robin."

"That isn't true!"

"Isn't it? The way I see it, it wouldn't matter who that kid was or what he looked like. You don't want Robin to have anything to do with any boy."

"She's a child!"

"She's almost sixteen."

"And that's too young. Besides, he's too mature."

"Lacey, what is this really about?"

She buried her face in her hands. "She's been seeing him all this time and she never told me."

"Kids don't tell their parents half the things they do."

"Not Robin. She always tells me everything. And she didn't tell me about Kyle because she knew I wouldn't approve."

"She told you now."

"Only because she wants to go to this Winter Dance."

"It's just a school prom."

"With a boy that she looks at as if the sun and moon revolve around him! That's exactly how I looked at the boy who got me pregnant with Robin!"

Taking measured breaths, Lacey went into the apartment, then headed straight for her bedroom. Flinging open her closet, she started pulling clothes out and tossing them on the bed.

Bobby followed. "What are you doing?"

"Packing."

"That's the craziest damned thing I've ever heard."

Maybe, but he didn't understand. Everything she had worked so hard for was unraveling. She had turned into everything she hated—lying, lusting after a man who was a known womanizer. And now Robin, falling for the very kind of boy that had been Lacey's downfall. Sexy and daring. Cool and wild. And no amount of warning or threatening from a parent would make her see straight. Lacey knew that story all too well.

Bobby strode over and shut the closet doors. Lacey only went to the dresser, adding sweaters and belts to the pile on the bed.

"Damn it, Lacey. Stop."

"No, I'm leaving. It's best this way."

Her mind whirled with plans, the exercise familiar. But thoughts cut off when Bobby grabbed her and turned her around. "Stop this. You're acting crazy. You can't keep running, you said so yourself. You'll never gain the kind of control you want. It doesn't exist. Face the problem head-on, just like you did not a half hour ago. You lied, and you owned up to it. You faced me and explained why you did it. I can live with that. Now, face the fact that Robin is growing up. Accept that you have taught her well and that she'll do the right thing."

"Easy for you to say. You're the grown-up version of Kyle Walker. You woo and seduce, then break a woman's heart."

He jerked away from her, his eyes strangely burning. "The women I date always know where they stand. And it doesn't take a genius to figure out that if you don't stop running, if you don't let Robin grow up, eventually you'll lose her anyway."

Her chest contracted.

"Don't hold on so tight that you push her away."

She hugged the sweater she was holding to her chest, then pressed her eyes closed. "One night I saw him getting into his truck behind the bar. I knew he looked too young to drink, and Peter swore he couldn't have been in the bar. He must have slipped up here to see Robin."

"You don't know that."

"What else could it be? Why was he parked out back? Has she been sneaking him in here while I've been downstairs working all this time? The fact is she lied!"

The words froze in the room.

"She didn't lie, Lacey. She just didn't tell you about him. Based on your reaction, you can hardly blame her."

She jerked away, hating that he was right.

Bobby came up behind her and put his hands on her shoulders. "Go talk to her. Letting her grow up shouldn't be a bad thing."

"I don't want her to get hurt."

"Bad things happened to you. But that doesn't mean those things happen to everyone. Most people go through their whole lives without the kind of trauma you faced."

She turned slowly. "Or the kind you faced, either."

His jaw ticked; his eyes went suddenly glassy. Then he drew a deep breath and said, "This isn't about me. This is about Robin. Go talk to her. Then stay at Bobby's Place where you have done a great job of turning the place around. You can't run forever, Lacey. Eventually you'll run out of places to hide."

Robin sat at the kitchen table with a glass of milk and a plate of Oreos in front of her. She looked young and sweet in her oversize sweatshirt, socks, and clogs, and more dear than Lacey could stand. Her heart leaped and surged, and she wanted nothing more than to wrap her child in her arms and run—run to a new city far away where no one knew them, where it would be just the two of them.

And that was wrong.

As Bobby had said, she had to stop running.

"Hey," Lacey said.

Robin whirled around in confrontation, her face stained with tears, mixed with a stubborn scowl. "How could you have done that?" she demanded.

Lacey walked forward, wishing for a second that Bobby hadn't gone back to his apartment. How was it possible that a football jock suddenly had more insight than she did after she had been a mother for nearly sixteen years?

Because he didn't look at the situation through the blurry eyes of love—not to mention that it wasn't *his* daughter who was faced with the world of sex and boys. He could afford objectivity. But objectivity wasn't a mother's luxury, especially toward a daughter who was all she had in the world.

"I was caught off guard," she explained softly, as kindly and regretfully as she could.

"Like that is an excuse for being mean?" Robin shot back.

"Robin," she warned. "I know you're mad at me, but I'm still your mother."

The teen's scowl deepened, then she *humph*ed, folding her arms on her chest.

"I wish you had told me about Kyle before he showed up so unexpectedly, surprising me as he did."

"Kyle is totally mature and faces issues head on."

Lacey remembered all too well the feeling that her boyfriend had been the smartest, most thoughtful person in the world. At least that's what she thought until she told him she was pregnant and he said someone else must be the father.

Lacey shook the thought away.

"I'm sure Kyle is very mature. But you know what I've told you about dating."

"Yeah, that I have to wait until I'm sixteen! I know! You've pounded it in my head since I was twelve. And I have waited. I haven't been out on a date, ever, despite the fact that most girls start going places with guys when they're fourteen."

"Fast girls," Lacey clarified.

"That isn't true. But whatever. The fact is, I'm asking to go to a high school dance, and by then I'll be sixteen!"

If only she had thought to set the age at seventeen, but back then sixteen had seemed a lifetime away.

"How about a deal," Lacey offered, scrunching her shoulders like a teenager, "I'll teach you to drive if you give him up."

"Mom!"

"Okay, okay. Can't blame me for trying."

"Does that mean I can go?"

Lacey sighed.

"It's not the end of the world," Robin pointed out.

"Are you sure?"

The teen groaned.

"All right," Lacey said reluctantly. "You can go."

Robin leaped out of the chair, squealing and dancing around the kitchen.

"But you have to be home early."

"No problem."

"A conservative dress."

"Fine," she said, still dancing.

Then the teen stopped and took her mother's hands. "I'm a good kid, Mom. You don't need to worry."

Lacey smiled over the poignancy that filled her. "I know that, sweetie."

Then she hugged her daughter close, and after not enough seconds of holding tight, Robin twirled away, dancing back to her bedroom.

Lacey watched her go, and couldn't help but whisper, "No sex, no sex, no sex," as if the simple words would somehow cast a spell around her daughter and keep her away from the same mistakes she had made at her exact age.

Reaching across the table, Lacey took an Oreo cookie and dipped it in milk. The dance was almost a month away. Who knew, but a lot could happen in that time—namely, Robin could get tired of Kyle Walker and call off the date.

Lacey scoffed out loud. Just like she was getting tired of Bobby McIntyre and his disarming smile and wicked good looks.

CHAPTER TWENTY

"HAVE YOU SEEN LACEY?"

Beth spoke the words as she barged into the office.

Bobby rocked back in the leather chair and studied his sister over steepled fingers. As always, she appeared a contrast of earth mother and errant schoolgirl. Fine lines had just started to appear around her eyes, though he felt certain she was proud of those lines—would have said she'd earned every one of them. He couldn't help but smile.

"Not this morning. Why do you ask?" he wondered.

"I thought I'd see if she was free for lunch, and while I was at it, I'd ask her to Thanksgiving dinner."

He leaned forward, the chair springs protesting as he returned his attention to the financial ledger he was going over. "No, Beth."

Beth marched forward, but Bobby didn't look up.

"How can you possibly object? It's my party."

He concentrated on the X and O diagrams of the new plays the Lone Stars coaching staff had sent him.

Beth pulled the pencil from his grip. "Tell me, Bobby."

He gave a weary sigh, rubbed his face with both hands, then took in her belligerent stance. "Because."

"Not good enough," she replied, tossing the pencil on the notebook.

"Beth, I don't want her there."

"Well, I do."

"She lied to us," he stated, blocking out emotion.

That softened her stance, but only a little. "I know. But it's Thanksgiving."

Slowly he stood from behind the desk and shook his head. "I don't get it. How can you bend over backwards for a woman who out-and-out lied to us?"

"I prefer to think that Lacey fudged on her résumé, and now she's sorry about it."

"And that makes it okay?"

"Yep. And you must feel the same way since I see you haven't fired her."

He scowled. "How do you know I haven't?"

"When I asked Peter if he'd seen her, he said he had, working on some order sheets. He said she was giving him a hard time, I might add. I gather he requested five more bottles of tequila, saying he's nearly out, when the accounts show that we've only gone through four. There's a bottle missing."

"That's down from the usual four missing out of five," Bobby stated. "And so what if I gave a few drinks away. I own the place."

"Nothing gets past Lacey. And if I were you, I'd let her know what happened to that bottle, since I bet Peter will eventually crumble under pressure and give you away."

Bobby groused and knew she was right. Peter couldn't hold out for long under Lacey's interrogation, though they all knew she was wise to the only person in the place still giving away free drinks. Him.

And no, he hadn't fired her. Though how he had gone from ready to toss her out on her ass to telling her she had to stop running, then nearly making love to her in the hallway, he couldn't fathom. Not that he should be surprised. Her twisting up his thoughts happened so often these days that it was like a repeated refrain in a really bad pop song.

But the truth was, he knew why he hadn't fired her. He

had believed her story, believed that she had been desperate to start a new life in a new place far away from the past. He could hardly blame her.

"Just because I didn't fire her doesn't mean I want to spend Thanksgiving with her."

"You'd rather she and Robin sit upstairs in that tiny apartment and have Thanksgiving by themselves?"

"Don't try the guilt stuff on me. It won't work."

"That's a shame. It used to work so well." She smiled at him. "No matter. But be warned, I'm going to ask Lacey whether you like it or not."

"Ask me what?"

They turned to find Lacey standing in the doorway, Peter's liquor request-form in her hands.

Bobby took her in, seeing the same woman he had seen since he first got back to town. Prim, librarian-ish. Woolen slacks and one of her damn sweater sets. But now he knew about the lush beauty that she hid underneath the modest clothes. More than that, he could no longer deny the true beauty of her. Clean and fine. Not flashy or fast. And her skin, like the petals of white roses with hints of pink.

"Bobby and I were just talking about asking you and Robin to join us for Thanksgiving dinner."

Lacey's reaction was swift. Amazement, excitement, a yearning that she couldn't hide. But as quickly as her emotions surged, she brought them back under control.

"Oh, we couldn't," she said hastily. "You are so nice, but Thanksgiving is a family day."

"Everyone here at Bobby's Place is family," Beth explained. "Peter's coming."

"He is?" Bobby and Lacey asked in unison.

"Well, he said maybe," Beth clarified. "But he's joined us before. So you'll fit right in. Won't she, Bobby?"

He looked hard at his sister. He really didn't want this. A "family" dinner was hard enough to take as it was, then adding Lacey to the mix, when all he wanted was to be back in Dallas playing the Thanksgiving Day game, made it damn near unbearable. He had put a call in to the team, and for the first time since Bobby was hurt, Coach hadn't sounded so desperate to get him back. Hell, he had even been reluctant to send the new plays. The last thing Bobby needed was this distraction.

But at the glower Beth shot his way, not to mention the look of puppy-dog hope written all over Lacey's face, he had little choice. "Yeah, you'd fit right in."

Lacey looked back and forth between brother and sister. "If you're sure . . ."

Beth smiled grandly. "Of course we're sure."

"Then we'd love to come," Lacey enthused, her face lighting up with a nearly palpable joy. "What can I bring?"

"Just yourselves," Beth said.

"But surely there is something I can contribute? Candied yams, spinach casserole. A pie."

"What kind of pie?" Bobby asked with a sudden spark of interest.

Beth laughed. "My brother doesn't think I can bake to save my life."

"You can't." He focused on Lacey and stated, "You can bring a pie. As long as my protein and whey shake regimen is shot to hell, it might as well be worth it."

"Any preferences?"

"Have you Northerners ever heard of a Black Bottom pie, or Bourbon Pecan?"

"No," Lacey admitted. "But I love a challenge. I'll bring one of each."

"Well, then," he conceded, "maybe Thanksgiving won't be so bad after all."

Two weeks later, Lacey stood in the kitchen wondering what had possessed her to offer to make not one pie, but two that were as foreign to her as Greek or Latin. Beth had provided her with a stack of cookbooks, but in the end, she went with one called *Joy of Cooking*, since she had high hopes the experience would be a joy.

Or not.

Halfway through the project, Bobby had wandered across the hall, a towel slung around his neck, his T-shirt dripping sweat from his workout, one of his disgusting whey shakes in hand. Despite the sweat and the whey, he looked great. Lacey wondered if he ever looked bad.

Disgruntled, she turned away. Every counter was filled to overflowing with cups and bowls and anything else the tiny apartment had provided for cooking. She had used baker's chocolate for the Black Bottom pie, then at the last minute, she had gotten a creative urge and turned the Bourbon Pecan into a Chocolate Bourbon Pecan. And of course, Bobby had to notice.

"I see you're on a chocolate binge again," he had the audacity to say.

Lacey shot him the same look she had mastered to keep the regulars in line. Unfortunately it didn't so much as faze Bobby McIntyre.

"I am not having any kind of a binge." Though of course they both knew that wasn't true, since even the bar crowd had begun to comment on the chocolate fest she had been on recently. But better that than give in to the very real urge she had every night to cross the hall and have him do . . . touch . . . bring . . . well, whatever it was he did that made her body tingle just by remembering.

"Are you sure you know what you're doing?" he asked suspiciously, following her into the kitchen.

No. "Of course."

"It smells like something's burning."

"I don't know how you can smell anything over that vile concoction you drink."

He smiled and moved closer, like a predator stalking its prey, tugging the towel from around his neck. Her heart lodged against her ribs, her tongue sticking to the roof of her mouth.

"Now, Bobby, what are you doing?"

He backed her up until she bumped into the table, the tin and utensils rattling around them. Standing so close that his thighs pressed against hers, he leaned down and planted his hands on either side of her. "What does it look like I'm doing?"

She didn't get a chance to answer when he bent his head and kissed her. As always, the touch sent warm feelings coursing through her, her body melting into his. She had the fleeting thought to crash every baking pan and ounce of chocolate to the floor so he could lay her back on the table and have his way with her. And when his tongue slid along her lips, all she could do was reach out and wrap her arms around him. Good sense be damned.

"Mmmm," he murmured. "Chocolate."

Then he actually licked her.

Her hands flew to her mouth.

"I got it all," he said, with a maddening chuckle as he straightened. "Or maybe not."

He leaned forward, but this time she leaped away. "Out! Get out!" she demanded, shooing him away. "Unless you want to end up with a frozen store-bought pie."

That stopped him in his tracks. He went, but not before grabbing a handful of Hershey's semisweet morsels and tossing them in his mouth.

Fortunately, by Thanksgiving Day, Lacey managed to produce the promised two pies without further incident. Though she could only pray that they tasted as they should.

"Robin," she called. "We're going to be late."

"I'm coming!"

Her daughter appeared wearing a white blouse, navy

blue skirt, matching socks, and a pair of penny loafers. Robin hated the outfit, but Lacey had insisted, and Robin had been on her very best behavior since she was getting to go to the school dance.

Proms and boys. Lacey sighed. Kyle had become a regular fixture around the place. In the mornings, he picked Robin up for school, and he came over every chance he got on weekends. Thank goodness he had a job that kept him working much of the time. But even with gainful employment, the boy spent every free second he could with her daughter. Lacey didn't know how it had happened, but the two had become inseparable.

She hated the way the kids looked at each other, hated the way Robin touched his shoulder or held his hand whenever she thought no one was looking. First love, and too intense for Lacey's liking. But she had agreed to the prom, and had even faced the fact that it was unreasonable not to allow Robin to go out for a Coke on a Saturday afternoon.

Please don't have sex, she whispered every time her daughter walked out the door with Kyle.

Though thankfully, that wasn't a worry today. Today's concern focused on pies and meeting Bobby's friends and family. Beth had assured her she and Robin would fit in fine. Lacey wanted to make sure she looked respectable, but she also wanted to look . . . pretty.

Taking forever to dress, she had ended up wearing a flowy kind of skirt that went with her silky blouse with ruffles. Then she had added a pair of high heels.

"You look beautiful, Mom."

Lacey cupped her daughter's cheek. "So do you, sweetie."

"Mom?"

"Yes."

"What am I going to do about a dress for the Winter Dance? It's barely a week away."

Lacey had wondered the same thing. At first she had

truly held out hope that Robin would get tired of Kyle, and had put off questions about what to wear. But now, conceding that this wasn't going away, she knew what she had to do. "We'll go to the mall and buy you a gown."

"Really?" Robin asked, her eyes going wide.

"Yes, really. I've been saving for something special. I guess this counts. We'll go on Saturday and join the rest of the post-Thanksgiving shoppers and find the perfect dress."

Robin threw her arms around her mother. "Thank you!"

"Come on, grab a pie. Bobby will be waiting."

The bar was closed for the holiday, and Bobby waited in the downstairs office with the television turned on, the remote in his hand, a football game playing across the screen. He hadn't heard them enter, as he stood there completely absorbed in the game, a strange look on his face.

"Who's playing?" Robin asked.

He didn't so much as flinch, but Lacey knew that they had surprised him.

"The Lone Stars," he said, a distinctly wistful note in his voice.

"Hey, that's your team," Robin said. "They aren't half as good without you there. Everyone says so."

The edge left his features, and he grinned softly. "Spoken like a true El Pasoan. I appreciate the loyalty, kiddo."

He clicked off the television and noticed Lacey. She saw the heat that flared in his eyes.

"You look great," he said, his voice a deep rumble. He took a step toward her.

Lacey felt the blush rise in her cheeks, and her breath caught.

"I told her the same thing!" Robin chimed in. "She looks totally great."

Bobby stopped in his tracks at the reminder that they

weren't alone, cleared his throat, then he ushered them to the door.

They bundled up into the Jeep, since Bobby had returned his SUV to the dealer. Lacey hadn't realized it was a loaner. Bobby drove, even though both Lacey and Robin had jockeyed for the position.

"I thought you said it was my car," Lacey stated.

"It is. But I'm a Texan, and Texas men don't let women drive them around."

Lacey and Robin squealed in disgust.

"That's archaic!"

"That's ludicrous."

"So sue me. I drive."

Amazing good cheer surrounded them as they headed down Mesa toward the valley. The desert hills gave way as they drew closer, slipping onto the winter-barren cottonwood trees that lined Country Club Road.

It was four-thirty in the afternoon when they arrived at Beth's. Lacey and Robin glanced at each other at the sight of the sprawling home of adobe and terra-cotta tile. *Wow*, Robin mouthed to her mom.

Bobby let them in the front door without knocking. The inside of the house was as beautiful as the outside. They started back toward the sound of people talking and laughing, but a wall of photographs caught Lacey's attention. An assortment of photographs of Beth and her family. And Bobby. Photos of Beth and Bobby through the years, proudly framed. But something seemed different between the photos of Beth versus the ones of Bobby.

"There you are!"

Beth strode into the room. She hooked her arm over Robin's shoulder as she kissed Bobby on the cheek; then she pulled Lacey into a hug. "I'm so glad you're here," Beth said with genuine feeling.

Lacey and Robin were pulled into a crowd of friends

and family that spilled between the kitchen and a den. Bobby laughed and joked, and the party seemed perfect until an older couple walked into the room and were introduced as Nigel and Hannah Hartley.

Curious, Lacey studied Bobby. No one, including the Hartleys, seemed aware of the change in him, at least no one else did but Beth, who looked on as the couple greeted her brother with a strange mixture of futility and a strained discomfort.

"Bobby Mac," Nigel said, his voice overloud, almost bellowing. "It's good to see you."

Hannah's smile was as forced as Bobby's. "Hello, dear," she said with an awkward formality.

Beth turned away, her brow creased, to finish cutting up a head of lettuce. Bobby nodded his head. "Nigel, Hannah. It's been a while." Then he moved away from the couple. As he turned, his gaze caught on Lacey. He looked at her, his blue eyes dark with an unsettling vulnerability.

A charged awkwardness filled the air as Beth started chopping the lettuce harder and harder. Hannah appeared at a loss, then she noticed Lacey.

"I'm so glad you could join us," the woman said to Lacey, clearly relieved to change the subject. She was a handsome woman, close to sixty, with a soft round face. "Beth told us how well you have done managing Bobby's Place."

"Thank you." Lacey looked at the older couple curiously, trying to place them. "Are you a neighbor, as well?"

Hannah and Nigel exchanged a surprised glance. "Well, no, dear. We're Beth's parents."

At the words, Bobby hesitated just as he was pushing out the door, though only for a half second before he continued on.

Lacey tried to understand. "Oh, I see." But she didn't.

Clearly sensing the discomfort, Beth wiped her hands

on a towel and announced that dinner would be ready in a few minutes. She shooed everyone out. But Lacey couldn't bring herself to leave.

Beth poured a glass of wine, then went to the window.

"Can I help with anything?" Lacey asked, not knowing exactly what to say.

Beth didn't look at her. "No, everything's just about ready. I'm waiting for the potatoes." She took a sip of her wine, and an achingly sad smile pulled at her lips as she continued to stare out to the backyard.

"I love him so much," Beth whispered.

Lacey walked up beside her and followed her gaze. Bobby stood tall and so full of life on the winter-dried grass lawn, tossing a squeezable Nerf football with Beth's young son.

Beth sighed. "He hurts so badly."

"Your son?" Lacey asked in confusion.

"No, no. Never my son. I make sure of that. I don't want little Jason to ever hurt like Bobby does."

Lacey hesitated, then had to ask. "I know this is none of my business, but I thought you and Bobby were orphans."

"Yep."

Unable to stop herself, Lacey plunged ahead. "But the older couple I met earlier, Nigel and Hannah? They said they're your parents."

"They are."

"Sorry to be dense here, but what am I not getting? I thought you and Bobby were brother and sister."

"We are." Beth's throat worked. "The Hartleys adopted me."

A slow dread started to fill Lacey. "And?"

"They didn't adopt Bobby."

Lacey's head reared back.

"They brought us both home," Beth added in a strangely disconnected monotone, "but Bobby was so mad—certain that our mother would come back. So he fought. If only you could have seen him then, five years old, filled with a stubborn rage. He stopped eating. Wouldn't talk. Even then he had an ironclad control. My parents gave up after a month." Her voice cracked, and she set down the glass of the wine. "The day they took him back to the sisters, I remember him standing at the front door, his little suitcase clutched in his hand, his obstinate face set. He looked me right in the eye and said, 'Come on, Boo. It's time to go.' "

Beth turned to Lacey like a sinner entering a confessional, her face lined with despair. "I said no." She closed her eyes. "I was a child." She drew a deep breath. "And I didn't want to give up my pretty pink bedroom."

Hastily, Beth wiped away one single tear.

Lacey wanted to comfort this woman who had become her friend. But something held her back.

Beth bit her lip hard. "Over the years, he went from the sisters to foster care. The only concession the state made to the fact that we were brother and sister was to keep us in the same school system." She looked up, her blue eyes tortured. "I saw him every weekday." She turned back to the cold winter yard and Bobby throwing the ball with her son. "Sometimes I wonder if seeing me at school wasn't worse. I was given so much. That silly pink bedroom. Clothes, toys, trips. And he had nothing. No love, other than what I could give him. No hugs." She wrapped her arms around herself. "No one ever touched Bobby after our mother left us, no one held him. To this day, Bobby doesn't let anyone get close."

"But what about all the women he's been with?"

"Meaningless sex with a long line of women is safe. They don't touch his heart. But mark my words, he'll push away any woman who comes close to making him feel."

Lacey's mind churned back over the time she had been

in El Paso, and she remembered with a start that Bobby hadn't allowed himself to feel. He gave her pleasure, but took none for himself. And she had wondered why.

"The only concession he's given to me," Beth said softly, "is locking fingers, and an occasional hug if he's been gone a long time—and only if I catch him by surprise."

"That explains why he's so strained with the Hartleys."

"Yes. And I hate it. It tears me apart. God, how many times I've wished that it were different. All three of them are an important part of my life. But Bobby won't budge."

Lacey worried her lip in thought. "Seems to me that it would be hard to budge. They were the adults—he only a child. And one short month to adjust to a lifetime of change isn't a very long time. They should have tried harder."

Tears flooded Beth's eyes. "I know, I know." She inhaled sharply, suddenly bitter. "Why did Bobby have to fight? Why did my parents have to give up so easily? Some days I feel like I hate all of them for making it so difficult."

"They turned him away, Beth, just like his mother did. And no matter how you look at it, that's difficult. Wishing it were different only makes you crazy."

Then Beth caught her off guard when she looked her in the eye. "I guess you're a champion of that."

"Of going crazy?"

Beth gave her a watery smile. "Of understanding that there are some things you just can't change in life, no matter how much you want to," she clarified.

"Ha! I'm only just beginning to understand that. For years, every time I couldn't make things work as I wanted them to, I . . . moved on. Not a great way to deal with life."

"Do you want to move on now?"

Lacey looked out the window to where Bobby caught Jason's wobbly pass, then zigzagged across the yard, circling the little boy before sweeping him up into his arms to great whoops of gleeful laughter.

"Yes. And no. But old habits die hard."

It was dark when Lacey, Robin, and Bobby pulled away from the rambling ranch house. Beth stood next to Ray in the drive, and his arm slung casually and lovingly around her as they left. The kids waved madly, little Jason racing the length of the front yard. Robin sat in the back, silent and content, stacks of leftovers beside her. Lacey looked out the passenger window, the sky so black, dotted with crystal stars.

Bobby drove, a barely contained tension running inside him like a sleek sports car idling in neutral. But with every mile that rolled by, the tension eased, until they pulled into the Bobby's Place parking lot. When he put on the brakes, he exhaled and just sat there.

Robin popped open the door and grabbed a stack of dishes. "If we hurry, we can get upstairs before *The Sound of Music* starts."

That got some movement out of Bobby. He raised a dark brow.

"It's a tradition," Robin explained, doing her best to cover the simmering enthusiasm. "Mom and I watch it every year. You can watch it with us if you want."

"Thanks, but I'll catch whatever's left of the football games," Bobby said with a distasteful grimace.

"You don't know what you're missing."

The three of them carried the dishes up the back stairs, then down the short hallway to where their doors faced each other like bookends. Lacey and Bobby hesitated, while Robin dashed inside to check the answering machine. The sound of Kyle's voice echoed into the apartment. "Hey, Rob. I'm working late at the station. I'll call when I get home."

Lacey grimaced. "They're getting too serious."

"They're kids," Bobby said.

"I'd prefer he was a kid who would move to a faraway country like Paraguay with no access to my daughter," she answered wryly.

"Now, what kind of a mother wants her daughter's heart broken?"

"Not broken, just sad for a bit until the boy is forgotten."

"You don't mean it."

"I'd like to mean it."

They stood awkwardly for a moment. "Are you sure you don't want to watch the movie with us?"

"No, thanks."

"Well, then," she shifted her weight, "thanks for including us today."

He looked at her and her breath caught. When he leaned close, her lips tingled in anticipation. They were alone in the hall, with Robin in her room, the bar empty below. He tilted her chin with one strong finger, meeting her eyes, and she was certain he knew what she was thinking.

But he only kissed her on the forehead, the touch lingering for a second as if he wanted something from her other than heated desire, before he pulled away and set the dish he carried on top of hers. "Good night, Lacey. I'm glad you and Robin had a good time."

He disappeared into his own apartment, leaving Lacey to stare at his closed door.

After a second, holding back a growl of frustration, telling herself it was for the best, Lacey went inside, toed her door shut, then went to the kitchen. Once everything was put away, she went back to her room to change. Wanting to be comfortable, she pulled on a bulky sweater of Robin's and a pair of long-forgotten leggings, then returned to the living room. Just as she sat down on the sofa, a loud clank sounded. "What was that?"

Robin sat curled up in the oversize chair and smiled just as Bobby materialized out of their kitchen, two extra-large slices of pie served up on a plate, fork in hand. With his face clean of expression, he walked over and sat down on the sofa next to Lacey as if they did this every night.

"I thought you didn't watch movies like *The Sound of Music*," Lacey said with a teasing grin.

"I don't. But you took all the pie. Besides, the games are over."

He took a big bite and moaned with exaggerated ecstasy. "Beth should take lessons," he commented.

"Ah, I recognize another of your veiled compliments in there."

"Shhh," Robin hushed them, after which they settled back and watched the show.

Once Bobby wiped the plate clean and set it aside, he didn't leave, though he offered an unappreciated commentary every few minutes on the absurdity of people launching into song at the drop of a hat.

"Shhhh!" This time both Robin and Lacey hushed him.

And when they got to the part with the yodeling puppet show, Robin and Lacey leaping up and singing along, Bobby looked at them as if they had lost their minds.

But eventually Robin slipped back into her chair, and before the movie was over, the telephone rang.

"That'll be Kyle!"

She dashed to her bedroom, the door banging shut just as the phone rang a second time.

When she was gone, Lacey and Bobby sat alone with Captain Von Trapp and Maria filling the screen. Bobby took off his boots and propped his feet up on the chair's footstool with a contented sigh. Then he leaned back against the sofa. When an advertisement came on, Bobby turned to look at Lacey.

She felt the shift in him immediately. The ease turned to awareness, the comfort turned to heat.

"You should wear bulky sweaters and those tight things more often. You look sexy as hell."

She felt the blood rush to her cheeks, and she stammered. "You certainly are in a better mood now than earlier." She covered her awkward embarrassment with her old standby. Propriety. "Did you even thank Beth for dinner?"

"Yes, I thanked her. I also told her I shouldn't have gone."

"Because of the Hartleys?"

He eyed her. "What did Beth tell you?"

She considered her answer before she spoke. "She told me that the Hartleys adopted her . . . but not you."

His countenance closed off; then he turned back to the television and said, "My sister doesn't understand the word privacy."

"I think she was just trying to explain the tension between you and them."

"There's no tension. I'm nice. I'm polite. But Beth wants me to act like they are my long-lost family. And that's not what we are no matter how much she'd like to think we are."

"I understand."

His gaze jerked back to her.

"I do. I also understand that they should be shot for returning you to the orphanage."

He looked back at the screen, and she could see that his jaw muscles worked. But Lacey didn't let up.

"They should be shot for breaking the two of you up."

She sensed the tight rein he held on his emotions. He sat there for an eternity before he turned away and watched Captain Von Trapp come on stage at the music festival with his family.

Bobby stared hard, and just when she thought he truly was watching the movie, he spoke. "The day the Hartleys showed up to take us home with them, Beth and I raced each other to their car. A station wagon with wood-paneled sides. I was so excited. When we got to their house, the first thing they did was show us this fairy-tale room for Beth. All pink and white, just for a girl. I couldn't wait to see mine."

Without thinking, Lacey reached across the cushions and threaded her fingers through his. He closed his eyes and curled his hand around hers.

"But mine was just a room filled with huge dark furniture that they wanted me to be really careful of." He laughed without humor. "I remember getting it right away. They wanted Beth, not me. Later I realized the sisters must have made them at least try."

"Oh, Bobby."

He sat up and pulled away. "I didn't care," he said with a shrug. "They took me back, and it was no big deal. Over the years, I made friends. It wasn't so bad."

"Because you found football."

Even the word brought a sparkle of fire back into his eyes. "Yeah, I found football."

"That was your family. The coaches, the players."

And since he had so much talent, he got the cheers and adulation from fans that most children got from their parents.

It all came together then, so clear that it was painful. She wanted to cry for this caring man who wrapped up his sensitivity in bravado.

"That's why you want to get back to the Lone Stars," she said. "You need your family."

At this he grew uncomfortable and scowled. "I want to get back to Dallas because the team needs me. Stop psychoanalyzing and watch the rest of this damn sissy show."

She almost pushed the issue, then thought better of it. truth was, she was no one to demand explanations about people's pasts. She settled back and watched, and by the the credits rolled at the end, she looked over and found Bobby was sound asleep.

obin had finally finished up on the phone, then had to bed. When Lacey turned off the television, the ment went quiet, and she expected him to wake. But n't. For long seconds she looked at him. A lock of air had fallen across his forehead. Sleep made him ung and carefree, and that vulnerability surfaced.

le to stop herself, Lacey reached out and gently the hair away. Bobby murmured, but didn't wake. d herself to send him home. But somehow she 't. Finding a blanket in the linen closet, she covered p, turned down the lights, and went to bed.

seemed like hours that she lay awake, staring at the ng, restless. She wanted to go out and see him again. she didn't. Though just when she finally started drift- off, she heard a low moan.

She blinked in the darkness as the sound grew louder, aking it impossible to believe she had imagined it.

Pulling back the covers, she opened her bedroom door nd tiptoed into the living room. Bobby was still asleep, but all traces of ease were gone, his face creased as he muttered and whimpered.

Without thinking, she went to him, reaching out to wake him. But the second she touched his arm, his moan turned to a scream, deep and guttural, horrifying, bringing him up off the sofa like a lightning bolt, one simple word filling the air in an echo of sound. *"Mama!"*

He stood before her, wild, cornered, seeming not to know where he was as his strong hands clutched her upper arms.

"Bobby," Lacey called to him, her voice filled with a calm she didn't feel. "It's me. Lacey."

It took a second, but recognition came slowly, and he took a deep, ravaged breath. Relief winged through him like a sigh; then something else followed when his breathing finally settled. Despair, utter sadness. After all these years, this strong man was still the boy who had been left behind at an orphanage. The child left first by his mother, then again by a couple who wanted only his sister.

Lacey felt as if her heart would break apart.

"Mom?"

They both turned to find Robin standing in the hallway, her young face lined with concern.

"It's all right, sweetie," she said in her most reassuring voice. "Bobby just had a bad dream."

With that, Bobby's face shifted as understanding finally hit him—understanding where he was, what had happened. And Lacey would have sworn shame was hied across his face.

Robin disappeared behind her bedroom door.

"Sorry," he mumbled. Then he made a jerky effort to fold up the blanket, finally tossing it aside.

"Bobby, it's okay." She touched his arm.

He tensed as he always did when she touched him. But he didn't push her away.

"You're okay," she whispered.

Then he clutched her to him, his grief real and heartbreaking. Without thought for consequences, Lacey wrapped her arms around him, and his mouth found hers with a desperate groan. He kissed her like a dying man, drowning in things he didn't understand. She tried to comfort him, but even in need he built a fire deep inside her.

He laid her back on the sofa, then came over her. He held her face and looked at her, just looked, then he kissed her again, long and slow, deep and wet, and she clung to him. Their mouths came together, each seeking, each yearning. Kissing, hands finding places that fueled the desire. But just when she started tearing at his shirt, he groaned fiercely, heatedly, then pulled away.

"I've got to go," he managed, pushing up and grabbing his boots to leave.

"What? Bobby—"

He wrenched open the door, then looked at her for one long drawn-out moment, his face ravaged. She understood then what had been coming to her since Beth had told her of Bobby's past. Unlike the other women in his life, she had touched him as he couldn't bear to be touched. Her determination to keep Robin when his mother hadn't kept him made him feel, brought up emotion that left him crying out in the night as if he were still a five-year-old child. He needed a careful distance in order to be safe—from emotion, from feeling too much.

Bobby Mac McIntyre, legendary football quarterback and renowned ladies' man, couldn't afford the emotions she made him feel.

CHAPTER TWENTY-ONE

IT WAS STEAMY and hot. His muscles strained and contracted, as he pushed himself to the limit. He felt the burn.

Fifteen. Twenty. Twenty-five.

He kept going. He wouldn't give in, refused to think about the pain.

Thirty. Thirty-five.

"Bobby? What the hell are you doing?"

Forty. Forty-five.

"Damn it, McIntyre."

Fifty.

Bobby dropped the weights to the ground with a roar, adrenaline pumping through him.

His trainer eyed him. "I'm not sure what's up with you, man, but you're pushing too hard."

But Bobby didn't respond. He went to the bench press and started in, barely waiting long enough to let his muscles recover. He was straining—he knew it—but he needed the release. He felt cornered, caged, ever since he woke up to Lacey in her apartment, her eyes wide with worry.

How many times had he woken up screaming in the past? Too many times to count. But he made a rule of never falling asleep with women, always leaving or sending them home so that no one would ever know. It had gotten better over the years, only surfacing when he was really tired or beat up from a game. Until Lacey.

What the hell had he been thinking to let himself fall asleep on her couch?

He hadn't been thinking. He had let himself settle into the ease of Lacey's company and an idiotic movie that foolishly captured his attention. A damned stupid chick flick about love and family and doing whatever it took to stay together.

With an animal cry, he pushed the bar up from the bench press, all three hundred pounds, then grunted with each repetition as the trainer sounded the count. He should have stopped at fifteen, but he kept going.

"Hey, Mac, I'm telling you, man, you're pushing way too hard. If you're not careful, you're going to strain something. Then where will you be?"

The bar clanged down on metal when he jerked it back into the holder. His arms felt weak with relief, but his mind still spun. He needed to regain control. He needed his life to fall back into the careful order he had built around himself. Football and women. Women who took what they wanted from him, then went off when he was done, well-rewarded, happy to brag that they had been with Bobby Mac McIntyre.

His age, his knee, and returning home had changed all that. And Lacey. Like that damned complicated refrain, her name whispered through his head. The complication of Lacey Wright and the way she made him feel. Frustrated, lousy, pissed off. And cared for. *Fuck.*

He yanked up first one hand weight, then another, standing in front of the floor-to-ceiling mirrors as he did dumbbell curls. The muscles bulged, veins popping out on his neck and forearms, his expression fierce.

"Smooth it out, Bobby Mac," the trainer said. "Don't jerk the weights."

The rest of the session went much the same, Bobby pushing too hard, the trainer trying to hold him back. By the time Bobby headed for the showers, he was spent. Too tired to think. Exactly what he wanted. And when he headed down Mesa back toward the bar, for half a second he thought about making a U-turn and going to his house overlooking Rim Road to get away. But when he came to an intersection where he could turn around, he continued on. He rarely ever went there, had a staff that took care of it. It was big, beautiful. And lonely. He might not want to see Lacey, but he also knew that he didn't want to be in that house alone.

"It's not fair!" Robin groused.

"They say that about life," Lacey shot back.

"It's a dance, Mom, not Saturday night with the big band at the local old folks' home."

Lacey's mouth fell open. When had her daughter become sarcastic? Yet more proof that her little girl was growing up. Not that she needed any more proof after spending the afternoon with her at the mall trying on prom dresses. Robin had developed a figure, which promised to be as lush as hers, and the nearly-sixteen-year-old wanted to show it off.

Those same old prickles of fear had rushed through Lacey so strongly that when Robin walked out in the first low-cut, tightly fitting gown, she had thrown her coat over her shoulders. Literally.

Things didn't get much better after that.

"You want me to be the laughing stock of the Winter Dance!"

"Don't exaggerate. That last dress you tried on was cute."

"For a four-year-old flower girl!"

"Okay, it was a little frilly. But the one before that wasn't."

"It was a granny sack! Long sleeves, high neck. A hundred tiny buttons down the back that I'd never get undone."

All the better, Lacey thought, though thankfully didn't say so. "I'm sorry, Robin. But I will not allow you to wear a dress more suitable for a strip club than a school dance."

"Then I'm not going."

Dear Lord, dreams do come true. "Fine by me."

"Ahhhg!" Robin slammed the car door and stomped away, taking the back stairs up to their apartment, unlocking the outer door, and flouncing inside.

Still in the driver's seat, Lacey watched her go. She felt an urge to slip the car back in gear and drive, out onto the highway, let the rhythmic feel of rubber on asphalt sooth her. But as quickly as it came, the desire fled.

Taking the keys from the ignition, she got out, locked the door, then headed around front. Best to give Robin time to cool down.

The minute she entered the bar, the usual Saturday afternoon crowd called out her name. Silly joy washed through her.

She waved, and continued toward the office.

"How'd the shopping go?" Rupert wanted to know.

"Marginally well," she answered.

"Does that mean you found something or not?" Jazzy asked.

Lacey tilted her head from side to side in consideration. "She found something, and I found something, but we didn't find the same thing."

Jazzy laughed. "Same with me and my kid. My teenager wants to look like a hooker. I want her to look like she never heard of s-e-x. You know what I mean? It's a parent thing. As long as there are mothers and daughters, there will be disagreements about prom dresses."

The idea that a hard-core Las Vegas bar waitress could spout such true words of wisdom made Lacey wince.

"I'll give you a little advice," Jazzy continued, leaning close. "Take her across town to Cielo Vista Mall and find her something in velvet. Doesn't matter how long the sleeves are, kids like velvet, makes them feel pretty. Works every time."

The waitress didn't wait for a response. She walked away, took an order, then called it out as she headed to the next table where she planted a pint of beer.

Lacey turned to make her way to the office, but stopped when she saw Bobby sitting at the far end of the bar, a beer mug in front of him. This time it wasn't a dark stein concealing a thick whey shake. He studied her with that same glittering intensity that unnerved her and made her skin tingle. Then he lifted his glass in salute and drank.

"I thought you were on a strict diet," she said when she came up to him.

"The diet went out the window when I ate turkey with dressing, candied yams, and four slices of your pie. I hardly realized how starved I was after a two-month high-protein diet. But now the knee is back, and it's time to build up my strength."

"Yep, beer or spinach. I'm sure Popeye would agree they're interchangeable. In fact, I think I saw an episode once where he slugged down a tall one himself."

He looked at her. "Popeye has nothing on me," he gloated. "I am back in shape. Bench pressed three hundred this morning."

"Am I supposed to be impressed?"

"Damn straight, you should be."

The Texas twang was back in a big way, and Lacey knew it was his means of keeping her at a distance. Which was fine by her. Once she had gotten over the emotion of his bad dream, she had come to her senses and remembered that the two of them had no business together. They had their moment of insanity in his bedroom, but each of them had their own share of problems and didn't need to get tangled up with the other. She had a daughter to raise, and he was going back to the Lone Stars to play football.

"Then congratulations," she said.

She left him at the bar and went to the office. But when she started to close the door, Bobby was behind her, so close that she could feel the heat of him. As always, he was so tall, so ruggedly male, exuding a strength that made her shiver with awareness. If only things had been different. If only their worlds weren't so opposed.

She wanted to lean into him, place her hand on his chest to feel the strong, reassuring beat of his heart. For a second, she thought he felt it, too, when his gaze drifted to her lips, those blue eyes burning like icy licks of fire.

But then he flattened his palm on the door above her head and pushed it open the rest of the way. "I've got work to do."

"Oh, yes," she stammered. "Of course."

They retreated to their respective desks across the real and imaginary boundaries that separated them. Each got to work, or at least Lacey tried to, since she was much too aware of Bobby across the room to get anything done.

"Were the dresses really that bad?"

Bobby had leaned back in his chair, and he was tapping a pencil eraser on the desk.

She shrugged. "Worse than bad," she explained. "I find it amazing what people call proper clothes these days. When I was a teenager—"

"You walked to school in the snow, uphill both ways."

Lacey blinked, before she slowly met his wry smile. "The snow part is true. Unlike around here. Does it ever really snow?"

"Sure it does. Three inches, maybe four or five. Prettiest snow you've ever seen. Then the sun comes out and melts it away in a matter of days. It's the best way to have snow, as far as I'm concerned."

A companionable silence settled between them, the tension easing away as it always did with them, before Bobby got that devilish look about him and asked, "What did you wear to your prom? I'd bet it was something with a high neck, lots of buttons, and mounds of ruffles. Probably in pink."

Lacey laughed at the image that leaped to mind. When the laughter trailed off, she inhaled. "I never went to a prom." She said the words, and even she heard their wistfulness.

"And you wanted to," he said with great knowing.

"Yes, yes," she stated, like admitting to a horrible sin. "I wanted to go to the prom . . ." She leaned forward, planting her elbows on her desk. "I wanted slumber parties with girlfriends. I wanted to sign annuals at the end of the year. Graduation. I wanted it all. But somehow what I remember missing the most is the prom, that idyllic night where all things seem possible. Silly, isn't it?"

He pushed up from his desk and crossed over to her, sitting on the corner of her desk. She felt surrounded by him, this pure, hard-edged male that somehow always made her forget everything but an intense yearning to lose herself in his strength.

"It's not so great," he offered kindly. "I hated my prom."

"But at least you went to one."

"Yeah, I did. I'm sorry that you didn't get to go." He hesitated, his expression sharpening. "But don't ruin Robin's Winter Dance by making a huge deal out of the dress because you still can't accept that she's going." He took her hands in a kind but stern grip. "Or because maybe, just maybe, you're a little bit jealous."

Insulted, she jerked away from him. "I am not jealous of my daughter. I want only what is best. And an indecent dress is not what is best."

He shrugged unapologetically. "Maybe you aren't. But since seeing you and Robin together, it's made me look long and hard at myself. I see Beth and me. Beth as the little princess. Me as the kid who had to struggle to survive. She had it handed to her. I had to scrape and claw for everything. And as much as I loved her, I wanted those things, too. I wanted the toys, the nice clothes. A room of my own. A car at sixteen. Not to have to white-knuckle life in my attempt to hold on."

Lacey felt a sizzle of aching emotion for that little boy, but when she started to reach out to Bobby, he stood apart, his expression unrelenting.

He looked her in the eye. "I was jealous of Beth. You and Robin, my knee, Thanksgiving . . ." He dragged his hands through his hair, trying to find a way to explain. "I'm thirty-five years old, and I woke up in your apartment screaming like I'm still five, wanting life to be different. And hating Beth because her life was. For years I couldn't admit that somewhere inside me I could feel anything but unconditional love for someone who had never done anything but try to help me and love me. It's taken me until now to realize that. And I've made a lot of mistakes in my life because of it. Don't make the same mistakes, Lacey."

Her heart pounded; her palms were clammy. She didn't want to believe for a second that his words could in any way apply to her. He was wrong. She and Robin were different.

Flushed and burning, she pushed up from her desk, the chair sliding back, banging into the metal cabinet with a clang. "Don't compare your life in an orphanage to my relationship with my daughter. I am not jealous of her," she said coldly. "The issue at hand is nothing more than a dress and a dance."

"It's about more than that, and you know it. Get her a

dress, and pretend you're thrilled for her. Let her go and
have a time she will always remember. She deserves that,
just as you deserved it."

CHAPTER TWENTY-TWO

FRIDAY NIGHT, the Camino Real Hotel ballroom glittered with hundreds of tiny white lights, like stars dotting a blackened sky. The simple beauty of white flowers and shimmering silver decorations made Coronado High School's Winter Dance look like a true winter wonderland.

Robin gasped her delight as they entered through a glimmering light- and snowflake-covered archway. "It's beautiful," she breathed.

"You're beautiful," Kyle said, tugging her close to his side, his gruff voice tingling along her skin. "Have I told you that yet?"

Robin laughed happily. "Yes, about a hundred times. But I don't mind if you say it a hundred times more."

She did look wonderful, and she knew it. Somehow her mom had gotten okay with the whole dress thing. On her birthday, she got to miss school so the two of them could drive out to Cielo Vista Mall. The day had been perfect. That morning her mom had woken her up by rubbing her back and singing "Happy Birthday to You," just as she had when Robin was a little girl. Then a birthday breakfast of a scrambled egg face, with blueberry eyes, bacon lips, and pancake ears.

"I'm sixteen!" Robin had protested, but she had loved every second of it.

Her mom hadn't even gone down to the office once; instead she had presented Robin with a single box. Inside there had been a hand-written coupon for "One Winter Dance gown of your choice."

"Even if you hate it?" Robin had asked carefully.

Her mom had wrinkled her nose, then sighed and said, "Yes, even if I hate it."

They had taken all of Tuesday afternoon, having a lunch of incredible deli sandwiches, potato salad, and the creamiest homemade chocolate milk shakes Robin had ever had. Then shopping, going from store to store, talking and laughing like the old days. Everything had gone so well that Robin hadn't even tried to buy something slinky, didn't know why she had pushed it the other day.

By the fourth shop they had found the perfect thing. The top was made from the softest dark blue velvet Robin had ever felt. It might have been long-sleeved, but the neckline very nearly fell off the shoulders. And the long skirt, made from a shimmering midnight blue taffeta, was fitted at the hips, then slowly flared out in an A-line sweep. She felt sexy and elegant all at the same time, and with her brown hair pulled up loosely, soft curls falling free to make her look just a little bit wild, Robin felt like a fairy-tale princess swept away by the prince.

"You look beautiful, yourself," she said to Kyle, meaning it.

She had never seen a guy look so great—like a model from a glossy magazine ad, his dark hair swept back from his face, then trailing down to brush the collar of his tuxedo. No ruffles or colored cotton shirts for Kyle. His was crisp white with black onyx studs marching down the center.

When he had arrived at Bobby's Place to pick her up, her mother had taken pictures of them in the Tiffany window, and several of the regulars had whistled and said he had good taste. Kyle had draped his arm around her and said, he thought so, too. The crowd had hooted; Robin had blushed. But her mother's pasted-on smile had faltered. For half a second Robin thought her mother wasn't going to let her go after all.

Thankfully, Bobby had come to the rescue, actually putting his arm around her mother's shoulders—how amazing was that?—and distracting her by telling her he had a surprise for her.

That had gotten her mom's attention. But Bobby wouldn't breathe a word about his plans. Just told her to go upstairs and change into the prettiest dress she had.

Robin smiled and wondered what Bobby's surprise had turned out to be. Whatever it was, though, she was happy that her mom had let her out the door.

"I was going more for handsome," Kyle said, then curled her closer in the crook of his arm and dipped his head to brush his lips against hers.

The gesture had become as much a part of her life as breathing. They were inseparable at school, and were known as a "couple" by the other kids. The only hard part was the way he made her feel when they kissed. Like she wanted more, even though she knew she shouldn't. But when he kissed her and his hands ran over her body, she always wanted to press close. Every time they were alone together, they had gone a little farther.

Her heart sped up, and forgetting the crowd around them, she started to lean into him.

Kyle's palms traveled over her. "Mmmm, let's blow this pop stand and head out. I can think of better things to do than hang out with this crowd."

Instantly Robin pushed back. "We can't leave yet," she squeaked. "We haven't even danced."

Kyle groaned. "All right, let's get this over with."

He took her hand and tugged her along toward the crowd.

Robin glanced down and admired the corsage of red roses on her wrist. As much as Kyle hadn't wanted to attend, he had worked late nights and weekends to save up for the event. First there had been the flowers; then he had taken her to a beautiful restaurant that was across the street from the hotel. She had felt grown-up and special, and tremendously grateful that he would spend his hard-earned money on her.

The menu had been so fancy and so expensive that it had overwhelmed Robin. When the waiter approached, she asked for a salad and water, saying she wasn't all that hungry. Kyle had said no way, then proceeded to order warmed, herbed goat cheese with walnuts over mixed field greens, chicken cordon bleu for the entrée, and crème brûlée for both of them. When she ate every bite, he had teased her about not being hungry.

Kyle pulled her out onto the dance floor, which was crowded with couples. It amazed Robin how many people were there that she had never seen before. But within seconds, other couples came up to them. None of them stopped dancing as the guys did the whole cool handshake thing with Kyle. Robin couldn't believe it when she recognized them as football players and cheerleaders, all of them really popular kids. But other than the handshake, Kyle kept himself apart from the others, and Robin could tell this made him all the more intriguing. It was clear that he had no interest in going along with the crowd.

He danced with Robin, holding her close, barely moving. When the song ended, the group moved to the side. Robin had a moment of sheer panic when Kyle gave her a possessive kiss and said he'd get her a Coke. But she about passed out from shock when Debi, the head cheerleader, said, "Hey, Robin."

Robin about keeled over since she couldn't believe the girl would talk to her, much less know her name.

"Hi, Debi."

"Your dress is awesome. And I love the way you did your hair. Who did it for you?"

"My mom."

Oh, no! So uncool. She couldn't believe she said it.

"Wow, your mom must know how to do hair. My mom did mine, too, but it isn't half as great as yours."

Like it was perfectly okay to talk about moms!

"I love your hair," Robin said. And she did. It was a huge mass of curls. "It's like Andie MacDowell from that major old Tarzan movie."

"Oh, yeah, the one where they used someone else's voice 'cause she couldn't talk like a normal human being."

Lana, Debi's best friend, overheard. "I saw that video like a hundred years ago. I thought it was kind of great, especially Jane's hair. Robin's right, Debi, yours looks just like it."

They talked as if they had been friends forever. A year ago, if anyone had told Robin that she'd be having a regular conversation with any kids, much less the popular ones of any school, she would have thought they had a screw loose.

As soon as the guys came back, Debi and Lana asked if Robin and Kyle had gotten their picture taken yet. Kyle immediately said no.

The couples returned to the dance floor, but Robin kept hold of Kyle's hand, keeping him back. He looked at her curiously.

"Let's get our picture taken," she enthused.

Kyle grimaced. "Rob, I don't do lame photo ops."

"Just one," she said with a laugh, "for me." Then she tugged him toward the streamer- and flower-covered latticework where a photographer was taking posed photos of each of the couples.

They waited in line, Kyle shaking his head at the stiff,

unnatural stances of the couples. He laughed along with the rest of them when a group of guys formed a cheerleader's pyramid, crashing to the floor as soon as the flashbulb went off.

When their turn came, Kyle took Robin into his arms, pulling her back against his chest in a pose that many had taken. But somehow with Kyle an innocent pose seemed intimate. Robin blushed, the photographer cleared his throat, then snapped the picture as quickly as he could.

"Kyle," Robin admonished as soon as they stepped away.

"What?"

They stood to the side, and Kyle took her hands. "I'm not crazy about this tux or the people, or even the pictures. But I'm crazy for you, Rob. Come on, let's get out of here." He wrapped her arms around him, then held her close as he kissed her.

"But we've hardly danced."

He looked down into her eyes, the dark depths growing heated. "A couple more. Then we'll go. Deal?"

Her heart leaped, and her pulse raced nervously. "Deal," she whispered.

"Then come on, let's dance," Kyle said as a wild and fun anthemlike song blared through the ballroom.

Within seconds, there wasn't a square inch left as everyone there crowded together and danced to the raucous fun. Robin felt a wealth of emotion. Excitement, joy. Happiness to be spending such a magical night with this wonderful guy.

"You dance great," she practically had to yell across the few inches that separated them.

"You're not bad yourself," he added, putting his hands on her waist, bringing their hips together as they swayed and bent to the rhythm.

She lifted her arms, letting loose. They danced together

as if they had spent their whole lives following the same steps.

"I thought you'd step all over my toes," she teased.

"No way." Then he wrapped his arm around her shoulders and dipped her in time with the music, holding her there for one long beat, his eyes locked with hers. And just when she thought he would kiss her, he swung her back up, and they held together, twirling around, laughing. Exhilarated.

They caught their breaths on the side during a really bad song that no one liked except for Mr. Martin, who, they were sure, had been forced to chaperon or get fired. The hated math teacher was out on the dance floor with Miss Lopez, a favorite Spanish teacher. He probably had to beg to get her out there, otherwise she'd be dancing with the likes of Coach Carter, who even the high school girls had to admit was totally hot, if old.

Coach stood at the edge of the dance floor, sipping a tiny glass of punch in a tiny glass that looked dwarfed by his gigantic hands, and he shot daggers at Mr. Martin. The song ended, and another total oldie came on, and Mr. Martin and Miss Lopez started dancing to it.

"Oh, no, you don't," Coach muttered. He slapped the empty cup into some kid's hand, then marched out onto the hardwood floor like marching out onto the football field to pummel some poor misguided referee.

He tapped Mr. Martin on the shoulder none too delicately. The math teacher stammered and sputtered, but Coach Carter didn't wait for a yes. He swept Miss Lopez into his arms and danced her across the floor in a Western two-step that had nothing to do with the beat.

After that, the music changed, finally slipping into a set that the teens recognized. Kyle tugged at his bow tie until it came untied, hanging down from either side of his crisp white collar. Then he grabbed her hand, pulling her out onto the floor.

This time he didn't let go of her hands. He was moving to the music, singing to her without embarrassment, charming her with his uninhibited dramatics, making her never want the night to end.

"I look at you . . ."

"What do you see?" she asked impishly, twirling underneath his arm.

"You look at me . . ."

Coming face-to-face, she did just that.

"Making me love you constantly."

His eyes darkened.

"Because I'm crazy for you." He drew her closer despite the fast beat. *"I'm crazy for you,"* he sang against her ear.

The music trailed off, but he didn't let her go. He held her until the DJ launched into another tune, this one with a slow pounding beat that filled the ballroom. For half a second, Kyle didn't move at all. He just looked at her, his smile lost, the throbbing chords seeping deep into her. Then he wrapped her close.

His arms surrounded her, much like the music. He was a full head taller than she was, but he held her securely against his chest, her arms wrapped around his waist. His palms flattened on her back, gently rubbing as they moved to the music, moving so slow and steady that each gentle dip brought his thigh sliding between hers, their legs a seductive joining. He pressed his lips into her curls.

"You smell good," he breathed.

They hardly moved from the spot, just a slow undulation that made Robin's body yearn. And when Kyle gently grasped her chin, tilting her head to him, then leaned low, she closed her eyes, inhaling just as their lips met.

They kissed in the darkly starlit room, its ceilings so high that they felt like painted heavens. His hard thigh grazed against her intimately as they dipped from side to side. He kissed her barely, once, then again, his lips brushing against her so softly that she wanted to weep with some intense emotion she didn't know how to name. As always, he made her want more—more of his kiss, more of his touch. When she felt his tongue against her, she opened automatically, her breath escaping at the feel as they intertwined.

She groaned when the song came to an end. Kyle pulled back and cupped her cheeks with his hands.

"It's time to go," he said in a whisper against her temple.

Her breath caught. "Are you sure we should leave?"

"Yes." One word that drifted down her spine like a promise of what was to come. Then he took her hand and pulled her from the dance floor, gathered their coats, and headed out into the snowy night.

CHAPTER TWENTY-THREE

"WHERE ARE YOU taking me?"

Lacey sat next to Bobby in the Jeep, dressed in an elegantly simple black velvet sheath that fitted her form and stopped just above her knees. She'd had it for years, though she'd never had an opportunity to wear it. With each move she told herself to sell it in one of their inevitable moving sales—they could have used whatever money the dress would bring—but somehow she never could. Her one luxury, allowed when most everything else had always been left behind.

Having no clue where they were going, Lacey pulled her coat tightly around her against the cold winter night. Bobby drove with the confident skill she was growing used to. They shot along Mesa toward downtown, but cut off before they got there.

They turned onto a gently curving road lined with some of the most beautiful homes she had ever seen on one side, and on the other side the earth dropped away as they sped along the very edge of the mountainside. Just when she thought they couldn't go any higher, Bobby turned into a small, gated community that wound its way farther up the hilly terrain. They were climbing up into the dark sky, which had grown thick with clouds, though there was a stillness to the night that made the world seem peaceful rather than ominous.

"Bobby, really, where are we going?"

"It's a surprise," he reminded her.

"I shouldn't have left the bar."

"Why not?"

"In case something happens to Robin."

"Why are you so worried?"

"Because I'm afraid she'll have sex!"

Bobby glanced over at her, his brow lifted wryly. "And you think she'll call to ask for instructions?"

Lacey choked.

"Sorry," he said sincerely. "I should know better than to joke with you about Robin. But remember, Lacey, it's a school dance."

"A school dance with a boy."

"And other kids, not to mention chaperons."

"Chaperons can't patrol an entire hotel."

"You make it sound like a military event."

"I wish it were," she grumbled. "I know teenagers. And I know guys like Kyle Walker. They're like snake charmers, making girls want to do things they shouldn't want to do."

"Kyle isn't a snake charmer," he answered softly, reaching across the console and squeezing her hand. "Just try to relax and enjoy tonight. Robin knows to call the bar if anything comes up, and Peter knows where to find us."

They drove in silence then, the CD playing softly in the background. The Thompson Twins, Simple Minds, Duran Duran, and just when she finally realized that all the songs he had played during the drive were from her days in high school, they pulled up in front of a stunning house so high up on the mountain the world seemed remote.

"Bobby, really, where are we?"

He pulled on the parking brake, turned off the ignition, then shrugged, suddenly looking unsure of himself. "It's my house."

Leaping from the car as if he were afraid that if he didn't get out right then he'd leave, he came around to open her door. He took her hand and led her inside. They walked through a Spanish courtyard, then entered through carved-wood double doors.

"Bobby, it's beautiful."

It was also empty. The foyer consisted of a landing that looked over a massive living room of tile floors and barren fireplace, then it led straight out into a wall of windows that framed the night sky. The thousands of flickering lights down below were downtown El Paso. Beyond downtown, she could make out the haphazard lights of Mexico just across the border, nestled at the base of the Sierra Madres that Lacey had learned formed the south side of this expansive valley known as the Pass to the North.

"No wonder you don't stay here," she said. "You don't have any furniture."

He shoved his hands deep in his suit pockets. "Yeah, well, I guess I never got around to it. It's easier to stay at Bobby's Place when I'm in town."

"If you don't like it, why not sell?"

He shrugged, then took her coat. "Come on. I'll give you the grand tour."

She could tell he was excited to show her around, making him seem more like a schoolboy than the ultracool star quarterback for the Texas Lone Stars.

His mood was contagious, and she felt a bubble of laughter surge up inside her. He grabbed her hand, then pulled her from room to room, none of them lived in, except for one. His office had furniture.

Like his apartment, this room had no evidence of his stellar career as a football player. There were certificates of achievement from charitable organizations. Photos with presidents. Several more with Bobby surrounded by a slew of little kids, and Lacey felt certain every one of them was an orphan. There was also a stack of unopened envelopes.

"Don't you read your mail?" she asked.

"Sure. I might not stay here, but I come by at least once a week. I have a housekeeper who brings the mail in and takes care of the place."

Turning away, she accidentally hit the stack, sending it tumbling to the floor. "Sorry!"

Kneeling together, they sank down and started gathering the envelopes. "I'm such a klutz," she said, their faces so close that if she moved just so she could kiss him.

"I'll get it."

With her hands full, she pushed back. And when she stood and started to set the pieces down, she noticed an American Airlines envelope.

She tilted her head and looked closer, then glanced at Bobby. "Are you going somewhere?"

Standing, he noticed the envelope. All lightness fled. "Back to Dallas."

He said the words simply, straightforward, the impact hitting Lacey like a blow to the midsection.

"For good?" she asked.

"For the play-offs."

"But they don't start until after Christmas. The guys in the bar said so."

"I need to get back. I need to make sure Sutter doesn't—" He cut himself off. "The team owner called and said if I return tomorrow, he'll see to it that I play on Sunday."

Her mind jarred. How many times had she prayed for just this, for him to return to Dallas, to get out of her hair. But now that it was real, she couldn't imagine him leaving.

She realized that she had come to care for him. Depend on him. Like a friend. Like a confidant. Like someone who actually cared about her even though he knew the worst about her past.

"I know this is what you have wanted, so I'm happy for you," she said honestly.

Bobby's smile returned. "You'll be glad to see the back side of me heading out the door, and we both know it. But don't get too excited, because I do come back every now and again. Got to watch out for my investment."

"Yeah," she said softly. "I'm sure you'd hate to see anyone giving away free drinks or buffalo wings."

"Yep, it'd kill me." He tossed the mail aside, then grabbed her hand, his Bobby Mac smile wide and playful. "You've seen the place. Now it's time for your surprise."

He tugged her along after him, down first one flight of stairs, then another, like descending the mountain in levels of the house. She stopped dead in her tracks when he pulled her into a sprawling room, barely lit by hundreds of tiny silver lights reflecting on glass. Ceiling and walls, all made of sparkling clear windowpanes, made it possible to see a hint of snow starting to fall from the dark skies.

Almost hesitantly, she stepped inside toward a glistening pool at its center. Everything she had heard about his house and this glass room didn't compare with the actual beauty of it.

A giant, oversize crystal blue acrylic raft floated in the water like a sparkling jewel. The space was stunning, made even more magical by the strands of tiny white lights strung about with shimmering streamers.

A sound system piped music, more songs from her past, into the grand room. A table covered with a white linen cloth and set with tall crystal and sparkling silver sat at the far end, like it was perched on the edge of the world, drifting over the city of lights below.

The contrast of the snowy night and the warm, almost tropical room of glass wrapped around her.

"Your corsage," he said.

She blinked and turned to him in confusion.

"No girl can go to her prom without a corsage." With care, he pinned the winter white roses to her dress.

"A prom?" Her chest felt tight with emotion. "Why did you do this?"

"Every woman deserves a Winter Dance of her own." The confusion stayed with her.

"I hated that you never got to go to your prom," he finally explained. "It's not exactly the same, but short of turning back time, this was the best I could do."

With those words, it was all she could do to hold back a flood of emotion. The snow visible through the glass. Being dressed up. This magical place. "Oh, Bobby. This is crazy." She looked at him. "Crazy wonderful, and I love it."

"Good. Now, come on. A good song is playing. Would you like to dance?"

The sounds of the funky, lively, and very popular 1980s song, "Raspberry Beret," filled the space, and Lacey couldn't help but laugh. "You like Prince? You strike me as more the Merle Haggard or Garth Brooks type."

"It's not a matter of what I like or don't like, sweetheart. This is your prom, not mine." He turned up the dial on the stereo system. "But just wait. I got Monster Rock of the Eighties, too."

He tugged her out onto the makeshift dance floor next to the pool, where she watched somewhat skeptically as Bobby started dancing just like she remembered kids dancing in high school.

"Come on, loosen up," he admonished her.

He certainly was. This tall, rugged man was no more inhibited on the dance floor than Prince himself.

Self-consciously, she started moving to the music. Step, step, swish, swish.

"You can do better than that," he scoffed.

And then, something took over. Her steps loosened up,

her swishes got swishier, and suddenly she was truly dancing under the glittering lights and falling snow, losing herself to the fun, to the beat.

They twirled and spun, but when the CD changed and Prince's "Purple Rain" came on, the deep, slow beat changing the mood, Bobby dashed over to the stereo and switched it to some indiscriminate song she had never heard before.

"I used to love that song!" she complained.

"I knew you would. It's such a girl tune. But no slow dancing for you." He smiled. "At least not yet. Dinner first."

He led her to the table, candles lit, and held her chair, then miraculously produced a meal. She stared, stunned. Moved. He poured her a glass of champagne. Any other time she would have declined, but tonight was different, special. And when he lifted his glass in a toast, she accepted.

"For everything you missed," he said softly.

"Oh, Bobby." Words escaped her, so instead she sipped, savoring the rush of warmth.

Dinner consisted of veal stuffed with herbed bread crumbs, Gruyère, and sausage, covered with a sauce at once light and creamy. There were perfect green spears of asparagus, a potato casserole, and she could make out just a hint of swirling chocolate cake in the pool-house kitchen set off to the side.

"I don't think they have dinners like these at most high school proms," she mused.

"You'd be surprised the kinds of restaurants kids go to in this day and age. But they don't serve champagne. As long as I was improvising, I thought why not improvise across the board. Better refreshments, skip the crowd—" He reached across the table and took her hand. "—forgo the chaperons."

A shiver of something ran down her spine. She felt the need to be free of long-held responsibilities, to be young again. The desire to forget, even if it was just for tonight. And when he poured her more champagne, even though he hadn't had more than a sip of his, she let him. She absorbed the warmth and pleasure of the room and his company, felt years of struggle and inhibition melt away like snowflakes hitting the warmed glass that surrounded the pool.

They talked and laughed; he told her stories of his days growing up, of his hopes and dreams. He talked like she was sure he had never talked before—open, with a self-deprecating humor about his adventures and misadventures as he made his way through his precarious world. The champagne settled through her, and by the time he told her the story of how he had walked into a pole while trying to see the very popular Tina Davies in seventh-grade English class, she was laughing harder than she had ever laughed before.

"I don't believe for a second that Bobby Mac McIntyre ever was a dork," she said, catching her breath.

"I don't think there is a guy alive who didn't go through some sort of dork stage in his life. Mine was in seventh grade."

By the time they finished the cake, Lacey pushed up from the table with a heady lightness filling her. She swayed softly to the music.

He stared at her for one long minute, then a new CD flared, a slow, pounding beat. "Let's dance."

Taking her hand, he pulled her to him, moving to the music.

" 'High Enough'? By the Damn Yankees? I think this is a little after my time."

"The way I look at it, it's the eighties. Close enough."

Then he turned her in perfect circles, their bodies moving together. She felt hot, every place he touched her sensitive. She wanted something—something she couldn't have.

Security. Safety. A relationship with Bobby that wasn't about two people using each other and then moving on.

Frustration sizzled up inside her, and when he leaned down and kissed her neck, she jerked away.

"No!"

"No, what?"

What could she say?

"I know you're doing this to keep my mind off Robin, and I appreciate your kindness down to my soul. But—"

"This has nothing to do with Robin. I'm doing this for you."

The words filled her heart with emotion—joy and panic. Joy because of his kindness. Panic because nothing had changed between them. This man still couldn't afford to feel. This man would leave in the morning.

The world seemed suddenly unfair. She spun away and searched for laughter. "No more dancing. I want to swim."

The shadow swept over him again, and he stopped. His hand dropped away. "I'd rather not."

"Come on," she whispered, the champagne making her bold. "It'll be fun."

"Lacey, this is a prom, not a pool party."

Something snapped inside her, the past colliding with the present, and an unfamiliar recklessness pushed her on. She took another long sip of champagne then reached behind herself and started tugging at the fastening. His dark eyes went darker as she pulled the zipper down. She hesitated for just a second, then let the sheath fall to the ground. She watched as his features became a sharp blank, his eyes narrowing as she stood before him in a delicate black slip.

Caution pushed aside, that careless desperation from her past filling her, she pulled off her high heels and panty hose from beneath the slip. Then she extended her hand to him. "Swim with me, Bobby."

He still didn't move, didn't seem to breathe, though she could see the dark heat flare in his eyes as his gaze traveled over her.

"Just tonight," she added. "Please."

His features grew ravaged, but his chin rose defiantly while an eternity passed. "I don't know how to swim," he replied finally.

The words hit her, as only his words had the power to hit her time and time again. This man and his outward strength, never able to completely move beyond the little boy, just as she had never been able to truly move beyond the girl who got pregnant at sixteen. She felt sad and defeated, not knowing how to change their pasts.

"I can't swim either," she whispered, and took his hand. "How is it that you and I are so different, but so much the same? Like opposite sides of the same coin. You're the bad boy and I'm the prim girl, each covering up who we really are, scared kids trying to make it in the world."

His expression hardened, a wildness igniting, and she turned away. From him. From the world. Then she walked to the edge of the deep end.

"Lacey," he said sharply.

She stood there looking into the depths, an all-too-familiar fear consuming her. But desire to be free snaked around her, gripping, holding tight, pushing her, until gravity gave way—or was it fear losing its stranglehold, pried away by champagne and a need to fly free?

"Lacey, don't."

But it was too late. She leaped in, felt the waters close around her, a cocooning warmth making her feel safe, secure, suspended from the world. Her body sank, drifting lower, her hair coming lose from the pins.

She thought she heard her name, distant and muffled. And she thought of Bobby. Bobby whom she loved.

The thought hit with a force that wiped away the security of the water. She loved Bobby. She didn't want him as a friend. She didn't want him to leave for reasons that went beyond this indefinable coexistence they had established. She wanted to break through the wall he kept securely around him. Because she wanted him to love her, too.

Her mind reeled, and in that second the cocoon of water felt like a trap, her lungs starting to burn. Suddenly she had to find air. Her feet touched bottom, and just when she started to push up, she felt the water explode and surge, then a hand grabbed her wrist, pulling her up and up until she broke through the surface.

Sheer strength surrounded her, pulling her through the water to the shallow end of the pool. When he let go of her, she finally saw his face. Lined and ravaged.

"You scared the hell out of me!" he raged, his voice echoing against the glass walls and ceiling.

But she didn't care about his anger. She curled her fingers into his soaking shirt and pulled him to her. She gave in to the very thing she had guarded against for so long. The desire to be free. Her passion for this man. And after one tension-filled second, he gave in, as well. He grabbed her up, swirling her through the shallow water, his mouth covering hers in a desperate hunger.

They clung together, their mouths slanting in need, the taste of tears mixing with chlorine. Pulling back, they looked at each other, and only then did she realize that the tears were his.

Her heart felt as if it would burst. She felt a smile tremble on her lips. "Hey," she said, the sound barely heard, "that's one way to learn how to swim."

"Damn you," he breathed against her, both benediction and curse, then pulled her back.

They kissed hungrily, his hands skimming over her body as if having to prove to himself that every inch of her had survived. But she didn't want this gentle reassurance. She wanted him.

Impatiently, she tore at his shirt, the black onyx tacks popping free, drifting to the bottom of the pool like stones settling in a river. But he resisted her.

"Why?" she demanded. "Why won't you let yourself feel?"

The darkness turned stormy. "I feel."

He straightened, but she clung to him. "No, you don't. You make others feel. But not you."

With measured restraint, he unwound her arms from around his neck, then started wading toward the stairs.

"Bobby, please, stop. Don't you think I understand?"

He hesitated and glanced back at her, the caged animal returned.

"Look at this house, this pool," she demanded, coming to him through the water. "Don't you think I understand what all of this is about?"

"It's nothing more than what you see."

"Wrong. You're trying to rewrite history by gaining everything you thought you'd never have. The cars, the women, the pseudofamily around the bar. This house and pool."

He jerked away and got to the stairs.

"Oh, Bobby," she whispered, following him, grabbing the back of his soaking shirt, stopping him. "Don't you see? Once you start lying to yourself, it's easy to lie to others. I know all too well."

His expression grew fierce. "I haven't lied to anyone."

"Perhaps not intentionally. But you have a house that you won't live in, and this pool when you don't even know how to swim. Let me in, Bobby, don't push me away. I really do understand the need to erase the past."

His body tensed, as if holding on to a lifeline as she

drew closer, coming up to stand behind him, her chest to his back, her arms wrapping around his waist.

"Let me touch you, Bobby," she said, tugging at his shirt.

He flinched when she finally found bare skin, and she pressed her fingers to him. Reverently, she traced each chiseled contour of his hard-carved back; his body was so taut that she thought he would break. But she didn't give in. She waded around him, coming up on the first curving tile step to stand in front of him, face-to-face.

His eyes bored into hers, his jaw working.

"You deserved a better childhood than you got," she said, the words a pledge.

With that, he broke, his roar of fury echoing wildly. Then he pulled her into his arms, holding tight.

"Let me love you, Bobby," she whispered. "Scars from your past and all."

And when she reached through the water and worked the belt on his pants, he helped. Suddenly the rest of his clothes and hers floated free.

Then he laid her back against the tile steps and braced his hands against the smooth stone lip of the pool.

CHAPTER TWENTY-FOUR

"MY MOM AND STEPDAD are out of town."

Robin felt a shiver of anticipation race through her as Kyle put the truck into gear and they slipped out into the deserted downtown streets.

"I love you," he whispered. "And I want to be with you."

She knew he did, could feel it in the way he looked at her. And when they pulled up to his house, she let him lead her inside.

The house was dark, and he switched on a few lights as they went, until the kitchen and den were dimly lit. Next he turned on a CD, a slow, driving hard rock that pulsed with a sensual beat. Despite his rented tux, he looked as out of place in this fancy room as he had on her white eyelet comforter. She wondered where he did belong.

She went to a window that overlooked the moonlit golf course, the long fairway painted with snow. Kyle came up behind her, wrapping his arms around her.

"You are so soft," he murmured, then slowly turned her around to face him.

They began to move to the music, dancing in a way that had nothing to do with silver streamers and prom corsages. He kissed her then, gently, his hands skimming down her back until their bodies touched. Gentle turned to needy when Robin wrapped her arms around him. Their kiss grew intense, their tongues twining. He cupped her round bottom through the shimmering skirt, pulling her up against him, and he groaned, shifting his hips so that she could feel his hardness.

"Let me make love to you, Robin."

She wanted to be as close to him as possible, wanted to feel loved and cherished in a way that she hardly understood. Biting her lip, she looked at him. "I don't know, Kyle."

He ran his hand down her arm. "We'll go only as far as you want. The minute you ask me to stop, I will."

They stood facing each other, and she didn't respond, didn't know how to say yes—though she wanted to. Every time he brought her home after making out in his truck, she felt an inescapable need. He made her want more, to go further, and more than once when her mom thought they were at the Charcoaler, they had driven out to the river and parked where they could be alone. Two Saturdays ago, he had slipped his hands beneath her panties, then slid his finger deep inside her in a way that made her want more and to cry at the same time.

When he had tasted her tears on her cheeks, he held her and told her he wouldn't rush her. They had all the time in the world. But tonight, alone, after he had taken her to the dance even though he hadn't wanted to go, she wanted to show that she loved him, and she wanted him all the more.

As if understanding, he carefully stepped closer, then put his hand to her waist, his palm sliding up beneath the velvet of her top.

She sucked in her breath at the touch, then closed her eyes as his hand slid higher, not stopping until he cupped her breast. She felt his shuddering exhale, felt the way his body hummed with life as his other hand slid inside, gathering the velvet against his wrist as it rose.

"Lift your arms, Rob," he murmured against her neck as he leaned close.

She did. For right or for wrong, she raised her hands, let him pull the top over her head. The material fell away, and he took her in with awe in his eyes. He might be used to being with girls, but Robin could tell that the sight of her moved him. A strange sensation of power filled her, which quickly turned to wonder of her own when he tossed his tuxedo jacket and shirt aside.

His chest was broad and well-muscled like an athlete. She wanted to touch him, but couldn't bring herself to do it until he reached around her, gathering her close, and unsnapped her bra. A moment of panic froze her to him, clutching his arms, too embarrassed to step back.

"Shhh," he whispered, setting her in front of him. Her bra fell down, catching in the crooks of her arms. "It's okay."

With an easy smoothness, he peeled the black lace away. His chest expanded as his eyes drifted over her. Then his palms, skin barely touching bare skin until the heels of his hands grazed over her nipples. She felt a burn in her face when they tightened into hard buds.

He watched her, mesmerized, his thumbs suddenly circling, and her embarrassment fled, replaced by something hot and pounding. Something that felt deep and primal, basic and primitive. She wanted him to touch her. And when he reached around to unzip her skirt, she reached around, as well, and helped.

Within minutes, they stood together in the room, he in his pants, she in a thin wisp of panties, the dark night just beyond the window, the rest of their clothes forgotten in piles on the floor around them. Taking her hands, he walked backwards until his knees hit the arm of an oversize leather sofa. He sat, bringing his head level with her breasts.

"Kyle?" she asked, her voice shaking, only to gasp when his mouth closed over one nipple.

Instinctively, her hands came up, tangling in his hair.

With one quick movement, he took a mink throw from the sofa cushions and tossed it on the floor. He lay down, pulling her on top of him, wrapping his arms around her as she rested against his chest. He rubbed her back, bringing his knees up to cradle her hips between his thighs as he murmured into her hair.

They kissed, then rolled to the side. He skimmed his hand down her body, then cupped the warmth between her legs. Instinctively she sucked in her breath at the contact, but he circled his palm over the juncture, making need slice through her.

Their embrace became even more heated, and he kicked out of his fine wool pants. He wore white Jockey shorts, and his hardness strained against them.

Holding her tight, he rolled them again until he was on top, his thighs alternating with hers, his hands sliding between her and the mink, pressing her close, his strong body arching, moving with a rhythm that made her body hum. Soon they were both panting.

"I want you, Rob. I want to taste you. Breathe you in. Lose myself inside you."

Like a wisp of air, he pulled her underwear away, then his, until they lay together, their bodies naked, intertwined. He lifted her knees and placed himself between her thighs. She felt young and old, each pulling at her. The need to be close to him tore her up, and when she felt the hardness of him pressing against her intimately, she knew her life was about to change forever.

A memory reared up.

"One moment in time has the power to change your life forever. A moment that can't be erased."

Her mother's words.

"Kyle? Do you really love me?"

Time spun to a halt, frozen, suspended, as he pulled

back to arch over her. "You know I do, Robin. I love you as I have never loved anyone in my life." He lowered himself to kiss her forehead. "And I'll love you forever."

CHAPTER TWENTY-FIVE

"LOVE ME," she whispered, as he drove between her knees, his hard shaft finding the sweet heat of her.

With his arms spread wide, his hands clutching the curving sides of the pool, Bobby floated like an eagle in the sky, soaring just barely over her as she lay back against the gradual incline of the steps, the water lapping at her chin, her body submerged. He didn't penetrate, only shuddered at the blinding intensity she knew they both felt as his tip brushed against her.

"Lacey," he murmured, his voice ragged as he brought his legs down to stand before her.

His movements were slow and dreamlike through the water, his hands running along her shins, bringing her knees up as he stepped closer. She felt his heated gaze as he watched her, his palms trailing down the tender flesh of her inner thighs until his fingers found the secret folds of her womanhood. Gently he parted her with the callused pads of his thumbs.

A slow, deep moan escaped her at the exquisite rasp of skin mixed with the caress of water against her open center. Her skin seemed to tingle, the water caressing her in time with the movements of his arms under the surface. She braced her elbows against the second step, the edge arching her spine.

He slid one strong arm beneath her back, arching her

farther until the tips of her breasts broke the surface. At the same moment, he leaned forward and took one nipple in his mouth, his finger circling the secret folds between her thighs.

He kissed her hungrily. Their tongues tangled together, making her body leap like fire. Never had she felt so alive. Never had she wanted anything so badly.

Her mouth fell open, and her body cried out for him. For a minute. For an hour. Nothing else mattered but her need to feel him inside her.

But in spite of his kiss and his hands working magic with her body, she could tell he remained elusive. She sensed an impending repetition of the night in his apartment when he held himself separate, giving to her, but not taking for himself.

Lacey focused on him, a knot of self-conscious fear trying to form. "What's wrong, Bobby? Do you really not want me?"

Humbled beyond imagining by the clear sight of her genuineness, he felt young and exposed, and he hated the emotion. But this woman made him act and think in ways that were foreign to him, making him care when he had learned long ago that caring too much only got him hurt.

Frustration assailed him and he raked his hands through his wet hair. "Yes, I want you. So much that when you're around I can't think straight. When you're gone, I want you back at my side. I think about you, I dream about you." He grasped her arms. "I want you every second of the day. And that's the problem," he accused raggedly. "I need you. I need you too much."

He didn't wait for a response, didn't want one. He pulled her close, crushing her to him. Lowering his head to hers, he captured her lips in a punishing embrace. With one hand at her back, he traced a path down her spine, pressing their bodies together as the kiss became a demand—long and slow, deep, unyielding.

She returned his embrace uninhibitedly. That was one of the many things he cherished about her. The boldness that mixed with a startling innocence, the touch of her tongue, the nip of her teeth showing just how much she truly desired him.

He groaned as he trailed his lips down her neck until he kissed the swell of her breast that just barely broke the surface of the water.

She shuddered when he ran his tongue along the pulse in her neck. Very slowly he returned to her mouth, kissing her in a sensual dance of lips and tongue, tantalizing, tempting.

He felt her answering moan deep inside him as water surged when she encircled his shoulders, clinging with a fierceness that amazed him. Their mouths crashed together desperately. She opened to him, then nipped at his lower lip, clearly wanting him as much as he wanted her.

Dear God, he felt it, understood it down to his soul. Never had someone so good and kind, someone who didn't care about how famous he was, felt such emotion for him. She knew how his mother had left him, how the Hartleys had returned him, how even all these years later he could scream out in the night. And still she wanted him.

The realization nearly brought him to his knees. Instead he stood up on the step, intent on pulling them both from the pool. But before he could take her hand, she drew a deep, shuddering breath.

"You're beautiful," she whispered in awe.

And he was. Lacey had known he was exquisitely carved and more handsome than any one man had a right to be. But standing there, his sex hard and heavy with arousal, the muscles along his chest and abdomen quivering with his barely maintained control, he was glorious and perfect.

She wanted to touch, to feel. Boldly, she did. She reached out and ran her palms up the wet swirls of hair on his thighs, gliding over his hipbones to his abdomen, feeling the contours, reveling in the sheer sculpted planes of him as she slowly stood, her hands grazing over his chest. They stood facing each other, her head tilted so that she could meet his eyes. Their gazes locked, and she didn't look away as she let her hands trail back, lower.

His body quivered as he sucked in his breath and his eyes closed. Then he groaned when her fingers slipped lower still and she wrapped her hand around his length.

Bobby opened his mouth, his head falling back, his commanding hands coming up to clutch her shoulders. The power she had over this invincible man amazed her, and awed her in turn.

She cupped and stroked, sinking lower in the gently lapping water until she took him in her mouth. She felt the tremors shudder through him, felt the strangled groan as he placed his hand on her head, and moved her gently on him. She had never done such a thing, could never imagine it. But she wanted him in every way. Her body burned with a need to give him everything he would never take.

His muscles began to tremble; his breathing went ragged. But just when she felt that his body would explode, he broke free with a roar and jerked away, pulling her to him with a force that was as desperate as it was passionate.

He kissed her then, urgently, his palms molding her to him. She matched his desire, melting against him, seeking what she knew he could provide.

He lifted her up, sweeping her through the water, and before she knew it, they were on the oversize raft that floated in the shallow end of the pool, her thighs straddling his, her knees pressing into the crystalline covering. His male flesh was hard and insistent between her legs, and her hands braced on his shoulders.

She looked out into the sky, the black pierced by falling snow, and had a moment of hesitation. He was leaving tomorrow.

But her desire for this man won out when his strong hands began to guide her down to his shaft. He nudged her knees farther apart with his own, bringing the juncture between her thighs lower, closer.

When the secret folds of her flesh touched his slick hardness, the sensation took her breath, and she couldn't hold back the moan that started deep in her throat as her body quivered with longing.

But when he carefully pulled her down on him, his sheer size made her tremble with trepidation. With his hands instructing, he moved her on him, slowly circling her hips, tantalizing, until she felt her body open to him. Her head fell back, and all concern evaporated. She only sought the pleasure he had given her before—though this time she sought something greater, something that pulled at her, something primal and innate. Instinctually, she understood that she yearned to feel him deep inside her.

Seeking, her body began to move without his guidance. She felt him suck in his breath when she tried to slide lower, taking more of him.

"God," he whispered on a strangled breath.

Expelling sharply, he grabbed her hips and guided her away from him until they were nearly parted. But then he pulled her back. Over and over again, barely a movement, slowly, deliciously, until she starting moving again on her own. Moving and sliding, still seeking.

She looked down at this man. His jaw was locked, his body hard and tense like stone.

Unable to help herself, she leaned down, her hair falling free to drape about them. She brushed her lips over his, back and forth as he had shown her. For one long, breathless moment, his hands just barely held her, as he reveled in the feel. But then without warning, he lifted her up with sheer strength, water sloshing violently beneath the raft as he rolled her on her back.

He pinned her down. His eyes met hers, and he planted his elbows on either side of her, his hands framing her face. His gaze locked with hers, as he sank between her knees, almost reverently, lowering himself slowly until the swollen tip of his manhood brushed against her. She lifted her knees to accommodate him, because this time there was no thought that he was too large—no thought that he would leave. She only wanted him.

"You make me crazy, Lacey," he accused.

"You make me love you," she responded.

And with those words, he slid his shaft deep within her flesh, calling out her name, the sound echoing against the glass.

Their bodies pressed together until there was nothing between them, joined as they were meant to be. For long seconds, he remained still, and she knew that at some level he was trying to control his emotions, control his body's response to her. He was giving in, though not completely.

Determined, she moved her hips, her body arching instinctively to take more of him. She felt the tremor in his muscles, watched as his eyes darkened with a quiet desperation. Reaching up, she traced a line over his chest. "Let go, Bobby. Let me inside your heart. I promise I'll never hurt you."

With that, his body shuddered as his control snapped and he gave in. He buried his face in her neck, moving inside her, slowly, deeply, obsessively as if he could drive out the demons of his past. She clung to him, the raft rocking around them as they moved together with passion, their bodies seeking one another. His movement grew faster as he thrust inside her. They were hot and wet, and deliciously wild as he drew up on his hands.

His hips arched into her, and her body tilted to take him more deeply. He had never penetrated a woman like this before—completely, his whole length taken, an acceptance of all of him. He had never felt anything so amazing, but when he adjusted his weight, the motion unsettled the raft.

Time hung suspended as the crystal blue acrylic upended, a moment of sheer surprise, before they spilled into the pool. They clung together, their bodies still joined, though barely, his tip throbbing just at her opening as they sank to the bottom of the shallow water. Everything felt slow and wonderful, like falling through cotton, until Bobby touched down with Lacey straddling him, and his shaft slid back inside her with a sweetness as smooth and thick as molasses. Every sensation was exaggerated, like moving in slow motion, before he grasped her tightly and exploded to the surface like a warrior.

Restraint spent, the need to keep himself separate gone, he wrapped her legs around his waist, held her body close, and waded to the steps with such force that waves crashed over the sides. With little effort, he climbed the stairs, his arms cradling her bottom, his body rock hard and throbbing inside her. Carrying her to a single lounge chair that was large enough to support them both, he laid her down, their bodies parting for only a second before he found her again. Then he slid between her swollen womanhood with shuddering intensity. He moved slowly, not wanting to hurt her.

With a frustrated cry she moved against him. Amazed, he laughed, then matched her movements until they were both seeking. He cupped her hips, pulling her body up to meet his bold, fevered thrusts.

She clutched his shoulders, panting, needing him. And then it happened. He felt her body convulse with spiraling intensity, his every sense reeling and alive. Only then did he allow his body's explosive shudder to race through him. He cried out her name, grasping her tightly to his heart as he buried his face in her hair.

CHAPTER TWENTY-SIX

THEY LAY TOGETHER, naked, their legs twined. Kyle arched over Robin, his eyes questioning.

"I love you, too," she whispered, red staining her cheeks, tears burning in her large hazel eyes. "But I'm not ready. Not for this."

Kyle felt a tremor carve through his body, and the yearning to damn all else and plunge deep sliced through his mind. But he would never do that to her, or anyone. Ever.

With a groan, he collapsed against her. For half a second, he lay on top of her as he reined in his body. Finally, thinking that he never would have guessed he'd end up with the unwelcome Christmas gift of blue balls, he rolled away, taking Robin with him until she was at his side and curled into his embrace. He was still hard as hell, the need for relief burning him up.

Shaking his head and chuckling grimly, he flipped the throw over his middle, then stroked her hair.

"It's all right," he murmured.

"I wasn't trying to be a tease."

"I know you weren't. I love you, Rob, whether you're ready or not." And amazingly, he realized that he meant it. He tilted her chin so that she looked into his eyes. "You're worth waiting for."

"You're not mad?"

"Hell, no. Though I could use a cold shower."

Her face started to crumple again.

"Hey, that was a joke."

He kissed her forehead, not with passion, but gently to reassure her. "Come on, let's get dressed. We'll go pig out in the kitchen, then I'll take you home."

They drove through the late night streets in silence, Kyle careful of the snowy roads, pulling up to Bobby's Place a good ten minutes before twelve. He turned off the truck, and they sat together for a moment.

"Thank you for a wonderful night," she said quietly.

He turned to face her, and took her hand in his. "I've never been much for proms," he said with an indifferent shrug, "but going with you made it all right."

He pulled her close and kissed her, softly at first, but in seconds it turned hot, as if now that they were in the safety of the truck in a parking lot, and not alone, lying naked in his house, they were back on safe ground. They clung together, kissing, feeling. But then he groaned and pulled away. He realized his body really couldn't take too much more in one night.

With a grim chuckle, he leaned back, his hands braced against the steering wheel. "I can tell I'm in for a lot of cold showers for a while."

"Me, too," Robin said honestly.

Kyle laughed out loud at that.

"When will your mom and stepdad be home?" she asked.

"They say a week, but who knows." He locked his hand with hers. "Hanging out with you makes everything seem easier."

He kissed her one last time before he walked her to the rear entrance of the bar. "Good night," he said. "I'll call you tomorrow."

* * *

Lacey heard Robin the minute she entered the back door of the building. Sitting on the sofa, Lacey waited as calmly and as patiently as she could, while Robin came down the outer hall. With a squeak, Lacey quickly turned on the television so she'd look as casual as possible. Just as the news leaped onto the screen, Robin's key slid into the lock; then she pushed inside their apartment.

Looking dreamy and euphoric, the teenager floated into the living room, swaying from side to side like music still played in her head.

"Hi, Mom," she said, smiling, her arm drifting out to set her tiny clutch bag on the entry table.

Lacey stretched, yawned dramatically, and turned off the television. "How was the dance?"

"Great, wonderful, heavenly."

She pulled off her winter coat, danced a few steps with it before she set it aside, then stopped and showed off her corsage, leaning so close that Lacey could tell for certain her child hadn't had any alcohol that night. That was one concern scratched off the list.

"Look what Kyle gave me." She extended her wrist showing off the corsage.

Lacey's hands fisted impatiently into the pillow she held in her lap.

Did you have sex?

The question erupted in Lacey's head, nearly slipping off the tip of her tongue, but she held it back, though only barely.

"Yes, it's beautiful," Lacey said, with a gaiety she hoped sounded sincere. "Sounds like you had fun."

"Lots."

"Everything worked out all right?"

"Perfectly."

"How was dinner?"

"Great."

"Did you dance much?"

"Tons."

Lacey decided Chinese water torture had to be easier to take than her teenager's elusive, one-word answers regarding the Winter Dance.

"I'm going to bed," Robin said.

"So soon?"

Robin smiled that dreamy smile, floating out of the living room. "I'm exhausted." But then she stopped, surprising Lacey when she returned to lean over the back of the sofa and give her a tight hug. "I love you, Mom. Thanks for letting me go. It was a magical night that I'll never forget." Without another word, the teen whirled away, then headed down the hall.

Lacey nearly groaned in frustration when she understood that her daughter wasn't going to offer the details she wanted. If Lacey wanted to know if Robin had been intimate with that boy, she'd have to ask outright.

"Robin?"

Her daughter turned back, her expression open and caring, not closed off and belligerent like so many kids these days. In that moment, Lacey realized that if she asked her daughter if she'd had sex, it would change their relationship forever. Tonight, something had happened and Robin had grown up. Lacey could see it in her eyes. She could see something older, wiser, more mature. But whatever had caused the change, her daughter wasn't going to tell her.

And that had to be okay.

The realization sank in as it hadn't all the weeks that the understanding tried to break through her stubborn mind. She had to let her daughter go, had to let her fly free. Lacey had to trust that she had taught her well, and that Robin had the tools to make her own decisions.

At this stage of the game, if her daughter made mistakes, all Lacey could do was be there for her. That had to be good enough, because everyone made mistakes at one time or another, no matter who they were, no matter how prepared, no matter how hard they tried to do the right things.

That was when Lacey understood she had to fly free, too. She had made a mistake—but that was all it was. She hadn't committed a horrid sin that could never be forgiven. Just a mistake that she had paid for and learned from, and gained a beautiful, loving daughter in return.

It was time to move on. Time to forgive herself for being young, impetuous, naïve. Just as Bobby had said so many times before.

Bobby. Who knew about her past, and didn't care, didn't turn her away because of it. Bobby, whose control she had broken. She had made him feel. But after their bodies had settled, he had only held her close for one long second before reminding her that they had better get home before Robin did.

Now, with her daughter home safe and sound, and Bobby leaving for Dallas tomorrow, she could only pray that he could accept what she had given, accept the fact that she truly did love him.

Lacey woke late the next morning. Afraid she would miss Bobby before he left, she jumped into the shower, brushed her teeth, did her hair, threw on the bulky sweater and leggings he liked so much, and went down to the office to wait for him to come downstairs.

Attempting to busy herself, she tried to concentrate on the books and order forms, advertising plans and time sheets. But as hard as she tried, all she could think about was last night—and the fact that Bobby was going to leave.

She paced and planned every little thing she would say to him. But what could she say?

Ask him to stay? That hardly seemed fair.

Ask him to take her with him? That certainly wouldn't work since she had a daughter to raise and a bar to run.

Besides, he had never made one mention of them being together after last night.

Her heart started to pound.

But then she chided herself. Whether he had admitted it or not, Bobby cared for her. The question was, how much?

At ten-thirty, with still not a sound of him rustling upstairs, she put on a pot of coffee behind the bar. Sipping a cup, she heard Peter come in the front door of the bar to set up for the Saturday noontime crowd. He was fifteen minutes early—a switch from when she first started there and he regularly showed up fifteen minutes late.

She smiled her contentment at how things had changed at Bobby's Place. She wanted to share all of this with Bobby—the success of the bar, the way the employees and regulars had warmed up to her. She had turned things around. Now to tell him how she felt.

Looking for anything to take her mind off the wait for him to come downstairs, she flicked on the television. As always, Bobby's usual ESPN blinked onto the screen. It was just when she raised the remote to switch the station that an announcer caught her attention.

"Leslie," a commentator said to a woman reporting remotely from a football field. "What can you tell us about the news that Bobby McIntyre is returning?"

"Chris, if you'll remember, it was while playing the Browns in September that The Bathtub pummeled Bobby Mac McIntyre, putting him out for what most people had assumed would be the rest of the season. But the Lone Stars' head coach, Dan Streamer, confirmed this morning that Bobby Mac will start in tomorrow's game against Miami. This, despite reports that doctors have advised the three-time Super Bowl champ to retire."

Lacey set her coffee aside and turned up the volume.

"Leslie, did the coach offer any further details about this news?"

"No, Chris, he didn't, other than to angrily deny what he called 'misinformed rumors,' then added that Bobby Mac was a hundred percent. But my sources tell me that during the September game against Cleveland, Bobby Mac not only sustained a knee injury, but a concussion, as well— the third for the thirty-five-year-old quarterback."

"Sounds like what happened to fellow quarterbacks Troy Aikman and Steve Young."

"Exactly, Chris. And like Aikman and Young, if the reports are true, Bobby Mac is faced with the very real possibility of serious and long-term physical damage if he receives another concussion."

The coffee cup clattered against the saucer when Lacey staggered. She couldn't believe what she was hearing.

The commentators moved on to another team, but she didn't listen. Instead, she looked up and found Bobby standing in the doorway, staring at the screen. Instantly she saw the fury that raced through him, his tightly held control returned.

"Is that report true?" she asked incredulously.

He strode over, grabbed the remote away from her, and turned off the television. "Fuck."

"It is true! You can't really mean to return to Dallas to play."

"You better believe I am. The car service picks me up at noon."

"And risk permanent injury?"

"It's not a certainty."

"Just like it's not a certainty that you'll wreck while driving ninety miles an hour on a rain slick road after drinking, but it would be a stupid thing to do."

His jaw cemented. "You don't understand."

"Hmmm, what don't I understand? That you could ruin your knee? No, I get that. That you could sustain permanent brain damage if you get hit in the head again? Nah, get that, too. So what could it be?"

He held the remote fisted at his side. "Football's my life."

"You're wrong! You have so much more than that! You have a sister who loves you, and an entire town full of people who adore you. You have more money than you know what to do with, not to mention three Super Bowl rings that you don't even bother to wear. That's more than most people have in a lifetime."

"It's not enough."

He said the words with such quiet intensity that she knew he was speaking with a candid honesty. But honesty didn't make it any more acceptable.

"Then grow up and make it be enough."

He started to pace, then stopped and whirled back. "What am I supposed to do with the rest of my life? Sit around, play golf?"

"Get a job," she threw out relentlessly.

"Doing what?"

"Become a sports announcer. The networks would give their eyeteeth to have you. You'd be every bit as good as that Chris fellow I just saw."

"I don't want to talk about the game. I want to play it. Football is what I do. It's who I am. If I don't have Sunday games and training camp, who am I?"

He looked as lost as she had ever seen any man, and she thought of the little boy who had found a place in the world through the game of football—a place where coaches were like fathers, and mothers didn't leave.

She went to him, wrapping her arms around his massive frame without a trace of inhibition. "You are a kind and good man, Bobby McIntyre."

She felt him tense. His breathing grew labored, and she could feel the strength of him holding a tight rein. But still she wouldn't step away. She curled beneath his arms, pressing her cheek to his chest. "Don't go, Bobby. Stay here with me. I'll help you build a new life."

His body shuddered as if the control he held cost him. Shaking, he brought his hands up to her back, holding her—though just for a second before he grasped her by the shoulders and set her away from him. "I can't change who I am, and neither can you."

Her heart knotted in her chest.

"I want you, Lacey. I do. Last night proved that. But not yet. I have to go back to Dallas. The team needs me." He hesitated. "I need the team. After the season's over, I'll come back. We'll figure out what to do then."

"But what about that report?" she demanded.

"I have to take the chance."

He let go of her and went to his desk, making it clear he wasn't going to change his mind.

She slapped her hand down on the papers. "If you leave now," she said, "when you are faced with the very real danger of permanently harming yourself, you'll never be able to stay. Not with me, not in El Paso." She straightened. "I'll always know that I wasn't enough for you."

He stared at her long and hard. But in the end he put the last of the papers in his bag, then headed for the door.

"Damn it, Bobby, stop running. You told me to stop running. You told me I had to have courage to stay."

He sighed. "What you don't understand, Lacey, is that you've always had more courage than I ever had. You raised Robin. You fought to give her a decent life—no matter what the cost was to you. And you did it all the hard way, by yourself, with low-paying jobs. I did it the easy way. Through sports."

"Oh, Bobby. You have courage. You always have. It took courage to survive. It took courage to make something of yourself. And one day you are going to realize that you have a great deal more to offer than a smile and a passing arm."

He looked at her, and she could see the raw hope that flared in his eyes. But just when she thought he would give in, he bowed his head. "I'm sorry, Lacey. Just give me the rest of this season. Then I'll be back."

He left her in the office, stunned. She could hardly believe he was truly leaving. She started to sink down in the chair, started to give in. But then a slow burning anger rose up in a rush. Without thinking, she wheeled after him.

The regulars had already arrived to see him off.

"Damn it, Bobby," she called after him.

He stood in the middle of the swarm of men wishing him well, and the group froze and turned to her. But she didn't let the mass of curious stares deter her.

"I love you, Bobby McIntyre. I love you as I have loved little else in my life. But if you walk out that door, I won't be here when you return."

Bobby glanced at the regulars, who raised their brows in quiet speculation, at Jazzy who shook her head in disgust, then back at Lacey, his eyes imploring her with a pleading darkness not to do this. But she couldn't give in. She stood her ground.

A car horn sounded outside, and his nostrils flared like a cornered panther, caged and desperate.

But the regulars didn't see the desperation. They hooted and whistled. Rupert slapped him on the back. "Bobby, my man, don't tell us you're going to let this little lady run you around."

With that, Bobby smiled, that famous, lopsided grin Lacey had seen a thousand times. Cool as you please, he strolled back to her, his trademark swagger and the bone-deep sensuality making the women who had started to filter in sigh. Using his free arm, he pulled her close, then kissed her with a showmanship worthy of an Academy Award. The crowd roared their approval, whoops and woofs careening off the walls.

When he pulled back, his eyes bored into her, the smile fading. "Stay. Don't leave. I *will* be back," he said for only her to hear.

Then he waved to the crowd and walked out, the front door swinging closed with finality.

Lacey stood there, stock-still, every ounce of courage and determined pride seeping away at the reality of what just happened. Seconds passed before she realized the regulars had quieted down and were staring at her, their excitement having clouded over with shades of embarrassed pity.

She blinked and focused, finding a smile. "In the kind of movies I like, that would have turned out a little differently."

Then she turned and fled up the stairs before any of them could see her break down and cry.

CHAPTER TWENTY-SEVEN

LACEY STUFFED CLOTHES into her soft-sided suitcase with a vengeance. "I hate football," she muttered.

It was Sunday morning, and while all of yesterday she had held out hope that somewhere between the bar and the limo ride to the airport Bobby would regain his senses and return, he hadn't. He had left El Paso and flew back to Dallas—and he hadn't called.

"Fine, don't pick up the phone, see if I care," she grumbled, shoving a stack of sensible cotton panties into a corner of the suitcase.

She wanted to curl up on the sofa with a whole bag of Reese's Peanut Butter Cup singles, topped with chocolate ice cream and hot fudge, then watch weepy videos like *Black Beauty* and *My Girl* until she had cried her eyes out or gotten sick. Whichever came first. But thankfully, the anger overrode everything else, renewing her conviction that to remain in El Paso would be a mistake.

Marching over to start on the second drawer, she froze at the muffled sound of someone coming up the stairs.

Foolish, idiotic hope surged through her, and she raced across the apartment, turning the knob, hope beating like a drum.

"Robin," she gasped, her face falling with disappointment.

"Don't look so excited, Mom."

Lacey returned to the bedroom.

Robin followed, chatting the whole way, going on about Kyle Walker. But when the teen came to her mother's doorway, her story cut off midsentence. "Oh, my gosh! What are you doing?" she blurted out at the sight of the clothes and suitcases.

"I'm packing. We're leaving."

"No! Not again! Not anymore. I want to stay here!"

Lacey didn't meet her eyes; she continued to pull out stacks of clothes.

Frantic and crying, Robin grabbed a pile of sweaters from Lacey's hand. "Stop! Talk to me. This is my life, too."

"I'm sorry, Robin, really I am," Lacey replied honestly. "But it's time we move on."

"Why are you doing this?"

"It's for the best, Robin," was all she said.

"It's because of Bobby Mac, isn't it?"

"Bobby?" she asked, trying to act innocent.

"I heard about the ultimatum you gave him in the bar."

Lacey grimaced. "Not one of your mother's finer moments."

"Not one of Bobby's finer moments either. The whole thing makes me mad. He's running. You're running."

"No one's running, sweetheart," she lied.

Lacey didn't know how to explain that she couldn't sit around waiting for Bobby to return. He'd come back, she knew he would, but then he'd leave again, and again, and she'd sit there year after year, waiting for that day when he could finally give up the spotlight, finally give up the adulation and praise that had provided him with the only love he had known in his life. The only kind of love he knew how to accept—and how to give.

"It wasn't meant to be, Robin. And there's a whole world out there just waiting for us." She tried to sound excited. "We'll take the map and start driving. It will be like old times. You and me on the road, finding the next place that's going to be even better."

"No, Mom. Not this time. I'm not going."

Lacey's hands stilled in a neatly folded scarf. "You have to go, young lady. You can't stay here without me."

"I can and I will. I'll get an after-school job. Or I'll quit school and work full-time if I have to. I'm sixteen and can get a license. I'm old enough to live without you," she added with a bravado that sounded forced and shaky, "whether you like it or not."

"You are my daughter," she railed. "You will not disobey me. We are leaving, and that is final."

Robin flounced out, crying, slamming the front door. Lacey felt panic swell inside her, like bands squeezing her chest. She remembered telling Beth that old habits die hard. Was that what this was? Just an old habit?

No, she assured herself, wanting to believe. She was the mother, she knew what was best, and it was best for both of them to leave El Paso. Christmas vacation was right around the corner. Robin wouldn't miss much school before they landed someplace new, someplace better.

Lacey was uncertain what to do about the car and the lifetime of payments she had left that tied her to Bobby, but it was also the means that made it possible for her to leave. With a determined nod of her head, she decided she would send him the money from wherever she and Robin ended up.

She hated to leave Beth in the lurch. But the bar was running smoothly, the books in order, time schedules made out for the next four weeks. They would leave in the morning, head west with the promise of a new future. Robin would get over her upset and be fine, she told herself, praying she was right.

By noon, with the apartment a jumble of half-packed suitcases and boxes, Lacey went downstairs to check on the bar. It was filled with the usual Sunday football contingent. But today, Bobby's Place was even more crowded as regulars and a whole slew of others came to watch Bobby Mac make his grand return to the playing field. If anyone else had heard the report about his concussion, no one was mentioning it.

Local reporters were there, waiting to see the prodigal son show what he was made of. Friends she recognized from Bobby's birthday party circled around to get a glimpse. They toasted with beers and ordered up buffalo wings, filling the place with fun, laughter, and eager anticipation.

Every television, including the big screen, was tuned to the pregame show as they counted down the minutes until kick off. Robin had called Kyle, crying. He had come by and picked her up, holding her tightly, in shock.

Lacey felt stress rise inside her. She was angry and sad, the emotions twisting together so tightly that she turned on the radio in the office to tune out the sound of the television. But still the voices drifted in to her, and she knew the second the Lone Stars came out onto the field, followed by the roar of an echoing cheer that erupted when she was certain Bobby must have appeared on the screen.

She sat back and closed her eyes, seeing him in her mind, her fingers itching to turn on the television across the room. Just to see him, take in his face, his smile. Like a drug, she wanted just a bit more. And that was why she had to go.

Sadness and fear gripped her until she couldn't breathe. With a frustrated cry, she leaped from the chair and took the stairs to the apartment two at a time, slamming inside, ripping off her clothes, turning on the water so hot that steam rose in the shower, clouding the glass walls. She was tired of hurting, tired of worrying. She wanted to wash it all away. Stepping into the biting stream of water, she relished the heat.

Bracing her forearm against the cool tiles of the back wall, her forehead on her arm, she let the water wash down her.

But suddenly, slowly, she felt an amazing ease seep inside her, a sense of peace she hardly understood. In a matter of seconds, something had changed, though she didn't know what. Somehow she felt whole, the sadness gone. Her brow furrowed as she tried to understand.

She whirled around and could see the faint outline of a man. Her heart stopped as she wiped a streak across the glass.

"Bobby?"

He was there, his gaze meeting hers. He didn't say a word, only shed his clothes and pulled open the glass door. An instant piercing joy spread through her, followed quickly by shock and confusion.

"What are you doing here?" she breathed.

Her mind tried to assimilate this change, from her certainty that he was on the television screen downstairs to the reality of him standing in front of her.

He stood on the threshold, naked, his chest hard and muscled, a light dusting of hair trailing down to his narrow waist, his shaft hanging between his thighs, thick and just starting to swell.

"I need you," he said in a hoarse demand.

The words were a curse and a plea. She heard it, and a shock raced along every nerve ending as he stepped into the flow of water, pulling the door shut behind him, taking her into his arms with a moan like he was drowning.

"You're like a fever," he murmured against her neck, his hands shaping to her body, molding her against him. "You burn me up, turn me inside out. Consume me, until I want nothing else."

She knew that they couldn't exist in a place of such demanding need, a need that he didn't want to feel, but just then her need matched his. And for that second it was enough. When he lifted her up, pressing her back against the tiles, she wrapped her legs around his waist, holding tight, kissing his hair, his eyes, never wanting to let go.

"I can't wait," he groaned, urgent, guiding himself to her, spreading her as gently as he could, before thrusting deep inside her slippery wetness.

Every muscle went taut as he held his body completely still. After he regained his breath, he pulled nearly out, then slid back, hard, deeper, just once before his entire body shuddered with an instant release. "Lacey," he groaned into her neck.

She held him with every ounce of her strength. "I'm here."

Just as he was.

She held tight until she felt the tension finally give up its grip on him, and she stroked his hair. "Why did you come back, Bobby?"

He raised his head from her shoulder, the desperation gone, replaced by one of his famously crooked grins as she felt him stiffen inside her. "I'm here to make love to you," he said with satisfaction. The smile faltered just a bit. "And to see if the one person in the world who truly makes me whole will have me back."

His eyes dilated, growing so dark and intense that the blue was almost black. "I love you, Lacey. I have since the day I walked into the office and saw you standing there in your prim little sweater, giving back as good as you got. When I'm with you, I understand what love really is. It fills my heart, fills my soul in a way that football never can."

He covered her mouth with his own, kissing her as he inhaled, like breathing her in, long and lingering. "I've been afraid of that love. Afraid to give in to it." He pressed his eyes closed as if he didn't want to say anything more. But something else, something relentless, pushed him on. "I have a bad habit of losing the people that I love."

She touched his face. "So better to leave me than lose me."

He shrugged, fighting off emotion. And when he started moving in her again, she held on, relished the feel, and then forgot when he ran his fingers along the cleave in her bottom to the sensitive lips of her sex. He moved inside her, taking her higher until her body trembled with release. Only then did he thrust hard, calling her name once again as he came inside her.

Her legs were weak, her muscles spent. He turned off the water and carried her onto the bathroom rug, setting her down on her feet. With loving reverence, he took the towel and dried her off, then wrapped her tightly as he brought a brush to her wet hair.

They sat together on the rug, she curled in his embrace as he worked long, smooth strokes until every tangle was gone.

"Does this mean you're finished with Dallas?" she asked hesitantly, turning just enough so that she could see his expression.

"Yes. Coach had prepped me with the plays. We stayed up late talking everything through. The team doctor felt good about my knee. Everything was set to go."

"Except the concern about getting hit again?"

He looked at her. "I would have taken the chance, but I realized that I wanted you more."

Trembling with a wealth of emotion, she touched his cheek, nervous now that she had gotten what she wanted, nervous that he would blame her years from now for making him give up his days of glory. "Are you sure this is what you really want?"

"I've never been more sure of anything in my life. But it took getting back and seeing the guys to really see myself.

I looked at them, younger than me, just as driven, striving for the kind of success I've already had. When Coach drew out the plays on the chalkboard, all I saw were Xs and Os, a black-and-white world that has always been my escape." He grimaced. "Sitting there in the prep room that has been more of a home to me than any house or apartment, I realized that the talent and determination I've always thought made me a great quarterback was actually just me chasing the shadow of my mother running down that walkway."

Her soul felt as if it ripped open for this man that she loved, and she leaned her forehead against his shoulder.

"Returning to Dallas," he added, stroking her hair, "made me realize what I want." He tilted her chin so that she met his gaze. "I want you. I want your strength and caring. Your passion." He took her hand and placed it over his heart. "And if you'll have me, I want you to be my wife."

Tears burned in her eyes. "Oh, Bobby." She kissed him in response.

"I want to take you to the house above Rim Road and carry you over the threshold as my bride. I want to fill the place with love and laughter and a lifetime of permanence. You and me, putting down roots." With every word he spoke, his excitement grew. "And I want to be a father. To Robin, in whatever capacity that she needs a dad in her life, and to a child of our own." He smiled his endearingly crooked Bobby Mac smile. "I don't know how great I'll be at it, but I want to try."

She realized how far he had come in his journey, far enough that he was willing to risk his heart as he hadn't since his mother left him years before.

She clung to him and made a promise, to him and to herself. "It's worth the risk, Bobby. You won't lose me. Just hold on tight. Because I'll never let you go."

EPILOGUE

"COACH!"

Bobby looked up from the clipboard where he was drawing out a series of plays for the team. The stadium was filled with crowds decked in blue and gold, cheerleaders cheered, and the opposing team was warming up on the field.

His first-string running back stood on the sidelines, trying to get his attention.

"What is it, Metcalf? And where's Jenkins?"

"In the bathroom, Coach. Crying."

Bobby hung his head and groaned. If it wasn't crying, then it was gossiping. Learning plays and even *playing* plays came a distant second to the vagaries of life at Coronado High School. Why he ever volunteered to coach the once-a-year girls' Powder Puff Football scrimmage, he didn't know.

But then he saw his starting quarterback sitting on the bench and he knew. Robin. And her mother, Lacey, who was just then climbing out of the stands and heading their way.

"What's wrong?" Lacey asked, her blue-and-gold scarf highlighting the gold in her eyes.

Whenever he saw her, it was the same. A sense of peace and ease softened the hard edges in his mind.

"Carter Whitman dumped Sally Jenkins," Nettie Metcalf

explained with a disdainful sigh. "And now Sally won't come out of the bathroom."

The entire team of sophomore and junior girls gasped, leaped up from the bench in unison, and headed for the bathroom. The only consolation was that half the opposing team of senior and freshman girls overheard and followed, as well.

"Hey, come back here," Bobby called after them. "The game starts in four minutes."

But the girls weren't listening. Not that Bobby was surprised. In the very long three weeks he had been coaching the team, he had found that current and potential boyfriends overrode anything that had to do with football. Who did what to whom was a close second, with clothes, hair, and fingernails tying for third. He still wasn't sure why any of them had signed up for the team.

"Go talk to her," Lacey said, placing her hand on his arm.

"Me?" he barked. "You go. You're a woman. Go do whatever women do when this stuff happens."

"Bobby, I can console her, I can tell her about how we all get our hearts broken, but this is just the kind of thing that one word from a man could easily fix." Her brow furrowed. "That is if you say something nice and supportive."

"No way."

"You want your team on the field, don't you?"

Bobby let out a long grumbling sigh, hitched the clipboard under his arm, his whistle clanking against the metal, and headed for the girls' locker room. At the door, he pounded.

No one answered, but he could hear the girls' voices and what had to be Sally Jenkins's tears echoing against the tile walls and floors.

"Sally," he called out. "Stop crying, and get the hell out here."

The crying only got louder.

Okay, so maybe that wasn't so supportive.

Again and again he forgot that what worked with guys really didn't work at all with their group. You had to reason with girls, where guys did better with commands.

He searched his brain and plunged ahead. "Forget about that moron, Sally," he called through the open window.

Voices trailed off, and he was sure there was a slight hesitation in the tears. Encouraged, he glanced at his watch. Three minutes to go. "He doesn't deserve you," he added.

After a second, the bathroom door cracked open, and Nettie Metcalf stuck out her head.

"Sally wants to know what you mean," the running back inquired. "About the moron thing."

"Tell her that Kotter—"

Nettie rolled her eyes and scoffed. "Carter."

"Tell her that Carter doesn't know squat if he broke up with her. She's too good for him, anyway."

The door opened a little wider, and this time he could see Sally, her eyes red and tearstained.

"Do you think?" she asked hesitantly, the number 23 on her jersey catching the overhead light.

"I don't think," he stated, "I know. Show him what you're made of. Get out on that field and let him see that you don't give a flying flip what he does. In fact, you're glad he broke up with you because you're moving on to bigger and better things. If he sees that, you'll have him eatin' out of your palm by the second quarter."

Robin slid out the door to stand next to him, giving him a look because they both knew that had Lacey been there, she would have heartily disapproved of his tactics. Playing games was not high on her list of how to get things done. But just then, Bobby was willing to risk it. He had a game to win.

"Well, maybe you're right." Sally wiped her tears away, a fire starting to burn. "I'll show him." A determined smile surfaced through her red-splotched face. "By the time I get through with him, he'll be begging me to come back, and I'll tell him to kiss my a—"

"Okay, save the trash-talking for the field. Let's go, girls."

"Wait! Where's my mascara? I can't go out there looking like this!"

"Mascara?" Bobby choked. "This is football. Get out there!"

"Hello! How do you expect me to make Carter Whitman weep if I look horrible?" she scoffed, helmet dangling from her manicured nails.

Bobby shook his head and returned to the field alone. He had to beg the referee for an extra few minutes, promising the guy a signed poster from his Bobby Mac days, then breathed a sigh of relief when his entire team ran onto the field like a jersey-clad girl band that brought up a cheer from the crowd. Somehow they made it look planned.

Bobby returned to Lacey's side. "I'm impressed," she said. "There aren't many people who could have gotten a heartbroken teenage girl out of the bathroom so fast." She looked at Robin. "How'd he do it?"

Robin and Bobby exchanged a guilty glance, but were saved from answering when the announcer's voice filled the stadium.

Bobby found his football scowl, called out the play, then sent his team to the field.

Lacey watched them go. "Be careful," she called after them with a sighing grimace. "I guess I should go sit down."

For half a second, Bobby watched Lacey make her way through the cheerleaders to the stands before he smiled and turned back to his players.

The game went about as well as a once-a-year sport named after a makeup application device could go. Nobody got killed. No teeth got knocked out. The final score came in at sixty-three to fifty-six because neither team wanted to block an oncoming player and risk a black eye the week before the homecoming dance.

"At least you won," Lacey said, hooking her arm through his after the game as the crowd filed out of the stadium.

"Yep, I'm da man," he strutted. "And the team wasn't half bad for a bunch of girls."

Lacey gave him the look.

Bobby stopped, and he pulled Lacey close as people streamed by on either side of them. "The cheering section wasn't so shabby either," he said with a teasing smile.

Inhaling deeply, Lacey felt the sense of ease that had become so much a part of her life in the last eleven months since she had married Bobby.

Mrs. Bobby McIntyre.

It was still hard for her to believe.

She had a life for the first time, a real life that wasn't about running away. She and Robin had a family—in Beth and her husband and children, in friends and neighbors. And she had a house. High on the mountain, looking over the city she had come to love, filled with furniture that she had spent months picking out.

"Mom! Can you believe it, we won!"

Robin laughed with a free abandon that filled Lacey's heart. Her daughter was truly happy and at ease. Lacey's smile faltered only slightly when Kyle walked up behind Robin. No question, he was handsome, and despite his bad-boy good looks he was nothing but respectful of her daughter.

Kyle stood in his leather jacket and black boots, his dark hair brushing his collar. He looked as bad as he had the first time she saw him, and she still wasn't all that crazy about the way he held Robin's hand. But every night she reminded herself that she had taught Robin well.

"Hey, Miz Mac," Kyle said in a deep rumble.

"Hello, Kyle," she managed, her smile wry at the name he had taken to calling her.

Suddenly they were surrounded by the entire team, the girls cheering Bobby. They chanted and circled around, leaving Kyle and Lacey alone. Suddenly the rugged bad boy shifted his weight uncomfortably, and Lacey's heart started to pound. Oh, no. What was wrong? she wondered. Was he going to ask to marry Robin? Tell her that Robin was pregnant? That they were going to go off and live together in a commune?

Lacey's mind ran away with her, and it took a second for her to focus when he spoke. But it wasn't his words that snagged in her mind at first, rather his tone and the look in his eyes. Dark and vulnerable, making him look far younger than she could imagine.

"Thanks for inviting me to Thanksgiving dinner," Kyle said. "It's really cool of you."

The day before, she had extended the invitation to the dinner she planned for the following week. Lacey knew the boy's mother and stepfather were heading off for some exotic vacation, leaving Kyle alone for the holiday. From what she had gathered, they left him a lot.

Before, she had simply worried that this kid was left too much to his own devices. Now, for the first time, she saw something in him she hadn't before—the desire to be a part of a family. *That* was what drew him to Robin, she realized. A sense of belonging. And Lacey felt her heart twist just a tiny bit for this boy.

She reached out and gave his forearm a quick squeeze. "You're welcome, Kyle. I'm glad you can come."

As soon as she said the words, a smile flashed on his

lips. Only then did she feel her husband's strong arms circle her waist from behind.

"Bobby!" Lacey squeaked.

Kyle grinned and Bobby chuckled as the two guys did some kind of handshake thing before Kyle turned and headed off with the group of teenagers.

"He's a good kid," Bobby said, holding her securely to him.

"You knew that all along, didn't you?" she said.

"Knew what?"

"That beneath that gruff exterior is a little boy just wanting to be loved."

Slowly he turned Lacey around until she faced him. "I understood that he needed to know that someone out there cared about him. I'm glad you asked him to Thanksgiving dinner. But I knew you would."

"How did you know?"

He kissed her on the forehead. "You have a soft spot for little boys who want to be loved. Even if it takes you a while to realize it." He reached down and placed his hand on the slight curve of her belly. "Just like I know that our little boy is going to have the greatest mom around."

She laughed into the brilliant blue sky. "*He* could easily be a *she*."

Bobby made a big production of groaning. "Then I better work on my Powder Puff coaching skills."

Throwing her arms around this wonderful man, she held tight. "Oh, Bobby, I love you."

He stroked her hair. "I love you, too. I've been looking for you my entire life, and I didn't even know it." His smile cracked on his handsome face. "Who would have guessed that I was looking for a sassy, prim little thing that would turn my life upside down?"

She worried her lip with her teeth. "Do you ever wake up and wish you were back on the field?"

All traces of humor fled, and he held her by the shoulders. "My only regret is that I didn't recognize what I was looking for sooner. You are my life, Lacey McIntyre." He pulled her close until she could feel the beat of his heart. "And I wouldn't have it any other way."